THE FACTORY

Also by Jack Lynn

The Professor
The Turncoat

THE
FACTORY

JACK LYNN

1817

HARPER & ROW, PUBLISHERS, New York
Cambridge, Philadelphia, San Francisco, London,
Mexico City, São Paulo, Sydney

FIRST U.S. EDITION

Designer: Sidney Feinberg

Library of Congress Cataloging in Publication Data

Lynn, Jack, 1927–
  The factory.

  1. Kennedy, Robert F., 1925–1968—Fiction.   I. Title.
PS3562.Y444F3   1982   813'.54   82–48837
ISBN 0–06–015162–5

---

83 84 85 86 87 10 9 8 7 6 5 4 3 2 1

Dedicated to
my wife Linzi and my son Alexandre

THE FACTORY

"I THOUGHT ELEANOR GARTH was finished as a writer," the small man behind the large desk commented, in that voice which seldom gave away his feelings. "You told us months ago that the disease had progressed and she would never produce another book."

Douglas Foreman was precise in manner, carefully dressed, with a pair of alert and piercing gray eyes. His reputation stood very high, after many years as senior editor of Colt and Lance, one of America's better-known publishing houses.

"Why did Eleanor suddenly ask for a meeting?" He posed in front of stylishly designed windows, obviously aware that the lofty view of New York City was particularly impressive on this clear April morning in 1978. "I'm anxious to see her again," said Foreman. "But what do you imagine she has in mind?"

"Probably a final story idea." The literary agent reflected for a moment with a grave expression on his face. "Eleanor was unusually secretive," he added quietly.

"Have you stayed in touch with her?"

"Only by correspondence," he answered. "My client's door is now locked to everyone."

"You received new plots?"

"A few," the agent replied. "They were unacceptable."

"Tragic," said Foreman. "A brilliant career washed up at thirty years of age."

"She has ability and determination," the agent reminded. "Ellie probably wants to succeed again before the illness cripples her." He met Foreman's steady gaze. "A talented woman's race against multiple sclerosis, Douglas."

Jim Hatfield's frame was six feet tall, carrying one hundred and eighty pounds of solid, conditioned flesh. His features were pleasant-looking, almost handsome, especially in profile. At fifty-seven, he wore a modishly trimmed crop of brownish hair still full and untouched by gray.

The popular New York–based literary agent had parlayed a warm personality, brains, experience, and shrewd business tactics into a first-class representation office. Unlike many of the brash hustlers in his profession, Hatfield was admired and respected by associates, competitors, a wife, and three children.

For a moment, he thought of Ellie Garth, her predicament, and the years before. She had come to him at the start of her career, glowing with beauty, talent, ambition, and strong ideals. Hatfield's personal interest and respect had grown as their working relationship continued.

"Why is Steve's name off the front pages?" Foreman asked bluntly. "Did they fire him at the *Times?*"

The cold questions about Eleanor Garth's husband snapped Hatfield back to the present. "No," he replied, looking up quickly. "They put him on routine assignments with lower pay."

"A pity," said Foreman, checking his watch. "The man is a bright investigative reporter."

"I know," Hatfield agreed without a pause. "But nursing Ellie and sharing the ordeal might have weakened his job performance. Visualize being chopped down suddenly by an incurable disease when everything is going for you."

A desk intercom purred softly and Foreman touched a button.

"Mr. and Mrs. Garth are in reception, sir," a young woman's voice announced.

"Thank you," said the editor, glancing at Hatfield. "Please have them brought up right away."

"Listen to me, Douglas." The agent rose and moved briskly to the desk. "We'll be smart and very tolerant."

"Of course."

"Ellie has been isolated since the diagnosis," Hatfield continued intensely. "She mailed three outlines and received negative responses from me."

"You explained."

"My offers to visit and discuss the material were ignored."

"I understand." Annoyance was beginning to register in Foreman's voice. "What's your point?"

"Only something extraordinary could have persuaded Ellie Garth to call and face us today." Hatfield spoke with friendly authority. "We should be unusually considerate regardless of what she has on her mind. Symptoms, drugs, frustration, and bitterness can produce unpredictable behavior."

The editor glared at Hatfield, and then smiled, and his appearance softened instantly. "Don't worry," Foreman advised. "The lady gave us two successful novels and a brief opportunity to admire her beauty and intelligence. Rest assured that Ellie and Steven Garth will be treated with unusual respect in this office."

A few seconds later, the machine buzzed, and a secretary announced that Douglas Foreman's visitors were ready to enter.

If the agent and the senior editor had been expecting to welcome a drooping invalid and her caretaker, they were mistaken, because Eleanor Garth was generating her usual brand of quiet excitement, and Steve was at her side contributing support, as the group exchanged greetings, and then settled down for the unexpected reunion.

Shortly afterward, Ellie mentioned her recent move to the suburbs, as hints of discomfort were becoming evident. "Cayuga Lake is a remote dot on your map," she explained, rather haltingly. "My husband found a good place for me to write, and plan, and slip away from things which are now beyond my grasp."

The smartly dressed brunette was a natural beauty, with an elegant figure, animated green eyes, and the facial bone structure of a glossy fashion model. In her productive days, before the diagnosis, Eleanor's straight back and clipped-voice self-assurance made her appear to be aloof, yet just beneath the frosty exterior lay a sensuality and warmth that cracked the reserve.

"My setup at the Lake has been ideal," Eleanor remarked, glancing at Steven. "Although it was a punishing commute."

"Past tense," Foreman noted, sitting on the edge of his desk, next to Hatfield's chair. "Are you giving up the place?"

"Yes," Eleanor replied. "We're leaving the country."

"Really?" Hatfield's curious stare moved to the journalist. "And what about your job at the paper?"

"I'm resigning," Steven Garth answered flatly. "Ellie has all the details."

The author's thirty-four-year-old husband had a rugged body, thick and unruly dark hair, bushy eyebrows, and a roughly chisled face. His features were a little out of shape and much too prominent, but the overall blend was unusual, and mannishly attractive. Years before, Eleanor had been won over by his genuine smile, open manner, and direct approach. Now, as Steve looked thoughtfully at his wife, waiting for her to speak, Jim Hatfield's inspection revealed a few disturbing changes in his very genial style.

"First a brief medical report." Eleanor started in a quiet, level tone of voice, although her audience detected traces of strain, probably efforts to control a delicate balance of underlying emotions. "Multiple sclerosis is an incurable disease of the central nervous system. And I have a bad case. Hit and run monsters are tormenting me and eventually they will put me to bed for good. The symptoms are cruel and ugly. At times unbearable. Remissions tease and make the next assault seem even more devastating. I take medication. Large doses. For pain, and fear, and disappointment, and insomnia, and a variety of other reasons. This illness will progress. A slow but absolute disintegration." There was silence for a moment. "End of brief medical report," Eleanor said in a near whisper.

Foreman cleared his throat before speaking. "Want to answer a few questions about the disease?"

"No," Eleanor responded at once. "I called a meeting to discuss a fascinating new project."

"Go ahead," said Hatfield earnestly. "What's this business about leaving the country?"

"I'm going to deliver one last winner before the sickness destroys me." With excitement flushing her pale complexion, Ellie stared at the agent, and he noticed what Doug Foreman and Steve Garth also noticed, a pronounced squint in her right eye, and a distinct trembling in both of her hands. "You were correct about the story ideas, Jim," she admitted. "A damn humiliating experience."

"Forget the—"

"No problem," she interrupted, attempting to ignore the appearance of her symptoms. "A miracle happened."

"We all need one." Foreman walked behind his desk and sat erectly in the chair. "Let's hear about it."

She gripped the purse in her lap and tilted her head to one side in a futile attempt to conceal the worsening signs of illness.

"This will be a very quick pitch," Ellie explained. "Details are sketchy right now." Her voice was low, and huskier than usual. "Even so, I want a promise of strict confidentiality, from both of you."

Foreman nodded and Hatfield gazed at Steve until the journalist looked down at the floor.

"Jim?" Eleanor was anxious to continue. "Agreed?"

"Agreed," said Hatfield, switching attention back at once. "This is a private meeting."

Eleanor leaned forward. "A few nights ago, I was contacted by a man who is setting up an incredible opportunity, the basis for an explosive novel." She took a deep breath and exhaled unevenly. "Someone, apparently a very knowledgeable someone, is willing to give me the facts, the real story behind the assassination of Robert F. Kennedy."

The office was quiet, until Foreman muttered, "A conspiracy?" He blinked his eyes repeatedly. *"Robert* Kennedy?"

"Yes," Eleanor snapped back with assurance. "The secrets will be revealed to us in France."

James Hatfield was examining her carefully. "Did the advance man visit or phone?"

"He visited," she replied, smiling uneasily. "I anticipated your reactions. Ellie Garth's final, desperate bid for recognition. A story idea based on pills and fantasy. The imagination of a crippled author with a rusting brain."

"Nonsense," said Foreman. "We know that—"

"Please, Douglas." Her smile vanished as she faced Hatfield. "I can only say this. An electrifying confession is waiting in the south of France. A fantastic piece of luck. With Steve's help, I intend to race this bastard disease, and produce a best-seller." She clamped one hand over the other to reduce the quivering. "I would never embarrass you by coming here with a fairy tale."

"When are you leaving?," Hatfield asked seriously.

"Very soon."

"Any date for the French contact?"

"No," Eleanor replied. "Our source is on the move. Problems may delay him. We have instructions to wait at a particular location, and carry on normally, until the approach is made."

"Where in France?"

"Sorry, Jim." Looking pale and in need of support, Ellie leaned back in the chair. "No forwarding address. For many personal reasons, I have to go ahead without sympathy or encouragement or curiosity from anyone, except Steven. You and Douglas will hear from us, when I beat the odds and complete a manuscript."

"A sure thing," Foreman remarked, overplaying. "Can you furnish any more details?"

"Ellie must be tired," Hatfield interrupted. "Let's wait for the product, Douglas."

The senior editor watched Steve Garth rise to his feet. "Did you meet the visitor?" Foreman asked.

"No," Steve replied. "Ellie briefed me."

"You covered Bobby Kennedy all the way," said Foreman, marking up a pad with scribbles. "His campaign, the killing, Sirhan's trial, and beyond."

"That's right." Steve moved to Eleanor's chair and rested on the arm beside her. "My files will be useful."

"A modest evaluation." Slowly, and with exaggerated care, Foreman laid a gold pencil along the margin of his desk blotter. "A plausible Robert Kennedy conspiracy project would strike oil for all of us." He looked up and focused on the reporter, avoiding Hatfield's glare. "Do you also believe in miracles?"

"Not usually," Steven replied, controlling his annoyance. "But I respect my wife's instincts."

"And so do I." Jim Hatfield smiled broadly at the author. "Doug will have celebration props ready for your next visit."

"Take my word," Foreman stated, after observing her deteriorating condition. "Remember the last one?"

"Yes." Eleanor's voice was unsteady. "We have pictures."

Her tremors had increased, and she appeared to be bracing against vertigo, and other disorders. Steven checked her frequently, without making a fuss, so Hatfield and Foreman remained seated, not wanting to aggravate the situation.

Proceeding carefully, Eleanor explained her reasons for crawling away from the Lake and visiting in person, when the new project could have been announced by Steve, or by mail, or by telephone. "I wanted you to receive the news directly from me," she told them. "Otherwise, it might have been ignored, or sneered at, or filed as a sick woman's dream sequence."

"We have first refusal," Foreman stated, in a businesslike tone of voice. "Nobody is laughing, Ellie."

Growing weary and impatient to leave, she nodded her thanks, and then stressed the importance of confidentiality, especially with the press, law enforcement, and government representatives. "Please keep your word," she reminded. "A leak might frighten the source and ruin our chances."

"Produce a manuscript," said Hatfield. "This discussion will be forgotten until we get together again."

"No, Jim." Eleanor looked at him sadly and brought up the final reason for appearing in Doug Foreman's office. "My visiting days are over." She explained that Steven would deliver the next property and manage her affairs. "I wanted to be upright, and mobile, during this last conversation with you."

Foreman protested, claiming that Eleanor was underestimating her courage and tenacity, but Hatfield watched in silence as Steve helped the author prepare to leave.

"We'll be anticipating a Robert Kennedy shocker by Eleanor Garth," Foreman continued, grimacing at her efforts to leave the chair. "Are you writing a book of truth or fiction?" he asked, when everyone was finally standing.

"I don't know, Douglas," she replied, clutching Steve's arm and beginning a cautious move toward the door, with Hatfield also beside her. "Everything depends on time—and symptoms—and our adventures in France."

The afternoon sun glared down on Berwyn Heights, Maryland. It was a cloudless day in 1978—June 16—and young children were bicycling, playing ball, and romping happily in this orderly residential area just outside Washington, D.C.

A car pulled up in front of a modest detached red-brick house, and four men with briefcases climbed out and moved along a narrow cement walk to the door. Just as the visitors entered, another vehicle stopped at the curb and unloaded a few more somber businesslike men; they followed the others inside.

Within minutes, these veteran agents of the Federal Bureau of Investigation were reviewing a very important ultrasecret government project. The Justice Department was in the early planning stages of a major two-pronged attack on labor union fraud and political corruption. Each of these wide-ranging undercover investigations would have its own code name: Abscam and Brilab.

For the former, Bureau agents were being enlisted to pose as representatives of fictitious Arab businessmen willing to pay for legislative help to enter and remain in America. Electronic surveillance and other modern techniques were bringing in information that members of the United States Congress and other public officials had taken, or had agreed to take, bribes in return for influence and favors—mainly to help smooth away immigration troubles encountered by wealthy foreigners.

At the same time, Brilab (an undercover federal operation in the southwest) was being set up to investigate organized crime, labor racketeering, and political corruption—focusing on the manipulation of labor union insurance plans.

The American government was determined to file solid evidence and ensure federal grand jury indictments for bribery, conspiracy, fraud, unlawful receipt of gratuities, interstate travel in aid of racketeering enterprises—and more. Bosses of organized crime in the region were, of course, primary targets, but sophisticated Justice Department weapons would also be leveled at political figures, and public officials, in order to prove that they conspired to demand and accept benefits in return for their being influenced in their performance of official acts.

"Our unit will operate independently," the Bureau senior told his agents in Berwyn Heights. "We have orders to deal exclusively with one delicious aspect of this probe." He looked at the others and smiled. "The Rajah is our baby."

Joseph Napoli was an undisputed leader of organized crime in the southwest and his tentacles branched out in all directions. The Rajah generated vast profits from casinos and prostitution, drugs and labor racketeering. His upper-echelon connections with the trade unions had spliced him neatly into pension fund fraud and kickbacks, bribery of public officials, and the misapplication of union funds. Carefully hidden interests in Las Vegas gambling joints enabled his group to skim off fat casino income without reporting to Internal Revenue or to the Nevada gaming authorities. Joe Napoli was the master of loan schemes and insurance plots. In fact, every criminal profit angle in his territory, and beyond, had been explored, activated, supervised, and protected by the former backyard numbers runner and his experienced team of specialists and hit men.

But Napoli had been paying a high price for his gravy. After being deported to Caracas, Venezuela, by Immigration on October 14, 1961, Napoli had re-entered the country illegally in the early hours of July 24, 1963, and so became the subject of a second deportation order. However, this second federal order had still not been enforced by the time the FBI agents met in Berwyn Heights—nearly fifteen years later (although Napoli's movements had been restricted by order of the INS).

"This unit was put together for one reason only," the agent was saying. "Get Joe Napoli!"

Others would be involved with the overall concept and eventual execution of Brilab and Abscam. Others would bait the congressmen and public officials. The investigation had given this FBI task force an opportunity, a very special ticket—a legitimate reason to go undercover in an attempt to compile new and more damaging evidence against Joseph Napoli.

"His connections with terrorist groups in Europe," the senior agent lectured. "Fresh international drug routes and new peddling methods." He tapped his briefcase. "We'll chase every Napoli lead while the main probes are under way."

"Never a better opportunity," somebody commented. "The whole damn system is tuned up for indictments. Drooling prosecutors and strong grand jury action waiting right down the line. But the usual gangster crap won't score points in the case of Napoli. Fresh drug routes and terrorist links might help, if we can build a responsible dossier and present breathing witnesses." He thought for a moment. "A rough assignment. Especially the breathing witnesses."

"What about his black file?" another asked. "Do we open it again and pray for a miracle?"

"The contents are legally primitive and practically useless," an agent reminded. "Get a reading from the House Select Committee members."

President John F. Kennedy and his brother, the Attorney General, had waged the strongest battle in history against organized crime. Joseph Napoli and his connections were prime targets: the Justice Department's sophisticated weapons had been used to disrupt lucrative operations, cancel plans, delay progress, and complicate the lives of syndicate members, from punks to the big-time leaders.

Napoli and others had sworn revenge against John Kennedy and his brother, Robert. Government investigators had already underlined the Rajah's name as a logical accomplice if conspiracy could be proven in the assassination of the President.

"I know the problems," said the agent in charge. "But we'll be on a quiet hookup to global law enforcement, intelligence, and every other source of potential business. We should be optimistic. There has to be a convincing neutralizer out there somewhere. Joe Napoli can't thumb his Roman nose forever."

"How much time?"

"The department hopes to finish up both investigations before the end of 'seventy-nine," he answered. "I predict courtrooms and news releases at the start of 'eighty."

"A career."

"The others are covering a lot of sensitive territory for VIP convictions," the agent proceeded. "We just dig in the garbage to help cripple one man."

"Starting when?"

"Now." The man in charge opened his briefcase. "Deportation is too goddamn easy for this animal," he said coldly. "I want Joe Napoli to burn in hell for every rap he should have taken over the years."

"Already my head aches from the brick walls," an agent moaned. "We'll need plenty of gutter cooperation and—"

"Luck," the group's leader interrupted. "The key to Napoli's extermination might be dangling anywhere."

On October 29, 1979, a French duty nurse glanced up from her desk on the third floor of Hospital Saint Roch in Nice. An emergency signal on the wall was humming and blinking repeatedly; the patient in 305 was having a problem.

Without a change of expression or any noticeable sense of urgency, the woman switched off the device and nudged her young companion. "The American," she announced quietly. "Madame Garth."

"I had a feeling." The junior attendant was busy finishing some routine paperwork. "And what now?"

"Better check right away," the duty nurse instructed. "They are quite concerned upstairs."

The patient in 305 sat rigidly in a wheelchair, eyes fixed on the door, waiting anxiously for a response to her frantic buzzing. She was clutching a large brown envelope.

As requested, window curtains in the room had been drawn tightly, blocking out the hazy afternoon sun. Only claustrophobia and fears of possible suffocation had kept her from issuing orders to roll down and lock the wooden shutters. Instead, anticipating the nurse's entrance, and a shaft of light from the hall, she had positioned herself in the dimmest corner, far out of range, so that no more than a silhouetted presence would be seen—although Eleanor Garth would have preferred complete invisibility during this critical period of her life.

The young nurse entered the room without knocking, squinted at the patient, and closed the door gently behind her, as she had been asked to do on previous occasions.

"Someone has been tampering with my papers." Eleanor's accusation was delivered unhesitatingly, in proper French, but the words ran together, and slurred out of her mouth. These symptoms were familiar now, but still they angered and frustrated her.

Expecting more details, to be followed by a jumble of unreasonable demands, the nurse stood motionless, giving the American time to deal with her problems.

"A professional thief was here," the patient said, obviously deciding to simplify a lengthier statement.

"Impossible, Madame Garth."

"During the night."

"Impossible, Madame Garth."

"What good is a bedside drawer without a lock and key?" she asked. There was no reply. "From now until completion I'll sleep with the manuscript under my pillow."

"A practical idea."

"Don't be so goddamn cute!" Eleanor blurted in English. She took a deep breath, paused, then reverted to French and struggled through a choppy monologue. "This is a formal complaint. Report it to the hospital authorities immediately. Somebody has been tampering with my papers. Four pages are out of sequence. Others were handled by a person in a hurry. This was probably an attempt to make photographic copies." She waited, cleared her throat, and rolled the chair an inch or two forward. "Listen to me," she went on. "The medics had me drugged out last night. But I know that a professional was operating in this room. Following orders to copy or steal my work."

"I can assure you—"

"You can't assure me of a damn thing," Eleanor broke in. "Report my complaint to your superiors at once. And make sure the security is doubled on this floor. Especially at night. God help all of you if something happens to me—or the manuscript. Do you understand?"

"Yes, Madame Garth," the nurse replied obediently. "I will report your complaints to my superiors right away."

"Mademoiselle Gautier!" Eleanor stopped the nurse just as she was leaving the room. "Please allow me to explain something to you."

The young girl turned abruptly. Her blank expression and complete lack of animation did nothing at all to compensate for a pale, thin face, heavy spectacles, and a rag-doll physique. The neatly tailored blue and white hospital cap and uniform were her most interesting features.

"Take a look at this!" Eleanor ordered, holding up the large brown envelope. The contents were heavy. In seconds, her fingers were trembling, and she was forced to lower the package. Numbness and tremors and vertigo and other reminders of her deteriorating condition had made it almost impossible for her to cope with recent events. But she remembered her pledge: to exercise control, finish the project on time, and avoid infecting others with her own bitterness. "Unlike some others in your hospital," she said, "I am battling for a great deal more than personal survival."

The nurse's deadpan gaze was difficult to interpret. It might have been interest, boredom, or stupidity. Eleanor carried on without making a selection. "I have almost completed my work on this manuscript," she explained. "The information is private, confidential, and very, very explosive."

"Explosive?"

"Yes, Mademoiselle Gautier. Secret and explosive. This shocking material will eventually alter the world's history books."

The nurse stared without commenting.

"Report to your superiors," Eleanor ordered, realizing that she had been wasting her time and energy. "Please emphasize the importance of my complaints."

"Of course, Madame Garth." She moved to the door. "I will certainly repeat everything."

A loud, piercing howl sliced the midnight quiet and froze Hélène Gautier as she traveled to the third floor in the staff elevator. Although most hospital employees are accustomed to the groans of suffering patients, Mademoiselle Gautier had difficulty associating this chilling sound with any others she had heard during her two years in the old building. It was definitely not a typical scream of pain, the French nurse analyzed, but more like a shock reaction linked to fear or panic. The high-pitched cry was repeated, with more intensity and volume as she walked out of the elevator and moved quickly to room 305. It was eight days since Madame Garth had first made her accusations.

Nurse Gautier opened the door and switched on the bright overhead lights, ignoring all previous orders to respect the American's desire for shadows and extraordinary privacy.

In bed, apparently conscious, Eleanor Garth moaned, and stayed rigid as a corpse. Her long brown hair was mussed and perspiration-drenched. She had thrown a slender arm up to cover her face, shielding her eyes from the glare and the nurse's presence. Her bedsheets, and a thin blanket, were crumpled and disordered. A pillow was on the floor.

Two other nurses had heard the cry and dashed into the room as Mademoiselle Gautier recorded Eleanor's rapid and uneven pulse rate. Then, after several attempts to discover what had happened, Nurse Gautier received a sketchy explanation, leaning close to the patient and unraveling her advanced speech irregularities.

"Attempted murder by suffocation," according to Madame Garth. She claimed that while she was dozing a person had entered the room and forced a pillow over her mouth, until death was close. Her physical handicaps, including paralysis of the left side, had made it almost impossible to fight off this strong and determined attacker. Luckily, a noise in the corridor had startled him, and he quit and ran without ever speaking a word. Aided for a second or two by the hall lights as the intruder opened and closed her door, she had been able to note some identifying features.

In her faltering delivery, the American described a tall muscular Scandinavian type, with blond wavy hair and gorilla features. The man, probably a young intern, was dressed in a white uniform.

"He is an orderly," Hélène Gautier corrected. "Claude Jourdan."

"A hired killer."

"No, Madame Garth," the nurse insisted. "A respected member of the hospital staff."

"On duty tonight?"

"Yes," Gautier replied. "But without a logical reason to visit any room on this floor."

"He was in mine."

"We should bring Claude upstairs now, Madame Garth," one of the others suggested. "Accuse him face to face."

"Get out, you idiots!" With an effort, Eleanor propped herself up on one elbow, and screamed. *"Out!"*

The sight of the enraged patient caused two of the nurses to leave, and Eleanor slid back to her former position on the bed. Nurse Gautier picked up a washcloth, soaked it, wrung it nearly dry, and walked toward the American.

"Stay away from me," Eleanor warned softly. "Don't touch me."

"I want to—"

"Call Dr. Roger Lambert," the patient interrupted. "Ask him to report here at once."

Still holding the washcloth, Gautier nodded, then reached down for the pillow.

"Leave everything alone!" Eleanor was now beginning to tremble. "Contact my doctor!"

The nurse stared for a moment sympathetically, and the patient covered her face again.

"Mademoiselle Gautier," Eleanor whispered. "Can you imagine

. . . being a stationary target . . . for the American Mafia?"

Instead of responding, the young woman backed away, turned, and headed for the door.

"Lock it securely," Eleanor ordered. "Make certain that no one enters this room until Dr. Lambert arrives!"

Monsieur Léon Dumas had a long, narrow head, and this squeezed his features together like an image in a carnival distorting mirror: a puckered mouth, tapered nose, and hardly any space between his eyes. Every part of his thin face, including his chin and forehead, seemed to come to a point. His shiny black toupée was obvious and his ears were pinned flat back to it. He was an unusually tall and skinny and militarily erect man; a conservatively dressed matchstick, a scarecrow, but the overall effect was rather fascinating and in no way clownish.

At a conference-room table at Hospital Saint Roch, Léon Dumas fidgeted, smoothed his hands over the back of his wig and coughed frequently, indicating that he was running behind schedule. On the first of November, three days after her last outburst, Dr. Roger Lambert and a Saint Roch official were discussing the case of Madame Eleanor Garth.

Dumas was one of the most respected of the administrators of Les Mimosas, a private neuropsychiatric clinic in Mandelieu la Napoule. This modern institution, which resembled a luxury hotel, had an excellent reputation—and a corresponding room tab. Dumas and his associates were in a position to be selective.

"My patient is now dealing with acute exacerbations," Dr. Lambert stated. "Her multiple sclerosis history and notes on her present condition are in a separate folder, together with Dr. Vassolo's psychiatric reports."

"I understand the woman is confined to bed," Léon Dumas said matter-of-factly. "Paralysis?"

"The entire left side of her body," Dr. Lambert answered. "Also the third and sixth cranial nerves are—"

"Spare me," said Dumas, raising both hands and lowering them quickly. "Confer with our specialists."

"Of course," agreed Lambert, a balding thickset man with a cool professional manner. "We should talk in general terms," he added, nodding to Dr. Pierre Favre, a hospital supervisor.

Favre was repeating statements he had made earlier to Dr. Lambert, as well as to his own Saint Roch colleagues, as he recommended Madame Garth's immediate transfer to Les Mimosas. It would be for the good of both the patient, and the hospital. The small elderly Frenchman ticked off the list of bizarre ravings which had been upsetting other sufferers and members of the staff. Her groans and screams and formal complaints about thieves, abductors, and murderers were now becoming habitual, and more difficult to control.

"Everything is detailed medically in Dr. Vassolo's file," concluded Favre. "Your people will appreciate the seriousness of this woman's physical and mental deterioration."

Léon Dumas glared for several moments before speaking. "Who is supposed to be chasing Madame Garth?" he asked bluntly. "One person or a group?"

"A group," Favre replied without hesitation. "The American Mafia and others."

"I see." The administrator did not appear to be particularly shaken by Favre's words, possibly because he knew that his staff would soon brief him, after they had examined the medical records. He bent forward, muffled a cough with his fist, and changed tack abruptly. "What about Monsieur Garth?"

"He deserted five or six months ago," said Favre. "Madame Garth prefers to be vague about the details. She promises that many startling facts will be revealed in her latest novel." He looked at the neatly stacked clinical folders in order to point up his skepticism. "The American has nearly finished a 'history-shattering exposé,' " he added quietly.

Dumas made a groaning sound as he eased his beanpole frame back in the chair. "Have you examined these papers?" he asked, after some thought.

"No one has examined these papers," Favre replied, apparently enjoying his role as spokesman. "She guards them carefully, day and night, under sheets and pillows. It seems that most of the world is after Madame Garth and her top-secret information." He sighed out a deep breath. "This pathetic fantasy is creating serious problems for the patient and for our hospital. Please study the files and make arrangements for an immediate transfer to Les Mimosas."

"Is there any way for Eleanor Garth to write a coherent piece during this stage of her illness?" Dumas had shifted his gaze to Roger Lambert. "Produce a sensible book?"

"Doubtful," Dr. Lambert answered. "However, there were several brief remission periods earlier."

"You're talking about MS only," Favre reminded. "Vassolo's psychiatric reports indicate that she—"

"No one has examined the papers," Dr. Lambert interrupted, doing his best to ignore Favre's sharp tone and pompous attitude. "I can only state that Madame Garth is a talented and determined woman," he continued, his voice sincere. "My patient has been struggling against formidable odds to complete some kind of manuscript. In a short time the work will be handed over to her literary agent, a man called James Hatfield, from New York. He's the only person she genuinely trusts."

"Perhaps James Hatfield will consult with you and Lambert after he reads the material," Favre suggested to Dumas. "Her gibberish might add a new dimension to Dr. Vassolo's findings."

Dumas stared at the white-haired supervisor without a trace of enthusiasm. "Has anyone spoken to Madame Garth about being transferred?" he asked.

"I have," said Dr. Lambert. "She is very anxious to make the change."

"Was our clinic described accurately?" Dumas hesitated before rephrasing the question. "In other words, did you talk neuropsychiatric and give her a complete picture?"

"Yes," said Lambert. "My patient understands."

"Good," Dumas remarked. "Such easy acceptance is unusual in delicate cases of this kind."

"Your tight security convinced her at once," Lambert told him. "This seems to be Madame Garth's prime concern."

"A speedy transfer will benefit the patient in every way," Favre broke in, attempting to finalize the negotiations. "How soon can you proceed, Dumas?"

The toothpick-shaped administrator puckered his lips into something resembling a grin. "Are you paying all her bills, Dr. Favre?" he asked.

"Don't be ridiculous," Favre retorted. "Will tomorrow be acceptable?"

"Possibly." Dumas had adjusted his bony features. "What about the financial arrangements?" he asked Lambert in a flat tone of voice.

"Monsieur James Hatfield has accepted full responsibility for all my patient's charges," Lambert explained. "I am in touch with him frequently about Madame Garth's condition."

"His credentials?" Dumas asked. "This patient will need specialized care."

"Impeccable," Favre responded. "I gather that James Hatfield is one of America's most respected literary agents."

"Monsieur Hatfield is now in London completing a business deal," said Lambert. "He intends to fly here in a week or two. You and your staff will have an opportunity to chat with him personally, Dumas."

A week later, James Hatfield was on his way to Nice. Ordinarily, turbulence on the short flight from Heathrow would not have bothered him, an experienced traveler. But on this occasion every irregular movement upset his stomach and jangled his nerves. At first he put the blame on a combination of familiar evils: a lack of sleep, too many grab-and-swallow meals, pressured conferences, stubborn publishing executives, unrealistic film producers, double-talking lawyers, and an overpaid, egotistical, thoroughly disagreeable client.

In time, however, he realized that one perturbing element had been downplayed, a major contributing factor, possibly the main reason for his uneasy state: Eleanor Garth.

He shrugged, leaned back, and forced himself to disregard the aircraft's bumps and vibrations. As the plane neared France he closed his eyes and thought of Ellie. The bits and pieces of her life, as he knew them, flashed by and deepened his sadness.

Eleanor Coleman had been born in Los Angeles, California, on March 6, 1945. The family made a good living from real estate. She had confidence, a touch of aloofness, and a fanatical passion for writing. Ellie majored in English literature, was a brilliant student, and had a book of short stories published while she was still in college. The girl received encouragement from her parents, and from teachers and literary critics. As far as the people around her were concerned, her success was assured.

At twenty-six, Ellie was handling an executive job with a top public relations firm in New York City. All her spare moments were devoted to writing a first novel. Feature articles and short stories had already been published in leading magazines. The girl was desirable, a veteran of all pitches from men with brains and looks and wealth. But both the funny games and serious links were avoided as Eleanor concentrated on her schedule.

Highly strung, the dedicated young woman began to suffer from double vision, a pronounced squint in the right eye, and unsteady balance during this period. Vertigo sometimes troubled her, especially when she first stood up in the morning, or perhaps if she changed from a sitting to an upright position. Various parts of her body would go numb or tingle—and there were other problems, including muscle spasms. These unpredictable signals would come and go. Completely unaware that she was experiencing the first symptoms of multiple sclerosis, Eleanor worried; but she blamed the pressures of her job, the book, and late hours. Anxiety, and tranquilizers, both entered her life at the same time.

After landing and checking out of Nice Airport, Jim Hatfield was traveling again, by taxi, heading for his booking at the Negresco Hotel, on the Promenade des Anglais. He would clean up, relax for a while, have lunch, and then join Dr. Roger Lambert, Léon Dumas, and his associates at Les Mimosas.

He thought about the neuropsychiatric clinic's new arrival. Although Lambert and the others had prepared him for the worst, Jim Hatfield was still profoundly affected by the news of Eleanor's rapidly deteriorating condition, especially her recent transfer from Saint Roch to Les Mimosas. After consultations with doctors and Eleanor, he would decide on the best timing for a move back to the States.

As they sped past the beachfronts and caught up with traffic, Hatfield's mind drifted again to what he knew of Eleanor's life when she had been battling the first waves of her illness, and blaming them on a job, a book, and late hours.

At a company barbecue, just before her twenty-seventh birthday, Eleanor had met Steve Garth, a twenty-nine-year-old journalist, and she liked what she saw.

Steve's parents had owned a grocery store in a black and white Philadelphia ghetto. The boy used to deliver on a bicycle. He was street-wise—bright, tough, but good-natured. He had attended the City College of New York, where he was a mediocre student with no driving ambition, living for the moment, hanging out with jazz musicians and very hip types. Yet he managed to stay clean. He was known for his generosity and interest in others. As a member of the school boxing team, the powerful slugger had won a state championship—and offers to become a professional, which he refused. Aware of his own strength, Steve kept his fists to himself when out of the ring. With all kinds of people, male and female, during college and later, he was a popular young man.

At the time he met Ellie, Steve was an investigative reporter for a New York daily newspaper. He worked with John Conway, and their team had gained recognition for busting front-page criminal and political stories. John Conway handled the bulk of the writing, but Steve was excellent for digging, making rough contacts, gaining entry, and applying pressure. He was also strong on research and had an unusual memory for details and faces.

John Conway received most of the credit and a higher salary, and Steve accepted this without a fight—his partner had a wife and daughter to support, and to hell with back-slapping and press awards. Many of Steve's associates were allowed to challenge him and move ahead for one reason or another. He detested the race for power and glory;

he felt that his allotted time on earth was short and very unpredictable, and he wanted to move forward at a slower pace in order to absorb the beauty and excitement. But the former boxer was still geared up and ready to deliver a crushing left hook or a deadly combination, as a group of journalistic rivals had been forced to recognize during heated debates. Someday, they realized, if he was motivated by someone or something, the affable Philadelphian might block the road and grab his piece of cake.

A steady friendship became love, and nine months after their first meeting, Eleanor Coleman married Steven H. Garth on October 14, 1972.

A telephone call had interrupted James Hatfield's cold shower. Naked, except for a towel around his middle, he was dripping water on the Negresco carpet while speaking to Léon Dumas at Les Mimosas.

"Madame Garth had a very unpleasant night," the administrator was saying. "Dr. Lambert will explain."

"How is she now?"

"Under heavy sedation," Dumas replied. "Will you join us for lunch?"

"Yes," said Hatfield, anxious to receive a detailed report on Eleanor's condition. "One o'clock?"

"Fine." Dumas waited a few seconds. "We have a package from Madame Garth," he said. "Dr. Lambert wrapped and sealed it late yesterday afternoon."

"Oh?"

"Strictly private and confidential, for James Hatfield," Dumas went on dramatically. "The contents will be of great interest to our psychiatric staff."

"And to me," Hatfield snapped back. "See you at one o'clock, Monsieur Dumas."

The literary agent hung up, returned to his shower, and wired in on Eleanor Garth again, the roller-coasting pattern of her life, abridged version.

Eleanor's first novel was published shortly after she married Steve Garth. The romantic thriller received a large advance, fine reviews, and public acclaim. Ellie Garth, at twenty-eight, was on her way.

Happy days and nights followed. Eleanor felt she'd made a giant step, a confirmation of many things past, and had been offered a reassuring glimpse of the future. The worrying symptoms had faded as the undiagnosed multiple sclerosis went into remission. But Eleanor took this as solid proof that all her problems had been minor—caused by anxiety, relieved by success.

She had resigned her public relations job. Then there had been a brief vacation and cocktail party time with Steve at her side whenever possible. A forced hiatus to meet the literary crowd, and Ellie Garth charmed them with her beauty and intelligence.

A few weeks later she was back at her desk outlining another project.

Steve continued with his newspaper assignments. He was thrilled by Eleanor's success. Proud, respectful, and deeply in love. Using research contacts and expertise, he assisted his wife with her controversial new book of political fiction set in Washington, New York, and Los Angeles.

Unexpectedly, as the work neared completion, symptoms returned with a new and punishing vengeance. The shock of it, the unbearable weight of it, disrupted her entire nervous system, and pills flowed. There were outbursts and dark moods and sleepless nights. Steve dug in and waited patiently as he sampled a depressing preview of the future and of their lives together.

Although she finally realized the significance of her physical and emotional trouble, Eleanor hardened and overruled Steve, refusing to consult a doctor, while racing in the home stretch. Instead, she finagled her husband's sympathy and encouragement and more of his journalistic assistance. She plunged ahead, treating each word as her last on paper, until the manuscript was completed and typed and submitted for publication.

Eleanor Garth's realistic blockbuster about the wives and lovers behind America's power brokers quickly bettered her previous novel in cash, sales, noise, and acclaim.

But even before the applause had faded, she was on her way to a hospital for tests after suffering a choking spasm of the larynx and a severe attack of vomiting. Specialists discovered that Eleanor, at thirty years of age, was a victim of an incurable disease of the central nervous system: multiple sclerosis.

Eleanor broke off normal contacts and ran. The Garths rented a home in a remote New York suburb. She remained behind locked doors with a nurse and cleaning woman. Steve, reluctant to discuss the matter, commuted and worked on the paper as usual; but, according to colleagues—especially John Conway—the strain had weakened his job performance.

An outline for a new story was eventually delivered to Hatfield by Eleanor. A soft rejection followed. His requests to visit her and his offers of help and advice were ignored. Later, Eleanor submitted two plots, both unacceptable. Again she refused to open her door for any kind of meeting.

A complete news blackout followed. Not a word from Eleanor. Steve refused to discuss his wife's sickness or their personal lives. The journalistic relationship with John Conway had been ended by Garth's chief, and he was now operating on routine assignments, taking lower pay. There were no complaints, frowns, or pleas for sympathy. Even so, the people nearest to him were able to detect many signs of his tormented existence.

Finally they met with Doug Foreman, in April of 1978. Then, Steve left his newspaper job, and the Garths moved very quietly to Europe, leaving no forwarding address. They were out of the picture entirely, until Steve made an unexpected contact during the summer of 1979. Right after that, by phone to New York, Dr. Lambert made himself known, and reported Eleanor's problems—which now included the sudden disappearance of her husband. Regular notes and calls from the French doctor had led to this meeting at Les Mimosas, the neuropsychiatric clinic, in Mandelieu la Napoule, France.

"Think of the central nervous system as a complicated telephone network," Dr. Lambert was explaining. "The nerve sheath is protected by a substance called myelin. Like the insulation covering an electric wire. During acute attacks—we call them exacerbations—this myelin destroys itself by some unknown process. Each nerve is left bare to infection and trauma, just as decaying insulation would leave a wire exposed."

"Unpredictable and incurable," added Léon Dumas. "The cause is still a mystery."

James Hatfield was sitting in the conference room with its modern furnishings, listening to a medical briefing on Eleanor's primary illness, multiple sclerosis. During each pause, he would glance at a bulky, carefully sealed brown envelope which had been positioned on the table directly in front of Dr. Lambert.

Although Hatfield had a layman's understanding of the problem, he sat patiently while the doctors lectured in French and English about signs, symptoms, attacks, remissions, and treatment. Monsieur Léon Dumas, the skinny administrator, insisted on tagging a line or two of his own after each point was made.

"Remission periods may occur at any time during the course of the disease, and symptoms have been known to subside, or disappear for weeks or months or even years," Lambert continued. "Some patients, unfortunately, never have a remission at all."

"On the other hand," Dumas added professorially, "a patient who has been seriously affected for years may, for unknown reasons, have a complete remission." He stretched himself up a head taller than Roger Lambert. "A very complex affliction, this damn multiple sclerosis."

Knowing there was no cure available, Hatfield was very curious about treatment, especially during the rough stages—what Dr. Lambert called "exacerbations."

"Along with other procedures, Madame Garth has been receiving short courses of ACTH, by deep intramuscular injection," he explained. "This drug helps relieve symptoms during crippling attacks."

"*Not* a cure," Dumas reminded. "And there are some nasty side effects."

"Quite true," the doctor agreed. "We proceed cautiously with the treatment."

Hatfield's concern was evident as he studied Dr. Lambert's somber expression. "What are the side effects?" he asked bluntly.

"ACTH may produce euphoria, hallucinations, a strange feeling of unreality," the doctor answered. "The drug is in the cortisone group. We have to cope with the moon-faced appearance, increased growth of hair on the legs and upper lip."

"I understand," Hatfield commented thoughtfully. "Anything else?"

"This drug sometimes causes fluid retention in the body cells and also appears to make extra fluid," Lambert answered. "Various other side effects may be produced. ACTH is a hormone secreted by the anterior lobe of the pituitary—"

"Dr. Lambert," Dumas interrupted, "all this medical jargon will be in his briefcase very soon."

Lambert glanced at the administrator. "You have a point," he conceded. "Madame Garth's records, including psychiatric findings, are now being prepared for you, Monsieur Hatfield." He relaxed in the chair. "However, Dr. Vassolo of Hospital Saint Roch—and other specialists here—would like to meet with you and discuss the patient's sealed notes and her background, as your friend and client, and as a writer."

"With pleasure." Hatfield's eyes moved from Dr. Lambert to Dumas and back. "Could this hormone treatment, ACTH, be responsible for Eleanor's struggle with phantom murderers?" he asked.

"Not on an isolated basis." At first Roger Lambert appeared ready to expand on the remark, but suddenly he decided against it. "That's just my personal opinion. Better examine her papers, meet with the staff, and wait for medical documentation. Serge Vassolo and the Mimosas specialists will deliver a comprehensive report."

"Can the disease lead to insanity?" Hatfield persisted. "Is Eleanor Garth mentally ill?"

Léon Dumas folded his thin arms and sat like a wooden Indian, demonstrating that Dr. Lambert was responsible for the answer.

"Multiple sclerosis is not hereditary, it is not infectious or contagious, and it is not a mental disease," Dr. Lambert told them. "I will restrict my comments to MS, the emotional attitudes of the patients, and Madame Garth's special difficulties. Consult psychiatrists for the rest."

"Fair enough," said Hatfield. "Go ahead."

"Although euphoria is very common in the early stages, it soon changes to extreme mental depression, frustration, and irritability. Suicide is by no means a rare event." He allowed time for the line to register. "In this particular case, we are dealing with a young, beautiful, talented person. Visualize her battle with the symptoms we talked about earlier—including agraphia, a loss of the power to express thought in writing."

"Pathetic," Jim Hatfield commented. "The frustrations must be unbearable for someone like Ellie Garth."

"And for all the victims," said Dr. Lambert. "At times, they are unable to communicate properly because of speech irregularities, word blindness, incoherence, and dysphasia."

"Minor factors, compared to the prospects of living in a chair or a bed for the rest of her life," Dumas stated. "MS can lead to progressive paralysis, and Madame Garth might be on the way right now."

"What are the odds?" Hatfield asked.

"The course is variable," the doctor answered. "Some patients, usually young women, can have a rapidly progressive disease lasting months, or perhaps a few years, without severe disability."

"And how do they eventually finish?" Hatfield asked without a pause. "The cause of death?"

"The cause of death, ordinarily, is uremia from urinary-tract infection or bronchopneumonia," Dr. Lambert answered. "Infected pressure sores and renal failure also have to be watched."

"Wait for the conference and the files," Dumas advised. "Rest assured, you will have a much better picture after studying Madame Garth's new work and conferring with Dr. Vassolo and our people here at the clinic."

Dr. Lambert slid the brown envelope over to Hatfield. "She must have been racing against time and symptoms," he remarked solemnly.

"A frantic effort to complete and deliver a final script before accepting the physical and mental handicaps of her illness. Yesterday afternoon she gave me the envelope, fell back on her pillow, and went to sleep at once."

In his rooms at the Negresco, James Hatfield walked to a puffy sofa, gripping a bourbon in one hand and Eleanor's sealed manuscript in the other. He sat, kicked off his shoes, put the drink on a low table, and started to rip the edge of the large manila envelope.

Hatfield had left the clinic in Mandelieu without visiting his friend and client. Eleanor had been drowsy from sedatives, when she had unexpectedly developed severe head pains; powerful injections were given to calm her and induce sleep. Dr. Lambert, Dumas, and the others had expressed puzzlement and concern. They had promised to phone the hotel with a report later in the evening.

He removed Eleanor's pages very carefully and stacked them on the carpet next to his feet. The literary agent took a long swallow of whiskey and gave it time to warm him and settle him and brace him for absolute gibberish or a history-shattering exposé—or, possibly, further evidence that his client was a definite candidate for Dr. Vassolo's psycho files.

At last he leaned over and flipped through Ellie's papers; they were all sizes, some typed, others written—a mixture of exaggerated neatness, clumsy handwriting, and scrawled indifference.

The literary agent picked up the first batch, sprawled full-length on the velvet cushions, and prepared to examine Madame Garth's secrets. Among many other things, James Hatfield was extromoly curious about the disappearance of Steve Garth, a man of solid character, loyal and understanding, a most unlikely deserter.

Anxiously he removed the blank cover piece, glanced at her title, and started the book.

SANDCASTLE

by

ELEANOR GARTH

with the indispensable assistance of

STEVEN H. GARTH

Sandcastle is based on truth. Some names, dates, and places have been changed. The others are valid. I assume responsibility for the contents, and hereby pledge my cooperation and support to all interested law-enforcement and investigative agencies.

Eleanor Garth

———————

PROLOGUE

(My dear Jim,

In this space, please have a writer describe me, and Steve, as you remember us, before the MS diagnosis and our swift move to Cayuga Lake. Tease with our meeting in Foreman's office. Use available biographical material, sketch both characters, and hurry them along to France. The rest is mine. You see, Jim, my brain has been programmed to handle today's experiences only, and screw the past, as far as our personal lives are concerned. Fond recollections aggravate my present state of health, and writing becomes more difficult, almost impossible. There is a time limit for me. I want to concentrate on the details of this incredible adventure. Please help. As usual, I trust your judgment, appreciate your understanding, and cherish your friendship.

E.)

1

Beaulieu-sur-Mer
France
Afternoon
Sunday, June 3, 1979

The ugly child rebelled by mutilating her beautiful sister, and a kamikaze-trained commercial pilot smashed his bomb-loaded aircraft into the White House, and a Cuban murderer was released from a federal prison in order to spy for the United States, and there were drug ideas and a black man's vengeance and whore heroines and regal villains, and Eleanor Garth continued to explore and reject a wild assortment of plot lines, knowing that she was emptying her professional insides and discovering garbage.

Over a year had passed in France without a contact, and Ellie's dream of creating another literary success had become a nightmare. With her back propped securely against a kitchen chair, she had spent an hour outlining a new book, and, by gauging her husband's polite remarks and lack of real enthusiasm, she knew that her latest attempt would have to be discarded with the others.

"Please go," Ellie pleaded. "I need privacy and medication."

Steven knew from experience that further conversation would only irritate his wife. He nodded, got up, walked through the modest rented apartment, and stepped out on a cigar-box balcony. The place was old and neglected, cluttered with a ripped sun umbrella, two rusted metal chairs and a table, a few withered plants, and a clumsy rack for drying laundry.

He leaned on an iron railing and stared at the Mediterranean, dotted with bright sails, yachts, and a luxury cruise ship. This was Beaulieu-sur-Mer. France's Côte d'Azur. To the east, Menton and Italy, with three corniche roads and spectacular cliffs. And westward, Villefranche and the Cape of Nice. Monte Carlo less than seven miles away, Nice just under six, and in the season snow-covered mountains after a one-hour drive.

Then he looked down three floors to the busy lower Corniche, and the transformation was startling. Cars and trucks and buses and motorcycles and noise and pollution. Certainly not a scene extracted from the Riviera holiday brochures, or a backdrop normally associated with the villa people or the yacht people or the beautiful people in the golden circles.

"Steven." Ellie was calling him. "Please come here for a moment."

He moved inside and found her stretched across the bed, fully clothed, in a pensive mood. Apparently she had finished popping a normal dose of Dr. Lambert's capsules, with her usual "one for good measure." The familiar bottle and glass of water stood on a table nearby.

"The sclerosis ghouls are feasting on my creativity," Ellie complained in a dreamy whisper as her husband sat and took her hand. "We'll never control them," she added.

"Help me lower the odds," Steven said as she relaxed, and conditions seemed balanced enough for a rational exchange. "Will you listen?"

"Oh, Christ," she murmured. "Do it gently."

"Examine the problems and face reality," he said. "Consider an immediate move back to the States."

"Not until we receive a message," she responded quickly. "This is my final chance to score."

"Ellie—" The reporter shook his head dejectedly. "Forget it, huh?"

"What about the phone ringing and the fast click-offs?" she asked. "Three times last week and once yesterday afternoon."

"A kook," he replied patiently. "Or wrong numbers."

"Or someone with a confession." She narrowed her eyes. "Do you really believe that I had a visitor at the Lake?"

Steven hesitated. "I do," he answered. "You should be convinced by now."

"Then why doubt the existence of a contact on the run?" Eleanor asked, her voice rising. "I was told that problems might delay him."

"For over a year?"

"Why not?"

"Listen to me." He released her hand and spoke firmly. "I'll go along with you. There could be someone out there getting up the nerve to approach us. A nut. Or a petty hood with a clever scheme. Or a group of these funny characters. You're a recognized author and I'm an established journalist. And our problems are not exactly secrets. We are perfect targets for a wild commercial plot. Legal or otherwise. It's late now, but I still wouldn't be a damn bit surprised if you heard from your contact, Ellie. But remember this, if it happens—which I doubt—we'll either ignore it, laugh it away, beat hell out of it, or recruit the gendarmes, because we are in no position to get messed up with fruitcakes."

"I'll wait—and have faith." Eleanor glared defiantly at her husband. "Only my illness can stop me."

"And money," Steven reminded, toughening his approach. "We need income. Your royalty figures are zero, and our savings won't feed us past Christmas."

"We'll have a marketable property by then." Ellie insisted wearily. "Gamble on a long shot."

Steven lit her fuse by coming right to the point. "Ackerman opened a spot for me on the *Washington Post,* Ellie," he said. "I heard from him last week."

Ellie pressed her lips together, and turned away from him. Her voice went cold. "I will never go back to America as a cripple, and a loser as well."

"The best way—"

"I want to sleep now." The capsules were taking over. "You should go out and walk and breathe some fresh air, Steven. The weather is perfect."

Garth walked the streets of the busy resort town, glancing blankly at the shopwindows and the passing tourists with their jabbering children, oily pink skin, and gaudy beach paraphernalia. Occasionally a familiar local would emerge, nod robot-style, and force a quiet "monsieur," as a matter of duty, but Steven Garth's mind was on Ellie, her sickness, and their predicament. From the nerve-battering days and nights at Cayuga Lake, up to the present, they had been existing in a state of isolation and futility, and Garth was rapidly approaching his saturation point.

The Café de Beaulieu, a typical coffee and snack bar on the main drag, was an unpretentious establishment with a cramped assortment of sidewalk tables and chairs, and a young, inexperienced-looking waiter responsible for serving the mixture of bored regulars and curious visitors.

Fatigued and thirsty after doing a zigzag course around the village, Steven went inside and found a corner booth, away from the pavement view and the waggle of foreign tongues.

He was seldom a customer in this place. Steven spent most of his time at home examining research papers, correspondence files, and a shelf of reference books, anticipating possible feature articles on a range of subjects. Deep inside, however, the former reporter knew that the project—like others conceived on his own in the past —was strictly a form of therapy, an exercise designed to occupy his mind during this period of stress and unemployment. Mostly he looked after Ellie and did everything in his power to keep her level and away from excess medication. But time was running out for both of them.

Yesterday's telephone ring and swift disconnection were gnawing at him, although he had said nothing to Eleanor about his feelings. Previous calls and quick hang ups had been written off as errors or nuisance, yet these minor disturbances, along with other signals, real or imagined, had added to a growing suspicion that his wife's mysterious contact was about to surface.

Tactics had already been formulated, in case someone had actually taken advantage of Eleanor's unstable condition by visiting the Lake with an outrageous plot and intentions of following through. Garth would listen calmly, fake ignorance, and do everything possible to avoid trouble and involvement. The connection would have to be minimized and terminated, right at the start, before Eleanor could grab a straw and wreck all prospects of employment for him, and a sane convalescence in the United States for her.

On this date—Sunday, June 3, 1979—Edgar P. Rand, known as the Major, entered the Café de Beaulieu, scanned the clients, then headed straight for the corner booth where Steven was finishing a cold mug of beer.

"I didn't want to bother you at home because of the missus." The Major, a bundle of nerves, was mopping his sweaty brow with a handkerchief. "In fact, sorry to disturb you here without a formal appointment."

"No problem." Steven watched the spreading red blotches on his neck. "Want a drink?" he asked.

"Yes, a cold beer, please," Rand answered politely. "Many thanks."

The Major was a dark-haired, beefy character in his early sixties, with a large oval face, a neat mustache, and a humorless expression. Layers of his flab were stuffed expertly into a tailored jacket and trouser outfit. Steven had spoken to him previously, casually, over a coffee or an afternoon drink. Although it was a guess, the former reporter considered Rand to be a shady type, with illegal connections somewhere, not really a working hood but obviously a man earning quiet cash payments from unorthodox wheeling and dealing on the side.

Unfortunately, Rand was a book-a-day reader, familiar with Ellie's novels and background—including her marriage to the award-winning investigative reporter. To his credit, the Major was tight-lipped about the Garths and their reputations: a big help in a small, gossipy community. Indeed, the man handled his own affairs just as discreetly, and Steven had no desire to probe for details.

Years ago, Edgar P. Rand, a veteran of World War Two, had left a divorced wife and two grown children in the States and moved to Beaulieu-sur-Mer. The Major's French apartment was a rental, but he also owned a house over the border in the mountains of Italy, and he made frequent trips in order to enjoy the change of scenery.

And that was all Steven Garth knew about the man. And that was all he cared to know about the man. But on this afternoon, over a beer, and not by chance, Major Edgar Rand was anxious to reveal some very personal information.

"An unbelievable thing happened to me last night," the Major whispered, leaning forward in his chair. "My head is still reeling from the impact."

The young waiter plunked a mug of beer in front of him, slid a bill under the ashtray next to Steven, and then moved lazily to another table. Rand straightened up and drained half the contents in one long swallow. "Many thanks," he repeated gratefully, dabbing the corners of his mouth with the same handkerchief. "A real thirst quencher."

Steven nodded and waited rather impatiently for him to continue.

"You know I own a shack in the mountains," he said in a low, confidential tone of voice. "Perinaldo."

"Where?"

"Perinaldo." He was leaning forward again. "A remote Italian village just over the border."

"And?"

"I drove up there yesterday morning to spend a week or two," he explained. "But this incredible experience rushed me home. As soon as my brain cleared, I thought of Eleanor and Steven Garth, and here we are."

Steven frowned and looked at his watch. This was not a phony show of restlessness; he checked the hour and decided that it was late. "Please get on with it, Major," he said. "I want to leave."

Genuinely troubled, Rand gulped more beer, inched even closer to Steven, and finally stated his business. "I found a strange man hiding in the barn," he said, nervously. "He was pointing a loaded revolver."

Steven sat back, folded his arms, and studied the Major before reacting. "Were you attacked?" he asked calmly.

"No."

"Threatened?"

"In a way."

"Have you contacted the police?" Steven watched the perspiration drip from Rand's forehead and begin to moisten the brightly patterned tablecloth. "Your friend is probably an escaped convict or a lunatic," he added, still examining the Major thoughtfully.

"No," Rand blurted. "The man wants to give us a shocking confession in exchange for special favors." He paused and then accented each syllable for maximum effect. "His unique story will electrify the world."

"Marvelous," said Steven. "Call the police."

"Absolutely not." The Major looked around at the other customers and brought his voice down a notch. "He'll commit suicide if police, reporters, or strangers come to the house. We've had a long discussion, and I believe every word. There are no official charges against the man. He is being hunted by certain dangerous people, and he needs assistance in order to survive. Unless his requests are granted, without tricks, the story will never be told." Rand took a deep breath and sighed out his final statement with great intensity. "I've agreed to help in every possible way."

Steven started to gather up the beer tabs. "Why are you pitching me?" He was becoming irritated. "And how dare you think about involving my wife in this damn nonsense?"

"Please, Mr. Garth." The Major's flesh was starting to puff around his eyes and make them slits. "Give me time for an explanation."

"Do it quickly," said Steven. "I want to get back right away."

"This is a rare opportunity for us all," the Major said without a pause. "An exclusive story, a confession, worth a million dollars or more. Your experience and—"

"What the hell are you selling?" Steven motioned to the waiter. "I am really late now, Rand," he said. "My wife is home alone."

Rand turned and saw the waiter was occupied at a crowded table on the sidewalk. Taking advantage of the delay, he faced Garth again, determined to build some enthusiasm in the closing minutes. "With your journalistic experience, and Ellie Garth's publishing contacts, we'll be guaranteed a fortune," he went on excitedly, keeping the volume a mark above zero. "Mainly, I trust you and respect you, and the man in the barn will accept your participation."

Steven was unable to stifle a laugh. "Sorry to be rude," he told the Major after settling down, "but you have to be putting me on with all this crap."

The look on Edgar Rand's blotched and swollen face said he wasn't. "Every word is true," asserted the Major. "So help me God."

Steven sat back in his chair and mumbled something about the waiter, showing that he thought the serious part of Rand's meeting was now over. "What's your boy confessing to, Major?" he asked lightly. "You know, it takes a hell of a lot to electrify this world in 1979."

"Maybe." Rand paused. "Stun is a better word." Abruptly, he twisted his large body, glared through the front plate glass at a customer's head, then swung back to Steven Garth. "Boland is out there," he complained.

"So?"

"This café is probably loaded with spooks like Boland," he replied. "I was a damn fool to blow off in here."

"Hell, yes," Steven agreed facetiously. "A screw-up."

Both men were quiet for a moment. Rand evidently thinking about his possible blunder and Steven staring restlessly in the direction of the slow-motion waiter outside. Jefferson Boland could be seen drinking coffee alone at a sidewalk table. Steven had spoken to

him occasionally while they were buying American newspapers in
the railroad station. Boland was a lanky, obnoxious southerner with
a crew cut and a thick drawl. The man looked to be in excellent
physical condition at forty or forty-five.

Once, while shopping in the morning, Steven had taken a quick
coffee break at the Beaulieu and Rand had moved from another table
in order to join him for a cup and a croissant. Steven recalled his
derogatory observations when Boland had sauntered by the café.
According to Rand, he was a suspicious recent arrival, a man with
a shadowy past—and present. Interpol, the CIA, Internal Revenue,
and undercover drug busting had been mentioned as possible links
for Jefferson Boland. According to Rand, the leathery southerner
was evasive about his background and about his reasons for settling
in the area. The Foreign Legion code had always been understood
and tolerated by the American exiles here, but—according to the
Major—Boland was a sleazy piece of work; he should never be
allowed to roam the vicinity and mingle and be accepted without
revealing a few more personal details.

According to the Major, Boland had disclosed two facts over a
few strong drinks, although he had refused to elaborate on them or
answer any questions. His wife had died of cancer, and he had
worked in London, England, for six years, assigned to the American
Embassy. Nothing else was known about Boland. Except, according
to Rand, he had mean eyes that locked on and glared even when he
was smiling.

"Come to my apartment tonight." The Major was scribbling his
telephone number on a scrap of paper. "I'll give you all—"

"No chance," Steven Garth broke in at once. "Find some other
playmates, Major."

"I am not playing a game, Mr. Garth," said Rand indignantly.
"There is a man hiding in my barn with a loaded gun and a brain
full of secrets."

"Call the police."

Ignoring the words, Rand folded the paper neatly, and shoved
it across the table. "My telephone number." He waited until the

former reporter picked it up and crumpled it into his back pocket. "Call me this evening if you change your mind." The Major straightened his jacket, put away the stained handkerchief, and made a final appeal. "Better listen to my complete story before turning away," he advised firmly. "This is a golden opportunity for all of us."

"Save your breath, Major." Garth watched the young waiter's lazy approach. "I have enough problems of my own," he said, and he meant it to be final.

2

Beaulieu-sur-Mer
France
Late afternoon
Sunday, June 3, 1979

Ellie opened the door for him and smiled when he arrived at the apartment. She was moving without a support, hesitantly, a bit wobbly, and dragging her left foot; but she was moving on her own, and this warmed Steven's insides.

And she had changed out of her nightdress into slacks and a smart blouse—the difference was spectacular. And she had combed and brushed her long brown hair and made it shine. And she had applied just enough make-up to accentuate her green eyes and delicate features. Steven kissed her tenderly and gave her compliments. Ellie Garth was up during a slight remission, and every second had to be recognized and appreciated, because the downs were abrupt and devastating.

"You were late, so I decided to cook my own meal," she said playfully. "To hell with your spaghetti bolognese."

They were in the front room, Steven relaxing on a sofa, and Ellie facing him in a pillowy wicker chair.

"How did it go?" he asked.

"A real disaster," she admitted. "Can you believe a seven-egg omelette?"

"Why not?"

"Five on the kitchen walls and two still in the pan." She brushed hair away from her eyes, a girlish habit, a reminder of days before, and Steven watched closely. "All of a sudden," she went on, "the ghouls arrived with uncontrollable muscle tremors, and dystaxia, and I splattered yolks everywhere and sat on the floor and laughed my guts out, because it was perfect slapstick and I was the audience."

Steven waited for her to look up at him. "Excuses, excuses, excuses," he said, attempting to smile her back to the previous mood. "You were a lousy cook from the beginning."

"Agreed." Ellie softened again. "Now go make your damn spaghetti bolognese."

As usual over dinner, Steven did what he could to pull the concentration away from Ellie's difficulties at the table. She had to bend her head forward and place her face very close to the rims of bowls and plates to shorten the traveling distance for all cutlery, or the contents would spill or tremble off before reaching her mouth. Drinking from a cup or a glass was always a problem, and the consequences of double vision and other symptoms were frustrating enough to make her curse and quit and burst into tears.

On this particular evening, instead of television or plot ideas or the rehashing of newspaper and magazine features, he knew that his outlandish conference with the Major at the Café de Beaulieu would be diverting enough to cover Ellie's battle with pasta and meat sauce.

Speaking in a glib, almost joking manner, he recounted the Major's story of finding a hunted man in his barn with a loaded weapon and a burning desire to trade his confession for special favors. Without glancing in Ellie's direction, Steven mentioned Rand's claim that the intruder had threatened to commit suicide if police, reporters, or strangers came to the house.

"Major Edgar Rand has invited me to a private briefing at his apartment tonight." Steven laughed, tasted his wine, and shook his head in exaggerated disbelief. "The man is a complete dingdong," he said. "A perfect example of what happens if you stay too long in these exotic boondocks, Ellie."

"Are you going?"

Ellie's blunt question and serious tone of voice were expected. He gazed across the table at her and was forced to squint because of the dim, flickering candlelight which had become an essential prop for his wife at their evening meals.

"Well?" She was resting after a brief contest with Steven's spaghetti. "Are you going?"

"Of course not," he replied emphatically. "I just told you that Rand is a nut."

"I met him about a year ago," said Ellie. "He seemed to be reasonable."

"We don't know the man."

"Aren't you interested?" she asked. "Curious?"

"No."

"Edgar Rand seeks you out in a café, babbles about a fugitive, a loaded gun, and the possibility of an electrifying confession," Ellie went on, brewing up steam. "And you're not interested or curious?"

"No."

"Can you tell me why?"

"I don't believe a word out of his fat mouth." Irritatedly, Steven placed his spoon and fork on the table and sipped more of the wine. "Guaranteed, nobody is in Rand's barn waiting to make history, my dear."

"What's his angle?"

"I don't know."

"Do you—"

"Give me a break, Ellie," Steven interrupted sharply. "This is the wrong time for a Cayuga Lake put-down."

But Ellie carried on anyway, in a quiet, steady, catlike fashion.

"If John Conway, or any hack in the business, had tagged the Major as a possible source, you would be rushing to his apartment tonight," Ellie chided. "Am I right, Steven?"

"Wrong." Steven had returned to his spaghetti and picked at it with a lack of interest in order to avoid eye contact with Ellie. "Rand is a zero," he stated.

"But he told you about a hidden fugitive, a loaded gun, and a possible confession." Ellie was beginning to lose her gentle touch. "The Major has to be our contact."

"Very likely."

"Go tonight and investigate," she persisted. "Take a little step on your own."

He looked up and their eyes met. "Rand is either a liar or a con artist or a psychopath," said Steven, pushing the food away. "Maybe a sick blend of all three," he added. "We are not getting involved with him."

"Suppose everything is true," Ellie snapped back. "He could have found a gunman hiding in the barn."

"I advised him to call the police," said Steven. "We'll stay away from this village barracuda, Ellie."

"Why?" Her left arm was trembling, and Steven noticed. "Did it ever occur to you that a liar, a con artist, a psychopath, and a village barracuda might be the link to our man on the run?"

"You know better." He watched her fight to control her movements. "I should never have mentioned the bull session with Rand. Forget about—"

"Paul Ackerman has a spot for Garth on the *Washington Post*," she interrupted, straining to conceal the results of her losing battle. "Do you honestly expect me to go back now as a goddamn vegetable?"

During an uneasy silence, Steven stared at Ellie, and his frown eventually developed into a smile. "What a jealous broad you really are," he teased her. "And stubborn too."

"Visit the apartment," she urged again. "Listen to Rand's proposition, for the sake of curiosity and for me." Ellie was near the candle, and the light shaded her features dramatically; Steven studied the effects with interest. "Even a dingdong situation is worth exploring, because my creative time is about up, and I know—" She broke off, sighed wearily, and tapped her forehead. "All the machinery inside has started fading to black, Steven."

"Edgar Rand is a flimsy last straw," Steven said. "We have to plan for the States."

"Later," Ellie replied. "Organize things before the end of the year."

"Without a doubt."

"Go see Rand," she persisted. "I have a deep feeling that you'll bring something home."

"A headache and nausea," Steven predicted, reaching into his back pocket for the crumpled phone number. "You will never be a vegetable, Ellie, take my word." He smoothed the piece of paper on the table and glared at the Major's handwriting. "But I am certain to become a horse's ass, tonight."

Located in a newly constructed building, Rand's apartment was clean, modern, and tastefully furnished, unlike most of the long-term rentals for budget-conscious Beaulieu residents. Steven realized at once that some of the art objects and expensive bric-a-brac had never been recorded on an estate agent's inventory. Rand had money and possessions at least, more than he was likely to report officially.

The Major had changed his outfit and his entire attitude. He was cool and deliberate and primed for serious business. After locking the door, he thanked Garth for coming, motioned to a small table in the front room, and offered drinks. Garth sat, and in minutes Rand had provided a fifth of Scotch, two glasses, a pear-shaped ice bucket, tongs, and wooden bowls full of salted peanuts.

When Rand lowered his plump bottom to a chair and started pouring whisky, Steven Garth was lecturing himself about tolerance and manners, for the sake of curiosity, and for Ellie.

"The fellow in my barn is called Muazzam Labadi," said the Major, coming right to the point. "He talks like a born American but his passport is Jordanian."

"I love him already," Steven remarked with a straight face. "What's his problem?"

Evenly this time, and not perspiring, Rand explained that Labadi claimed he was being tracked by many deadly hunters, although the Arab had refused to be explicit. "I figure the Mafia," Rand said, "and union muscle and some American Intelligence agents and probably a few sensitive Middle Eastern characters." He waited for an audible reaction, heard nothing but a grunt, and decided to finish. "Labadi thinks he lost most of them on his run from Le Havre."

Disregarding ice and peanuts, and maintaining his control as promised, Steven sampled the whisky and noticed that Edgar Rand was doing the same. "Quite a chase," he said doubtfully. "How did your Arab guest become so damn popular?"

"Labadi claims that he participated in the assassination of Robert Kennedy," the Major told him after swallowing hard. "And I believe every word," he added.

Steven had an immediate urge to blast off about ignorance and gullibility and the lack of respect for a man's knowledge, experience, and time, but instead he attempted to correct the statement. "Your guest means John Fitzgerald Kennedy," he pronounced acidly. "Dallas in 1963."

"Robert Francis Kennedy," the Major slammed back without a hesitation. "June fifth, 1968, in Los Angeles."

"You fucking idiot," Steven fumed. "I covered the Robert Kennedy story all the way."

"How well I know," Rand said patiently. "That's part of the reason I approached you and why you should be fascinated, and eager to visit Muazzam Labadi as soon as possible."

Steven filled his mouth with Scotch and held back an ugly outburst. He allowed the drink to go down slowly and deaden his temper. Without being aware, Rand had fingered an open wound, the Robert Kennedy murder, a very special case in Steven's research files, and still a fresh memory for personal reasons.

"The Senator was killed by Sirhan Bishara Sirhan," he recited in a monotone. "There is no official evidence of any conspiracy."

"Meet with Labadi," Edgar Rand advised. "The Arab has a different version."

For the sake of curiosity and for Ellie, and possibly for himself, Steven decided to sit back, pull in his claws, and give Major Rand the floor. "Proceed," said Steven, lifting his glass as in a toast. "I want to hear the rest of this fantasy."

Rand grabbed a handful of peanuts, flipped them into his mouth, chewed like a monkey, and then washed them down with a large gulp of whisky. "Labadi was paid off by certain people in New York City, on June seventh, 1968," he divulged. "The Arab made a hasty exit from the States on June ninth."

Ever since, according to what he'd told the Major, Labadi had been living undercover in Beirut with close friends and sympathizers. To guarantee privacy, the grapevine had spread a faked obituary two months after his arrival; and evidently the plan had worked in America and elsewhere. But in time Muazzam Labadi's money, patience, and welcome had faded, and he was forced to scramble and take his chances.

A blank expression camouflaged the former reporter's thinking as Rand spoke about Labadi's unique familiarity with Sirhan, the plot, the conspirators, the assassination, and the startling events which had followed, just before his rapid departure on June 9, 1968.

"Labadi's facts are based on personal involvement," said the Major. "And privileged information."

"He gave you details?" Steven tried a few salted peanuts. "Names, dates, places, and so forth?"

"Of course not," he answered. "His inside information is the man's only bargaining tool."

Steven Garth smiled, but wiped it off quickly after inspecting the grim-faced lump sitting opposite him. "What turns on his machine?" he inquired, playing along. "How do you extract all this incredible material?"

Abruptly the Major slammed his empty glass down hard on the table and glared. "I think you've squeezed my balls long enough, Mr. Garth," he said without raising his voice. "You accepted this invitation, and I demand a reasonable amount of courtesy and respect."

"I've reacted normally, Major," said Steven, refusing to compromise. "Your statements have been outlandish."

"An honest account of a jolting experience," Rand replied. "Take it or leave it."

"Complete your exercise." Steven finished his drink and turned down another. "Labadi talks about the Kennedy murder and gets a cut of the publishing action," he said, doing his best to move things along. "Am I correct?"

"Oh, Lord, no," the Major answered promptly. "He'll be gone forever once his confession is delivered."

"Why?"

Rand hesitated, evidently choosing his approach smartly, to placate Garth and keep the meeting rolling. "Labadi has to make this deal for his personal survival," he replied in a brisk, military way. "There are no practical alternatives for him."

Labadi, he explained, had agreed to audio-tape the story of Robert F. Kennedy's assassination from his own point of view—that of a conspirator responsible for certain key elements of the plot. During this tape session, he would also submit to questioning by an "expert," and record all known facts, including names, dates, and places.

"Fascinating proposition," Steven remarked, trying to keep impatience and skepticism out of his voice. "What does Labadi receive in exchange for this historic contribution?"

"Plastic surgery," the Major replied crisply. "A new identity."

Steven Garth sat still as Rand outlined how the Arab had to change faces and obtain an American passport and other relevant documents in order to walk free and start a different life. Otherwise he was a dead man, waiting to be crated and put under.

"Safeguards to protect both sides have already been lined up and approved," Rand continued. "For example, there is no way for Labadi to disappear after surgery unless an acceptable tape has been produced and handed over. The rules also work for him. We honor our terms as scheduled, or the confession will be lost forever. I'll explain—"

"Major," Steven interrupted harshly, "what do you expect me to do about this strange happening of yours?"

"Join us as the expert," Rand stated. "Question Labadi and record his story," he continued. "And then I have a very exciting business arrangement to discuss with you and your wife."

The former reporter glanced at Rand's whisky bottle. "Pour us both a short one," he advised. "My closing remarks are going to be offensive."

Rand was about to protest, but he changed his mind, followed instructions, and braced himself for another dose of humiliating unpleasantness.

"First of all, I don't believe that a man is hiding in your barn, Major," Steven started point-blank. "And if there is such a creature, he is obviously a fraud and he is bullshitting you, or for some unknown reasons both of you are doing the same to me, and I do not particularly like the idea."

"How can you—"

"Just a goddamn minute," Steven Garth broke in again. "Let me finish."

The blotching and perspiration started to reappear on Edgar Rand's face and neck as Steven's speech continued. "Now, if by chance there is a man hiding in your barn and he does know something about the murder of Robert Kennedy and wants to sound off about it"—Garth paused long enough to down the shot of whisky —"contact the Italian police and the American consulate at once," he warned. "Take my good advice, Major."

"Labadi's secrets will never be revealed if the authorities close in," said Rand firmly. "He'll trade his Robert Kennedy information for a face change and pertinent documents. Survival. Our deal is wrapped up. Make any other move and the Los Angeles conspiracy facts die with him."

"That's enough." Garth stood and prepared to leave. "Find some other helpers, my creepy friend," he growled. "Knocking on the Senator's tomb is very sick business."

"Visit Muazzam Labadi tomorrow in Perinaldo," Rand insisted as he also got to his feet. "You'll realize the significance of my discovery."

"See you around town, Major." Steven walked across the room, stopped at the door, turned, and faced him. "I still don't know what the hell you're peddling." His delivery was cold and tough and it matched his expression. "But whatever it is, we are not customers," he said with finality. "Do you understand?"

An awkward quiet followed, until Rand spoke again. "Give me your word of honor to maintain secrecy forever," he said, "and I'll back up all I've told you with a confession of my own."

"The meeting is over," Steven reminded him bluntly. "Unlock the door."

Rand sat and poured himself a large whisky. "The Arab did not turn up at my shack by accident, Mr. Garth." He stared into the glass, and his tone was hushed and circumspect. "Many people have used the barn as a safe house." Rand looked up and noticed that Garth was interested. "I have a contact across the border in Italy," he whispered. "Muazzam Labadi *will* be able to change his face, get an American passport, and other relevant documents. And we'll record the story of Robert Kennedy's assassination."

The Major grinned, and reached for his Scotch again as the former investigative reporter walked back to the table. "Like I said before," Rand told him, "I trust you."

3

Ordinarily, at two o'clock in the morning, Ellie would have been positioned on the bed, medicated, uncomfortable, and waiting for sleep. But Steven's cautiously phrased report about his meeting with the Major had pumped her adrenals and rouged her cheeks, and she was leaning forward in a chair reacting to every word. They were on the cramped balcony under a moonlit sky, and he was pleased to see his wife tuned up and energized, the first time in months.

Even so, he had attempted to keep her on a rational level by smacking down Rand's assassination talk and references to a confession and plastic surgery. Using his professional knowledge, Steven had shot large holes in the Robert F. Kennedy conspiracy theory, in order to prove that Muazzam Labadi was a figment of Rand's imagination or a bum on the run, an escaped convict, or a maniac or a partner in some kind of confidence game.

"I was ready to leave the goofy bastard," Steven explained calmly. "Then he mentioned an Italian setup over the border, and it rang a distant Conway bell." He thought about this for a moment. "We had reliable tips on a similar operation in the area, but it was impossible to glue enough facts together for solid reporting. Remember our three-part run on international terrorism?"

"Of course." Ellie's face suddenly reflected a pain as she adjusted her body in the chair. "Tell me the rest, Steven, please."

Knowing his audience, he nodded and went on about the Major's border contact, remembering to use a soft pedal.

For over a year, according to Rand, his barn in Perinaldo had been used as a safe house, a waiting room, the jumping-off pad for clients who had legitimate appointments at the Factory: a unique expertly staffed, well-equipped, and heavily guarded identity-changing facility. Every aspect of the process, from surgery to forgery to psychological guidance, was handled in this place.

The Factory, according to Rand, had been servicing tricky customers from all over the world. They included qualified loners, fanatical Arabs, Israeli hit squads, and organizations like Baader-Meinhof, Red Brigades, the Japanese Red Army, IRA, and friends of Carlos the Venezuelan. Even former Nazi brass had passed through.

Rand claimed the house rules were observed fanatically by all staff members. Once admission had been granted, a code of ethics as tight as high-level Mafia guaranteed respect for all contracts, prevented questioning, harassment, and invasion of privacy. On the flip side, the entire organization had been fused to vanish in a quick puff of smoke at the first hint of trouble. So far, rigid security, grateful clients, and loyal employees had kept the business moving with few problems. And God help the body and soul of anyone caught whispering secrets or plotting against the Factory.

"Where is this place?" Ellie asked. She was taking it all very seriously. "Did Rand give you any hints?"

Steven shook his head and explained. The Major had sworn that he was just a trusted intermediary, like others on the fringe assigned to strategic areas. He would care for each traveler at his barn in Perinaldo, handle the preliminary details, coordinate with the traveler's sponsor, make delivery, and then walk away holding a small percentage.

"Rand must know the location," Ellie insisted. "He delivers the packages, the clients."

"To a drop. Never to the Factory. Usually an apartment in a crowded residential district. And even these addresses switch frequently. According to Rand's story, he completes all his business at the drop, returns home, and that ends his linkage until the next client shows up in Perinaldo."

Ellie listened intently as her husband emphasized Rand's claim that the Factory address was unknown to him and to most others—including the customers. They received needles, and went under before arriving or departing. A very healthy arrangement, the Major had stressed. It was best to retain as little knowledge as possible about the Factory, the customers, and the sponsors. Rand had been getting steady assignments as a trusted helper because he was able to manage his fringe piece of the action and keep his nose clean at the same time. His prime rule for success: never, under any circumstances, become involved with a traveler.

"He did with Muazzam Labadi," Ellie broke in. "What's his excuse?"

"A special case," Steven answered. "Rand was unable to blink away the missing pages of American history."

"Oh, God."

"That's an exact quote," Steven announced, raising both hands as a sign of futility. "Are you getting a better picture of this nut?"

"Yes," Ellie replied. "The whole damn thing is outrageous, and I am positively fascinated."

"Really?"

In a disparaging manner, Steven explained that Edgar Rand had important plans and a business proposition to outline in detail. A chance of a lifetime. "But first, our Major wants me to visit Labadi, audition him, and convince myself that he participated in a Robert Kennedy assassination plot."

Ellie laughed, and the sound was unfamiliar after so many days and nights of symptoms and depression. "Here I am, straining for a lousy plot line, and Garth comes home with a thousand scenarios."

"A booby-hatch jumble."

"Our miracle," said Ellie excitedly. "How do you read all this now, Steven?"

"The same as before," he replied. "Rand is either a liar, a con artist, a psychopath, or a very sick mixture of all three."

"His Labadi confession?"

"Absurd."

"You once questioned the handling of the Robert Kennedy case," she reminded, wagging her finger. "The investigation, evidence, *and* trial."

"Many years ago," Steven said irritatedly. "I was young, cocky, and suspicious of everything." He paused and seemed to flash back for an instant before finishing. "Sirhan was the killer of Robert Kennedy. There is nothing on record to prove a conspiracy of any kind."

She watched carefully as he picked up a pack and tapped out a cigarette, one more than his self-imposed limit of six a day. "The Major's talk about an Italian contact interests me," he said, lighting up. "All the rest is pure crap."

"You believe the Factory exists?"

Steven took a long drag. "Rand probably exaggerated the customers and the facilities and their code of ethics," he said while exhaling smoke through his nose and mouth. "But I have a gut feeling there *is* an operation like it just over the border."

"And Rand is connected."

"Maybe," said Steven. "The barracuda is pocketing extra money from somewhere."

"What about his conspiracy pitch?"

"I don't know why he's using this freak approach." Steven leaned back in the chair and propped his shoes on the balcony railing. "Unless Kennedy is bait and Rand expects to hook us for some devious reason." He gazed straight ahead at the dim glow on the Mediterranean. "I can't untangle his motives."

There was silence until Ellie asked, "Do you have any plans?"

Without looking around, Steven knew that it was time once

again to shift gears and float her down to earth. "I refuse to blow this situation out of proportion," he stated. "We're dealing with a village idiot."

"Regardless," said Ellie impatiently. "Do you have any plans?"

"I figure three options," said Steven. "We'll select one right now." He yawned and closed his eyes. "Are you feeling strong enough?"

"Of course," Ellie responded without hesitation. "Go ahead."

"We turn Rand off, ignore him completely, scrub our ears with soap and water, and plan an immediate move to the States for a touch of normalcy and other benefits." He grinned and let the statement register. "A very practical selection," he added.

"Next?"

"We turn Rand off, ignore him completely, and I get in touch with the American or French or Italian authorities and repeat all his secrets, just in case some part of the fantasy happens to be true." Steven nodded approvingly. "After receiving our medals for civic responsibility, we plan an immediate move to the States for a touch of normalcy and other benefits."

"Next?"

"Steven H. Garth, investigative reporter, takes one step and visits a barn in Perinaldo to determine whether Rand is a liar, a con artist, a raving maniac, or a sick mixture of all three." Steven faced her and smiled again. "After completing this evaluation, we take appropriate action and then plan an urgent move to the States for a touch of normalcy and other benefits."

"The final option." Ellie's face brightened. "Have you made a choice?"

"Yes."

Steven would visit the Italian barn.

"Suppose you do find a man in Rand's shack, and his name is Muazzam Labadi, and he is a Jordanian, and he did participate in the assassination of Senator Kennedy?" Ellie was asking. "And what if the Factory is the same operation that you and Conway were unable to document?" She moved closer to him and rested her head on his shoulder. "Can you imagine the payoff if by chance the Major and Labadi are for real?"

"Ellie." Steven spoke firmly. "Keep everything in focus, or you'll scare me away."

After a pause, without changing position, she nodded and whispered agreement. The nearness of her face reminded him of things past, and he wondered if his decision had to do with getting an idea for Ellie, or was it really for Ackerman of the *Post,* or had he decided to visit the barn in Perinaldo just to disrupt the monotony of his Beaulieu existence?

Late afternoon
Monday, June 4, 1979

After leaving Menton and crossing the border to Italy, Edgar Rand's gray 1974 Fiat stayed on the lower coastal road and moved slowly through Ventimiglia, a crowded, bustling little town.

The somber-faced Major, outfitted in safari khaki and dressy half-boots, had been unusually quiet since leaving his apartment in Beaulieu. Ordinarily, a closed mouth would have pleased Steven Garth, but on this occasion it was strange—almost disturbing—to watch Rand ignore a captive audience and remain silent about the Arab, the Factory, the Robert Kennedy plot, a million-dollar audio tape, and the rest of his outlandish conspiracy package.

Steven had dressed for the trip in blue jeans, a tapered shirt, and loafers, and was casually inspecting the muddle of pedestrians and traffic on the busy Italian streets. "What's on your mind, Rand?" he asked finally, still gazing out the window.

Rand was slow to answer. "My gamble with Steven and Eleanor Garth," he said, keeping his eyes straight ahead.

The seriousness of Rand's tone prompted Steven to look over at him. "I'll be damned," he said, jokingly. "Do you mean there really is a guy hiding in Perinaldo?"

He studied the driver's trimmed mustache and bloated flesh, which had been cleanly shaved, powdered, and lotioned. There was no sign of amusement or any willingness to answer, so Garth made a fast transition. "Why did you approach us and take risks?" he asked, becoming ruffled. "Obviously I can set you up for a stiff interrogation based on assassination talk and Italian underground connections. Fantasy or not. You must have known that before we met in the café."

Edgar Rand nodded his large head several times. "Forgive me for being uneasy," he pleaded. "The stakes are very high, as you will discover in my barn later this evening."

Unimpressed, Garth continued to glare at the side of Rand's face until the man bit his lip nervously. "I'm curious," Steven said. "How can you sound off like a mental case and gamble that I won't blow a whistle?"

The car stopped at a red light. "I approached you for many reasons," the Major answered, glancing at his passenger brazenly. "You're a dynamic, experienced investigative reporter." There was genuine admiration in his voice. "You covered every phase of the Robert Kennedy story. A professional, a journalist who understands and respects confidentiality and the need to protect exclusive news sources."

"I might fool you."

"A slight possibility," Edgar Rand admitted. "But the odds are with me."

"Why?"

"Circumstances."

Rand looked away, changed gears, and inched ahead when the signal turned green. "Steven and Eleanor Garth are in desperate need of a big plot, fresh recognition, and quick money," he said rather arrogantly. "I'll bet on my hunch."

"Good luck to you."

"A publishing bonanza shows up on a haystack," Rand continued. "And two qualified, available made-to-order partners are living right down the street. Can you blame me for making the approach and taking risks?"

"I'll answer on the way home."

Along with irritation and resentment, Garth felt an urge to talk about the Factory: his personal interest and the abortive Conway mission and the importance of the facility and the chance that Rand might be associated—and to hell with the Kennedy foolishness. Instead of questioning the Major, he decided to sit back and wait for developments.

"We turn off here," said Edgar Rand. "Prepare yourself for a very bumpy ride."

Leaving the main street of Ventimiglia, they made a sharp left turn at Vallecrosia, just before reaching the outskirts of another scrambling frontier town called Bordighera. They were on a narrow road, a twisting climb, going up and up to a mountain village. An old sign at the intersection pointed to Perinaldo.

The frequent clink of bottles on the back seat prompted Rand to speak. "Labadi is probably starving again," he said. "That moody Arab will gobble up everything in my bag." He laughed and wiped a pudgy hand across his mouth. "And wait until he starts uncorking the vino."

There was no response. Pensively, Steven stared out the open window as twilight created fascinating shadow patterns in this quiet border district. Habitations were becoming more isolated—modest homes and small farms were growing scarcer. They heard the rushing sounds of a torrent on the left.

"I'm hungry myself," said Steven, covering the fact that he was anxious to inspect the barn. "Do we have far to go?"

"A few kilometers."

"The village?"

"No," the Major replied. "We detour up ahead."

After passing through a cluster of houses known as Soldano, the asphalt shrinks and the earth drops off on each side as the steep, lightly traveled road snakes its way up. This is the hilly region of Monte Peiga, Monte Caggio, Monte Rebuffao, and Monte Mera.

The Major squinted at the rearview mirror, although no other cars had been seen for miles. "Clear," said Rand as he slowed down and checked for a landmark on the right side of the road. Abruptly he veered off into what seemed to be a clump of bushes and thick weeds, but the vehicle plunged through and dropped easily to something resembling a widened footpath, choppy and pebbled and overgrown with foliage.

"What the hell is this?" The sudden maneuver had caught Steven unprepared. "An obstacle course?"

"I'm sorry," Rand answered, moving the car jerkily past a tangle of overhanging leaves. "We're pulling out now."

After a fast left, he was on a smoother trail, with fewer green plants scratching at their windows and clawing the doors. Steven looked at the puffy, unsmiling driver and felt a strong twinge of uneasiness as night started to close in and darken the area. Rand switched on the foglights as they moved closer to his place in the country.

"A shortcut," the Major explained. "Better than driving the long way around from Vallecrosia. I also wiggle down from the village on my own route," he continued. "These diversions are quick and private. A very important factor when I'm doing business at the shack."

Steven watched dim scenery and kept quiet as Rand geared his way through a maze of natural obstructions. Shortly after passing under a neglected arch, they were in a field, bouncing over mounds of earth and patches of tall grass.

"I want to apologize for the mess," said Rand. "We're on a remote hill. The properties are either unoccupied or going to pot or in the process of being renovated by local families in need of cheap housing." The Major was serious. "I've been doing some work on the interior," he said. "Expensive changes on the outside might spotlight my presence here and attract my distant neighbors. I've owned the shack and grounds for years and have never had a problem, with anyone."

The Major drove up to a dilapidated wooden structure, two floors almost completely hidden by trees with matted leafage and low branches.

"My dark corner," he said. "Primitive and isolated, but quite suitable for weary travelers."

Unexpectedly, Steven Garth's heart beat a little faster as he opened the car door, stepped out, and took a deep breath of fresh mountain air.

4

Perinaldo
Italy
Early evening
Monday, June 4, 1979

They were in the barn. Steven carried the Major's shopping bag and followed his large behind up a ladder to a hay-strewn loft. Despite all the build-up, including a hurried lecture in the shack, Steven was still dubious about the existence of a Muazzam Labadi, or any other weary traveler.

His thinking was altered instantly as they stepped off the last rung and touched down on some crude planking. A lantern's glow illuminated the outline of a man sitting in a corner with his back propped against splintered wood and both hands aiming a heavy revolver directly at Steven's chest.

"Put it away," ordered the Major. "This is our unofficial interrogator, Steven Garth."

"How do I know?" a frosty low-pitched voice asked. "Show me documents."

"Accept my word," Rand said firmly as he walked over and deposited the bag next to his guest. "We've got food and drink in here, Labadi."

Ignoring Rand's offer, the man kept his eyes on Steven, and Steven stared back just as suspiciously.

"Are you really the tough bastard who used to go with John

Conway?" the man asked. "Sniping at hoods and politicians for the New York journals?"

"Lower that fucking weapon and I might answer you." Steven watched and waited, and so did Rand, and finally the revolver was brought down and placed on the straw, within easy grabbing distance of the man's hand.

"My name is Steven H. Garth, and I handled many assignments with John Conway," he announced bluntly. "And from now on I'll ask the questions."

The man failed to react, because he was already pawing his way into Edgar Rand's shopping bag, inspecting the contents and mumbling approval.

"How did you survive in Beirut?" Steven Garth asked. "What contacts did you have?"

"I knew two of Wadie Haddad's people."

Steven had to stop and think about that one, and then he smiled, and the reaction irritated Muazzam Labadi. "Do you think I'm a comedian?" the man asked.

"Hell, no," Garth replied. "Were you a member of the Popular Front for the Liberation of Palestine?"

"Not really," he explained. "I was just around doing odd jobs in exchange for strong protection."

"Does George Habash ring a bell?"

"Enough." Labadi narrowed his eyes and glared. "Why are you testing like I'm a punk in school?"

"Because my instincts tell me that you are completely full of shit," Garth leveled. "And if you fabricated this Beirut angle I can take off now and forget the rest of the Major's fairy tale."

"Take off!"

"Answer the questions, Labadi," Rand commanded. "You won't talk about the Kennedy conspiracy until we tape. So Garth has to find some way to gauge your authenticity."

"I refuse to be quizzed like a child," Labadi snapped back. "He's playing with me."

"Do you want to get serviced at the Factory?" Rand's expression was firm and convincing as he repeated Steven's question. "Ever heard of George Habash?"

Labadi studied the Major's face and recognized a lost cause. "He organized the Front with Haddad in 1966," said the Arab, giving in. "I only saw him a few times."

In picnic fashion, Rand, Labadi, and the reporter had shared portions of fried chicken and potato salad and fruit, and now Rand was pouring the wine into paper cups. His living quarters and furnishings were strictly off limits to all travelers, a condition respected by every member of the Factory network.

While they ate, Labadi had allowed Steven Garth to examine his Jordanian passport; in return, Garth had identified himself properly to the Arab. Edgar Rand seemed pleased with the exchange he'd organized. Now Garth looked closely at Labadi. He was thirty-four years old, medium height, and slightly built, with dark skin, black wavy hair, and good-looking features. He wore a leather jacket, corduroy pants, and battered military field shoes. There was a razor-thin scar over his left eye.

Short, deep lines furrowed down from either side of his nose, and gathered at the corners of his mouth, and this roughened up a boyish appearance. A very cold, suspicious, unemotional nature was also part of the first impression. Labadi seemed to be highly intelligent and unusually alert.

On the surface, and judging by types, Steven had to admit to himself that Labadi could have been a terrorist or an assassin. But the former journalist had prowled big-city streets and alleys for most of his life. He wasn't easily taken in by appearances.

"I'll dangle my limited Haddad knowledge," Steven said to Labadi. "And you can establish a trace of legitimacy or come off as part of a two-bit hoax right away."

"Like I said earlier." Labadi reached for his bottle and took a swig, ignoring Edgar Rand's paper cups. "You want to play games."

"Why not?" Steven asked sternly. "Let's drink and chat about Beirut and Dr. Haddad, and give me an excuse for being in this goddamn barn." He looked at the Major. "Either this character opens up about something of interest or we leave at once."

It was not until Rand repeated his threats about the Factory that the Arab pocketed the revolver and agreed to cooperate, within his stated limits. He stretched his legs out full, leaned back against the wood, and took frequent gulps of wine, facing Steven Garth, who sat cross-legged on the hay and fired questions about Haddad and Beirut. Rand's ungainly hulk was draped over a milking stool.

In a relaxed, confident, insolent manner, Labadi surprised Garth and fascinated the Major by proving that he knew a great deal about Beirut and Dr. Wadie Haddad—obviously more than his interrogator.

Answering with elaborations, he proved his awareness that the Popular Front's guerrilla activities were being financed by Arab interests opposed to all peaceful negotiations with Israel—among them, Libya. Haddad's connections were listed, including the Baader-Meinhof group in West Germany, the Japanese Red Army, and other notorious terrorist organizations. Offering extra details, Labadi claimed that he was present at but did not participate in the first hijacking by Palestinians, under the direction of Haddad: the seizure and diversion of an El Al plane in July 1968. He fielded a trick question easily and recalled that he went underground with Haddad and his associates after rockets pounded the doctor's Beirut apartment in July 1970.

The traveler said that he had been forced to use a code name, Abu Zaki, and to participate in one of Haddad's most startling actions: the hijacking of three airliners, and the attempted hijacking of a fourth, in September 1970.

Labadi was aware, very much aware, of a rift between Wadie Haddad and key members of the Popular Front. George Habash and his loyal followers had come to regard the seizure of airliners as more harmful than beneficial to the Palestinian cause.

"Are you convinced, Garth?" Rand was beaming. "Muazzam is legitimate."

"Sounds that way." Steven sipped wine from a cup and Labadi tilted his bottle. "Quite a performance."

The Arab had responded to every question calmly, accurately, with detailed personal touches, as a man on the inside. Labadi had lived in Beirut, close to Wadie Haddad, or he had researched and memorized a pile of documentation, or . . . a person or persons unknown had skillfully briefed him or programmed him for this special assignment.

"Want to hear more?" Unlike his other mannerisms, Labadi's smile was awkward and uncertain. "Have I established a trace of legitimacy?"

"Beirut and Haddad are covered," Steven answered. "Now tell me why you're running."

"I explained that one," the Major snapped indignantly. "He participated in the killing of Robert Kennedy."

Steven nodded, leaned back on his elbows, and studied Labadi very carefully. "True?" he asked.

"Stop jerking me around." Nonchalantly, Labadi slid down a few inches and rested his feet on a suitcase, which appeared to have been recently purchased. "Rand outlined my situation."

"Verify it," said Steven adamantly. "Did you participate in the killing of Robert Kennedy?"

Without a change of expression, Labadi tossed an empty wine bottle, and it landed on straw. "I was involved," he said. "And your interrogation ends right there."

Rand pulled his stool closer in order to break things up again. "You know that Labadi has a firm deal with me for the confession," he told Garth. "We'll talk about the particulars on the way home."

Steven's attention was focused on Labadi, and he hardly heard what the Major was saying. "You seem to be a very astute guy," he complimented. "Do you honestly expect a serious response from me?"

"I don't expect anything from you," Labadi replied. "My arrangement is with Edgar Rand."

"Rand didn't live with the Bobby Kennedy assassination," said Steven. "Try somebody who knows the facts."

"That's a funny one." Labadi uncorked another bottle of wine.

"Most of you people are still in the dark after eleven years." He poured with a steady hand and filled paper cups for Garth and the Major. "Nobody dug for worms."

"And you have the real story."

"Correct." He took a gulp from the bottle and swallowed hard. "All details, including names, dates, and places, will be audio-taped as soon as Rand follows through."

"The Factory."

"Right."

"A change of identity."

"Right."

"Are the police chasing you?"

"No."

"The Mafia?"

"Piss off."

"Fine idea." Steven sat up smartly and brushed straw off his clothing. "Rand wants me to play unofficial interrogator. And there are other considerations. My wife and I have—"

"Labadi knows," Rand interjected at once. "What do you expect him to do, Garth?"

"Answer a few Kennedy question on the spot," he replied. "Give me a reason to watch his arrogant face."

Unperturbed, Labadi set the bottle down, pulled his shoes off the valise, and leaned forward to challenge Garth. "I participated in a conspiracy to murder Robert F. Kennedy," he announced, without showing emotion. "The victim was stalked and finally hit by Sirhan Bishara Sirhan, at the Ambassador Hotel in Los Angeles, California, on June fifth, 1968." His dark eyes stared unblinkingly. "I was paid off on June seventh, 1968, in New York City, and left the United States on June ninth. End of statement. Our meeting is adjourned."

"Now don't get yourself all steamed up, Muazzam," said Rand in a comforting, fatherly tone. "Garth is responding as I anticipated. The man is an experienced journalist. We can't blame him for being suspicious and doubtful at this point."

Lunatics, thought Steven—or talented, cleverly rehearsed

hoods on a priority mission. He watched as the Arab returned to his flat-out shoes-up, head-back, wine-guzzling position. Major Edgar Rand unstuck himself from the milking stool. He bent over awkwardly and rubbed up the blood flow in his stumpy legs. A remote possibility crossed Garth's mind. Was Rand straight and gullible, and had Labadi actually sold him the Robert Kennedy plot in order to check in at the Factory?

Although he felt he could write off most of the Perinaldo episode as an affair staged for unknown reasons, Steven was still unable to suppress an instinctive belief that a face-changing operation did exist, and that Rand's attachments were legitimate.

"We *need* Garth's help." Rand was standing and glaring down at the inattentive Arab. "He's got a right to ask a few Kennedy questions."

Like a dream, thought Steven as he watched Labadi tip the wine and ignore the fat man. Regardless, certain facts had to be accepted and digested sensibly. An apparent fugitive was planted in Edgar Rand's Italian barn. The character had a gun and a Jordanian passport which identified him as Muazzam Labadi. He was bright and carefully programmed. Also, fantasy or not, he had admitted taking part in the assassination of Robert Kennedy.

Steven's thoughts were scattered by the Major's rough handling of Labadi.

"Put that damn bottle away!" he yelled. "I'll terminate our contract if we lose Garth and his wife. My big payoff depends on them. Just like the Factory is your only hope for survival. Bait him! Tease him! Convince him! Let him know that he's talking to the real thing!"

Impassively, Labadi sat up, corked the wine, and propped the bottle against his suitcase. He removed a clean handkerchief from his pocket and wiped his mouth. But he said nothing.

"You claim that Kennedy was stalked," the Major pressed. "At least tell Garth where and when."

"This information will be tape-recorded," said Labadi without glancing up. "After the Factory."

"Now!" Rand ordered. "Where and when did your people stalk Bobby Kennedy?"

Reflecting anger for the first time, Labadi's flesh tightened. His scar was gone, and the deep lines too, and his eyes became glistening black-centered marbles. The effect transformed his entire appearance and reminded Steven once again that Rand's sulky Arab could very easily have been a terrorist or a paid assassin.

"We made a deal, Rand." He looked up and warned him quietly but persuasively. "Follow the rules, or I'll split and play dumb until another opportunity comes along."

"Or they pulverize you."

"Whichever comes first." He shrugged. "This is a hallelujah finish."

Labadi's expression helped to underline the meaning, and Rand finally broke eye contact and turned away. "You make sense," the Major admitted. "We have to obey the rules and maintain a code of ethics."

Without comment, Steven drained the wine in his paper cup and then rose to his feet. He stretched lazily as Rand approached him. "Hope you understand," said the Major. "My bargaining position is very delicate."

Steven nodded and took his final look at the Arab. "It's been charming, Muazzam," he remarked sarcastically. "You must come to our place some evening."

The Major frowned as Garth turned abruptly and headed for the ladder. "Wait a minute," Labadi called just as Steven was putting his foot on the upper rung. "They stalked him for about two weeks before the assassination."

Rand's face lit up again. "Did you get that?" He checked to make sure of his audience.

Steven rotated slowly, folded his arms, and listened without a trace of enthusiasm.

"The first hit was scheduled for Pomona, California." Labadi was back to normal, relaxed, chewing on hay. "A Kennedy stopover at a place called Robbie's Restaurant."

"What happened there?" the Major asked. "Can you feed Garth any of the details?"

"Absolutely not," Labadi replied bluntly. "The story will be taped."

Expecting a positive reaction, Rand threw a quick side glance at the former reporter and drew a blank. Garth's eyes were fixed on Labadi, and his expression was frigid and contemptuous.

Rand continued to probe anyway. "Did you get instructions to strike again from another location?"

"They," Muazzam broke in at once. "I was never personally on the firing line."

"Understood," said Rand. "Go ahead."

"Next was the Los Angeles Sports Arena." He returned Steven's gaze evenly. "They had to abort for reasons unknown to me."

"Are you including Sirhan?" the Major asked.

"Jesus Christ!" Labadi spat hay and pulled himself away from the wall. "How many times do I have to blast you off, Rand?" the Arab griped. "We record after the Factory!"

"Of course." The Major lowered his fat head to emphasize the apology. "Just wrap up this stalking business for Garth," he said in a pleasant tone of voice. "Handle it your own way."

Without hurrying, Labadi got up and straightened his leather jacket, making certain that the gun was in place. He walked past the Major to face Steven.

"Kennedy was stalked at a rally on June second." They were eye to eye. Labadi dipped into his pocket and brought out cigarettes. "The Ambassador Hotel," he said, knocking the package against his fist. After a slight hesitation, Steven took one and Labadi did the same. "No positive results on that date," he added, ignoring Garth's unswayed manner. "Sirhan finally connected in the pantry on June fifth."

"And we'll get the details later," said Rand, moving over to join them. "A true history of the Bobby Kennedy assassination."

The Arab struck a match and lit Garth's cigarette and then his own. "I forgot a place," he muttered, exhaling smoke toward the rafters. "San Diego."

Steven heard a tap on his memory vault, a faint sound because of circumstances and the passing years, but it was audible enough to make him ask, "Where in San Diego?"

"A hotel." Labadi thought for a moment. "The El Cortez."

"When?"

"On June third, 1968."

The words poked at his senses, although he could only recall jotting something in his files about the El Cortez, one of dozens of question marks accumulated during the investigation and trial of Sirhan Sirhan. Part of the notation suddenly came back to him and he tested Muazzam's computerized knowledge. "Do you remember any politician who appeared with Kennedy at the El Cortez on June third?"

Labadi forced a smile. "Kennedy canceled at the last minute because of exhaustion," he responded. "They didn't have a target on June third."

"Satisfied, Garth?" Rand asked boastfully. "You won't trip him up."

"I can see that." Steven looked at his watch and then Labadi. "Anything else before we head back?"

"Just one point." Labadi moved a step closer. "The Major has all kinds of reasons for trusting you," he said, looking again like a terrorist, an assassin. "Please think of the consequences if you let him down."

"Are you threatening me?"

"No, sir," he replied in a quiet, almost gentle tone. "I feel that a good reporter knows when to break a story, and when to hold for maximum impact."

5

During the journey home from Perinaldo, Edgar Rand babbled incessantly about Labadi, his confession, a pot of gold, and the need for secrecy and immediate action. "This man participated in the murder of Robert F. Kennedy," he dramatized. "And we have an exclusive."

They were speeding back on the autoroute instead of using the low coastal road. Steven stared at oncoming headlights and replayed the insane barn incident while Rand continued to chatter.

Labadi was a shrewdly constructed robot, thought Steven, an obvious fraud. Probably an escaped convict or a thief, rapist, or murderer evading arrest and prosecution. An Arab terrorist spouting memorized copy from books and newspapers in order to promote a change of identity or some other favors.

"Kennedy was stalked," the Major went on. "Labadi has the details."

The Senator's appearances, Steven mused, could easily be lifted from any publication, although he did intend to examine his notes on the El Cortez. Regardless, the entire Kennedy presentation was farfetched and not worthy of serious thought. Labadi figured. But

Edgar P. Rand was a mystery: overacting, pretending to buy Labadi's product, audaciously insulting Steven's experience and common sense. Was he a fool or an accomplice? Either way, he still had a gambler's hunch about the Factory and Rand's connection as a fringe delivery boy. This angle had to be explored.

"Give me a one-word reply," the Major was demanding. "Yes or no?"

"Sorry," Steven apologized. "I missed the question."

"Are you with us?" Rand's eyes were on the road. "I have to outline my complete proposal."

Steven plugged in by shifting to a more upright and attentive position. "That depends," he finally responded.

"On what?"

"A few reasonable explanations."

"I'll do my best."

"How can you possibly accept Labadi's version of the Kennedy assassination?" Steven jabbed. "Did he open up and show any kind of proof?"

"Enough for me," Rand replied. "Mainly he found my place by traveling on a very exclusive circuit. The supervisors are rough and loyal." He checked the rearview mirror as they approached a row of floodlit toll booths. "Muazzam would never lie about the assassination and expect to walk away from the Factory with a new identity."

Rand slowed down, flipped the exact money into a bin, a gate lifted, and they were rolling again. "Anything else on your mind, Garth?" he asked, exaggerating his patience.

Unconvinced, Steven passed over the Muazzam Labadi affair, and moved toward his prime objective: the Factory. "Your confidence is baffling," he stated. "What makes you think I won't notify the police or the American government?"

"The question was answered earlier."

Steven inspected the Major's blotchy profile. "We're hard up for a story . . . and income . . . and recognition?" he asked, cynically. "Journalists understand confidentiality and protect their special news sources?"

"That's what I figure."

"You presumptuous bastard," Steven snarled, unable to control his anger. "Don't underestimate me."

After a long, uneasy pause, Edgar Rand broke the quiet. "My opinion stands," he declared firmly. "But I'm obviously aware of the consequences if you notify the authorities. Labadi will . . ." His voice trailed off for a moment as they overtook a heavy truck and then it picked up again on the normal run. "Labadi will kill himself, if he gets the chance, or seal his lips forever if he's booked and questioned."

"Screw the Arab!" Steven blasted. "What about you?"

Rand's smile was automatic. "The possibility of betrayal has crossed my mind," he said quietly. "But I'm ready to gamble."

In a detached and melancholy world of his own, the Major rationalized his unusual faith in Garth by chattering on about his life: the ups and downs, from birth to present. Eventually, Steven leaned back and closed his eyes until the words jumbled into a tolerable monotone. Once in a while a revealing comment would break through, dangle for an instant, and then float past with the rest.

Toledo, Ohio, had been repeated many times. Rand's father had passed away during the fat boy's eighth year, and his sharp-tongued mother had persevered by selling kitchen appliances in a local shop. References to an unstable childhood, a depressing adolescence, and a limited education had penetrated Steven's detachment.

"I was a corporal in the Army," said Rand. "Years ago at work some fellows came up with this Major label because of my appearance. It stuck, and, frankly, I have never resented the promotion."

After a fast left, they used a winding road for the steep descent to Monte Carlo. Steven opened his eyes and stared; he was fascinated, as usual, by the pattern of glittering diamonds below.

Segments of a tedious biography intruded. Rand's marriage had produced two children and years of boredom and restlessness. "Louise had decent qualities," he recalled unemotionally. "No glamour doll. But she was clean and faithful and intelligent. A perfect wife and mother type."

Feeling edgy, Steven lit a cigarette and prepared to break things
up as Rand was accepting responsibility for all trouble leading to his
divorce. "I was usually on the road selling for a gardening outfit,"
he jabbered. "That's why the relationship continued so long."

At home during breaks and holidays, with his family around
him, Rand was lonely and irritable, despondent and trapped, unable
to sort out the reasons. Then a promotion locked him behind a desk
in Toledo, and seven months later Louise filed and the marriage
ended.

"No tears and sympathy," Rand concluded. "She has a loving
husband and both kids are grown. I've been a distant memory for
years."

Steven interrupted. "Thank you very much for the background
piece," he told Rand. "But I want straight answers."

"Let me finish," the Major demanded. "You'll understand my
willingness to bet on instincts and risk betrayal in the case of Muazzam Labadi."

In time—possibly on the next delivery, or the next, or the next,
or the next—he would face the law or the Factory's inner circle or
unknown assailants, because of a leak from a traveler or a sponsor
or a disgruntled employee. A variety of rat traps were cocked and
baited and professionally hidden on this field. The growth and sav-
agery of crime and terrorism had aroused the public and most government enforcers.

"Regardless of how carefully I follow the rules," the Major said,
"my number will be up sooner or later."

According to the rambling monologue, he believed the Robert
Kennedy conspiracy theory and Labadi's involvement. It was his
opportunity to grab a substantial payoff and disappear before the
final whistle.

"I have outstanding debts and touchy moral obligations," he
stated. "My pipe dream is to settle and go to hell with a quiet
conscience."

They were at the bottom, on the coastal road again, leaving
Monte Carlo, speeding toward Beaulieu. "One phone call," Steven

warned, "and the pipe dream goes to hell with you."

"Quite true," said Rand. "But I've been doing some careful thinking lately."

Steven listened and gathered that Rand's thoughts had been about isolation and loneliness and unpredictability and the passing years and foreign soil and going back to America—either in a pine box or under arrest. There were no alternatives for him, because of the past, including creditors: nasty ones and relentless ones, like alley blackjack dealers and Internal Revenue.

"I'm frightened of death," said Rand. "However, prison in the United States has become easier to contemplate as I grow older and more vulnerable."

"Are you looking for a jail term?"

"Of course not," he stated. "I want freedom and a lump sum of money. But if you notify the authorities, which I doubt very much, my predicament will not be as horrifying as you seem to imagine. I might accept the development with a sigh of relief."

"You fucked-up lunatic." Steven pressed out his cigarette butt in the ashtray. "This whole damn thing is unbelievable."

"Very realistic," the fat man insisted. "Go along with me and extract the Labadi testimony. Our arrangement will guarantee you a fortune and new journalistic respect." He swallowed to moisten his dry throat. "Contact the police and you'll bury the Kennedy murder forever. Labadi dies or changes to stone, and Edgar Rand marches to jail in America, where he'll probably live happily ever after."

Steven switched off and thought about the Factory as the Major attempted to demonstrate that penitentiary living was no worse than peacetime Army duty. In fact, many similar benefits were available for men in his position: no rough competition or financial burdens, room and board and essential services provided gratis, a chance to bail out and wind down and chip away some guilt under protection of the law.

A sudden recollection lit up Steven's brain and drowned Rand's words completely. June of 1974. Queens, New York. On assignment for a John Conway piece. Terrorism and the possible existence of a key identity-changing operation in southern Italy. A daylight raid. Two suspects picked up. An Italian citizen from Sestri Levante and a radical American student.

Both of them were freed. A lack of solid evidence. Two weeks afterwards, Steven had cornered the Italian and paid for the information, that had been recorded and filed by the agents during questioning. He was never able to shake a suspicion that his rugged squealer was either holding back or lying through his big white teeth.

"I have a question." Steven trapped Rand in mid-sentence. "Do you know Victor Donato?"

The Major turned his head abruptly, gaped for an instant, then switched back to the road. "Who?" he asked unconvincingly.

"Victor Donato," Garth repeated. "From an Italian town called Sestri Levante."

"No."

"Ever heard of the name?"

Obviously stalling, Rand leaned forward and watched the traffic, exaggerating his attentiveness.

"Cooperate with me, Edgar." It was a threat. "Or find another stooge to handle Labadi."

Perspiring again, the Major unbuttoned his collar, allowing his large jowls to flop out. "I've heard of Victor Donato," he admitted carefully. "Many tourists will give you the same answer."

"What do you mean?"

"Donato operates three dumpy cruise boats," Rand explained. "A seasonal fleet. He takes people around the eastern Ligurian Riviera. Mostly out of Rapallo to Sestri Levante, Portofino, Santa Margherita, and San Fruttuoso."

The answer was correct but not particularly startling. Even so, the journalist's feelings about Edgar Rand and his connections were growing stronger by the kilometer. "Has Donato been associated with the Factory?" he asked, coming straight to the point. "Inside or on the fringe?"

"Victor Donato operates cruise boats around Rapallo," said Rand flatly. "That's all I know."

"Will you explain one thing about the Factory?"

"Later," Rand answered. "When I'm sure of you." He paused and wrinkled his brow. "Tell me how you came up with the name of Victor Donato."

"Later," Steven replied. "When I'm sure of you."

They were nearing Port de Plaisance on the edge of Beaulieu-sur-Mer. "Are you with us?" Rand inquired.

"I haven't made a decision." Steven Garth took one more nibble at the bait for the sake of curiosity, and for Ellie, and for his own personal reasons: some hazy, others unknown even to him. "What's your proposal, Major?" he asked.

6

The small, cluttered apartment was quiet when Steven returned from his Perinaldo visit. Ellie had gone to bed. Her portable typewriter was upside down on the floor. Pencils, a notepad, and crumpled bits of paper were scattered in all directions. A very low and sudden plunge on the MS roller coaster, Steven realized. Agraphia or dystaxia or diplopia or dyslexia, or God knew what else or which combinations had surfaced to plague her evening.

A deadly army of clinical tags representing punishment and prospects of wheelchairs and hospital beds: misting or blurring or double vision. The inability to express her thoughts on paper. Once, while organizing some research files, she wanted to use the letter H but could not remember what the damn thing looked like. A dictionary was meaningless, because Ellie did not know where to open it and begin a search. She was forced to wait until Steven came home and wrote the letter for her.

Typing was often a catastrophe. Striking wrong keys, either to the right or left or above or below. Picking wrong objects and screaming out her frustrations. And the devastating numbness. The need to see her arms and legs in order to know what she was doing.

With hands behind her back, Ellie would seldom be able to identify the objects she was touching. And the constant struggle to make a relationship with the printed word. A kind of obstruction between what the eyes see and recognition of what the word means in the thinking part of the brain. At times, Ellie was unable to utter a sound, because she could not find the logical words. And bladder weakness and gastrointestinal trouble and paresthesia and more and more . . .

Steven reached into a cabinet, took out a bottle of whiskey, and poured half a glass. He flopped wearily on the couch and glanced up at a shelf full of his research books. Then his eyes lowered to a drawer. Inside, locked securely, was a metal box containing an orderly file of typed and handwritten personal notes recorded while covering high-priority news events like the assassination of Robert F. Kennedy.

The bedroom door opened and Ellie stood there, checking her balance for an instant.

"How are you?" Steven asked.

"Just wonderful," she replied, glancing at the floor. "Haven't you noticed?"

Wearing a dressing gown and slippers, Ellie began an unsteady foot-dragging move to the wicker chair. Observing the rules, Steven remained in place while she made her own way.

Ellie's hair was uncombed, her flesh was chalk white, and her eyes were glassy and heavily ringed. She eased down to a pillow and sat rigidly until her breathing came back to normal.

"A bad one," Steven remarked.

She pointed to the typewriter on the floor. "Even that goddamn contraption joined the enemy." Her body was trembling as she looked up at him. "I want to hear about Perinaldo."

From the beginning, line for line and move by move, Steven told her the story of his visit to Rand's house, adding comments designed to emphasize the fantasy aspects. "But the man's knowledge of Victor Donato teased me along," he admitted. "I asked for his proposal."

This was the most outlandish feature of the entire charade. Edgar Rand's proposal, as Steven Garth outlined it in detail, was this:

The Major performs his usual fringe duties, with Labadi as a traveler and Factory client. But on this occasion he also operates in the background as Garth's silent partner. A fuzzy profile is essential because of the personal reasons he'd covered on the ride back from Italy. Rand comes up with the Factory's fee of $25,000, plus $5,000 for special attention. However, Garth actually makes payment, acting as Labadi's sponsor. Rand books Labadi into the Factory under his guerrilla code name, Abu Zaki. Rand clears Garth as Mr. Thompson. The backgrounds of Zaki and Thompson are off limits. Kennedy's assassination will never be mentioned. Questioning by Factory staff members or contacts is forbidden. Strict rules prevent invasion of privacy.

The Major, Abu Zaki, and Mr. Thompson report to one of the Factory's drop addresses. The locations change frequently. At the drop, before going for surgery, Zaki is photographed by his sponsor, Mr. Thompson. Also, Zaki writes a document in his own hand stating that a confession will be made freely, as Muazzam Labadi. A copy of his passport is attached. Identity-changing references are, of course, omitted. He is revealing secrets in exchange for an undisclosed amount of money. On schedule, Zaki takes a needle and leaves for the Factory. Thompson and Edgar Rand wait at the drop.

Soon after the operation, another jab, and Zaki returns to the drop. On schedule and under airtight security, a Factory inside man visits and removes Zaki's bandages. The client has an opportunity to inspect his appearance. Only the inside team will know Zaki's new face and identity. Not Rand or Garth or contacts at the drop or anyone else. The Factory's insiders have a reputation for becoming deaf, dumb, and blind after each job has been completed. A blood oath guarantees their reliability.

Abu Zaki's new passport and other identifying documents are withheld until he completes his end of the bargain. A pitch-black room equipped with a tape machine and unique security devices is provided as part of Rand's arrangements for Zaki and his sponsor, Mr. Thompson. The Factory has the best reputation in the world to uphold. The inside team wants satisfied customers. All deals are respected and policed to a handshake finish by the drop contacts acting on inside orders.

With all elements functioning, Zaki confesses for his sponsor, Mr. Thompson, and the words are recorded in absolute privacy. The Factory members guarantee satisfactory completion, without knowing or caring about the information being revealed. They have enough secrets of their own to guard. In addition, an unbustable code of ethics protects all clients and sponsors who deal with the Factory and honor the rules.

After the confession, a new passport and other documents are handed over to the person once known as Abu Zaki, and Mr. Thompson pockets his audio tape. The arrangement has been completed. Rand and the sponsor leave. A member of the inside team is responsible for their patient's first steps as a citizen of the United States, with a new face and identity unknown to others.

The Major's business proposal for Eleanor and Steven Garth was just as head twisting:

He is aware of the legal and moral complications and possible reluctance of some editors to buy the authenticity. But he knows that all problems will be solved once the facts begin to check out and the futile hunt for Muazzam Labadi gets underway. In addition, Sirhan and the others named in the confession will be bound to react in a violent and dramatic fashion, boosting the value of the Garths' property.

The packaging and sale of the Labadi material are the Garths' responsibilities. The Major has faith in their judgment, experience, and professional contacts. His numbers are easy. Garth credits the Major with 75 percent of the income until a $30,000 outlay is recouped. Then split fifty-fifty on everything.

Rand's shady lawyer draws up a paper. Mainly a rundown of the basic conditions, with instructions to pay the son if Edgar dies. No references are made to the Factory or plastic surgery. A $30,000 fee will reward Labadi for revealing his personal experiences. Garth owns the copyright, and Rand collects in the shadows, because of his taxes, creditors, and other problems. He admits that a legal document is worthless in his situation. Breach action and courtroom decisions are out of the question. Their pact is based on mutual trust. A necessity because of Rand's circumstances. He will be forced to depend on Garth's integrity.

"Nothing seems to penetrate his thick skull," Steven told Ellie. "Rand becomes one-directional and neurotic whenever he talks about the Labadi fantasy."

Along with other crushing negatives, Garth had explained to Rand the dangers of buying testimony from a hood and allowing him to walk free regardless of the offense. Instead of making a deal, the seller might face brick walls—and official charges of aiding and abetting. Of course, a Bobby Kennedy angle, if true, plus a face-lift to oblivion for the accomplice would surely guarantee a permanent ball and chain.

As might have been expected, the Major had disagreed vehemently, claiming that Labadi had sworn to die before revealing his information to the authorities. If the police or anyone questioned him, the hidden truth about Robert Kennedy's assassination would be lost forever.

Steven Garth studied his wife intently. He knew the signals well and dreaded the consequences. Tight lips, blinking eyes, heavy breathing, nerve twitches in her face: a jungle creature about to pounce, a volcano set for eruption.

"An unbelievable opportunity." Ellie battled with every syllable. "When do you contact him again?"

"Late in the morning," Steven answered, expecting the worst. "After I've reached my decision."

"Have you?"

"There are few alternatives, Ellie," he replied. "My first inclination is to notify the French gendarmes and the American consulate at once."

The moaning, the screeching, the disjointed verbal abuse, and the pounding of fist against fist and then fist against chair until blood showed was Cayuga Lake again. He jumped to his feet, grabbed her, pressed hard, and shook and shook and shook until finally the ghouls ran off and left her, with eyes closed and tears rolling down her cheeks.

Very early the next morning, after a hellish night, Steven loaded two books, a research file, and writing material into a plastic shopping bag and headed for breakfast. Ellie was in bed sleeping off pills, and he figured she would remain there for hours. Cayuga Lake had returned, and Steven questioned his ability to cope with the pressures once again. He loved Ellie, understood her predicament, and respected the emotional turmoil it generated. Garth believed he had proved his willingness to sacrifice, to alter his life-style, cook, sweep, bottle-wash, and pamper; but at times he wondered if the extra responsibilities and burdens of his present existence were truly appreciated by his wife.

Once, at the lake during a mind-splitting weekend, he had analyzed their plight to himself. They were victim and guardian, and he decided that the misery was equally split; frequently it even appeared that Ellie had the best part of the deal. This evil thought had brought on instant feelings of guilt, and he had been moody and tense for days and nights, adding to their problems.

Wanting to avoid tourists and gossipy locals, and fearing a chance meeting with Edgar Rand, Steven selected a grubby café instead of the popular Beaulieu. He found a table in a quiet corner and ordered. A book, the research file, a pencil, and a yellow notepad were taken from the shopping bag. He sat for a moment glaring at the pad, and then, deep in thought, Steven Garth printed MUAZZAM LABADI at the top of an empty page.

After coffee and a few bites of croissant, he pushed the dishes to one side and opened his research folder. In a short time he had found a rundown of the Robert Kennedy primary appearances in California, with a scribbled notation about the El Cortez Hotel, San Diego.

June 3, 1968. A question mark about Sirhan's movements on this date. First he was home all day. Then he tipped some reporter about a trip in the direction of Corona. Later Sirhan bragged to an investigator that he had clocked 350 miles on his 1956 De Soto and no one was curious enough to find out where he had gone. His tangled statements were labeled as insignificant. The discrepancy was never pursued. But a run from Pasadena to San Diego and back would have accounted for 350 miles. Bobby Kennedy had been scheduled to appear that night at the Hotel El Cortez in San Diego. The Senator canceled unexpectedly because of exhaustion.

Information from witnesses claiming to have noticed Sirhan in Kennedy's presence on May 20, May 24, and June 2 was played down, and out. And now June 3. Was Robert F. Kennedy stalked before the June 5 killing? Conway and the others say no.

Swiftly, by instinct, Steven jammed the paper into his file, closed it, and placed it over the yellow notepad, covering the name Muazzam Labadi.

Jefferson Boland had approached softly from behind. "Mind if I join you?" he asked. "Don't want to interrupt any work."

"No problem." Steven placed his material into the shopping bag. "Just finishing up some research."

The grinning, drawling lanky southerner watched carefully. "A new book for your wife?"

"Maybe."

"Odd," he remarked, glancing around for service. "Both of us picking this joint instead of the usual."

Very odd, Steven agreed to himself; it was a hell of a coincidence. He kept his eyes on Boland as the obnoxious intruder winked and gestured broadly to a man serving tables.

He turned back and leaned extra close to Garth's face. "I drop in at this place frequently," said Boland. "Mainly to lose Edgar Rand."

"I see."

"A fat bore," the southerner drawled. "Head in the clouds. Full of crazy schemes. Been in these parts much too long." He paused. "Are you friendly with him?"

"We speak."

"Don't hang around this guy and show interest," he advised. "Rand will never climb off your back."

"Thanks for the warning," said Steven, reaching for the bag next to his chair. "But I've had plenty of experience with all kinds of leeches."

Jefferson Boland flashed his teeth in what was meant to be a smile. "Good for you," he remarked acidly.

7

Beaulieu-sur-Mer
France
Morning
Tuesday, June 5, 1979

After his encounter with Jefferson Boland, Steven returned to the apartment and found Ellie in bed sitting up, waiting for him. She was taut and belligerent. James Hatfield, their old friend, had called from the International Book Fair, a short distance away in Nice. The literary agent was spending an afternoon there before flying to England for a promotional conference.

"Who gave Hatfield our number?" Her voice was shrill and ready to crack. "Did you?"

"Jim is working on a few prospects for us," Steven replied without shadow boxing. "Like Ackerman of the *Post* and Rowland of the *Daily News.*"

As he anticipated, Ellie blew off uncontrollably, and then went into a silent and detached world of her own. Much better, he thought, than using velvet gloves and enduring hours of constant nagging and harassment.

The recent discussion by telephone with Jim Hatfield was the first contact made since they left America early in 1978. Eleanor had refused to see visitors, and her literary agent was no exception, although she respected and admired him. During her ear-puncturing reaction to her husband's mention of Paul Ackerman, Ellie disclosed that she had once again refused to see Hatfield and that Hatfield had booked a table for lunch at one o'clock with Steven at the Negresco.

Before leaving the apartment, Steven prepared a salad on a tray, the way she liked it, and the best way for her to manage it, with hard-boiled eggs, lettuce, sliced tomatoes, cucumbers, and red peppers. Orange juice was in a plastic mug.

Carefully he placed the food on a side table next to the bed, an easy reach away. Ellie was lying motionless with her back to him. She might have been asleep or pouting or looking out the window at trees. Steven hesitated and then made a soft exit without disturbing her.

Garth was like a caged animal set free. The waiters and the platters and the clink of fine glasses made him think of similar times in the States. The adjustment was difficult to handle after being isolated with sickness and futility. The elegantly set tables and high-priced menus and smartly groomed customers, unimpressive before, were now triggering resentment by magnifying the extent of his backslide to obscurity. More than ever, he realized the seriousness of their plight and the importance of arranging a quick move to America, regardless of Eleanor's objections.

Encouraged by Jim Hatfield, Steven had taken advantage of the short reprieve and was enjoying his taste of freedom and luxury. Four big drinks, a good meal, wine, brandy, unlimited smokes, and civilized talk with a knowledgeable and genuine old friend. Personal affairs had been saved for last.

Finally Garth reviewed the details of Ellie's mental and physical condition, and Hatfield was disturbed. Garth stressed finances and morale and the need for an immediate withdrawal to America, where he could earn a living and begin to make their existence normal again. He didn't mention a word about Eleanor's contact in France, and Hatfield, presumably understanding his reluctance to comment, avoided the subject entirely.

"Did Rowland top Ackerman's offer?" Garth inquired. "My

preference is Washington unless the dollars are just too large to ignore."

Hatfield picked his approach swiftly. All facts on the line without holding back was the only practical way to manage Steven Garth. Ackerman had changed his mind because of high-level pressures. Rowland's interest had also faded. Others had given a variety of excuses for not wanting to hire Steven H. Garth. Mainly the employers felt that Garth's preoccupation with Ellie's sickness could affect his attitude on the job, and this had been proved without doubt, they claimed, during his assignments just before leaving the States. A few noted Garth's long absence since early in 1978, and they questioned his capacity to grasp current happenings without an extended period of reorientation. One editor pointed up his mediocre writing ability and the need to hire a partner, like Conway, or assign him to basic reporting instead of special features, when the newspaper was already staffed with qualified people in all departments. But it was clear that Ellie's illness and their worries about Garth's frame of mind had scattered the chances of employment with leading journals.

Steven pushed the cognac aside, or he would have downed it and ordered five more. He lit another cigarette instead. The unexpected report from James Hatfield had jolted him, and he was having a difficult time disguising the fact. "I do not have multiple sclerosis," he said bitterly. "Why the hell are they penalizing me for Ellie's disease?"

"That's baby talk," said Hatfield. "We've only checked a few prospects. You don't have to settle for New York, Los Angeles, or Washington. There are hundreds of papers in the United States eager to hire a man of your caliber."

"How about the Fartcreek Gazette?" Garth swallowed the brandy and glared at Hatfield. "Do you expect me to haul my crippled wife to a rube town and kiss ass for peanuts? Like a geek in a circus? She has pride. And I have pride. This fucking MS is not her fault. And it is not my fault that I love her and want to help and comfort her. The stuff won't rub off on them. Why the hell are they making us pay double for a lousy break?"

Instead of answering, Hatfield waited quietly for Garth to simmer down, finish his counterpunching, and begin to lick his wounds.

"Christ almighty," the former reporter mumbled disgustedly to himself. "I'm wallowing in my own slop."

Hatfield avoided patty-cake lectures and roundabout offers. "Do you need financial help?" he asked. "I'm in a position to make things easier."

"No, thank you very much," Garth replied instantly. "We'll survive."

In a warm and unassuming manner, Jim Hatfield made it very clear that he was available in the event of trouble, any kind of trouble, money or otherwise. "Contact me whenever you feel the need," he urged. "I'll be at Claridges in London for six days. You have my private New York line and my home phone number. Keep in touch."

"Thanks, Jim." Bitterness and humiliation made the words garble deep in his throat. "We'll see how things go."

"Rest easy," said Hatfield, motioning to his waiter. "Our job hunt continues when I get back to the States."

"That won't be necessary," Garth told him in a polite but firm tone of voice. "We'll have to return before October." He lowered his eyes. "And I know the suburban rag operators much better than you do, Jim."

After his lunch with Hatfield, Steven walked along the Promenade des Anglais in Nice, hardly aware of the sun or the beaches or the tourists or the restaurants or the hotels. He was hurt and dazed and trapped in a corner and weary of opponents who would slug harder as he fell. A clock on a building reminded him that Ellie was alone. Garth stepped out faster in order to catch his bus for Beaulieu-sur-Mer.

"Son of a bitch," Garth muttered to himself as the creaky elevator arrived at the third floor. "Bastards," he said aloud when he entered their cramped apartment and inhaled the rubbing alcohol and other sickbed odors.

He moved directly to the living room and froze. Partly closed window shutters were blocking out most of the light. In a dressing gown and slippers, Ellie sat posed in a chair, erect and regal, like a figure made of wax. Yet her eyes were clear, animated, playful. A taunting half-smile bordered on arrogance. She was in command. The woman had a secret, or a plan, or both.

Instantly he thought of Dr. Lambert's capsules, and more than one for good measure. But with Ellie, Steven could never be sure. Then, he noticed a bottle of whiskey on the table and a large drink already poured.

"For you, my dear." Ellie pointed a slender finger at the glass. "I've been waiting."

Completely deflated, and not thirsty for more booze, Garth sat and glowered and listened, without attempting to separate true reasoning from the haze of medication. Ellie had guessed about Paul Ackerman, Rowland, and the others; and there would be more disappointments, she assured him. Haltingly, and at times with great difficulty, Ellie preached about many things, and her husband took special note of a few.

They were drifting far off shore on the same raft, and a miracle was needed to get them back on a direct course. It had to be now or never, especially for her. Once they returned to the States and Garth reported for work—anywhere, big-time or small—Ellie would become a motionless piece of twisted flesh, pleading for death unless she had been given a final chance to score and bail out with dignity.

"You'll have a mad scramble for a Robert Kennedy conspiracy exposé," she went on fervently. "Tease Ackerman or Rowland with limited serialization rights in advance of the book. Watch them crawl on their hands and knees for Steven H. Garth. Picture the action. Both of us connecting against the odds. Jim would have a field day." She paused and took a deep breath. "Did you tell him?"

"No."

"Why not?"

"Because Senator Kennedy was assassinated by Sirhan Bishara Sirhan," Garth replied automatically. "There is no evidence of a conspiracy."

Ellie had obviously primed herself for negative responses. "What about the Factory?" She was calm but persistent. "You've admitted that it could be an important story."

Garth thought about it for a moment, then pulled himself up, and walked dejectedly across the room. "Two bums are playing a con game for unknown reasons." He glanced at the metal rod next to the shutter and was tempted to flood the apartment with light. "We can't get involved," he said with finality.

"Give up a miracle?"

"Stop it!" He turned abruptly and raged for the first time in many years. "I refuse to drift on your goddamn raft, Eleanor! You live in a world of pills and fantasy! One of us has to cope with the real thing!"

Instead of falling apart, Ellie was steady and unusually lucid. "You have an appointment tomorrow morning," she told him, ignoring the outburst. "A good chance to prove a few things—to me and to yourself and maybe to others in America. Let's see how Garth copes with the real thing."

"Make sense!" he ordered. "What the hell are you babbling about?"

"Major Rand phoned here today," she explained. "We had a long discussion."

Fuming inside, Garth moved back and took a seat opposite his wife. "All right, Ellie." The cards had been played. "I'm listening."

From her response, Steven realized that Rand had confirmed everything that he had told her, and more. She believed in Muazzam Labadi and the Factory.

Rand had been in touch with his Italian friends. Luckily, due to a cancellation, an early booking had been arranged, the only time available for at least a month. Labadi was cleared, as Abu Zaki, and Garth as Mr. Thompson. All Factory business had been discussed and approved. The execution of contractual obligations between Zaki and Thompson would be supervised until a farewell handshake. Garth had a 9 a.m. rendezvous at the Major's apartment. They would travel immediately to Perinaldo and collect Labadi. Then, as

fast as possible, on to the drop, where Factory associates were expecting them before midnight.

Because of mumbling and slurring, Ellie decided to repeat the
instructions a painful word at a time. The dim lighting, the blend of
ointment smells and perfume, her abnormal posture, and the odd
broken rhythm of her delivery created mesmerizing effects which
Garth had to fight against. His troubled brain scanned back to the
Negresco lunch and returned quickly with indignation churning
again.

"Tomorrow morning at nine," Ellie said finally. "Major Rand's
apartment."

Disregarding a need to curse, or ridicule or lecture or flee,
Steven lifted the drink, stared hard at the contents, and then gulped
it down to mix with Hatfield's offerings.

"Forgive my selfishness." Ellie was beginning to deflate. "You'll
be taking risks. But so help me God, I'll die now if you ignore my
last opportunity to be productive."

Garth poured another whiskey and remained silent.

Thoughtfully and rather sadly, Ellie inspected the dark-haired,
powerfully built, good-looking roughneck. There had been a few
changes over the years. A warm smile had faded along with his
easygoing manner. Lines were beginning to deepen and crease his
forehead and slice at the edges of his mouth and eyes. And Ellie was
able to detect other marks of strain. "Perhaps a world of capsules and
fantasy has more to offer than your sweaty days and nights of real-
ism," she whispered. "But I can only talk for myself during this
hopeless period." Eleanor slumped in the wicker chair, lowered her
head, and closed her eyes. "Do you understand, Steven?"

"Yes." Garth finished the bourbon, placed the glass on a table,
and lit a cigarette, his twentieth of the day. "Yes," he said again,
without glancing at her. "I understand."

In the morning, Garth was packed, and ready for his journey into
the unknown. All the necessities had been carefully arranged in one
suitcase. Ellie was also prepared. Manageable provisions had been

stored in the kitchen. A local restaurant was available in the event she needed catering. Emergency phone numbers had already been posted in each room: Dr. Lambert, SOS Médecins, Hospital Saint Roch, police, gendarmerie, taxis, *pharmacie de nuit,* the concierge, and every local merchant with delivery service. Ellie had money in her purse and a reserve supply in the bedroom closet.

"I'll manage." She was leaning on a cane in the doorway. "Take care of yourself, and bring home a winner."

Without commenting, Garth kissed her gently on the forehead and left for Edgar Rand's apartment in Beaulieu.

8

Holding the suitcase, Garth tapped lightly on Rand's door and waited for a response. No answer. He knocked. Silence. Becoming impatient, he pressed the bell—a short ring first and then a long one. He could detect no movement inside. As a last resort, he put his ear to the smooth wood and listened very carefully.

Garth heard a sound, a barely audible sound, almost impossible to distinguish right away; but seconds later he knew that it was a moan, a whimper, the low cry of an animal or a human being in pain. Fear gripped him for an instant, and he thought of backing off and running to avoid involvement. But rationality smothered the impulse. Cautiously he wrapped his fingers around a bronzed handle, applied pressure, and the door opened slowly.

After walking inside, Garth put his suitcase down, kicked the door closed with his foot, and stood gaping in disbelief. A cyclone had ripped through Edgar Rand's apartment. Lamps were overturned. The furniture was out of place. Every drawer had been emptied. Papers and other personal effects were strewn over the floor. Mirrors and pictures had been yanked off the walls. The contents of Rand's bar formed a puddle near the couch. Nothing in the living room had been spared.

A groan from down the hall jolted him, and Garth moved swiftly past a ransacked bathroom, kitchen, and linen closet. His wild run ended in the doorway of the bedroom. Edgar Rand, wearing green and white checkered pajamas, was on his back, sprawled across a thickly carpeted floor. Blood oozed from deep wounds on his face and body, evidently the result of a savage beating with heavy objects. The Major appeared to be dying.

After he'd taken in the grotesque sight, Garth hurried across the room, knelt beside the man, put his ear close, and listened.

"Three gorillas . . . from Italy . . . with questions . . . about me . . . and you . . . and Labadi. I refused to answer. They were experts . . . pistol butts . . . and knuckles." Rand was barely able to choke out the words. "Who . . . leaked . . . the . . . information?"

"Screw that now." Garth's voice was unsteady. "I'll call the police and an ambulance."

"No!" Rand ordered through swollen lips. "Dr. Bouvier . . . number by the phone . . . he's special . . . I always go private . . . do you understand?"

Garth started to move, but the Major pulled him back. "Forget the police . . . look at me . . . raw flesh . . . They want Labadi . . . he's the real thing . . . a Kennedy assassin . . . You'll lose the confession . . . and a lot more. . . . Don't be a fool."

An odd mixture of dread, curiosity, guilt, and excitement took hold as Garth struggled to understand Rand's throaty instructions.

"Briefcase . . . hidden . . . Perinaldo shack . . . everything inside . . . money . . . documentation . . . agreement for confession . . . location of the drop." Rand swallowed blood and coughed part of it up. Garth used a handkerchief to wipe him. "Take Labadi . . . and the case . . . follow through . . . on schedule. . . . You're authorized . . . without me." Rand's battered face turned white, and he shuddered violently. "Alert . . . Bouvier . . . then we'll talk . . . details . . . if . . . I . . . stay . . . conscious."

Garth took a long hard look at Major Edgar Rand's battered body. Then, after making a firm decision, he rose to his feet and worked quickly. Dr. Bouvier, contacted in Nice, promised emergency action. With the Italian gorillas on his mind, Garth phoned an SOS ambulance and gave instructions to pick up Madame Eleanor Garth at the apartment and deliver her to Hospital Saint Roch at once. He reported that the multiple sclerosis victim was experiencing severe chest pains and other alarming symptoms. Then he telephoned Ellie and gave her a rapid-fire briefing.

"Phone Dr. Lambert right now," Garth continued. "Tell him an ambulance is on the way. Fake and exaggerate your condition. Get into Saint Roch and stay there until you receive word from me. Don't mention our escapade. I'm away investigating a job offer." He felt perspiration moisten his forehead. "Be alert and suspicious of everything. We'd better take precautions in case Rand's assault story is legitimate."

Ellie understood. Garth hung up and went back to Edgar Rand. His face was a pulpy mess. Bruises, welts, and crudely split flesh were evident on his arms and neck, and they were probably just samples of worse damage concealed by his ripped pajamas. "Do you have any medical stuff in the bathroom?" he asked. "I'll patch you up until Bouvier gets here."

"Skip it," Rand wheezed. "We . . . don't . . . have . . . time." He motioned Garth closer and told him exactly where the briefcase was hidden. And he pointed to a radiator where keys for the Italian house and the car had been lodged in the back. Other details were covered. Finally, with his voice and strength failing, he told Garth to check the terrace.

"Flowerpot . . . bottom . . . special compartment. . . . They missed it . . . a Smith and Wesson .44 . . . with ammunition." He closed his eyes and turned away. "Good luck," he whispered.

Moving in slow traffic, Garth headed for Perinaldo on the lower corniche instead of the autoroute, because the frontier crossing was easier there, especially with an American passport. There were seldom delays, unless the cops had advance tips or suspected funny business.

Nevertheless, Garth fought his nerves and imagination, feeling that he was being followed and expecting complications at the border. One by one, images flashed across the windshield and blocked his rearview mirror. Ellie and Edgar Rand, Jim Hatfield and Muazzam Labadi, Conway, Ackerman, and Rowland, and the Factory. Then he thought of gorillas and risks and the possible leak, Jefferson Boland, and a loaded weapon under the passenger seat.

Steven H. Garth, investigative reporter, passed through a town called Menton, and sped toward Italy, at work again on a very special assignment.

●

JIM HATFIELD'S ROOMS at the Negresco were comfortable, and the view was good, but he'd been too engrossed in Eleanor's manuscript to notice. Now he stopped in mid-chapter, stacked her pages neatly, and put them on the low table in front of the couch. The literary agent sat for a moment digesting the experience. Considering the writer's physical and mental handicaps, he was impressed by the steady flow of her work, although the implausibility of the material would surely provide new clinical approaches for Dr. Vassolo and the other psychiatrists.

Most of all, Hatfield was curious about Steven Garth's reported desertion, something he refused to accept as a matter of fact. Perhaps clues were lurking in Eleanor's wildly fabricated story line.

After pacing the room, he called the desk and ordered a map of southern France and Italy. Then, just for the hell of it, he traced Garth's run on the lower corniche and found the way. Menton, the frontier, Ventimiglia, a sharp left turn at Vallecrosia, and a twisting climb past Soldano in the hilly region of Monte Mera, Monte Caggio, Monte Rebuffao, and Monte Peiga. A jungle detour before reaching Perinaldo. The agent slid his finger to the right and was able to circle the exact location of Rand's dark corner, according to Eleanor's papers. But had there ever been a Major? And had he survived a vicious assault by Italian gorillas?

On impulse, James Hatfield booked a taxi for a short ride to the Café de Beaulieu. By the time he had finished a Perrier and a sociable exchange with the owner, the Major had ceased to be an imaginary figure in Eleanor's disturbing manuscript.

Hatfield thanked his source, paid the bill, and left with Edgar Rand's address.

No one answered Rand's door. Hatfield took the elevator back down to the lobby and rang for the concierge. She was young, fat, and talkative, but Hatfield's French was able to cope.

"He's probably visiting Italy," the girl said in a high-pitched voice. "The Major owns a house there."

"I know."

"Any message?"

"No," Hatfield answered. "When do you expect him to get back?"

"A day, a week, a month," she replied, gesturing broadly. "Who knows? He comes and goes and never has a schedule."

"I understand." Hatfield proceeded cautiously. "Do you remember when he left this time?"

"On my birthday," the girl answered without hesitation. "June sixth."

"You have a sharp memory."

"Lovely flowers arrived for me," the concierge explained. "That evening I went upstairs to thank him but he was already gone."

"Nearly five months ago," said Hatfield, recalling Eleanor Garth's beating episode on the sixth of June. "That's quite a visit."

"He's been away longer," the girl told him. "Major Rand enjoys a change of scenery."

"Don't we all." Hatfield's smile was natural. "I guess you look after things while he's gone." The agent hesitated. "Care for the plants and so forth."

"Oh, yes," she responded. "Dust and keep the place tidy. I do my best for him. The Major is very kind."

"And lucky to have you as a friend." Hatfield was about to go, convinced that Eleanor's plot was sickbed imagination, hyped fiction, except for the June 6 date: Rand's departure, according to the concierge, and Rand's bout with the Italian gorillas, according to *Sandcastle*.

"Monsieur Poncet is a bad one." The girl's confidential tone stopped Hatfield. "A real troublemaker."

"Monsieur Poncet?"

"The owner of Rand's apartment," the concierge explained testily. "He's waiting for the Major to get back."

"Oh?"

"Poncet came by in August when I was cleaning," she went on. "A few minor things really disturbed him."

"Like what?"

"One glass table has a crack down the middle," the young concierge replied. "And a thick white scatter rug is missing from the bedroom. Poncet wants the Major to pay up like they were precious jewels. Ridiculous. You can hardly notice the crack. And I'm sure the Major took the rug in for cleaning. Poncet thinks he grabbed it for his Italian place." The girl made a vulgar sign with her right hand. "Poncet is fortunate to have Rand as a tenant. I always find everything clean and orderly after he's gone. Just like this last time. A busted table? Easily repaired. A missing rug? Out of the cleaners as soon as Rand gets back. Poncet is a bad one. Waiting for a chance to make trouble over nothing."

Back in his rooms at the Negresco, James Hatfield shoved aside images of a violent beating by Italian gorillas, which might have resulted in damaged furniture, and a bloodstained carpet. He ignored a flash of the victim's hasty removal and some frantic apartment straightening by a Dr. Bouvier or his associates or others. After a quick check, he was unable to find a listing in any directory for Bouvier, Rand's fictional physician. He thought of probing deeper for this name, along with others—especially Jefferson Boland.

Instead, he tuned out the guesswork section of his brain, picked up Eleanor's script, and continued with Garth's exploits in a world of fantasy.

After leaving Soldano on the hilly route to Perinaldo, Garth copied the Major by squinting in the rearview mirror, although no other vehicles had appeared for kilometers. He geared down, checked for a landmark on the right-hand side, then swung off into a clump of bushes and thick weeds. The car plunged through and dropped to a narrow road—more like a widened footpath—choppy and pebbled and overgrown with foliage.

Unable to shake the feeling that he was being followed or watched, Garth rammed past some natural obstacles, moved under the decaying archway, and entered the grounds. After bouncing over mounds of earth and patches of tall grass, he drove up to Rand's dark corner, the safe house—an isolated, dilapidated two-floored wooden building almost completely sheltered by trees with hanging branches and matted leafage.

Garth reached down, felt under the seat, and picked up the revolver and extra ammunition. He jammed them into his denim jacket pockets and stepped out of the car.

The windowless basement of Major Rand's house was damp and rat-infested. An overhead light bulb cast shadows on a pile of faded magazines, an old bicycle, and rusting garden equipment. A metal table and two lawn chairs were spiderwebbed. So was an antiquated Baldwin piano. A moist green fungus had streaked the walls, ceiling, and floor.

Although he hardly believed what Rand had told him, Garth followed instructions and located a partially dismantled oil stove at the far end of the cellar. Working in bad lighting and anticipating zero results, he examined the junk pile, using both hands. Later, to his surprise, Garth found Rand's briefcase under a covering of moldy rags.

On a storage box, in the glow of the overhead fixture, Garth opened the Major's briefcase and inspected the contents. Everything was in order. The victim had been truthful and precise. A heavy manila envelope contained exactly 30,000 American dollars. Garth knew that $25,000 was the Factory tab and $5,000 represented very special attention. Another $5,000, in smaller denominations, was held together by rubber bands. This was expense money, and Garth had Rand's authority to use part or all of it during the course of his mission. A lengthy formal understanding between Abu Zaki and Mr. Thompson spelled out every detail of their arrangement: a private confession on audio tape in exchange for surgery and a fresh identity. Other documents referred to the policing of this agreement by Factory employees. And there was a typed sheet of house rules and back-up credentials for Zaki and Thompson signed by Major Edgar Rand. And more. Much too much for Garth to digest at this early stage of the journey.

However, the Major's artistic printing on a neat white card glued him to the spot.

MARIO, CONDOMINIO FERNANDA, VIA TUBINO

RAPALLO, ITALY

The Factory drop information was starting to build the kind of excitement Garth had been missing during the last few years of his life. He replaced the contents of Rand's briefcase. Then, after a thought, he put in his gun and the extra ammunition.

●

"Labadi!" Garth was in the barn, shouting from the bottom of the platformed loft. *"This is Garth!"*

In seconds, movement could be heard and a light streamed down, almost blinding the former reporter. "All right." Labadi was at the top of the ladder. "I'm waiting."

"Get your ass ready to move out right now," Garth ordered. "We have a date at the Factory."

"Yeah?" There was a pause. "Is the Major with you?"

"No."

"What?" Labadi hesitated again. "How come?"

"I'll explain in the car." Garth watched the Arab's hazy outline, pistol in one hand, flashlight in the other. *"We'd better move, Labadi!"* Authority had to be established right from the start. *"Do you want a new face?"*

9

Jefferson Boland, outfitted in a nautical blazer and a polo-neck shirt, was visiting Port de Plaisance in Beaulieu. The southerner moved along jauntily near the water examining a line of bobbing yachts. Finally he stopped at a gangway belonging to a compactly built Riva, a sleek model: *Princess Rainbow,* out of Antibes. Noticing a man at the rail, Boland grinned, saluted exaggeratedly, and strutted aboard without receiving a hint of acknowledgment.

In comfortable quarters down below, they sat together having a drink. Andrew Tolkin was a soft-voiced man with rimless glasses and straight dark hair parted close to the middle. His complexion was pale and lifeless, and his evenly modulated delivery had a school-teacherish quality. In fact, Tolkin looked more like a hick-town banking official than a veteran member of the Central Intelligence Agency, an active officer with battle scars from ultrasecret operations in all parts of the world. He was now attached to the American Embassy in Paris.

"Get this over with fast, Jefferson." Tolkin's dislike for the other man was obvious. "I'm on vacation."

"Lucky fella." Boland smirked as he glanced around at the plush furnishings. "You certainly do it in style."

Andrew Tolkin was on a short break in Cannes as a guest of old friends. He had reluctantly accepted Boland's demands for an urgent conference, mainly because a one-day visit to the Beaulieu port had been scheduled anyway.

The gangling, drawling, crew-cut southerner had worked on numerous free-lance assignments over the years. A roving asset for Andy Tolkin, Jefferson Boland had been rough, dependable, and well connected in many specialized areas of interest. But for various reasons—including the Agency's recent clean-up and shakedown operations—his usefulness was nearly finished. Now Tolkin saw him as a potential embarrassment, or worse.

"I want lump money for this one." Boland rubbed his palms together. "Prepare to drain the Company's budget."

"Get to the point," Tolkin said irritably. "My friends are expected back in twenty minutes."

"You'll have time." Boland narrowed his eyes. "Labadi is out and roaming the neighborhood," he whispered. "And I'm in a position to help."

"Labadi?"

Boland was disturbed for an instant. "Muazzam Labadi," he repeated slowly. "The corpse from Beirut."

Andrew Tolkin glared at him. "I don't understand you," he said. "The name is unfamiliar."

"Really?" Boland removed a thin cigar from his jacket and lit up defiantly. "Ask your station chief in Paris."

"Ask him yourself and get off my back."

"Oh, no." The southerner was grinning again. "Labadi was meaningless to your boss Draper. Just another informant picking up small disbursements under a crypto. A name lost in an old file." He inhaled and then blew smoke discreetly. "However, I do believe that your connection with Muazzam Labadi was personal—and very sensitive, Mr. Tolkin. And you cannot possibly allow this man to walk free and shoot his mouth off."

Andrew Tolkin removed his glasses. Without them his placid expression was cold and tough and he appeared much younger than his fifty-eight years. "Our meeting is over," Tolkin announced. "You have nothing to sell."

Boland tapped his cigar ash in a golden tray. "The customer is always right, Mr. Tolkin," he drawled. "You probably know more than I do about this Labadi development."

"Step carefully, Jefferson." The agent was rubbing his glasses with a handkerchief. "I might forget old times and line you up with the gendarmerie."

"Now you wouldn't do a thing like that," said Boland. "We know too much about each other, and this is the wrong climate for digging up the past and spilling more Intelligence guts. My information is for you, and you alone. I can't do business with anyone else. There are too many personal risks. Agreed?"

"You are trying my patience."

"We need a couple of minutes," said Boland. "Then you can pipe me off this fancy motor launch."

Tolkin stared disdainfully. "You have a couple of minutes," he agreed. "The last we'll ever spend together. Rest assured that our professional relationship is over, Jefferson."

Boland ignored the ultimatum and moved ahead quickly. "Whether you know it or not, or whether you care or not, Labadi is alive—and on the run—here in Europe. The man needs cash and favors. He is a very bad risk."

With arms folded, Andrew Tolkin sat impassively, refusing to make a comment.

"Some nasty gentlemen from Italy are right on his tail," Boland proceeded. "American brains and muscle are probably set to move in case the locals screw up or take too long."

"Have you finished?"

"Another minute." Boland squashed his cigar in the tray. "I'm at ringside with confidential information and an opportunity to get more, depending on a briefing from you."

"What are you talking about?"

Boland straightened up and smoothed his lapels. "Give me orders," he said. "Labadi, along with a few others, is marked for instant execution. Do you want it to happen that way? Or maybe you have a different plan." Andrew Tolkin's former asset leaned closer. "In other words, tell me if you need this character for some reason, or whether you'd like him to disappear permanently." His grin was more obnoxious than ever. "You see, I'm in a great position to help, either way."

Tolkin got to his feet and stood motionless, both hands at his sides. "We'll go up on deck now," he advised quietly. "Our meeting is over." A cluster of thin purple veins was beginning to swell on his forehead, and Boland noticed it right away. He followed instructions obediently.

On deck, in the sunlight, they paused at the gangway. "The Central Intelligence Agency has no official interest in a person by the name of Muazzam Labadi," Tolkin stated. "Understood?"

"Yes," Boland answered. "But I was referring to Mr. Andrew Tolkin personally."

"Get off this boat," Tolkin ordered in a firm tone of voice. "And stay away from me unless you want real trouble."

Arrogantly, Boland extended his right hand, knowing that it would be ignored. "Well, sir, if things change, you always know where to find me."

"Yes, I do," Andy Tolkin responded. "And don't ever forget it, Boland."

Hospital Saint Roch
Nice, France
Early evening
Wednesday, June 6, 1979

Ellie had followed Steven's instructions exactly; exaggerating her actual symptoms, she had assumed, would guarantee her a bed in a private room in the Hospital Saint Roch—and be a logical reason for asking for the emergency transportation. It had worked. She imagined Steven would be content, and rather proud of her achievement.

Now Dr. Roger Lambert stood at the foot of her bed and watched thoughtfully as she slept. An ambulance had brought her in the morning. Reports from an intern, given to Dr. Lambert on his first visit, indicated that various ailments had been detailed convincingly by the patient, including sharp pains in the chest, back, and left arm—a worry for the young apprentice.

Aware of her medical background, Dr. Lambert's inspection had ruled out everything but MS symptoms, a violent case of nerves, and a few baffling emotional changes. During his second visit, after a lengthy talk and a potent sedative, Eleanor had dozed off.

Later, in Dr. Pierre Favre's office, the situation was discussed.

"Madame Garth's husband is away," Roger Lambert told him. "This has obviously aggravated her condition."

"Awful time for a man to leave his wife alone," the small, elderly hospital official remarked. "Probably urgent business of some kind."

"A job opportunity, according to Madame Garth," Dr. Lambert explained. "He's an experienced newspaper reporter."

Favre was unimpressed. "What's your prognosis?" he asked. "Her neurotic behavior has already disrupted members of our staff. Questioning the nurses. Refusing to allow hospital personnel in her room. Asking for locked doors. Suspicious of food and drink and routine care. Your patient is a bundle of trouble. And we run a busy institution here, Roger."

"Give me time for more observation," said Dr. Lambert. "Along with other disorders, she has pain in the back, face, and limbs. Monsieur Garth's absence has probably lowered her tolerance."

"Not to any great extent."

"What do you mean?"

"Shortly after your morning visit, she finished one of her loud groaning sessions and then buzzed for the duty nurse," he reported.

"Madame Garth demanded and received a large quantity of writing paper and a box of pencils." The hospital official scratched his bearded chin. "Odd request from a lady suffering pains—in the back, face, and limbs, as you say—along with other crippling symptoms."

"Madame Garth is an author."

"We know," said Favre. "But she has just been admitted to this hospital as an emergency patient. Now, based on your knowledge of the case, is Madame Garth physically and mentally capable of writing a book, a letter, or anything credible today at Saint Roch?"

"Please don't play games with me," said Lambert, beginning to lose his easygoing attitude. "What's on your mind?"

"Nurse Odette Bouchard entered your patient's room at five o'clock this afternoon and found her scribbling away," said the wizened Frenchman. "Madame Garth howled obscenities, covered a page with her blanket, and ordered the nurse out in a tone and manner befitting a wild animal."

Dr. Lambert frowned. "I'll have a talk with Madame Garth," he promised. "Early tomorrow morning."

"Want my opinion?" Favre asked. "Serge Vassolo should be consulted at once."

"Premature," said Lambert, getting ready to leave. "Allow me to handle this case in my own way."

Italy
Evening
June 6, 1979

Muazzam Labadi had been very quiet until he removed a pint of whiskey from his leather jacket. Garth had declined to join him. His brain was pulsating with thoughts of Ellie and the briefcase and the gun and the consequences of embarking on a reckless adventure into unexplored regions. They were speeding on the autostrada heading toward Genoa and Rapallo.

"Do you figure the wops killed Edgar?" Labadi was slumped down in the seat with his battered military field shoes propped on the dashboard. "How did the fat man look?"

"Busted up good."

"A survivor?"

"I don't know."

Labadi glanced over at him. "You have plenty of guts," he commented sincerely. "The Italians might be on our tail lights right now."

"A possibility," Garth agreed. "We'll run up against them sooner or later."

"Are you nervous?"

"Yes."

The Arab gulped a quick shot and used his fist as a napkin. "You confuse hell out of me, Garth," he remarked, trying on his awkward smile for the first time since they'd left Perinaldo. "I thought you'd be climbing all over my head by now, probing and bullshitting and rationalizing your association with Rand, and things like that."

"Disappointed?"

"Just curious," he replied. "Still don't accept my Robert Kennedy experience?"

"You haven't disclosed anything yet," Garth stated. "I'll wait for a tape."

They drove on quietly. Labadi sipped whiskey and appeared to have focused his mind elsewhere. Garth felt like explaining the motivation for joining the group, in order to remind Labadi about his intelligence and experience and street knowledge of bums and fakers. And to prove that he was not a desperate man grabbing for trumped-up bait as a last resort. And to mock a theatrical con job, which had been put together by amateurs for devious and unknown reasons.

Frankly, I don't care what your real story is or why you have to get a new face, he wanted to say to Labadi. You are my ticket for admission to the Factory, and that's all I personally give a damn about. But instead of delivering the speech, Garth kept his eyes on the autostrada and said nothing.

"I'll be somebody else after the Factory," Labadi muttered

under his breath. "A wierd prospect."

Garth did not react.

"Born again," said Labadi, "without parents or a childhood to remember." He drained the bottle of whiskey, started to flip it out the window, changed his mind, and pitched it on the back seat. "Are you interested in my childhood?" he asked.

"Not particularly."

"You can have my childhood without strings," he went on in a fuzzy voice, ignoring Garth's remark. "People are willing to discuss childhood. Have you noticed? Movie stars, politicians, industrialists, gangsters, kings, and queens are usually ready to open up about childhood. Mine is unique."

"Why?"

"Because it is damn nearly an exact copy of Sirhan Bishara Sirhan's childhood." Labadi paused. "Do you have any booze in this car?" he asked.

"No," Garth replied impatiently. "Aren't you drunk enough for the moment?"

Labadi shrugged and closed his eyes. "A new identity will keep me alive. And I'm grateful," he slurred. "But it's also freaky and sad. Muazzam Labadi has to die. That's why I jump back to my childhood."

For some reason, Garth realized, the Arab was determined to sound off about his early years. Probably a strategic move to establish more authenticity before reaching the Factory drop in Rapallo. Was Labadi also magnifying the effects of whiskey from a pint bottle? So far, he'd always projected an image of telling the truth, being for real. A fantastic actor. A carefully programmed hoodlum. Unlike Rand and Ellie, Garth refused to accept the possibility that Muazzam was for real.

"Did you know Sirhan as a child?" Garth asked. "Was he a friend of yours?"

"I probably saw him around and he might have seen me," the Arab replied. "But we didn't know each other." According to Muazzam Labadi, he had been born in Jerusalem, the son of a Christian

Arab employee of the Public Works Department. This was Palestine under a British mandate. His Greek Orthodox family lived close to Musrara, a middle-class blended Arab and Jewish quarter.

Labadi was an infant when Jewish immigration to Palestine soared, during the Holocaust years. Britain set up limitations, and the Palestinian Jews resorted to violent action in order to obtain increased quotas. This problem was handed to the United Nations, and the organization passed a resolution in November of 1947. It partitioned the country into separate Arab and Jewish states. Then, on May 14, 1948, Great Britain withdrew from a divided Palestine.

"All hell broke loose," Labadi recalled. "And blood flowed." He glanced at the driver. "As a kid, like Sirhan, I watched Jerusalem being ripped in two."

Garth checked the rearview mirror, eased over, and a truck roared past.

"Am I boring you with my childhood?" Labadi asked. "Maybe the story is irritating?"

"Not exactly," Garth replied. "Why?"

"A fact has registered," said Labadi. "I'm wailing into a Jewish ear."

"That's your problem, Labadi," Garth told him. "You should have demanded a gentile associate."

Labadi was stopped before he could respond. "Carry on with the plot," said Garth. "This is a long trip and we don't have a radio to break the monotony." He became serious. "I would like to hear the rest."

During the Jerusalem violence, Muazzam Labadi's family left their personal belongings and fled to a Jordanian Arab sector. Labadi attended school there. Finally, under a program designed for Palestinian refugees, a group in Los Angeles sponsored the Labadi parents and Muazzam; they emigrated to California in 1957.

"Damn nearly a photostat copy of Sirhan's early years," said Labadi. "But in America we took different paths right away."

"And they led to the same junction."

"What do you mean?"

"The killing of Robert Kennedy," said Garth. "At least that's what you've been peddling to get a new face and a different life."

Labadi became sulky and tight-lipped again. "You know about my childhood." He forced the words. "That's it until we tape."

"Fair enough." Garth took a quick look and saw Labadi had closed his eyes. "Did our little therapy session help?" the reporter asked facetiously.

"Piss away," he mumbled. "I want to rest."

Garth turned him off and switched his attention to the side and rearview mirrors, wondering if any of the vehicles on the autostrada belonged to Labadi's supposed hunters: "the Mafia, union muscle, American Intelligence agents, and a few sensitive Middle Eastern characters," according to Edgar Rand. And he thought about Labadi's childhood, amazingly close to the published facts on Sirhan. Like the Beirut episode, all the material could have been lifted from books, magazines, and newspaper reports. But why in hell would the man select the background of Robert Kennedy's assassin? For the first time, Garth toyed with the remote possibility that a part of Muazzam Labadi, a small part, he emphasized to himself, could be for real.

"Jam your foot down, Garth." Labadi was inspecting him through half-closed eyes. "Our friends are waiting to greet us at midnight."

10

For once, Jefferson Boland was positioned upright in a chair, attentive, grim-faced, and unable to strike his usual pose of southern arrogance. Unexpectedly, two gentlemen from America were visiting his untidy studio apartment, and the sight of them had managed to rubberize his limbs and turn his flesh chalk-white.

Anthony Pisano and Gabriel De Luca were upper-echelon operators. They handled very special assignments for Gino Corletto. Boland knew that Gino was one of Joseph Napoli's most respected lieutenants.

Pisano was a tall, hefty forty-year-old man with full gray hair, coarse features, and a bulldog's expression. He spoke in a growl which hinted at a raging temper, difficult to control, just below the surface. His suit of quality material had been expensively tailored, but his muscles and shoulders bulged the sleeves, stretched the back, and pulled the buttons; this made him look like a wrestler dressed for a special occasion, something no one dared mention to Pisano.

De Luca, a fifty-two-year-old, was shorter and trimmer, with fuzzy black sideburns and a completely bald top. Deep wrinkles in his forehead, and a face apparently unaccustomed to smiling, showed the man to be a chronic worrier.

Gino's boys had to be sharp and professional. He knew the consequences of delivering apology reports to the Rajah, Joseph Napoli. Pisano and De Luca's tactics had chilled many subjects along the way, and now it was Jefferson Boland's turn.

"Our temperamental Italian cousins have already messed up good," Pisano was bellyaching. "Always get your facts before eliminating the source."

"The Major?" Boland asked. "Edgar Rand?"

"Yeah."

"Is he in rough shape?"

"Dead and buried," De Luca commented angrily. "Stupid in their fucking heads, these punks."

"Christ almighty." Boland yanked at his ear nervously. "What about the police?"

"That's our business." Pisano tasted Boland's instant coffee and made a sour face. "Explain it to him, Gabe."

"We'll run the operation from here," De Luca said. "Contacts have been alerted and leads are being followed right now. This chase is a priority. We're on the executive monitor." His forehead wrinkles seemed to deepen. "Muazzam Labadi will become dust. But this has to happen before yesterday."

"You're working for us. Boland," said Pisano. "At the usual rate."

"I'd like an increase," the southerner ventured. "The assignment is top-level and extremely dangerous."

"Whore," De Luca blurted. "You've got no fucking right to negotiate with people."

"The usual rate," Pisano insisted. "Or do you want to stay unemployed forever?"

"A deal," said Boland. "Give me orders."

"First a couple of simple answers." Pisano was moving along. "And then get lockjaw and paralysis and do exactly what you're told."

"I want the exact location of Rand's shack," De Luca broke in. "His Italian place."

"Just over the line," Boland replied. "That's all I know."

"We know that too," said De Luca. "Give us a better reading."

"Can't help you," Boland insisted. "Ventimiglia or Bordighera or San Remo or—"

"The guy doesn't know." Anthony Pisano was studying Boland's expression. "Ralphie and the boys will track it down, Gabe. They're on a full sweep of the area. Depend on professionals."

"*I* handed you Rand and the Garth connection," Boland reminded them, feeling hurt now. "And that was more than dumb luck in a coffee joint."

"We appreciated the information," said Pisano. "The leads were phoned home."

"And Garth's wife," Boland continued. "Hospitalized at Saint Roch."

"You get another trophy," said Pisano, winking at De Luca. "We'll have a friend operating in there as soon as possible."

"Then why can't you people deal with me—"

"*Boland!*" De Luca slammed his fist down hard on the arm of a tacky couch. "What the fuck are you looking for, a kiss on the lips?"

"Money," Boland answered. "And respect for services rendered."

"That's enough." Pisano stood and moved his giant frame close to the southerner. "You'll get orders early in the morning. Don't leave this apartment until you receive my phone call. Understood?"

"Yes."

"Our people in the States are waiting for quick and effective action," said De Luca, also getting to his feet. "Screw this up in any way and I'll cut off more than your paycheck."

After the visitors had left, Jefferson Boland pulled out a thin cigar, lit up slowly, and propped his boots on a low mahogany table. He was thinking about Andrew Tolkin of the Central Intelligence Agency—surely a potential buyer, despite his reaction at their meeting that afternoon. Tolkin would eventually realize that Boland had salable merchandise; but he'd have to proceed shrewdly, because of an unhealthy climate and his current low rating with the CIA man. And Boland knew that if the American guests, Pisano and De Luca, had been able to read his mind, they would have removed his crew-cut head a slice at a time.

Italy
Night
Wednesday, June 6, 1979

"Open your eyes and snap to, Labadi," Garth instructed. "We're here."

After speeding twenty-five kilometers past the city of Genoa, they were entering Rapallo, a popular Italian resort town on the eastern Ligurian Riviera. Labadi, who had been dozing, shifted quickly to an erect position and fixed his gaze on the driver.

"What's the address?" he asked tiredly. "Do you know how to get there?"

"Via Tubino," Garth replied. "There's a street map in the glove compartment."

Both men were pensive, touchy, fed up with the journey. Garth needed a shave, but Labadi's growth of beard and long shaggy hair were only two reminders of his rugged days and nights in the barn.

"This is Via Aurelia Ponente," he said, examining the map under the Fiat's ceiling light. "We have to cross the whole damn town."

"Probably a short haul," Garth remarked. "Alert me as we move along."

The reporter felt his breathing, pulse, and heartbeat quicken each time Labadi called out a street or a direction. In a short while, if Edgar Rand's pronouncements were valid, fantasy could become electrifying reality, and Steven Garth might be directly involved. The hoarseness of Labadi's voice and a fidgety manner which he had not detected in Perinaldo told him that the other man was also uneasy.

"Slow down," Labadi ordered. "Make a quick right turn just ahead." Thoughtfully, he folded the map, switched off the car light, and glanced at the driver. "Via Tubino," he whispered.

It was a narrow, poorly lit uphill street in a quiet residential area close to the Montallegro cable car. Moving slowly, they checked right and left for names, and began to worry as the vehicle approached a dead end at the top.

Eventually, Labadi gestured with his thumb. "Pull over now," he blurted. "Condominio Fernanda."

They were in front of a modest apartment building. A one-car garage was next to the entrance. Following Garth's orders, Labadi jumped out with a key, opened the door, and Rand's Fiat was rolled inside. Quickly he closed and locked the garage door and both men walked briskly to the Fernanda's steps, their destination.

Just before going in, they stared at each other for an instant, and Labadi muttered huskily, "Good luck." Without responding, Garth turned away and entered a marble-floored lobby, knowing that the Arab was right behind him.

The condominio was a drab structure in need of repairs and fresh paint. There were no tenants about, although the building appeared to be wired up and occupied. Labadi and Garth took a slow, bumpy elevator to the third floor. They approached a wooden door marked 304. A small metal-framed cardboard nameplate was blank.

After a jittery hesitation Garth pushed a buzzer, and the door opened. A short, bull-necked Italian man greeted them warmly.

After bolting the door, and introducing himself as Mario, their pleasant host led them to an old-fashioned high-ceilinged living room. They sat at a table under a dangling chandelier. Despite time-worn furnishings and a slightly musty odor, this apartment was clean and polished.

"Want to fresh up and eat?" Mario's accent was heavy in places, although he spoke English fluently and unhesitatingly, American-style. "Give me Rand's documents for inspection and we'll talk later." He noticed Garth's disapproving look. "I have to see validation first off, because you people are here without the Major," he explained.

"Does he usually show up?" Garth asked, deciding not to mention the problem in Beaulieu.

"Usually," Mario answered. "But other times Rand makes the arrangements, the clients report alone, and he receives a fee by special messenger." The Italian glanced at Labadi's leather jacket and turned back to Garth. "Everything depends on Rand's circumstances," he said. "The man is reliable, and we trust him all the way."

"You were offering food," Labadi interjected. "Any chance of a drink?"

"Absolutely," Mario replied graciously. "You can take a shower and—"

"No, thank you," Garth broke in fast, without consulting his partner. "I would prefer to start at once."

Labadi was about to object, but Mario held up his hand, authoritatively. "Mr. Thompson is your sponsor," he reminded. "He pays the bills." The young, dark, strongly built Factory associate was cordial, but his change in attitude reflected the importance of the business about to be discussed. "May I have your weapon, please?" he said to Labadi.

"Why?"

"All weapons are handed over on arrival," Mario answered patiently. "A hidden weapon found later will be considered a breach of house rules. Nobody wants trouble here."

Frowning, Labadi dug into his pocket, removed the gun, and placed it on the table in front of Mario, who smiled approval.

"Mr. Thompson?"

Garth stared, then looked down, opened his briefcase, and produced the Smith and Wesson .44.

"Well, I'll be goddamned," Labadi remarked, moving his head from side to side in amazement. "Never figured you to have a piece cached away."

"They'll be returned when it's over," Mario said quickly. "Understandable, eh?" Adroitly, he unloaded both weapons and dropped them into a brown cloth sack. "Now," he proceeded in an easy fashion, "I think we might have a drink and get down to business."

Mario inspected Edgar Rand's papers: they included a formal letter, signed recommendations for Abu Zaki and Mr. Thompson, a contract outlining the provisions of their deal, and a personal note in code, meaningless to Garth, but quite acceptable to Mario.

"Everything in perfect order," he said. "The Major is a dependable worker."

Labadi reached for a bottle and poured another large drink while Mario eyed him coldly. "Slow down," the Italian warned. "You might be admitted tomorrow."

"Give me a break, warden," Labadi flipped back. "I always handle the stuff very well."

"Our bar is closed to you until further notice." Mario demonstrated instantly that he was capable of enforcing his authority. "That's the way it is, Zaki."

Labadi nursed his last shot and glared at the man in charge without commenting.

Mario ignored his sulk and delivered what seemed to be a prepared lecture on the house rules, mutual trust, reputation, and the Factory's iron code of ethics, before asking for the payment. He opened Rand's heavy manila envelope and counted out 30,000 American dollars. The money was tied with a rubber band and placed in his attaché case. In a quiet, businesslike manner he removed a white card, scratched his name across the front, and handed it to "Mr. Thompson." "Your receipt," he explained. "Legal and binding in the proper circles."

Garth examined the unorthodox voucher. The card, about the size of a normal business card, had an unusual engraving of a black ship's anchor in the center. A name, G. ANDRETTA, was neatly printed in the upper left-hand corner. And Mario had scribbled his unreadable ink mark, from end to end, just below the middle.

"If a client or a sponsor has a legitimate bitch," said Mario, pointing to the card, "this receipt guarantees a full refund, damage money, and instant tombstones for the workers involved."

"Where do you register a complaint?" Garth asked, only half joking. "The local board of trade?"

"Your contact is Edgar Rand," Mario replied, failing to smile. "He knows exactly how to proceed without rocking the boat." The Italian was suddenly impatient. "My third year begins next month and I've never heard of a complicated problem. The operation is tight, and unique, as you will soon discover. Please listen carefully.

"Zaki is scheduled to get his injection and leave early tomorrow morning. After three days in the Factory, at a top-secret location, he takes another needle, and returns to this apartment for convalescence, with his new face under bandages. You wait at the apartment as a special guest until Zaki arrives. There are restrictions. You will not be allowed to leave the premises or make outside contact of any kind until the books are closed—satisfactorily."

Signora Rosa Gambino, Mario told them, was housekeeper, cook, and guardian responsible for the maintenance and supervision of the Factory's drop in Rapallo. They would meet her shortly. Mario himself lived and operated elsewhere, as the right hand to a fringe director of the organization, although he contacted the signora every day. The whole of the condominio was occupied by close and loyal tenants—a family in the lobby floor had been on the payroll for years. A cripple and his wife occupied front rooms, and two grown sons and a daughter had quarters in back.

"Condominio Fernanda is well policed," Mario stated. "Eyes and ears are tuned up day and night."

The paperwork between "Abu Zaki" and "Mr. Thompson" was discussed. Now that Mario's organization had agreed to supervise the arrangements outlined by Edgar Rand, no adjustments or cancellations would be tolerated. The Factory's reputation, he emphasized, was based on a code of ethics and a fanatical need for satisfied customers: backers and travelers.

He outlined the agreed procedure: Following the removal of

bandages by members of the inside group, a tape machine and facilities with unique security devices (he was not specific) would be made available to Abu Zaki and Mr. Thompson. Mario was under oath to guarantee absolute privacy and the satisfactory completion of this recording without knowing or caring about the facts being divulged. After their session, a new passport and other documents would be handed over to Abu Zaki, and Mr. Thompson would be given his audio tape at the same time.

"Deal completed," said Mario. "Mr. Thompson leaves and a member of the inside group will be responsible for directing Mr. X to the right path as a brand-new citizen of the United States. Absolutely no one, except the Factory surgical team, will know Zaki's new face and identity," he continued. "And these people are in the same category as God when it boils down to responsibility and trust. And the forgery experts who handle passports and documents are members of this surgical team." He glanced at Labadi. "The inside workers take blood oaths. You can forget about leaks and disclosures."

Steven Garth had been absorbing the Italian's speech. "Fascinating," he commented, hoping for more. "No wonder your organization has a brilliant reputation."

"Security is the key," Mario lectured. "Our present deal is a good example. Zaki traveled a widely respected circuit before finding the Major. Rand's history with us is spotless. You've been checked and authorized by Rand." His alert dark eyes shifted from Labadi to Garth. "But even if one of you did decide to jump out of line and cause trouble, the Factory would be protected. This drop is nothing more than a rented apartment in Rapallo. Rosa Gambino has a legitimate and positively unbreakable cover, and so have I. Our tenants in Condominio Fernanda are law-abiding citizens. What Factory?" He lowered his voice, automatically. "Very few have ever seen the place, and the address is guarded like Fort Knox. Imagine —my job is on an upper rung, but still it's considered fringe, and I have no idea where the Factory operates."

"Beautiful," said Garth, pushing again. "And the drops change frequently?"

"And the Factory dissolves in an instant if anything penetrates the radar and sets off the alarms." Mario was gathering documents. He placed them neatly into his case, zipped it shut, and glared at Garth. "Mr. Thompson, we have enforcement teams poised to smash from anywhere in the world. They are cold, experienced, and dedicated, and a good reason to obey the rules now—and long after you do business with the Factory."

"Zaki" and "Mr. Thompson" had been assigned to a large, comfortable room, with two beds and a mélange of old but practical furniture. Like the rest of the apartment, everything was clean and polished and tidy. A window overlooked terraces and the back yards of Via Tubino. The moon lit up a religious portrait and a cross on the wall.

Garth was awake, twisting, perspiring, feeling stomach jabs from every type of emotion. He couldn't go on thinking about Ellie or Rand and the gorillas or Boland and the law. He punched up urgent instructions for his weary brain, and at once only Mario remained, and the possibility that he was digging a journalistic gold mine.

Again he flashed back to June of 1974: Queens, New York, on assignment for a John Conway piece. Terrorism and the possible existence of a key identity-changing operation in southern Italy. Victor Donato, a suspect from Sestri Levante, freed because of a lack of evidence, had been lying through his big white teeth.

Mario had convinced him that a Factory did exist, and that he was sitting right on the doorstep.

A cough interrupted Garth's thinking. He could see a fuzzy outline of Labadi's bed in a corner across the room. The Arab had traveled over a highly respected circuit to locate the Major. Ruling out fantasy, like the Robert Kennedy murder, what act had been committed by this man? Something important enough to make him eligible for a new face and identity, Garth realized.

"Hey, Garth." It was Labadi. "Are you asleep?"

"No."

"Same with me," he complained. "I need a drink."

"The bar is locked," Garth told him. "You heard what Mario said about the rules."

"Yeah." There was a pause. "But in a few weeks I'll be on my own, pouring booze in a new mouth." He laughed. "And Garth will be exploding the Robert Kennedy truth for cash and standing ovations."

11

Condominio Fernanda
Rapallo, Italy
Early morning
Thursday, June 7, 1979

$\mathbf{A}$ tapping on the door roused Garth from a light sleep at eight o'clock. "Who is it?" he asked, cotton-mouthed.

"Signora Rosa," a gentle voice replied. "Breakfast will be ready in twenty minutes."

"Fine."

"Go directly across the hall," she went on. "Take seats and make yourselves comfortable."

"With pleasure."

The dining room matched the rest of the apartment: large, homely, and functional. Garth and Labadi seated themselves at a neatly arranged table. A bath, a shave, and fresh clothing had made Garth feel better, but as they waited in silence he began to feel anxious. He saw that his emotions were mirrored in Labadi's face.

A moment later, Rosa Gambino entered, introduced herself, and served them eggs, bacon, toast, and coffee. Labadi began to devour his food instantly. Garth proceeded slowly, taking notice of the cook, housekeeper, and guardian whom Mario had spoken of with such respect. The signora was in her middle thirties, dark, smooth-complexioned, and very attractive. An unsophisticated dress hung on a trim, well-proportioned figure. Garth surmised that Signora Gambino was educated, of good breeding—and completely out of place as a maid in a Factory drop. He had expected something quite different.

Rosa left the room and returned when they had finished eating.

"Your appointment has been canceled this morning," she told the man she'd been introduced to as Abu Zaki. "They have an unscheduled surgical emergency at the Factory."

"Balls!" Disappointment had turned Labadi's nervousness to anger. "When do I go?" he asked.

"Probably late tomorrow," Rosa answered. "We're sorry for the inconvenience."

A lousy, skittery beginning, thought Garth. "We counted on today," he remarked firmly. "Please notify your boss about our feelings."

"Mario knows," the signora replied. "I'm certain that Mr. Zaki will be admitted tomorrow."

"Let's hope so." The Arab was disquieted. "We have a formal agreement," he reminded.

"The agreement will be kept," Rosa assured him while glancing at his empty bread-wiped plate. "More food or hot coffee?" she asked.

"I want a bottle of whiskey," he answered without any hesitation. "For later today."

The Italian woman stepped closer to the table. "Mario has ordered me to emphasize three house rules." She looked at Garth. "No one leaves the premises. Outside contact is forbidden." She turned to Labadi. "Our bar is temporarily off limits to you, Mr. Zaki."

Labadi pounded both fists and made the breakfast dishes jump. "What the hell are you operating, a fucking prison?" Rosa's mild expression remained unchanged, but Labadi cooled at once when he saw how Garth was glaring at him. "I'll crack by tomorrow morning without a drink," he explained, running out of steam. "Understand that I'm not going in to have my piles removed."

"Exactly," said Rosa Gambino. "And that's why our bar is closed."

The Arab was sullen and deflated. "Getting a new face is a traumatic experience," he mumbled to himself. "I rate a pacifier."

"My heart bleeds for you, Zaki," Garth said roughly. "The bar is closed." He stood and faced Rosa. "Tell Mario we'll obey his rules. But I want my client admitted to the Factory by late afternoon tomorrow."

"I'll tell him," she promised quietly. "And thank you for being helpful."

He watched thoughtfully as Rosa left. Up close, Garth had detected unhappiness in her eyes, and he wondered about her story. Where did it feature in this dangerous, mystifying booby hatch? In a fantasy mood, Ellie had calculated there were a thousand possible scenarios.

Genoa
Italy
Thursday, June 7, 1979

Gabriel De Luca, Anthony Pisano, and Ralph Cecchi were finishing lunch in a quiet corner of a small restaurant, away from the main Genoa streets. The proprietor, his waiters, and many of the guests knew the Americans by reputation, and they had been receiving very attentive—but very discreet—service.

The representatives of Joseph Napoli's organization had enjoyed the meal and the vino, and they were now discussing the Labadi chase, serious upstairs business. Cecchi raised his glass to acknowledge Pisano's congratulatory toast. This young, good-looking, modishly dressed junior lieutenant had found Rand's house in the country—a swift and efficient piece of action.

Cecchi and members of his group had been covering the Italian border area systematically, using experienced help and proven techniques, when they were attracted by the narrow uphill road to Perinaldo. And eventually they interviewed a grocer's helper on a bustling Ventimiglia street, only a few blocks away from the mountain turn-off. The twelve-year-old delivery boy, fascinated by the United States and curious about his neighbor, had followed Rand one evening after making his delivery in Soldano.

After a search of the house and grounds, which the boy had led them to, Cecchi's men found a number of promising odds and ends, but only one turned out to be a workable lead. A partly charred scrap of paper yanked from under the grate of a living-room fireplace gave them a reference to some kind of an Italian connection. Ashes had nearly obliterated percentage figures, expense accountings, and other business computations, but a name was still readable: G. AN-DRETTA.

Gabe De Luca's extraordinary memory for names, dates, and places was well known in underworld circles. For him, G. Andretta rang a very distant bell: Napoli's people were on the hookup at once with their cousins in Reggio Calabria, Sicily, Milan, Palermo and elsewhere—including the States. Andretta's name was programmed into the network's reliable machines, along with a reminder bulletin on Muazzam Labadi and the Arab's possible traveling companion, Steven H. Garth.

"We have a report from the hospital," Anthony Pisano told Ralph Cecchi. "Garth's wife."

"That's fast," he commented. "Do you have somebody inside already?"

"Not a full member," Pisano answered. "But the character is dependable on a temporary basis."

"A fag in the records section," Gabriel De Luca jumped in unhappily. "We'll have to do better."

"The woman has multiple sclerosis," Tony Pisano explained to Cecchi, ignoring De Luca's remarks. "Do you know anything about this disease?"

"Yeah," he answered. "A broad I know is crippled up with it."

"Right," said Pisano. "According to her files, Mrs. Garth might also be a psycho."

"Did she mention the reporter?" Cecchi asked. "Have we got any clues?"

"She told her doctor that he's away being interviewed for a job," Pisano replied. "Maybe that's all she knows."

"Horseshit," said De Luca. "This is a smart bitch with plenty of information."

"Want to choke it out of her?" Pisano was sour. "All we need are French gendarmes and American law enforcement to bust things up right now."

"You might get ordered," De Luca persisted. "Gino has to report an instant Labadi smear or Joseph Napoli will castrate him."

"This lady wouldn't tell even if she knew," Pisano stated. "Use persuasion? Too risky. Wrong customer. Always get your facts before eliminating the source. Right, De Luca?"

"Garth won a trophy for his Bobby Kennedy coverage," said Cecchi. "He's the wrong partner for Labadi."

"Bet your ass," Gabe De Luca responded. "And his wife is scribbling notes and covering them with pillows."

"I don't get it," said Cecchi. "What do you mean?"

"A crippled psycho is writing in a hospital room," Pisano explained calmly. "You really are a worrier, Gabe."

"We should be very curious," said De Luca. "The reporter might be feeding her information on a private line."

"Eleanor Garth is being monitored carefully," Pisano told him. "And we'll soon have faster eyes and ears inside. Don't give me lectures. If anything develops and the woman's notes become suspect, we'll grab them and nail her instantly." He turned away, and faced Ralph Cecchi. "The hospital in Nice is under control," he summarized.

"Great," said Cecchi. "I'll work on a few leads while you and De Luca handle the syndicate. The Andretta name and some other items should be on the pipe right now."

"Examine the Beaulieu ideas we discussed," Pisano ordered. "And keep a finger on the revolving whore."

"Boland? I'd like to have been with you and Gabe on your visit with him yesterday evening."

"I've got plans for this cutie," said Pisano. "We'll use him later."

The big, muscular white-haired leader of Napoli's search partly focused his attention on Gabriel De Luca. The chronic pessimist was scowling at a wineglass.

"You won't find him in there." Pisano's bulldog features had softened. "Rest easy, Gabe," he said. "We'll deliver the package on time."

"The government means business," De Luca moaned. "Agents are snapping at Joe Napoli's ass. Can you imagine the fucking Arab whispering in their ears at a time like this?"

"Muazzam Labadi is a dead man," Pisano growled. "He will never whisper or testify or rise up again."

"You'll have to prove it to Napoli," said De Luca. "Gino claims the Rajah is nervous."

"We'll bring home all the skulls." Pisano glanced around the room. "Drink up," he instructed. "Let's move out of this place."

●

AFTER READING *Sandcastle* late into the night, James Hatfield continued during breakfast the next morning until the Negresco phone buzzed and interrupted him. He put the manuscript on the couch, lifted the phone, and heard the voice of Léon Dumas.

"We are quite upset," the administrator of Les Mimosas was saying in a brisk and formal tone. "Can you possibly visit my office at eleven?"

"This morning?"

"Yes."

"Of course."

"Dr. Serge Vassolo will be present," he said ominously. "A matter of importance."

"How is Eleanor Garth?"

"Best to discuss her situation over here," Dumas answered. "There are many complications."

Dr. Vassolo was a short, paunchy man in his early fifties, with steel-gray eyes, unusually wide nostrils, a balding scalp, and a pockmarked complexion. But the psychiatrist's direct manner and gently soothing voice made up for his botchy appearance. He sat at a table with Léon Dumas. Both men looked somber and concerned.

Eleanor Garth's acute exacerbation had become one of the most crippling since her multiple sclerosis had been diagnosed in 1975. In addition the head pains that had attacked her the day before were now more severe. Dr. Lambert and the Mimosas physicians were still attempting to determine the exact cause.

"I want Madame Garth flown to London at once," said James Hatfield. "Can she be moved?"

"It would be a risk at the present moment," Dumas answered. "This institution will refuse to accept responsibility for any of the consequences."

Hatfield looked at Dr. Vassolo. "What's your opinion?" he asked. "Can the patient be moved?"

"Bad timing," Vassolo remarked. "You might agree when our discussion is finished this morning."

"We've mentioned some of her physical ailments," Dumas lectured, glancing at Vassolo. "There are other disturbing problems to be considered."

"Nevertheless," James Hatfield insisted, "I want a top London specialist brought over for consultations as quickly as possible."

"That's up to Eleanor Garth, Dr. Lambert, and James Hatfield's pocketbook." Dumas maneuvered his features into a jovial appearance. "Our group has nothing against Harley Street missionaries."

Vassolo drummed his fingers on the conference table restlessly. "The patient's emotional state has deteriorated alarmingly," he informed Hatfield. "Once again Madame Garth had to be restrained and put under."

"When?" Hatfield asked. "And for what reason?"

"I'll explain in layman's terms," said Dumas, becoming an unsmiling beanpole again. "Dr. Vassolo is preparing his formal written report."

He began to review Eleanor Garth's neurotic behavior in the past at both Saint Roch and Les Mimosas, then he moved on to the latest —and most startling—of all the incidents.

"Her animalistic wailing froze this entire clinic just before mid-night," Dumas proceeded grimly. "Hysteria would be an understatement."

Again, she was making delirious accusations, similar to unproven charges she'd made against Claude Jourdan, the Saint Roch orderly, eleven nights before on October 28. On this occasion at Les Mimosas, according to Eleanor, she'd awoken from a drugged sleep and found a nurse examining her personal belongings in a wardrobe. The drawer of a bedside table and every other conceivable hiding place appeared to have been inspected.

According to the patient's report—which had been very difficult to understand because of her coughing and sputtering—the nurse had quickly realized that she was awake and battling to find her voice. The intruder dashed across the room and stifled all noises with a pillow.

A large woman, Madame Garth had been able to determine, strong and violent, although her features were hazy in the dim glow of a night-light. While applying pressure, nearly enough to suffocate her, the nurse leaned forward. "Expect another visitor later," she threatened in a hoarse whisper. "Have the manuscript available next time or you will die instantly."

Hatfield's mind was partly on the book as Léon Dumas continued about the patient's incredible ravings, and Vassolo followed with confirmation in his best psychiatric jargon.

"What about the nurse?" Hatfield asked during a brief lull in the report. "Anybody on your staff who fits the description?"

"Eleanor Garth is referring to Catorina Faugno," Dumas replied.

"Did she visit the room last night?" Hatfield went on. "Just before twelve o'clock?"

"She did," Dumas replied. "After passing the door and hearing moans and groans."

"I'll have all details on paper," said Dr. Vassolo. "And why not chat with the nurse yourself?"

"She's off today," Léon Dumas reminded. "Her duty begins at eight in the morning. If you want me to arrange—"

"Possibly," Hatfield interrupted. "I'll let you know."

"Caterina Faugno entered the room and found Eleanor Garth in a delirious state." Dumas was enjoying his own performance. "She was obscene and abusive and belligerent. The nurse tried to calm her, but the woman's screeching and psychotic behavior were uncontrollable. Caterina was forced to leave and get immediate assistance."

Hatfield thought a moment. "The nurse is a permanent employee of this clinic?" he inquired. "A regular member of your staff?"

"Absolutely," Dumas replied without hesitation. "And one of the most experienced."

"On the job a long time?"

"No," the administrator said matter-of-factly. "But she was highly recommended by people known to us."

"When did she arrive?"

"Caterina reported November sixth," Dumas replied. "Just a few days ago."

"Really?" Hatfield paused for a snap tabulation. "Madame Garth was admitted on November second."

"That's correct," said Dumas. "What's your point?"

"Did you find her in Nice?" Hatfield asked. "Or another part of France?"

"Italy," Dumas replied, becoming provoked. "The foremost clinic in Genoa."

James Hatfield was thrown for an instant, until he suddenly realized that the impact of Eleanor's fantasy was leading him down an embarrassing path. Dr. Vassolo confirmed his insight.

"Quite frankly," the psychiatrist muttered, "this Gestapo-type interrogation is rather bewildering."

"Curiosity," said Hatfield. "I'm doing everything possible to understand an old friend's actions."

Dumas smoothed his toupée with both hands and forced a crooked grin. "Oddly enough, we expected to probe you and gather more background information on the patient," he said. "We're talking about Madame Garth's notes."

"I'm just beginning," Hatfield stated cautiously. "An evaluation now would be premature."

"Gibberish?" Dumas asked. "Or can we all learn a few things?"

"Madame Garth has written a book of fiction," Hatfield replied somberly. "I'll analyze the material with you and others when I've read it all and the contents have been digested."

"Have you uncovered reasons for the patient's neurotic behavior with hospital staff?" Dumas asked. "What about a Mafia chase?"

"There are fictional references to the underworld," he answered, picking his words very carefully. "And—based on what I've read up to now—may I offer a few practical suggestions?"

"Go ahead," said Dr. Vassolo. "But you must realize that my files will remain incomplete unless you give me an opportunity to examine the patient's notes line for line."

"Something will be arranged." He was not enthusiastic. "In the meantime, you should take my advice and make things easier for the patient and the clinic. It's very important that you treat Eleanor Garth's fears with respect and understanding during this critical period.

"I want a security guard posted outside her door until further notice," Hatfield went on. "He will enter the room with all visitors and remain until they leave."

"Are you talking about clinic personnel?" Dumas asked incredulously. "Nurses and physicians?"

"Everyone," Hatfield replied. "Day and night. I want to minimize the patient's anxiety about intruders and death threats."

"An unethical approach," Serge Vassolo protested. "We have to convince her that—"

"Please," Hatfield interrupted, determined to organize the situation. "A guard will help Eleanor cool off until my London doctor arrives. I want her on a plane to England or America as quickly as possible."

"Our security people will cost you a fortune," advised Dumas. "Especially on a day-and-night basis."

"I'll hire my own," said Hatfield. "A more comforting arrangement for Madame Garth."

"Starting when?"

"Right away," James Hatfield replied. "As soon as I can make arrangements."

Dumas placed bony fingers over his mouth, coughed, and then glanced at Dr. Vassolo, who had been studying the American with cold professional eyes.

"You must be reading a very impressive book," said the psychiatrist knowingly. "I can't wait for my turn."

"All in good time, Doctor." Hatfield was preparing to leave. "Phone me at the hotel if something develops. I'll be in touch after lunch. And give my love to Eleanor when they bring her around."

"Of course," said Vassolo. "By the way," he continued, "we have all guaranteed the patient that the whereabouts of her manuscript will never be revealed."

"Good," Hatfield told him. "That plays along with the situation nicely."

"Yes." Vassolo buttoned a tight collar. "Thought you would approve."

"Caterina Faugno won't have to sneak into your bedroom just before midnight." Dumas laughed and it was a gurgling noise. "Sorry about that, Hatfield."

By three o'clock in the afternoon, James Hatfield had wolfed down a room-service lunch at the Negresco, made formal arrangements for Ellie's guards, coordinated a fast start at Les Mimosas, and left his number with Dr. Brandon Patterson's office in London.

He sat quietly for a moment, allowing his imagination to wink at nurse Caterina Faugno, orderly Jourdan, Rand's damaged table, a missing rug, and other unfounded links to Eleanor Garth's fantasy plotting.

Then, without expecting a positive response, Hatfield called the American Embassy in Paris, where they had never heard of a Draper or Tolkin. He also made a cursory attempt to find a listing for a Jefferson Boland. Without success. Fictitious characters, obviously, he realized—although the Major, Edgar Rand, had been a quick trace in Beaulieu-sur-Mer. He discontinued the exercise when the opening lines of Eleanor's novel reminded him that "some names, dates, and places have been changed. The others are valid."

On the sofa with a drink, Hatfield picked up the manuscript and located the page where he'd left off. Before starting, he reached for the house phone and gave instructions to a man on the desk.

"Put calls through," he said, "but I do not want to be disturbed in my room by anyone."

"Yes, Mr. Hatfield. What about the evening papers and—"

"Only the phone," he interrupted harshly. "Do you understand?"

"Yes, sir."

Hatfield replaced the receiver, got up, walked across the room, locked the door, and used the chain. He returned, made himself comfortable, and joined "Zaki" and "Thompson" in *Sandcastle*.

12

Condominio Fernanda
Rapallo, Italy
Noon
Thursday, June 7, 1979

Muazzam Labadi and Steven Garth were at the dining-room table sipping coffee after leaving most of their lunch. Few words had been exchanged between the two men since Rosa Gambino had announced the Factory cancellation during breakfast.

Labadi, tense and anxious to go, had paced the room cursing under his breath. Garth was suspicious and uneasy about the delay. And in addition, the reality of his involvement had taken a firm grip, blowing away the candy floss and pumping up wide-screen visions of his wife and Rand and Boland and Mario and a quiet pack of unknown hunters.

The existence of a Factory operation had now been accepted without question by Garth, and he was becoming more than inquisitive about the actual crime of Labadi.

Signora Gambino brought another pot of coffee, and Labadi asked her to join them. She hesitated, but to Garth's pleasure Rosa finally agreed. He was even happier when he discovered the reason for the Arab's unexpected invitation.

"I want to know about the Factory," Labadi told her right away. "The procedures when they get me in there for the job."

"I don't know the exact details, Mr. Zaki," Rosa claimed, but Labadi insisted. She proceeded reluctantly, emphasizing that her information was hearsay, based on gossip from the patients after surgery, nothing official or confidential.

Her understanding was that there would be a preliminary examination, followed by photography and X rays by specialized camera techniques, and still more inspections. Afterwards, the patient would be given three composites to analyze, photographs of faces unlike his own. A selection would be made. Finally the scalpel, and a new identity. Under the bandages, the new face would heal to be as near as possible the exact duplicate of his choice on paper, guaranteed by the Factory.

Meanwhile, forgery experts who belonged to the surgery group would be rigging up his passport, birth certificate, and other important documents.

Rosa Gambino finished her skimpy explanation of the Factory basics. "We know that our surgeons and the other insiders are competent, experienced, and trustworthy," she assured Labadi. "Members take oaths in blood to protect you and everyone associated, including fringe workers."

"That's wonderful," he remarked, in a grouchy voice. "But you people delayed, and there has to be some kind of compensation for us." He watched Rosa drink up and get to her feet. "I want a quart of whiskey right now," the Arab ordered.

"Sorry," the dark, attractive Italian woman repeated. "The bar is closed until further notice."

Labadi scowled, and Garth eyed her thoughtfully as she left the room without glancing back.

That evening Labadi was a vibrating bundle of discontent. Garth reclined on his bed pretending to read American newsmagazines while the other man paced and cursed and kicked imaginary objects across the room.

"I could whack her ass and go for my own quart," Labadi mumbled. "Screw the rules."

"Great idea." Garth kept his eyes on the magazine. "You'd get a face lift without surgery." He turned a page in a casual manner. "I have a feeling that Mario and his boys do a very effective job."

"Fuck him," said Labadi, beginning to deflate. "I need whiskey."

Garth finally glanced up, closed the magazine, and pointed to a chair opposite the bed. "Sit down over there and wipe your tears," he instructed. "I want to discuss a proposition."

"A lecture?"

"No," Garth replied. "Booze for information."

Labadi stared at him curiously. "Where the hell do you expect to find booze?"

"Right here." Garth shifted himself to an upright position, reached under the bed, and came out with a quart of whiskey. "Do you want to make a deal?"

Labadi gazed at the bottle in astonishment, and then he roared with laughter—the first time, Garth realized, that he'd heard the unfamiliar sound coming from this moody Arab. "Did you lay the wop broad already?" he asked, having a difficult time controlling his voice. "I noticed that she had big eyes for you."

"Signora Rosa gave me the quart after lunch while you were crapped out," Garth explained, ignoring Labadi's remarks. "I promised to supervise the contents and accept full responsibility for your actions."

"What a goddamn operator." Labadi flopped in the chair and laughed again. "Maybe your friend wants to attend our party."

"Knock it off." Garth's expression reinforced his words. "I told Gambino that I'd space out a few drinks to calm your nerves," he said. "The woman trusts me. And I intend to keep it that way."

"A noble gesture," Labadi announced, leaning forward in the chair. "Now, may I have my first pacifier, Doctor?"

"Booze for information," Garth reminded. "Give me straight answers or die of thirst."

"Everything will be on tape," Labadi snapped back. "We have a formal agreement."

"I don't mean your Robert Kennedy bullshit," Garth said harshly. "This is different."

"Come again?" Labadi was perplexed. "What information are you referring to?"

Garth had located a plastic cup under his bed. "I want everything you know about the Factory situation." He poured a large drink for himself, and Labadi watched. "Give me a factual briefing about the circuit. Names, locations, their operating procedures, and connections, political and otherwise." He topped the bottle and set it down gently. "Repeat what you've heard on the Factory's grapevine." He drank the whiskey carefully, as a tease. "Step by step. I want to know how you moved along the high-level paths and finally turned up in Rand's barn eligible for an identity change at the Factory."

Labadi leaned back, and his flesh seemed to tighten, so that he looked cold and evil; Garth was reminded again of terrorism and assassination. "I thought you were a clever piece of work," he snarled. "My evaluation is going to be drastically revised."

"Why?"

"Because millions of dollars wouldn't buy the Factory information," he replied. "How can you possibly expect to Jew me around with a shot of cheap booze, assuming I know some factual things about the route to Perinaldo? You heard what Mario said about going against the Factory. They've got enforcement teams out there to handle this kind of crap!" He sounded determined not to tell what he knew, if it was anything.

"Nobody questions what's on a patient's record," Labadi stated. "Assassination, terrorism, drugs, rape—forget it—they don't want to know. But screw with the Factory and you'll come through a grinder like hamburger meat."

Garth had seen Labadi's explosive reaction before. He swallowed the rest of his drink and worried about pushing ahead. Maybe later, using smarter bait, he decided.

"Wise up," Labadi lectured, keeping his eyes on the cup Garth had just shoved under the bed. "Don't act like a goddamn fool."

"Oh?"

"Kennedy is the story," Labadi carried on. "And you'll be alive to report it."

"Good," said Garth. "I'll wait for a tape."

Labadi folded his arms, and glared at the reporter. "Think I'm lying about the conspiracy?"

"Possibly."

"Stand by for a jolt," Labadi promised, obviously hoping to be rewarded with the whiskey. "I'll honor the deal and unload names and dates and places."

Garth grinned. "Anybody can hold a microphone and spout fairy tales," he taunted the Arab. "You come up with a plot, rehearse it well, sound off glibly, and then collect a new life for keeping a bargain. You'll claim it's true, I'll say it's a lie, but so what—the game is over because the deal has been honored." He reached for the bottle and sighed. "Oh well, too late now. My bet is on the line, so I've got to play out the hand."

"You're a winner." Labadi, as usual, was able to project sincere feelings. "The confession will be authentic."

He looked away from Garth and the cup and the whiskey, and began talking in a quiet monotone. He seemed to be caught up in his own bitterness and unpleasant memories—obviously a fabricated history would be easy to record, he admitted, but he was anxious to disclose the truth for his own satisfaction. Robert F. Kennedy's death had been plotted and executed as a conspiracy.

"Some bastards got away with murder," Labadi grumbled. "Operating now like nothing ever happened. Fuck 'em. I had to run and scrounge like a dog for years. Why the hell should they beat all the raps, when I can finger them and dissolve behind a new identity?"

Garth poured another whiskey for himself, lifted the cup, hesitated, and then set it down on the rug next to his feet. He was impressed and confused again by the Arab's seemingly genuine performance.

"Pity if Sirhan Bishara Sirhan walks out of Soledad prison as the lone assassin," Labadi continued. "You know the guy is up for parole and is pitching for an early release; I heard that the California board might shorten the date. They say he's been offered political asylum in Libya." Labadi's eyes flashed back to Garth and his whiskey. "Your tape will complicate this situation," he added. "Beginning to understand the importance?"

Instead of replying, Garth bent over, found an empty cup, and poured a modest quantity of whiskey. "Do you think Sirhan has a chance for parole?" he asked.

"A damn good one," Labadi replied. "His base term is sixteen years and nine months, and they might cut it for good behavior and rehabilitation. But my confession on tape will probably screw things around."

Garth got up with both cups of whiskey, moved to Labadi's chair, and delivered one. "Nurse it along," said the reporter. "My bar is closed."

With eyes fixed upwards and head back, Labadi was relaxed in the chair, making his last drink work overtime. Garth, reclining on the bed again, flipped through his magazines in a vain attempt to smother a feeling that he might have underestimated the Arab and the importance of his crime.

"Sirhan had better visit our Factory the minute they open the Soledad gates," Zaki remarked, almost to himself. "He's been cozy for years in PHU-1. Lots of mean people will be right on his ass, if and when they grant a parole and let him run free."

"You seem to know a bit about Soledad," the reporter commented without looking up. "Ever do time there?"

"Never," Labadi replied. "But I know facts about this guy Sirhan." He licked at the whiskey. "The prisoner is in the maximum security quarter of the State Correctional Training Facility, at Soledad. PHU stands for Protective Housing Unit. Semi-isolation. Things will be a lot more hazardous on the outside."

Labadi emptied his drink and glanced over at Garth, who was pretending to read. "I owe you a favor," the man acknowledged, tapping on the cup. "Do you want to hear a little story?"

"About the Factory?"

"Balls," Labadi replied. "About me."

Garth looked at him and realized that he was all business and eager to converse. "The Kennedy plot?" he asked while sitting up and leaning his back against fat pillows.

"Not exactly," Labadi answered at once. "But I'm sure you'll catalogue it as background material. A lead-up to my involvement."

"Are you pitching for another drink?"

"I could use one." The Arab managed to smile. "The whiskey jogs my recollections."

According to Muazzam Labadi, code-named Abu Zaki:

Adjustment was difficult for Muazzam and his family after they emigrated to California in 1957. He talked about unemployment, hunger, poor living standards, disillusionment, and violent arguments between his whiskey-soaked father and confused mother. Even so, he persevered with his education, receiving better than average grades and a special citation for mastering the English language in record time. But the quarrels and futility at home eventually broke him down, and Muazzam left school and family in order to make his own way in Los Angeles.

Constantly in need of money and recognition, he drifted from one job to another, searching for his base, a ladder, a goal. Muazzam was intelligent, ambitious, and respectful of the law, but he felt that the obstacles had been stacked too high for refugees, especially for the Palestinians.

On October 8, 1964, in Los Angeles, California, a man introduced him to a man who introduced him to a man by the name of Sanford Draper. Muazzam began to work free-lance as an informant, for the Central Intelligence Agency, reporting exclusively to the officer who had recruited him.

He was usually instructed to mingle with young Arab students, workers, and drifters who had been labeled by the intelligence group as political agitators or organizers with foreign connections. Muazzam's reports were always given top marks by Sandy Draper. The

CIA officer had also praised his loyalty and dependability.

The young man was in awe of the United States and honored to be a part of the system. He was impressed by Sandy Draper, the Agency officer, and his recruitment speech. Labadi had no allegiance to Jordan, no real pride in his Arab heritage, and no fanatical animosity toward the people of Israel. Draper's money was good, with bonus chances and recognition.

Starting on February 10, 1967, Muazzam Labadi—still working exclusively for Draper—participated in a top-level Agency checkout. Reliable sources had uncovered fresh new information about the existence of a very determined ultrasecret professional Arab murder team. According to formal reports, the organization was structured like an old Jewish Stern Gang—with active cells abroad, particularly among extremist Arab students. This group was pledged to destroy all foreign politicians who leaned toward Israel either by sympathetic words or deeds.

The investigation of the possible existence of an Arab murder squad was given a code name by the Agency: "Sandcastle."

Labadi was assigned to beat around the dingy Hollywood joints frequented by Arabs and other immigrants from the eastern Mediterranean. He talked and listened and passed on his information. Labadi was an effective radar post. A dependable asset for Draper and the CIA.

There were no startling reports. Labadi felt that the Agency was tracking ghost riders, exaggerating the importance of minor incidents, pressing for complicated networks based on whiskey rumors and doped-up chatter from unhappy aliens. However, Labadi had an unusual opportunity to meet and study various types of customers, and he kept a written and mental file on every one, along with their friends, enemies, contacts, and families. Draper's informant was becoming an expert on the Greenhorn Belt.

By July of 1967, he felt that the Agency was beginning to lose interest in Sandcastle and in his reports from the Hollywood clubs. Sanford Draper's payments were no longer flowing on a consistent basis. Now it was a spot arrangement, negotiated amounts for specified pieces of business only. And worst of all, soon after he was given a new contact. Draper had been replaced by a man known as Polk.

Labadi had respected Sanford Draper as a competent and honest man, a credit to his organization and to the United States of America. Now when he mentioned the replacement his voice tightened and anger brewed. A dirty bastard who used a code name, Albert Polk. Labadi was sure that this agent had played with bigtime organized crime figures, making all kinds of sensitive arrangements, including government leaks for payoffs. And the son of a bitch was probably caught in their web, tangled forever.

Labadi was certain of a few things. The intelligence operator had pocketed Agency funds, paid many of his assets on a half-and-half basis, and collected disbursements for a list of fictitious informants. The man known as Polk was a crooked rustler with a lot to hide. But, Labadi explained, the deadliest accusation, the shocker, Albert Polk's coffin lid, could not be revealed without the protection of a new face and identity.

During the final months of 1967, while Sandcastle was crumbling, Polk treated Muazzam like a used rubber. He made the Arab feel guilty and ashamed of his dealings as a paid informer, a whore reporting to the American government. Finally Labadi realized that his loyalty had been wasted; he accepted a final payment from the Agency on January 10, 1968, and went back to his job in a gas station.

On February 2, 1968, two smartly dressed Italian men from New York City visited Muazzam at one of the Hollywood nightclubs. To the best of his knowledge, no one outside of the intelligence group was aware of his connections and services. But word had apparently spread about his unique catalogue on immigrant clientele in the Los Angeles area.

These two visitors had a big-money proposition. They were hunting a particular type of employee for an important free-lance assignment. Local connections had named Muazzam as a responsible talent scout.

Labadi suddenly halted the flow of his reminiscences, and Garth prepared for a change of mood.

"You've had enough information for three lousy drinks." Labadi bent forward and gestured. "The house should pour one free."

"Was Sirhan on your list?"

"No comment."

"Two of his brothers must have been studied," Garth persisted. "Joe used to play drums in the joints."

"No comment."

Garth finally drip-dropped a reasonable quantity of whiskey into Labadi's cup, and the Arab settled back in place. "Is your wicked intelligence friend still operating these days?" the reporter asked. "Polk?"

"I have no idea where the guy is stationed at the present time. He might have been fired, or he quit, or he died. It's unimportant now," Labadi explained. "My confession on tape will guarantee instant destruction for this filthy bastard, whatever his real name happens to be."

"When did you—"

"Don't be greedy." Labadi pulled himself up and walked unsteadily to his bed, sipping along the way. "We'd better follow the rules."

Garth, acknowledging a dead end, stretched out and gazed blankly at a religious painting on the wall. Now he was even more hazed up and thrown off course by the Arab's unfaltering and realistic performance.

"Hey, Garth," Labadi called softly. "About Sirhan's two brothers."

"Always use 'Thompson' here."

"Yeah." Labadi paused and started again. "Joe is Munir Sirhan," he muttered. "The guy never worked any clubs as a drummer."

"Really?"

"Adel Sirhan was the professional musician," Labadi went on.

"Played the oud in a joint called the Fez."

"A what?"

"The oud," Labadi responded. "A big gourd-shaped guitar from the Middle East."

"Oh, yes."

They were both quiet, and then Labadi snarled, "As if you didn't know all this crap."

"I was just—"

"You'd better wise up," Labadi interrupted coldly. "And treat my knowledge with respect. The Robert Kennedy murder was a conspiracy. I want the facts and the people involved exposed for my own reasons. Edgar Rand told me that you were the best man to handle the job, because of your ability and experience and familiarity with the case. Quit testing me and busting my rocks. Or when recording time arrives, you might get the bullshit I'm supposed to be full of."

Garth thought before he reacted. "Don't lecture me," he said, exaggerating anger. "I'm not putting up time and over forty thousand dollars for bullshit. Screw me now and they'll bury you with the same ugly face. Am I getting the message across?"

Labadi was quiet for a while. "Piss away," he said in a tired voice. "I'm off to see the Wizard tomorrow."

Garth adjusted a pillow and closed his eyes, although he expected to be awake for the rest of the night.

13

It was nine o'clock on Friday morning, and Labadi was under-standably excited. During breakfast, Rosa Gambino had announced that the Factory was prepared to receive him. She gave him his instructions.

"Mario arrives at eleven," said Rosa. "He will escort you to a *funivia* located three blocks away. Ride the cable car alone. Get off at Montallegro eight minutes later. Walk a short distance to the Sanctuary. Go up the steps and continue left of the building until you reach a narrow footpath. Follow it through a densely wooded area. Eventually you will be met by a small group of Factory representatives. You can expect an injection and a blacked-out auto journey down the mountain road." She paused and then said in a formal tone, "Good luck with your new identity."

In their room, fifteen minutes before Mario was due, Garth sat on the edge of his bed watching Labadi pack a suitcase.

Suddenly his mind flashed back to the fifth of June 1968, the Ambassador Hotel, in Los Angeles. A shocking vision of Robert F. Kennedy's body on the pantry floor. His wife and others next to him as blood drained from a head wound. The Senator had been a man of accomplishments and potential, with driving force, character, intelligence, and noble ambitions. And this man who might have been President had died at forty-two.

Just for a moment Garth thought about the killer, Sirhan Bishara Sirhan, and then allowed himself to drift into Ellie's world of pills and fantasy. He toyed with the notion that Labadi *had* participated in a conspiracy to assassinate Robert F. Kennedy. The Arab would have a new face and identity, Sirhan would go free on parole, and others would do business as usual while Kennedy continued to rot in his grave. Garth stared at Labadi's back as the man fastened his suitcase, and then he glanced around and spotted the empty whiskey bottle; he had a passionate urge to crush the Arab's skull. But the Major's arrangements and the Factory's strict code of ethics would mean that the Kennedy secrets would be lost forever; and his life would have ended violently. Reason took hold again, and Garth blinked away the phantoms and got to his feet.

They were in the entrance hall ready to go. Labadi, holding a packed suitcase faced Garth, while Mario and Rosa Gambino stood nearby.

"I want to thank you for arranging my new life," Labadi said, without concealing his jumpiness. "Expect pure gold when they switch on the machine."

Garth eyed him contemptuously but made no effort to respond.

"Pay attention." Labadi stepped closer and brought his voice down to a throaty whisper. "Most of the players are still around," he confided. "A few years older now. Some have moved up the ladder. Others down. Two have retired. One is dead, replaced by a son." Labadi glanced around and saw that Mario and Rosa had walked out of hearing range. "The Kennedy brothers have always been ducks in a shooting gallery. Number one was hit and number two, and they are probably ready to eliminate number three, if he ever moves past their sights on a journey to the White House."

"Let's roll," Mario ordered from the doorway. "We've got a tight schedule."

Labadi inched forward until he was breath against breath with Garth. "Handle our tapes properly and you'll be a very rich hero." He was quiet and intense. "Finger the conspirators, botch up Sirhan's early release, and help to protect the number-three duck on the line."

Labadi turned abruptly and joined Mario. "See you in a few days," he announced, without looking back.

Garth continued to stare at the doorway after both men had left.

"Abu Zaki will be someone else when he returns." Rosa murmured. "The procedure is quite chilling."

"Yes," said the journalist, eyes still forward. "The procedure is quite chilling," he repeated mechanically as the attractive Italian woman locked and bolted the door of 304 Condominio Fernanda, Via Tubino, Rapallo, Italy.

A villa
Suburb of Genoa, Italy
Early afternoon
Friday, June 8, 1979

Resembling a hairy whale, Anthony Pisano floated on his back in the ornate swimming pool, using water wings and earplugs. He paddled and thrashed noisily with his brawny arms and legs, making very little progress, but the sky was clear, and the sun was bright, and Tony was enjoying himself, until Ralph Cecchi interrupted.

"Mister Spitz," the young American hood called from the edge of a diving board, "Gabe is waiting."

Pisano, outfitted in a robe and sandals, dried his gray hair vigorously with a towel and then joined the casually dressed Cecchi and De Luca at an umbrella-shaded table next to the pool. There was a pitcher of cold orange juice for De Luca, and gin and tonics had been put in front of Cecchi and Pisano. All three took uneasy sips, their expressions gloomy.

"I'm ready for a briefing, Gabriel." Pisano tapped his chubby fingers against the glass. "Was Andretta the bum you remembered?"

"The same one," De Luca answered, and the lines on his fore-head deepened. "We now have real trouble."

De Luca's investigations had produced from a friend in Reggio Calabria a brief report on Giovanni Andretta. He had worked numbers and some prostitution years ago in Jersey City, Newark, and in Paterson—which was where his name had entered De Luca's prodigious memory. Andretta had been small time. With no record in the States, he had come to Italy around 1966, played clean, and operated a seasonal fleet of three dilapidated cruise boats. They hauled tourists on the eastern Ligurian Riviera: Portofino, Sestri Levante, Santa Margherita, San Fruttuoso, Rapallo. The business had been sold to Ernesto Gallucci in 1972, and old man Andretta had retired. De Luca's friend had reported that Gallucci was dead, though the boats might still be floating in the area with new owners. He had no information on this, and the whereabouts of Andretta were unknown.

"Now, hold on to your balls, Pisano." Gabriel De Luca paused for effect. "My friend whispered a theory."

"Go ahead."

"Andretta might be operating again," he went on, using a somber tone. "Chief of the Factory."

Pisano's coarse features and bulldog expression turned to granite. "The identity switch in Marseilles?" he asked, dazed by the remark.

"Wrong address," De Luca blurted. "They've moved four times since Marseilles."

"Holy Jesus," said Cecchi. "A natural for Labadi on the run."

"All right." Pisano's temper was rising. "Where's the Factory now?"

"The Calabria guys don't know," De Luca replied. "And I believe my source."

"*Mother fuckers!*" Pisano roared and tossed his glass violently, splattering it nearby. "These pricks are hooked up to the Brigades and the other garbage eaters who run the fucking place! Of course they know the location!"

"Tony!" De Luca held up both arms. "Cool off and let me explain."

Pisano glared at him. "Make it real," he said, fuming. "Because I don't trust our Italian cousins." With the robe, he wiped gin and tonic off his barrel chest and then added, "Especially down south."

"I'll repeat." De Luca met his gaze without flinching. "My source in Calabria is very dependable. And we now have real trouble."

He went over the background: The southern brotherhood had pulled away from the Factory connection over a year ago. The Red Brigades and the Front Line and other groups like them had discontinued active participation in management. De Luca's source had heard that Andretta was running operations for a group of wealthy, dedicated revolutionaries—without a formal link of any kind: a well-equipped, tightly organized, independent service, available to all verified and eligible clients, regardless of political or underworld affiliations.

"The southerners don't know where the Factory operates now," Gabriel De Luca announced. "Because there is no high-level interest in the project."

"*Liars!*" Bulging veins deformed Pisano's neck. "Federal cops are on the Rajah's ass with this new investigation. I smell a deportation or even worse. Labadi could be atomic right now." He settled back. "They know the Factory address, Gabe," the big man concluded. "But these bums are probably operating with Houston."

De Luca frowned into his empty glass.

"Contact Gino with my remarks." Anthony Pisano was on top of the situation again. "Our guys in the States might press the right buttons."

"Expect a shit hemorrhage on the phone," Ralphie added. "Labadi could have a new face and identity by now."

"Doubtful," Pisano retorted. "Anyway, we get the face lifter or a nurse or a records man. Somebody will have a file on him." He noticed De Luca's concerned expression. "As long as we move fast enough."

"What about Garth?" De Luca asked. "The bastard is a reporter."

"And his novelist wife," Cecchi added. "The psycho in Saint Roch."

"I'll phone Gino," De Luca stated. "But, like I asked you before, what's next?"

A young man cleared his throat and then approached the table with a fresh gin and tonic. He eyed the broken glass nearby, but Cecchi motioned him away.

"We can't splash around waiting for the States," Tony Pisano announced in his typical growl. "I'll follow my gut instincts until something better comes along."

"That's good enough for me," said Cecchi. "What's on the agenda?"

Pisano tasted his drink, crushed hard and noisily on a lump of ice, and then addressed De Luca. "You'll stay here, Gabe, and keep on the hook with Corletto. Me and Cecchi and a few strong Italian boys are going down the road. The eastern Ligurian Riviera. We'll sail on three dumpy cruise boats and interview anybody who remembers Giovanni Andretta or Ernesto Gallucci or their families, associates, enemies, and pals."

"We'll dig up something." Cecchi was excited. "It's a tourist cluster with greedy locals."

"Remember a bum named Victor Donato, Gabe?" Pisano asked. "An Italian citizen from around here?"

"Just vaguely," De Luca replied. "A terrorist link and drug pusher."

"Associated with the Factory," Pisano went on. "He beat a 1974 rap in Queens and decided to rush home."

"It's a blur."

"Donato was from Sestri Levante." Pisano hesitated. "We might trip over the bastard or his family during our investigation."

"A long shot," De Luca remarked, dejectedly. "What about Boland?"

"Jefferson watches Saint Roch, and your Italian boys watch

Jefferson," Pisano answered. "Best to keep whores on the payroll until missions are completed." He looked at Cecchi. "This one will earn his salary before we're through. And that's a promise."

"I believe you," said the young Mafioso. "Anything new from Garth's wife?"

"No visitors, no mail, no calls, and no improvement." Pisano sipped gin and tonic. "The lady is being watched by insiders."

"Eleanor Garth is writing and stashing her notes under pillows," De Luca said. "Plenty of information could have passed already."

"A remote chance, Gabe," Pisano told him. "Besides, this crippled psycho will be ignored, no matter what she scribbles and hides."

"I want to be positive," De Luca insisted. "Boland could arrange—"

"Forget it." Pisano was adamant. "Garth's wife is under constant surveillance. And that's all for now. I won't risk a dumb move in a French hospital. You'll get a signal when and if a closer look becomes necessary."

Cecchi nodded and De Luca poured orange juice.

"The action is down the road." Pisano's excitement was building. "We'll use tact and dollars and muscles, until a finger points to Andretta, the Factory, the Arab—and his Jewish companion." He seized the wrists of both men and applied violent pressure. "My gut instinct," he said. "This chase will end in Portofino, Sestri Levante, Santa Margherita, San Fruttuoso, or Rapallo."

14

American Embassy
Paris, France
Morning
June 9, 1979

"Can you get up here for a visit, Andrew?" Sanford Draper asked politely on the interoffice hookup. "The FBI just left and I want to brief you."

Draper was forty-two, a Central Intelligence officer; he was blond, freckled, and blue-eyed, with a natural smile and likable manners. Tennis and golf helped to keep his body slim and well conditioned. Intelligence people and others in government had respected Draper for many years. His beautiful wife and two children felt the same way.

Without toughening his looks or using any dramatic voice inflections, the agent had a talent for emphasizing the importance of a situation, guaranteeing the complete attention of his audience. Andrew Tolkin was no exception. In this case, for many personal reasons, he was glued to his seat by Draper's account of the FBI meeting.

The morning visitor was representing a special task force. Part of a long, complicated, restricted ongoing Bureau investigation of political bribery and organized crime in America.

"Richardson is the agent's name," Draper was saying. "His

group wants cooperation on a particular OCT network development."

For eleven months the Agency and foreign intelligence services had been monitoring formal links between organized crime and international terrorism. The underworld syndicates and a network of Italian, West German, and Palestinian urban guerrillas were reportedly splitting profits from kidnappings, robbery, gambling, drugs, prostitution, and other activities. Italian terrorists such as the Red Brigades and the Front Line were being trained in Palestinian bases. Other locations in France and Switzerland had been reported. The Italians and the Palestinians maintained tight connections with the West Germans. Profit-sharing with organized crime had helped the groups finance their armed membership.

"Richardson wants to study the Nice possibility," Sandy Draper explained. "We'll give him full cooperation."

The Agency, using French and American drug officers, had been checking out a very recent lead which indicated that a large heroin storage and distribution center was situated in the Nice region. Italian terrorists, key French traffickers, and members of organized crime in America were rumored to be involved.

"The Bureau feels that either Joe Napoli or Beppe Sandalo is connected," Draper announced. "Napoli is their first choice."

Tolkin removed his glasses and blinked repeatedly. "I can't buy a Napoli link here." The agent's evenly modulated delivery was forced. "Sandalo is also doubtful. What's the basis for their sudden accusations?"

Draper, knowing the man well, attributed his uneasiness to a longtime resentment of outside interference by the FBI and other agencies.

"Richardson was candid," Draper proceeded. "His team's primary objective is to gather evidence against Napoli." He smiled. "They won't be under your feet, Andy."

Believing that his statements were eliminating Tolkin's apprehension, Draper explained that the Bureau's specialized task force had been working undercover for a year in order to compile new and more damaging evidence against Joe Napoli. They had updated his file by chasing and processing hundreds of leads and angles, but the material was still not powerful enough to guarantee immediate deportation, or a long federal prison term. The Bureau needed a few crushers: a verifiable drug link with French pushers and international terrorists would be difficult for Napoli to flick away.

"I disagree with you, Andy," Draper remarked without a trace of belligerence. "Richardson might be onto something in Nice."

"Why?"

"Ralph Cecchi was spotted two days ago in Ventimiglia near the border." Draper paused. "Were you aware that Gino Corletto had people over here?"

Tolkin replaced his glasses and then lied convincingly. "Yes," he said. "I'm finishing a report."

"And Jefferson Boland?"

"He's included," Tolkin shot back. "Pisano and De Luca have also been visiting."

"Richardson mentioned that." Draper was still pleasant. "So why can't you buy a Napoli link?"

Andrew Tolkin was not easily flustered. "I think Joe Napoli's people are over here to investigate Beppe Sandalo's foreign connections. Especially in southern Italy. And the guy has plenty. Nice is probably on the agenda because Gino thinks, as we do, that Reggio Calabria is involved. And if so, they might have pitched Sandalo as the American connection, a lucrative deal."

"You feel that Napoli is just an observer." Draper was slow to accept Tolkin's estimate. "His people are here on a fishing trip."

"We just picked up the lead, Sandy." Tolkin backed off an inch. "Nobody is certain of anything. That's the reason I questioned the Bureau's references to Joe Napoli and Beppe Sandalo at this early stage."

Draper penciled meaningless doodles on a yellow notepad. Tolkin felt his right foot go cold, as if it had been plunged in ice water —something which occurred every time he faced danger or stress conditions. No other part of his body was vulnerable, except for a tiny cluster of forehead veins. He wondered if Draper was about to mention Labadi.

"Contact Edwards in Nice and brief him," Draper ordered instead. "We'll do everything possible for agent Richardson and the Bureau."

Tolkin was making hasty plans while Draper talked about surveillance for Corletto's men and a possible chat with Boland and the offer of a detailed up-to-the minute rundown on the Nice file, and more. "I would love to see them puncture Joe Napoli," said Draper. "We might have a few items Richardson can use."

"Now you're getting me excited." The station chief's instructions had rattled Tolkin, especially the part about a chat with Jefferson Boland. "I'd better handle this affair personally, Sandy," he decided, adjusting his glasses for no reason. "There are many important and fragile points to be considered."

"What about your Marseilles trip?"

"Bob is reliable on his own."

"Start packing." Draper grinned. "The old Côte d'Azur is beautiful in June." He tore away the scribbled page from his notebook, rumpled it, and flipped a basketball shot into a waste container next to his desk. "I should have assigned myself."

Condominio Fernanda
Rapallo, Italy
Evening
Saturday, June 9, 1979

Since Labadi had left the Rapallo drop on the morning of June 8, Steven Garth had been working on a closer relationship with Signora Gambino during afternoon tea and later over a glass of brandy on their first evening alone. Obeying house rules, she had avoided references to the Factory, Mario, and the backgrounds of "Zaki" and "Thompson." But little by little, with soft and expert urging from an interested reporter, the attractive Italian woman had exposed the basics of her adult life. She had been married to a teacher of political science who had been active in the Workers Autonomy Movement, a University-based Marxist group of ultraleftists known to have direct connections with the notorious Red Brigades. In 1978, while serving his third year of a five-year term for armed insurrection, subversive activities, and the illegal possession of weapons and explosives, her husband had committed suicide in his Milan cell.

Answering Garth's questions hesitantly, Rosa Gambino explained her involvement with a young, good-looking teacher, a man resentful and disenchanted because of corruption and the economic tangles of a postwar Christian Democratic Party, and because of a shift away from a revolutionary program by the Italian Communist Party. He had other gripes, and she had agreed; then later, without really being aware, they found the cause had come to saturate their lives day and night. They met new friends with similar thoughts and feelings. And in time there were official contacts, followed by her husband's formal membership. Deeper and deeper, until what had begun as opinions were being translated into positive action. And Rosa was trapped with her husband in a dark underground world of terror and rebellion.

According to Rosa, she had never been a member or a participant in any of the Workers Autonomy activities. Her husband had tried to protect her by withholding facts about objectives, missions, and the press accounts following violent acts of terrorism by his organization. Signora Rosa Gambino—according to Signora Rosa Gambino—had been a complete outsider. Nevertheless, after Italian police had grabbed her husband, she too was arrested, interrogated at length, and then released. She believed that officials had kept her under surveillance for over a year. Eventually, with the help of Mario, Professore Gambino's friend, Rosa had left Rome secretly in 1977. As the wife, then widow, of an imprisoned hero, she joined other Factory recruits and had become a trusted member of the staff.

As they drank brandy in the evening, Steven Garth decided to gamble and ask a personal question.

"Are you unhappy here?"

"Perhaps." She hesitated a moment. "Have you been watching me?"

"Yes."

"I feel differently about certain things." Rosa became thoughtful. "Especially since the death of my husband." She sounded somber and distant as she explained that most of her earlier beliefs had mellowed—she no longer gave much thought to the need for drastic changes in Italy and in other parts of the world. Her husband's strong belief that force had to be used to exert pressure, gain attention, influence the public, sway governments, and eventually alter history was no longer hers.

"I feel now that violent revolution is evil." Rosa sipped her brandy. "Every day, I feel lonelier and more isolated here—the ugliness and secrecy . . . Everything is becoming more difficult to handle."

Garth was about to fill her glass, but she motioned him away. "Why do you stay here?" he asked, pouring a shot for himself. "Break and run and start again."

"Impossible," Rosa answered. "There is no way out for me. I am guilty; I must stay and take responsibility for my actions. Yet I dream of beauty and a normal life." Rosa shrugged and met Garth's eyes. "But this will never happen. And I'm resigned to my fate."

"Unexpected opportunities arise, Signora." As he spoke, he realized how much he admired her dark beauty. Mingled with this thought was self-congratulation for oiling a key to the Factory: a possible source of explosive information. "One more question?"

"No." Rosa toyed with her brandy glass. "May I also break the house rules and ask a few of my own?"

"Yes."

"Are you married?"

"Yes."

"To a beautiful woman?"

"Yes."

"Can you describe her for me?"

Garth frowned and then answered her question unemotionally.

"My wife has been ill for many years," he explained. "She's a cripple."

They were both quiet. Finally Rosa Gambino, with her eyes gazing into his, moved a glass slowly toward him, and he poured brandy. "I'm sorry," she whispered.

Later that same evening, Garth lay in bed pondering the entire Factory adventure. Labadi would soon return with his new face and identity. The confession was scheduled to follow after removal of his bandages. He attempted to visualize the blacked-out tight security facilities and procedures. How, he wondered, should he deal with Labadi and the bizarre event? Treat it seriously or as a hoax? What if the Arab had been involved as a Robert Kennedy conspirator? Outlandish. But anything now seemed possible in these fantasy trappings. Nevertheless, he would have to respect the confessional phase in order to appear legitimate: he was the sponsor, the investor demanding a genuine product, as arranged by the Major.

Garth decided to examine the Robert F. Kennedy murder from start to present. His unique ability to store and catalogue data would give him the edge without files. He intended to listen attentively to Labadi's conspiracy statements and then question him, trap him, bludgeon him—and finally expose the fraud by pointing a knowledgeable finger at the loose ends, the missing links, and the conflicting evidence. For some reason he was sure that Labadi would stand firm; he would hold his own and put up a hell of a fight, and the prospect excited him.

Even more importantly, Garth felt, bold plans had to be structured without delay, or his opportunity to break a Factory piece might vanish. He thought about his possible key: Rosa Gambino. A beautiful, confused, exciting, disreputable person, floating aimlessly in a sea of violence and terror. How strong were her feelings of loyalty and dedication to her dead husband, to Mario, or to the Factory operators and their revolutionary beliefs? Garth had a hunch that Rosa's loneliness, isolation, and guilt might lead to the Factory doors—if he proceeded cautiously, with respect and understanding.

15

Mist hazed the water and partly concealed a savage encounter near the bow of a rusty tourist boat docked here. Two of Anthony Pisano's Italian commandos were questioning the skipper. An earlier investigation in the area had led to this man: a muscular, pimple-faced, weatherbeaten English character with tangled red hair and a very stubborn manner. Anthony's persuaders were receiving more belligerence than cooperation.

"One more time." They had him propped against a deck rail. "Ernesto Gallucci?"

"No."

"Giovanni Andretta?"

"No."

Fists pounded at the man's ribs and stomach, until he groaned and doubled over. A knee came up fast and nearly back-flipped him over the side and into the water.

"Ernesto Gallucci?"

"No."

"Giovanni Andretta?"

Unexpectedly, the skipper howled like a mad dog and threw a

barrage of wild, dangerous punches, connecting with most of them.

"You son of a bitch!" One of Pisano's men rubbed his jaw. "Now we'll break your fucking neck!"

They walloped him professionally, unmercifully, only in the midsection, until blood trickled from the corner of his mouth.

"Enough!" a Pisano helper ordered. "We messed up his guts."

The glassy-eyed victim sank to both knees, swayed, and then crashed forward on the deck.

A Pisano man spotted a wooden-handled fishing knife in a toolbox nearby. They seized the tourist-boat sailor and roughed him into a face-up position, thrusting the cutting edge of the blade against his throat.

"Want to die?" They were stooping low. "Gallucci and Andretta."

"No."

"I'll have to operate." Pisano's commando made a tiny incision and the red-headed Englishman screamed, *"No!"*

"Talk!"

The skipper coughed and gagged and began to nod affirmatively. "A guy named Donato knows."

"Victor Donato?"

"Jimmy."

"Who the hell is Jimmy?"

"A brother."

"He lives with Victor?"

"Victor is dead," the sailor wheezed. "Jimmy runs the boats now."

"Give us the address."

"I don't—"

"Address!" The blade slid another fraction of an inch down his neck. *"Address!"*

"Condominio Miramare," he replied, giving up. "On Via Rosselli."

"Sestri Levante?"

"Yes." The Englishman swallowed hard and avoided their eyes. "But he travels a lot."

"What about now?"

"Probably home."

They stood and glared down coldly. "We just finished a very private discussion," an interrogator reminded. "Do you understand?"

"Yes."

"Jimmy Donato knows," the other man said, examining the knife. "Gallucci and Andretta."

"Yes."

"He'd better," the Italian warned. "Or we'll slice you from neck to asshole."

Beaulieu-sur-Mer
France
Late night
Sunday, June 10, 1979

Jefferson Boland entered his apartment, flicked on the lamp, and went rigid at the sight of Andrew Tolkin posed in a chair.

"What gives?" the southerner demanded nervously. "Do you have authority to break into my place?"

"No," Tolkin replied. "Seven or eight telephone calls were useless. Consequently, I invited myself over to wait on the premises and guarantee a meeting tonight."

"Funny deals are out." He began to roll up the wooden shutters, changed his mind, and lowered them again. "These people are watching."

"Relax, Jefferson," the intelligence officer counseled. "Expect a promotion from your boss."

"A what?"

"Sit down and be quiet," Tolkin ordered. "You are now my personal contact with Gino's employees."

Boland narrowed his eyes and stared, until the meaning registered and produced a crooked grin. "Have we actually joined the same team?" He laughed and pounded on his knees with clenched fists. "Quicker than I figured."

"Labadi's rapid elimination has now become a matter of urgency." Tolkin noted Boland's arrogance. "Gino's people have my full cooperation."

Boland ran fingers through his crew cut and drawled, "Well, I'll be dipped in pig shit." The former Agency whore laughed again. "You are really too—"

"Shut up!" Tolkin interrupted harshly. "This is very high-level business. Listen carefully and report to Pisano accurately." He removed his glasses. "Or you might end up being delivered to Joseph Napoli in small pieces."

Quiet descended over the room as Andrew Tolkin's warning finally settled Boland in his chair.

"We'll exchange pertinent information and coordinate our actions." He glared hard at the southerner. "Muazzam Labadi has to be apprehended and neutralized immediately. I'll show good faith by opening my files now."

Tolkin confided that an agent representing a special FBI task force was operating in the region. Luckily, to the best of his knowledge, they were not tracking the Arab. The visit was part of a large, complicated, restricted investigation of political bribery, organized crime, and formal profit-sharing links with terrorist groups. Mainly the Bureau's task force was interested in a drug lead, very recently picked up by the Agency. Reports that a major heroin storage and distribution center was functioning in the Nice area. According to Agency sources, it was supervised by Italian terrorists, French promoters, and members of organized crime in America. The Bureau had already guessed at Joseph Napoli or Beppe Sandalo, with the Rajah as first choice. Tolkin wanted Pisano to know that he did not figure Napoli as a connection.

However, the overall investigation and now the drug lead were helping the FBI justify its use of a special Joe Napoli hunting license.

The Bureau representative had admitted that his task force's prime objective was to rake up evidence, and pepper the Napoli files and stack the odds and buttress the government's case for rapid deportation or long-term federal imprisonment for the Rajah.

"What a mess if these hounds accidently stumble over the Arab," said Tolkin. "Or find out that we've pledged to chase and destroy him because of what he knows about Joseph Napoli, and some others."

"I'm getting a picture," Boland remarked with a straight face. "Anything else?"

"Cecchi was spotted in Ventimiglia," said Tolkin. "Gabe De Luca and Pisano are known to be around. Draper and the FBI representative assume that Gino sent them over to participate in the Nice operation. Regardless, your employers are marked, and booked for surveillance."

"Good Lord Jesus!"

"You were also mentioned by the agent," Tolkin continued. "Private discussions are being planned."

"Me?" For once Boland looked frightened. "Why the hell me?"

"They know about you," Tolkin replied. "Gino Corletto's workers are here and so is Jefferson Boland. You can't blame anyone for being inquisitive."

"I should have walked away." He kicked a table with his boot and a glass tumbled on the floor. "Quit while the chips are—"

"Jefferson!" The intelligence officer calmly positioned his rimless spectacles. "Brief Pisano and the others without dramatics. I've received permission to supervise the Bureau's mission in the Nice area. I'll be operating from a private residence: Les Oliviers, Boulevard Mont Boron. Telephone 353-64-50." He handed a slip of paper to Jefferson Boland with this information, saying that the FBI agent had no official authority to conduct any investigation on foreign soil. Cooperation would therefore be extended by Andrew Tolkin and his personnel.

"Do you understand, Jefferson?" He waited for a nodding of the southerner's head. "I'll be covering surveillance and any other requests made by the FBI or Draper in Paris."

"That's a help."

"We are focusing on the drug lead and a possible Napoli connection," Tolkin reminded. "Muazzam Labadi has nothing to do with the FBI visit."

"Right."

"And we have to keep it that way," he added. "While the hunt continues."

"A sensitive job."

"A balancing act," said Tolkin. "More delicate than you can imagine."

"Do we talk by phone?"

"I'll probably recruit you on a spot basis," he answered. "Our frequent contacts will then be understandable to the FBI, my associates, and Draper in Paris."

"Right."

"Handle yourself smartly."

"I always do."

"And be sure that Gino's people never approach me," Andy Tolkin warned. "You are the only link."

"Pisano is not dumb."

"Expect a call tomorrow afternoon," he said. "I have an important luncheon scheduled with the FBI man."

"Right."

"Put together your leads and background," Tolkin went on. "Give me a detailed report when I phone."

"I'll check with De Luca."

"Remind Gabe that brute force used indiscriminately will attract law enforcement," he advised. "We have to coordinate a sophisticated mission."

"Right."

"Wait by the phone." Tolkin rose to his feet. "This is your most challenging assignment, Jefferson."

"Hell, yes." Boland slumped low and peered up at Andrew Tolkin. "Quote me a figure."

"What?"

"My payoff from you."

The agent leaned over, picked up the glass, and set it down neatly on Boland's table.

"Let's wait and see how you play for one team," Andrew Tolkin remarked icily as Boland closed his eyes. "For the first time, both of your employers will have an opportunity to compare notes, during and after the game." The official turned and walked briskly toward the door. "How difficult for you, Jefferson."

"Wait a minute."

"Yes?"

"Did you break my lock?"

"No," he replied at once. "I have just explained that we are coordinating a sophisticated mission."

"I want to know—"

The front door had closed quietly and Jefferson Boland was interrogating himself.

Condominio Fernanda
Rapallo, Italy
Early morning
Monday, June 11, 1979

Mario had telephoned Rosa Gambino, reporting the Arab's successful operation. Labadi, healing a different face under the bandages, was in line for a needle and a return to the Rapallo drop at eleven the following morning. Subsequently, Factory insiders would visit and perform the unveiling at the appropriate time. Zaki had a right to inspect his face in a mirror before taping. An American passport and other relevant documents would arrive by special courier and be handed over when the traveler had fulfilled his obligations according to Rand's paper.

Muazzam Labadi, known as Abu Zaki, was almost somebody else.

Hospital Saint Roch
Nice, France
Evening
Monday, June 11, 1979

A blanket-covered patient was hauled out the rear exit on a stretcher and loaded gently into a waiting automobile. The vehicle pulled away quietly, heading for Saint-Jean-Cap-Ferrat, Beaulieu's neighbor, eleven kilometers from Nice on the lower corniche route to Menton and Italy.

To the relief of Dr. Favre and most of the hospital's staff, Roger Lambert had arranged Eleanor Garth's discharge from Saint Roch. The pains in her face, back, and limbs had eased, and the multiple sclerosis victim was in remission; it was not total, but enough to allow some mobility with a cane.

However, the patient's emotional state and disruptive neurotic behavior had grown worse. She had cursed away Dr. Serge Vassolo's involvement, and Dr. Lambert had refused to goad her into meetings with the psychiatrist. The cool-tempered Frenchman had ideas of his own about therapy for Madame Garth, and she was responsive.

Dr. Lambert had American friends, now at home in Boston, who owned a villa on the Cap. It was a modest place in beautiful surroundings, ideal for Eleanor's convalescence during Steven Garth's job-hunting (privately, Dr. Lambert wondered if it was desertion, as many believed). A reliable Frenchwoman lived on the premises and had agreed to cook, housekeep, and nurse the ailing writer.

In order to reassure Eleanor, Dr. Lambert was secretive about his plans, and extraordinary procedures had been used when moving the woman from her bed to his car. She had demanded an evening transfer, a blanket for concealment, use of the rear exit, and very tight lips with doctors, nurses, and other staff members. Firm orders were given to the phone operators and management: Eleanor Garth had been discharged from Saint Roch. No further information was available. However, in the event of a request from her husband, Steven H. Garth, he would be told to contact Roger Lambert, at home or in his office. Only when he was certain it *was* Steven would the doctor pass on the villa's address and telephone number. Eleanor was satisfied with the precautions.

Jefferson Boland trailed Dr. Lambert's car at a safe distance. An inside tip had been received while the doctor and his nurse were preparing Eleanor for the journey. Gabe De Luca and Tony Pisano had already been notified.

A squad of four, with Boland as top dog, would operate a two-man day-and-night shift, covering the front and back of Eleanor Garth's new home. Tolkin's suggestions had been accepted without debate. No breaking or entering or muscle action. The phone line had been tapped expertly. All visits and exits would be under close surveillance. Pisano had agreed with the CIA officer: very few leads were expected on the Cap. But the novelist wife of a sneaky reporter —diseased or not, a psycho or not—would have to be monitored as part of the hunt.

•

AT THE HOTEL NEGRESCO in Nice, France, on the evening of November 9, 1979, James Hatfield placed Eleanor's manuscript on the sofa, leaned back, and wondered about the contents. Definitely it was Steve Garth's research and theories, inflated and fictionalized by Eleanor's medication and hospital-bed imaginings. A reckless last-ditch collaboration, a wild goalpost sprint before the final whistle. Yet Hatfield was unable to ignore a growing uneasiness about Eleanor's material, and her peculiar behavior. He intended to finish the novel and check it out thoroughly before permitting Madame Garth to be sealed away in one of Serge Vassolo's psycho files. Steven's disappearance continued to mystify him. And there were other questions to be answered.

Hatfield reached for the phone. Lambert should be available at Les Mimosas now.

"What's her condition now?"

"Very serious," the doctor answered. "A devastating attack. Her entire body is numb. And the head pains are becoming worse."

"Have you found the cause?"

"No," Lambert replied frankly. "A specialist is due here tonight."

"Can I visit?"

"Madame Garth is drugged and under," he said. "I'll phone you when Dr. Joubert arrives."

"Fair enough."

"Are you still reading her notes?"

"Yes."

"Will they help us?"

"Probably." Hatfield was cautious. "Will you answer a question for me?"

"Yes."

"Did you arrange for Madame Garth to leave Saint Roch in June?"

"I did."

"Can you elaborate?"

Without a hesitation, Dr. Lambert repeated the details of Ellie's transfer—and they matched her fiction. Remission, secrecy, extraordinary procedures, a blanket-draped figure, Lambert's waiting automobile, the ride to Cap-Ferrat, her stay in a villa owned by his friends in Boston, the dependable housekeeper, instructions to phone operators, and the rest, just as she'd written.

"One more question?"

"Go ahead."

"Was Madame Garth living in the villa when she had to be hospitalized again at Saint Roch?"

"Yes."

"In bad condition?"

"Astonishing," said Dr. Lambert. "Multiple sclerosis was only a part of the worry. Bruises, sprains, and cuts were evident. Her dress was torn. A shoe was missing. Madame Garth was delirious. A shock patient."

"Why?" Hatfield asked incredulously. "Had she been attacked?"

"Madame Garth claims to have tumbled down a flight of stairs."

"At Cap-Ferrat?"

"No."

"This information should have been reported during my briefing yesterday."

"Dumas told you that Eleanor Garth's history, including psychiatric findings, is being prepared for you," Dr. Lambert reminded him. "Her condition upon arrival at Saint Roch, and other factors, will be detailed efficiently."

"How could—?"

"Just a moment." Dr. Lambert cupped the phone and had a fast talk with someone. Afterwards, he was back in a rush. "I must leave at once," he stated. "An emergency call from Nice. We'll discuss Madame Garth when you visit tonight or tomorrow."

The literary agent was still reviewing and dissecting his interrupted conversation when the phone buzzed.

"Mr. Hatfield?"

"Yes."

"Cliff Dwyer of King Features," the voice said. "I'm in the lobby."

"Who?"

"Cliff Dwyer," the voice repeated. "King Features of New York."

"What do you want?"

"About an hour of your time for a special piece," the voice replied. "May I come up?"

"Not this evening." Hatfield didn't try to hide his irritation. "Your approach is rather unorthodox."

"Sorry," the voice apologized. "I was having a drink just a block away."

"How did you find me?"

"Mutual acquaintances in London." The voice answered confidently. "Please give me an opportunity to explain my interest."

"Call in the morning," Hatfield told him. "Every day is booked solid."

"I'll be in Frankfurt tomorrow," the voice said. "An early plane."

"There is no other way," Hatfield insisted. "Call my New York office when you get back."

"A pity." The voice exaggerated disappointment. "My help would spark your latest venture."

"Young's book is number three and climbing fast," the agent said, losing patience. "We're moving extremely well, Mr. Dwyer."

"I was referring to Ellie Garth," the voice announced. "Her gallant battle for publication."

Silence crackled.

"What are you talking about?" Hatfield was obviously upset. "Be specific or I'll disconnect."

"An easy one," the voice replied. "Eleanor Garth and her husband live on the Côte d'Azur. She has an incurable disease. Multiple sclerosis. You are her best friend and her literary agent. A rumor is circulating that Ellie Garth has delivered a manuscript. I envision several human interest features to go along with your advertising and promotional campaigns." The voice paused. "Why blame me for doing my job?"

"Where did you hear this preposterous gossip?"

"Mutual acquaintances in London." The voice became a bit unpleasant. "Are you denying the reports?"

"Eleanor Garth is a very sick woman." The edgy reply was too fast and unlike Hatfield. "Janet Young's book and scenario are my latest projects."

"Message understood." The voice went cold. "Perhaps I'll be in touch later, here or in London or in New York or someplace when you're in a receptive mood."

The line clicked dead.

Hatfield stared at Eleanor's manuscript as a jumble of annoying thoughts wrestled his brain. Then he picked up the receiver again and questioned the hotel desk.

"Were there inquiries about me?"

"Sir?"

"Requests for my room number?"

"Hold, please." The clerk was back in moments. "No, sir."

"Earlier in the day?"

"I would have to check and phone you."

"Never mind," said Hatfield. "Get New York City for me. Person to person. Sebastian Baker of King Features."

"Yes, Mr. Hatfield."

Sebastian Baker was King Features' senior editorial official and an old friend. After exchanging greetings, Hatfield went straight to the point. "Do you have a Cliff Dwyer on the payroll?"

"In which department?"

"A feature writer."

"Cliff Dwyer?"

"Yes."

"He's not a staff man," Baker answered. "Unfamiliar name."

"Oh?"

"Could be free lance," the editor pointed out. "But I don't remember anything going under a Dwyer."

"That's interesting."

"Might be wrong," Baker admitted. "Want me to get a confirmation from Powers in Los Angeles?"

"No, thanks," James Hatfield replied. "I trust your memory, Seb."

"What's the problem?"

"Just curious," said Hatfield evasively. "He showed up in my hotel lobby without an appointment pushing for an immediate meeting."

"Sounds like our guys." Baker chuckled. "Used King for credentials?"

"Yes."

"Who doesn't?" The veteran editor dropped his voice in mock confidentiality. "Bet this fellow was looking for angles on your sexpot Janet Young."

"No," said Hatfield. "He wants a feature on Eleanor Garth."

The New York City end went quiet for a moment. "How is Ellie?" Baker asked, somberly.

"Worse than ever."

"Unfortunate." There was another pause. "Dwyer has the right idea, Jim. A human interest feature on Eleanor Garth. You don't want to exploit the lady. But this guy is a writer. And if he showed me a good piece on her I'd be a customer. He barged in and used our name. What the hell, eh?"

"Right," said Hatfield. "I was just curious because of his attitude."

"When are you getting back?"

"Don't know yet."

"Call me."

"I will," said Hatfield. "Thanks again, Seb."

James Hatfield sipped a whisky and calmly replayed the Baker dialogue. The old man was right. A glib, aggressive free-lance journalist had stormed the lobby in search of a human interest story on Eleanor Garth. King would probably be a customer. Faked background? So what. Besides, Dwyer might have submitted a piece or two over the years without Seb remembering offhand. But his rumors about an Ellie Garth manuscript? Presumption? A door-opening tactic? Or did he pick up a tip at Saint Roch or Les Mimosas, where her guarded notes were known by many? Perhaps he shouldn't have phoned Baker about such a triviality.

Another sip reminded him of Dr. Lambert's unexpected description of Ellie when she returned to Saint Roch from a villa on Cap-Ferrat. Bruises, sprains, and cuts. A torn dress. A missing shoe. Delirious. A fall down the stairs?

One long gulp brought him to nurse Caterina Faugno and orderly Jourdan, and Edgar Rand's damaged table and missing rug and—

Hatfield finished the drink abruptly, put a lid on his vivid imagination, and went to Rapallo, by way of Eleanor's *Sandcastle*.

16

Condominio Fernanda
Rapallo, Italy
Evening
Monday, June 11, 1979

At half past nine, Signora Rosa Gambino brought a quart of whiskey and some appetizers to Garth's room. They sat at the table prepared to enjoy their final evening of privacy; Mario and Labadi were due at eleven the next morning. A friendly relationship had developed between them without sex or discussions of taboo Factory secrets, Labadi's background, or Garth's reasons for visiting Fernanda as a sponsor. Following his plans, the reporter had been proceeding cautiously, with respect and understanding.

Progress had been made. Rosa was curious and fascinated by the rugged, outspoken American. He was unlike anyone she had ever met. A man of depth and quality, with manners and warmth, who had made her smile and think and dream more frequently about beauty and a normal life. Rosa wondered how such a person could have found the crooked Factory road.

Garth had taken every opportunity to pound away at the increase of violence and terrorism in Italy and the rest of the world, repeating stories they'd both read in the daily papers. He deplored the extremist activities of her husband's Workers Autonomy Movement, the Red Brigades, and others; fanatics exploding innocent human beings and wrecking property for obscure political reasons, cash, and notoriety. He also dramatized rumors that most of the groups were linked to organized crime, accepting money from prostitution, drugs, and gambling.

He even went so far as to speculate that the Factory was associated with organized crime, and that Rosa had been used—not as the wife of a radical hero with a political cause, but as a brainwashed accomplice loyal to a network of terrorists and international criminals. Her remarks two evenings earlier—that the evil aspects of revolution had caught up with her, and that the passing days and nights were exaggerating her isolation and loneliness—had given him an opportunity, an opening.

At first her reactions were the same as before; she was much too deeply entangled to flee and begin a new life.

But Garth continued to score his points every time they met, and the signora had become quiet, thoughtful, and more receptive.

Now, after a few drinks, the reporter was ready to aim for the bull's-eye. Mario and Muazzam Labadi were due the following morning, and the odds would go against him instantly.

"Your world is morbid and disgusting." Garth rose from the table and carried his drink to the bed. "Can you leave?"

"Never."

"Why?"

"It's obvious," she answered unemotionally. "I know too much."

"More than your associates?"

"Possibly."

"Do you want to break away?" Garth leaned his back against a pillow and sipped the drink. "I can help."

"Too late," Rosa answered solemnly. "You would be rescuing a corpse."

Garth examined her closely as she looked down at the table. Long black hair flowed over a tightly wrapped dressing gown, and the garment outlined her well-proportioned figure. Without any make-up, her smooth complexion was flushed from the alcohol, or possibly from the excitement the reporter was starting to feel.

"Come and sit over here, Rosa." She glanced up quickly as Garth made room on the bed. "We'll never have another chance to be alone."

Rosa hesitated, then finished her drink, stood, and walked to him.

"Listen to me," he said quietly as he eased her down to a sitting position. "You now have an opportunity to ditch this miserable life and play clean."

"A fairy tale."

"Stop dreaming, Rosa," he said. "I can make it all happen for real."

The dark-eyed woman stared at him curiously. "Are you the police?"

"No," he replied instantly. "A well-known journalist. In a position to arrange some kind of immunity and protection if you cooperate."

"I don't understand."

"Have faith in me." Steven Garth put his drink on a night table and sat up close beside her. "Rosa Gambino bungled her life," he said, moving his arm gently around her shoulders. "A self-imposed death sentence is too drastic a punishment for the offense."

"We all pay for our mistakes." Rosa turned and faced him, breathing unevenly. "God only knows what loathsome crimes I've been supporting here."

"There's a way out," said Garth intently. "An opportunity to buy a new start. Do a noble thing. Make up for every lousy mark on your conscience." Up close, he studied her eyes, mouth, and tilt of her head, and decided that Signora Gambino was ripe for a bold move. "Do you know where the Factory operates?" he asked softly.

Rosa frowned, then—with her eyes lowered—she nodded.

"Will you tell me?" he asked gently.

"Never."

"How do you know so much?" Garth demanded. "Mario pleads ignorance."

"My husband's friend is on the Factory staff." Rosa looked up. "A blood oath member."

"Surgeon?"

"The records division," she replied. "Handling photographs and other identity material."

The admission exploded in his brain. "You certainly are on the inside, Rosa," he stated in an awe-filled voice. "A trusted employee."

"Widow of a martyr," she corrected. With trembling fingers she loosened the dressing gown, and Garth caught a glimpse of her large breasts. "There is no possible way out for me, whatever I feel, whatever you do." Her body seemed to vibrate with emotion. "Can't you see that?"

"On the contrary," he replied. "I believe—"

Rosa had leaned closer to him, and her lips were on his, wet and passionate. Garth did not tell her what he believed, for moments later she was on her back, nude, with legs spread wide, and stomach heaving. "How long I've waited for a moment like this," Rosa whispered hoarsely as her arms reached out for him. "Make love to me," she begged. "I want you so very badly."

Steven Garth's key, perfectly shaped and well lubricated, was turned smartly and excitedly; and when it clicked, he wondered if the Factory doors would eventually open.

11:15 a.m.
Tuesday, June 12, 1979

Mario was in Garth's room explaining the latest developments. Although the short bull-necked Italian grinned frequently, he was unable to cover many obvious signs of worry and tension.

The bandaged "Abu Zaki" had just arrived. Mario claimed that the operation had gone without a hitch: a total success, a new person. Zaki, he said, was being set up in a large room down the hall, an off-limits area specially furnished to handle all his needs. But, as Garth had suspected, there were a few problems.

"Just rumors," Mario insisted. "Still, we have to be alert and cautious."

"Sure," Garth agreed. "What rumors?"

"Don't get mixed up," he answered flatly. "I'm here to outline a change of plans and some new rules."

Nervous and unable to hide it, Mario explained politely that "Thompson" would be restricted to quarters until further notice. Meals would be served in his room and he was ordered to use the adjoining toilet. His door would be locked from the outside and a guard had already been posted in the hall.

"What the hell are you doing?" Garth was confused. "Am I a prisoner?"

"Absolutely not," Mario replied. "We're taking precautions because you and Zaki are still in the apartment."

"Explain that."

"There are more important things to go over." Mario leaned forward. "A change of plans."

Mario had orders to evacuate the Fernanda by midnight. All tenants and employees staying in the condominio had been alerted earlier, and Mario had already discussed the unexpected revisions with the Arab. The American passport and other documents would be ready by six in the evening, and Labadi had agreed to have blind faith in the Factory surgeons. There was no time for complete healing or a mirror. He would confess through his bandages on audio tape at eight o'clock that very evening.

"Actually," Mario rationalized, "an early bandaged taping is a problem for Zaki. It has very little to do with your end of the deal, Mr. Thompson. You'll have the confessional tape, a document in Abu Zaki's own writing, the patient's original passport, and photographs of him taken before surgery. The restricted material was off limits to me and most of the others. Zaki's revelations are for your ears alone—members of the group, including Factory personnel, are under oath to steer clear."

After the finish of all business, he went on, a guard would escort Zaki to a new location, a safe house, for healing and bandage removal under the guidance of a Factory insider. Thompson would be free to go thirty minutes after Zaki's departure. Deal completed for traveler and sponsor. Mario and his people would then proceed to handle the latest batch of rumors.

"Special Factory guards have been assigned to the confession on tape," Mario explained. "I'll return before you leave."

"Are the police—"

"Rand's deal will be honored." The Italian got up. "Please excuse the inconvenience."

Condominio Miramare
Sestri Levante, Italy
Noon
Tuesday, June 12, 1979

Anthony Pisano and Ralph Cecchi were seated uncomfortably on tattered hassocks glaring at a young man. Orazio Torissi, a lean eighteen-year-old, had sun-baked fetures, grimy hands, and a dim wit. He returned their gaze vacantly from a chair which had been positioned directly in front of the Americans. Torissi worked as a handyman for Jimmy Donato, present owner of three rusty cruise boats, a tourist fleet on the eastern Ligurian Riviera.

One of Pisano's men had been watching the place for over two days. A neighbor had confirmed that Donato was away on a journey and would return this Tuesday. Pisano and Cecchi had found Orazio on the premises when they arrived an hour earlier. He occupied a room in the dingy apartment and had just returned from a vacation with his family.

Orazio claimed to be waiting for his boss to get home from a San Fruttuoso business trip. Donato was expected before nine in the evening. There was no reason to doubt this, but Pisano had decided to stay with the boy as a precaution. New facts whispered by Tolkin had revealed that Jimmy Donato might be a direct lead to Andretta and the Factory.

Cecchi had questioned Torissi about Gallucci, Andretta, and

the Factory, but had got nowhere. His knowledge seemed to be limited to boats, tourists, and odd jobs for Donato. Cecchi had agreed to suspend the interrogation until the arrival of their main target—and God help Orazio if his knucklehead act was a fake.

Based on information exchanged with Gabriel De Luca in Genoa, Pisano's men were checking other Factory leads supplied by Tolkin, Calabria, and the States. But a majority of the group believed that Donato was a reliable compass, and that he would point to Andretta and the Factory, depending on the skill and effectiveness of Tony Pisano's urging.

And so they glared at Orazio and waited, knowing that Andrew Tolkin was balancing on a delicate government tightrope, and Joe Napoli had already threatened Gino Corletto and his workers because Labadi was still moving on the twelfth of June, 1979.

17

Condominio Fernanda
Rapallo, Italy
6:30 p.m.
Tuesday, June 12, 1979

Steven Garth paced and circled and jotted notes as he reviewed his mental files on the Robert Kennedy assassination. The unemployed reporter was having a difficult time preparing for the eight o'clock confessional. A strong mixture of alarming thoughts was knotting his insides: Ellie alone, the Major's beating, the possibility of Labadi as a conspirator, a bolted door, a guard outside, Mario's anxiety and the unexplained change of plans, and the risk of deadly hunters.

Loud voices in the hall wheeled him around, and he stood motionless waiting. His door was being unlocked, and someone knocked gently.

"Yes?"

"Signora Gambino."

"Come in."

Rosa entered with his meal on a tray. As the door swung closed, he noticed that a burly Italian, the guard, wasn't in his usual place. The man had delivered his lunch, instead of Rosa, whom he had not seen since Mario's visit.

"The guard?"

"I sent him on an errand downstairs." Rosa walked to the table near the window, and Garth followed. "He'll return in a few minutes," she added, positioning the tray.

"What's going on?"

"Mario received a warning from Calabria." Rosa's voice and actions were shaky. "Leaders are being questioned about the Factory."

"A police investigation?"

"No," she replied. "American Mafia."

The reply dangled for an instant before registering. "Are they hunting for someone?" he asked carefully. "Or is this a gang war?"

"I don't know." She looked away. "Precautions have to be taken anyway. I've been organizing a new address for the evacuation." In a detached, mechanical way, Rosa continued. "We have time. No one answers questions easily in our group. The members are trained. All drops and the Factory will be gone when and if these people arrive." She sighed deeply and turned back to him. "Later, in some other places, we'll operate again."

"Why do they fear the American Mafia?"

"Only these particular members," she answered. "A very important and extremely dangerous organization."

"From where?"

"I don't care to know."

"You'd better."

Now or never, Steven Garth decided, and he toughened his approach. "Mario is a frightened little man," he said. "And the guy has a right to be." He gazed into her eyes and asked, "Do you hear the closing whistle, Rosa?"

"Possibly."

"This is your chance!" Garth took her by the shoulders and applied pressure. "Remember our discussion?"

"I'm frightened."

"Zaki is special," he whispered fervently. "Go to your husband's friend in the records section immediately. I want the photo of his new face, his name, the number of his passport, and anything else you can beg or steal. They must keep files at least until the bandages are removed."

"It would be suicidal!"

"Or perfect timing," he went on. "Mario's warning from Calabria might have disrupted the place."

"Arnaldo took a blood oath." Rosa choked out the words. "You're asking the impossible."

"Tell him a drunken sponsor leaked important facts," he advised, pulling her closer. "Zaki is a paid assassin, with lucrative contracts on you, Arnaldo, and some key members of the Workers Autonomy Movement. All of you will die if Zaki runs free with an unknown identity. Tell him anything! But get the material!"

"My noble deed?" she asked, with a slight trace of sarcasm. "A new life?"

"Yes."

"These files must be very important to you."

"Zaki reportedly helped to assassinate Senator Robert Kennedy," Garth blurted. "A special case, Rosa."

She pulled back in astonishment.

"A conspiracy," Garth proceeded. "Zaki and his friends slaughtered a brilliant and courageous young American on his way to the Presidency."

"I have to leave now." Her voice trembled. "The guard is returning."

"Listen," he commanded. "With a new identity, Abu Zaki roams free, eluding the government, avoiding punishment, confusing history. Unless I have flesh and bones to support my taped confession, Kennedy's death remains on the books as the act of a lone assassin. Sirhan Bishara Sirhan walks out of jail in 1985 or before. The other participants are never punished. And Robert Kennedy is dead."

"As you could be for revealing this information." Rosa walked away. "The confession is set for eight o'clock," she announced officially. "A Factory guard has been assigned to you."

Rosa opened the door. Garth, standing right behind her, noticed that the huge Italian guard was not in his chair, and he closed the door again.

"I'll risk anything for this story," the journalist whispered. "Help me and rescue yourself."

With her eyes shut tightly, Rosa rested her forehead against the old wooden door and mumbled in her own language—a curse or a prayer, he could not tell.

"Get the Zaki material," he breathed next to Rosa's ear. "And later, in a safe place, we'll talk and decide your best route to a new existence."

He waited for a reaction, but there was no movement or comment from Signora Gambino.

"My revolver is in this apartment." Garth was pressing against her. "We'll need a weapon." He could feel her body stiffen. "Join me, Rosa."

A light tap on the door from the outside jolted both of them into upright positions.

Rosa smoothed her dark hair, brushed down her dress, and left the room without glancing around or speaking a word.

At 7:45 p.m. Steven Garth had declared himself ready for the confessional, although his insides were still jelly and his mind was on Rosa. She had three choices: She could ignore his plea for Zaki material, or go to Mario or the Factory staff and report the incident. Or she could follow through, become his ward, and a primary source of information. Garth had already convinced himself that the last two options were both possible, but very doubtful. Even so, the risks chilled him.

Voices in the hall reminded him of the Calabria warning about the American Mafia. Were they actually hunting Labadi as a Robert Kennedy conspirator? If they were, he too was sure to be on the list, marked for instant elimination.

Garth hesitated at the window and went through his escape plan, a dangerous last resort in case a run from the apartment became urgent.

Easily accessible just under the window, a rusty third-floor balcony overlooked the back yards of Via Tubino. Using a firm grip, he could dangle from the lower rungs, swing out, then back, and drop to a similar balcony on the floor below. The same procedure would land him on the next, at the bottom, angled for an easy jump to the grass and running space.

There were, however, a few goose-pimpling considerations. His leaps would have to be executed with incredible precision and fault-less timing. The deteriorating condition of the old balconies might not support his acrobatics, and there were occupants on the lower floors. Still, if lucky on the way down, he would have a chance in back of the houses. There was a dead end to his left, but a sneak was possible to the right—across yards, over a wooden fence and a row of hedges. Then he would be able to choose a shaded passageway, duck under the ground-floor windows, and head back to Via Tubino.

Along with other worries, he imagined the neighbors and bark-ing dogs chasing an intruder off the premises. This would be a last-ditch escape route, something to keep in mind in case of a premature Mafia assault on Fernanda or a double-cross by Rosa Gambino or a trap by Labadi.

At precisely eight o'clock, a guard knocked twice on the door, then entered and informed "Thompson" that "Abu Zaki" and the others were ready for the audio-taped confession.

The journalist had been waiting anxiously with dry mouth, rapid pulse, and cold sweat. He tapped a notepad in his back pocket, took a deep breath, exhaled slowly, and walked out of the room followed by a large, unfamiliar escort.

They moved down the hall to a door on the right. "Our first stop," the guard explained when both men entered.

It was a large room, spotless as usual, furnished only with a narrow bed, two metal chairs, and a table. A window overlooked the garage on Via Tubino. Another door led to an adjoining room. Garth and his keeper were alone.

"Take off your clothes," the man ordered in a businesslike fashion. "Everything."

"What?"

"Inspection," he answered, not disrespectfully. "Part of the system."

The tall, athletically built Italian stood with hands on hips, making it very plain that griping and delays would not be tolerated.

Garth eventually obeyed. He was still firm, muscular, and close to his old ring weight as an amateur boxer. "My notepad is personal," he decreed. "Give it back."

After shaking the pad vigorously and flipping through pages, the guard returned it without reading a line.

"Hold up your arms and spread your legs," the man told Garth. "This is a body check."

"Aren't you people overdoing it?"

"Orders," the guard replied. "Zaki is in the other room bandaged and defenseless."

"How about me?"

"You get the same protection."

Minutes later, the door leading to the next room opened and closed; another man joined Garth and the guard.

Bono, as he called himself, was probably one of Mario's elite troopers. The swaggering young tough appeared to have brains, experience, manners, taste—and a gun holster inside his smartly designed jacket.

"Zaki is waiting for you," he announced, sitting on the end of the table. "My recording equipment is positioned and ready to activate."

"Fine," said Garth. "Is Zaki alone?"

"Of course." Bono straightened trouser creases. "I'll explain."

"We're late." The reporter was edgy and impatient with the burlesque formalities. "Our session was marked down for eight o'-clock."

"The procedure started at eight o'clock," Bono reminded, keeping a level temper. "Can I go ahead?"

Garth nodded approval.

"Our tape room was used for storage." Bono inspected a manicured fingernail. "One door. No windows. Practically soundproof."

"Any time limit?"

"You've got an hour reel," he answered. "Do it as fast as possible. I assume Mario explained that we have a little static tonight. Rumors and evacuation."

"He explained."

"One more thing." Bono eased down from the table. "We installed a buzzer on the arm of each chair. A basic device. You or Zaki can press if something is out of line, and we get the alert here." He pointed to a tiny makeshift contraption on the wall. "Expect a fast response," he added.

A thought crossed Garth's mind. "How do I know the room isn't bugged?" he asked. "You people are very inventive."

Bono's smile lacked warmth. "We have enough problems to juggle and a reputation to uphold," he emphasized. "Rand and Mario and Signora Gambino must have convinced you by now."

"That doesn't answer my question."

"Check the place." Bono's smile had faded. "We'll take Zaki out if Mario approves."

Garth noticed the guard looking at his watch and cursing quietly; it was late, he realized, too late for troublemaking. Besides, he felt confident that the interrogation room was as clean as the rest of Rosa's apartment.

"Skip it," he advised Bono. "I'm ready."

18

THE interrogation room was an enlarged broom closet, a glorified pantry, with a light bulb dangling on wire from a high ceiling. A standard tape recorder had been positioned on a table between two wooden chairs. Each arm had a black plastic button and makeshift electrical connections. A fan rotated stale air.

Garth went numb as somebody closed the door behind him. He stared in amazement at a mummy that had been propped in one of the chairs. The head was thickly bandaged and there were slits for the eyes, ears, and mouth. And, for reasons he didn't understand, the hands were swathed in gauze and white adhesive tape. A bright glare from the overhead light distorted the shadows and exaggerated the unreal sight.

"I have a great new face under these rags." The voice belonged to Labadi, certainly, although it was distant and tight-jawed and shaky. "They also removed two birthmarks and warts on my hands."

"Congratulations," Garth quipped nervously as he took a seat opposite the bandaged figure. "Ready to deliver my product?"

"Anxious is a better word." The mummy had a piece of cardboard leaning against the recorder facing him, and some full en-

velopes were piled next to it. "Did you hear about Mario's rumors?"
    "Yes."
    "Let's tape," he instructed. "I want my papers and a quick exit."
    Still unsettled by the fast movement of events, Garth reached for his notepad, placed it on the table, and gazed at the bandages and adhesive without commenting.
    "You should be just as eager to roll," the mummy went on. "The American killers are looking for both of us."
    Garth's trance broke off at once. "Pick up that damn microphone," he ordered. "Convince me that Muazzam Labadi helped to assassinate Robert F. Kennedy."

AUTHOR'S NOTE

The following are transcripts of audio tapes recorded by Steven H. Garth and Muazzam Labadi, on the twelfth of June, 1979, in Rapallo, Italy. Segments are missing because of events I will describe later as the book progresses.

Eleanor Garth

LABADI: I told you before that a couple of Italian men from New York visited me at a Hollywood joint on February second, 1968.

GARTH: You were an expert on the Greenhorn Belt and they needed an employee for special duty.

LABADI: Right.

GARTH: Did they explain the assignment?

LABADI: Somebody wanted a nervy educated guy capable of blowing away a political VIP and losing his tongue for lump sum retirement money.

GARTH: Was Robert Kennedy mentioned?

LABADI: Hints were dropped.

GARTH: You must have been shocked.

LABADI: I was pissed off at the world, and joyous to accept five hundred dollars in cash.

GARTH: Did they give their names?

LABADI: No.

GARTH: You handed over Sirhan's name as a candidate.

LABADI: With four other possibilities.

GARTH: Background material?

LABADI: As much as I knew at the time.

GARTH: How did the visitors react?

LABADI: I'd hear from them.

GARTH: And?

LABADI: Three days later they visited the club again and offered me a fascinating research job.

GARTH: I'm listening.

LABADI: Sirhan interested them. I was asked to write a detailed report without getting close or making him suspicious.

GARTH: A difficult assignment?

LABADI: I used to do the same work for Sandy Draper. Always received high marks. It was my speciality. Contact the Agency.

GARTH: Was Robert Kennedy mentioned?

LABADI: No. But I figured he was the target.

GARTH: What about the organization?

LABADI: Nothing. They concentrated on the Sirhan report that I was asked to deliver on February eleventh. A meeting in the same joint. No questions were answered. A step at a time, they said. Five hundred bucks more was an incentive to follow the rules and make a good impression.

GARTH: And you really wanted to become involved? Murder? The assassination of a great American? Employment with the Mafia as a paid killer?

LABADI: I only thought about big cash for reference work. Like they kept repeating. One step at a time. Besides, I was fed up. Disillusioned. Tired of eating crumbs and pumping

gasoline. I had brains and wanted a fat payoff for using
them.

GARTH: What convinced you that Sirhan was qualified?

LABADI: Pick up the envelope on top. It's a copy of the report
handed to Pella and Giannini at our meeting on the eleventh. Read it later. You'll understand why they recruited
me and Sirhan.

Copy of a report on Sirhan Bishara Sirhan. By Muazzam Labadi.
Dated February 11, 1968

BACKGROUND:

Born Jerusalem, Palestine, 1948. Violence. Flight to a rough
existence in Arab sector (sharing a house with about nine other
families, rationed food, very little money). Father strict in religious beliefs and discipline; reported to beat his children when
out of work. Sirhan did well in school there: intelligent; became
deeply anti-Zionist. 1956 family emigrated to America, sponsored by a Pasadena family under special program for Palestinian refugees.

(I can identify with Sirhan's thoughts and feelings as far as
early years are concerned.)

IN AMERICA:

Determined, learns English, pushes ahead. Father nervous
after seven months in California, leaves family and returns to
native village of Taibeh. Young Sirhan attends John Muir
High School, Pasadena, does well, graduates at 19. Older,
smaller, darker-skinned than most of his classmates. Goes on
to Pasadena City College for a year and a half but drops out.
Family claim reason is partly his sister's death from leukemia.
Goes from job to job: in gasoline stations, gardening assistant,
then at Santa Anita racetrack cleaning stables. Gets a chance
to exercise horses—he wants to ride, be a jockey, but at five

feet four, 120 to 125 pounds is too big. Also wonders about his nerve, confidence. Is interested in magazine advertisement: "Develop Inner Powers; Contact the Ancient Mystical Order of the Rosae Crucis in San José." This is the start of his hang-ups with occult sciences and Rosicrucian mysticism.

Disillusioned, he quits Santa Anita and finds work on ranch—Granja Vista del Rio at Norco, near Corona. Among his other jobs he exercises horses, but is still ambitious to be a jockey until September 25, 1966, when he is thrown by a filly racing in fog on an exercise track. Knocked unconscious, he is taken to a hospital; blood on his face. Discharged, no serious injury; but gives up riding anyway. He complains of blurred vision and pain in his eyes and files workmen's compensation claim; leaves the ranch December 6, 1966.

1967: Sirhan is uptight, out of work, bitter—discouraged about job prospects. He visits his brothers, Munir and Adel, and spends time home reading, brooding, practicing white magic (staring at candle flames in front of a mirror on his desk). Browses through occult volumes on shelves of used-book store in Pasadena. When he has the money he goes to Santa Anita and bets long shots.

Complete frustration, lack of work, mystic reading, weird experiments to bring out his inner powers are all shaking him up. Things begin to simmer, boil—he is underdog, and "underdogs" are "doing things" shown on television.

May: Armed Black Panthers march through Sacramento, and again in June. Night fires in Cincinnati for arrival of H. Rap Brown, who says SNCC has declared war.

June 5: Israeli jets attack Egyptian Air Force, rip them all on the ground. Israeli Army marches into Gaza Strip and Sinai Peninsula, right to shores of the Red Sea. In six days Arabs lose another war and control of land that was Palestine.

July: Things are busting open in Newark—fires, lootings, bombings. Guns and other weapons being used. More death statistics from Vietnam.

Pressure is building in Sirhan, and there is no practical outlet for him. The following months are disturbing as television, radio, newspapers, magazines all play up Israeli action. He fumes inside: he needs money, will have to organize himself and raise his voice against Israel and the United States.

He looks for work but has problems. He is a foreigner. Continues with occult, Rosicrucian experiments, personal magic. Claims to be able to see mystical figures. His mother is concerned; finally gets him a job in September working in an organic food shop in Pasadena owned by John Weidner, a Seventh-day Adventist.

Sirhan hates Jews—they took away his home and family belongings and his freedom. Had expected to have chance in States, but now believes little guys mean nothing. He has a lot to offer, but no opportunity. His job as a delivery boy is humiliating for him. Alone most of the time, he has few dependable friends. Money and *recognition* are the most important things for him now.

I believe that Sirhan is qualified to handle your important freelance assignment.

Muazzam Labadi

19

LABADI: On February nineteenth, 1968, I received a phone call from the New Yorkers. A meeting was held late that night. They were excited about my candidate's qualifications. A proposition was outlined. Five thousand dollars up front and the same money when the victim is canceled. How could I push away ten thousand bucks?

GARTH: Did they identify the victim?

LABADI: After I shook hands on the deal.

GARTH: Robert F. Kennedy?

LABADI: Yes.

GARTH: The organization?

LABADI: No.

GARTH: And?

LABADI: The visitors represented clients with a plot. I would concentrate on my own business and have nothing to do with the overall strategy.

GARTH: Had they pitched Sirhan?

LABADI: Of course not. He was being watched. Some kind of an approach would be made at the right time. The guy had no idea that he was being considered for a job.

GARTH: What about you?

LABADI: I was told that my prime contact would be a man called Franco. They described him. Young. Rugged. Bright. A junior member of the client's organization. Trusted on every level. All of my orders and reports would be delivered by Franco.

GARTH: His name?

LABADI: I found out later.

GARTH: His name?

LABADI: Frank Sindona.

GARTH: Alive?

LABADI: I think so.

GARTH: What else?

LABADI: A girl named Joan. They called her my responsibility. She was investigated and hired by the New York advance men. But I'd seen her around the clubs and in a few other places. Even had personal information on her.

GARTH: Like what?

LABADI: Franco's employers had a winner. She was perfect bait for Sirhan, practiced occult, belonged to a group of mystics like the Rosicrucians. She hated Jews and Israel, had strong political opinions about Arabs and the Middle East. A very intelligent girl. Not really a paid whore. But she used to make it with the brainy Arab radicals. And upcoming hoods.

GARTH: Her name?

LABADI: I came across Patterson and Gower and Nash and Hawkins, and they were all fake. The organization probably had the real one. But they ordered me to use Joan and Franco. And I was not about to rock the boat.

GARTH: Describe her.

LABADI: Joan was in her late twenties. Five feet four or five. Light brown hair. Often dyed the color. A very sharp mind. Dedicated. Lethal. A good-looking broad.

GARTH: Alive?

LABADI: We'll come to that.

GARTH: Her job?

LABADI: Joan would be a direct link to Sirhan. As soon as the time was right for a contact. I was reminded. Pay attention to Franco and Joan. My contact and responsibility. Ignore the rest. They asked me to sit tight. Be patient. And wait for a message. The New Yorkers also said goodbye.

GARTH: And?

LABADI: On February twenty-third, 1968, I was contacted by Franco. We met at a sleazy joint on North Vermont in Los Angeles. The candidate had not been pitched. Franco handed me a white envelope. Five thousand dollars in cash. He told me again that another five thousand was due and payable after the subject's elimination.

GARTH: Your fat payoff.

LABADI: Correct. He also gave me two thousand for Joan and said that her deal was unlike mine. I didn't ask any questions.

GARTH: Was she aware of your participation?

LABADI: Franco told me to expect a visit from her on the twenty-fifth. Same club. Around midnight. He wanted me to deliver the money and give her instructions.

GARTH: About Sirhan?

LABADI: Right. Keep moving around him. Smartly. Cautiously. Get him interested. Without being obvious. Talk him up —occult, politics, horses, Jews, Arabs—play on his weaknesses. Establish a relationship. Slowly and carefully.

GARTH: Using your background material.

LABADI: Yes. And he told me to warn her to stay away from the punk hoods and greaseball radicals. The organization wanted her clean and detached. Joan would soon get a message to proposition Sirhan.

GARTH: A high-level decision.

LABADI: Right.

GARTH: Based on what?

Labadi: Senator Robert Kennedy.

GARTH: Meaning?

LABADI: His ambition to climb.

GARTH: What?

LABADI: A presidential run.

GARTH: Let's stop jerking around. Give me the names of the principals. And the reasons for wanting Kennedy put away. Honor your end of the deal.

LABADI: I'm doing my best with cardboard notes! Give me a break!

GARTH: Carry on.

LABADI: Kennedy and Sirhan were being monitored. Joan had a good meeting with me. I gave her money and Franco's instructions. She understood and began operating at once.

GARTH: How did she progress?

LABADI: According to her reports, Joan was on friendly terms with Sirhan by March third. Franco was pleased. The girl and the candidate were naturals.

GARTH: When did things break?

LABADI: On March seventh. From the floor of the Senate, Kennedy spoke out against the fighting in Vietnam. According to Franco, the organization and many others believed it came across like a political move. Right after the Kennedy news, Sirhan became touchy. His boss mentioned a fouled-up delivery and the guy blew his job at the organic food shop in Pasadena.

GARTH: A more accessible candidate.

LABADI: Right. And then Kennedy moved. On the tenth of March he appeared unexpectedly in Delano, California, for the Mass of Thanksgiving—with Cesar Chavez, the leader of the Farm Workers Union. A few days later from the Caucus Room of the Old Senate Office Building in D.C., an official announcement on live television. Senator Rob-

ert Kennedy was a candidate for President of the United
States.

GARTH: What happened next?

LABADI: Franco went away for meetings and got back on March
twenty-fourth with a secret plan. My orders were to organize Joan's reports and make certain that Sirhan was
being propped up for a direct approach in the near future.

GARTH: And Sirhan?

LABADI: Floating, bitching, doing odd jobs—like taking care of
lawns. He picked up about seventeen hundred dollars of
insurance money on April fifth. Lost a few hundred on
bad shots at Hollywood Park. He was still playing with
occult and looking for power and recognition. Joan reported that he was ready and perfect for the assignment.

GARTH: When did they finally set him up?

LABADI: Franco called and gave me the word on May fourth, 1968.
I ordered Joan to pitch Sirhan right away. The next
morning she reported that our deal had been accepted.

GARTH: Explain the proposal.

LABADI: Can't. Sirhan's arrangements were never revealed to me.
Joan's either. Private business. Franco had orders to keep
it that way.

GARTH: You are totally full of shit.

LABADI: *Garth!* I can only tell you what I know! Do you want me
to exaggerate? Concoct a juicier story? This was a conspiracy. Many people were involved. I had some things
to handle. My own business. You can't expect me to
know all the facts!

GARTH: Didn't you brief Joan on the Sirhan pitch?

LABADI: Sirhan's proposal was given to Joan by the New Yorkers
just after they recruited her. Franco's organization
wanted to avoid contacts with the girl and Sirhan. Joan
was my responsibility. The proposal stayed locked in her
brain, ready to be activated on cue.

GARTH: She never leaked a word to you?

LABADI: Only that it was good money.

GARTH: Did anyone witness Joan's pitch?

LABADI: I don't know.

GARTH: And Sirhan's acceptance?

LABADI: I don't know.

GARTH: So all you have is a report from the girl. A money deal was offered to Sirhan and he accepted. There is no actual proof, as far as you know.

LABADI: Later developments prove that a contract with the guy had to exist.

GARTH: Only by way of reports to you.

LABADI: Want to press this fucking button and have the gorillas sort things out?

GARTH: Simmer down, Labadi.

LABADI: The first order to hit Senator Kennedy came on May nineteenth, 1968. Franco had called about eight at night. Later I sat with Joan and briefed her. She was ordered to meet Sirhan at Robbie's Restaurant in Pomona, California. At noon the following day, Senator Kennedy was making one of his California primary appearances upstairs—in the banquet room on the second floor.

GARTH: Your report?

LABADI: According to Joan, they forced their way up a stairway around twelve-thirty p.m. An employee of Robbie's allowed them to enter the banquet room after Joan insisted that they were in the Kennedy party. But later this same man noticed them hanging around the back of the room and he became suspicious. After being interrogated again they decided to leave.

GARTH: And the organization was angry?

LABADI: Right. And Franco told me to warn the girl. They were getting careless. An organization member had seen Joan and Sirhan together at Rancho, California, doing target practice.

GARTH: And the next order?

LABADI: The Los Angeles Sports Arena. On May twenty-fourth. A Kennedy rally. Joan reported a foul-up. They were never able to get close enough.

GARTH: Next?

LABADI: June second, the Ambassador Hotel. A Kennedy rally on a Sunday. Joan's report mentioned crowds and police and other difficulties. No possible way to score a direct hit. They gave up.

GARTH: Result?

LABADI: Franco phoned that evening, cursing. His people had been in touch. Kennedy was scheduled for the El Cortez Hotel, San Diego, on the following night. I was advised to sit with Joan and threaten rough conduct if the Senator wiggled off the hook again.

GARTH: Kennedy had canceled due to exhaustion. Why didn't Joan phone before leaving?

LABADI: She did. A guy confirmed the Senator's appearance. A bad piece of luck.

GARTH: And the organization?

LABADI: Trouble. Franco called my room at eight o'clock that night. All shook up. He asked me to visit his place on East Foothill at ten. An urgent meeting.

GARTH: Had you been there before?

LABADI: Once: a real dump, near a topless bar. Usually he would visit me. The last time I went there Joan had just propositioned Sirhan. His place was for emergency sessions, I assumed.

GARTH: So what happened?

LABADI: First of all I arrived twenty minutes early. Punks were congregated outside the topless joint close to the door leading to Franco's narrow walk-up. Just as I moved toward the entrance, two guys came down and stopped to light a cigarette. I eased myself back to the punks and took a good look at Franco's visitors.

GARTH: Did you know them?

LABADI: On sight. And I nearly crapped in my pants. Anthony
           Pisano and Gabriel De Luca.
GARTH: Corletto's boys.
LABADI: The someone behind the assassination of Bobby Kennedy
           was Joseph Napoli.

20

JAMES Donato had been gloomy and depressed since the cancer death of his older brother Victor in 1977. An emaciated, round-shouldered thirty-eight-year-old former insurance broker, and a discreet homosexual, Jimmy had acquired with Victor's passing a leaky tourist fleet and his brother's side operations. Love and devotion and memories had kept him going. Donato's boats and Factory connections were running smoothly.

His meeting in San Fruttuoso with a local tour operator had produced results, but he was exhausted and glad to be home.

A door on the lobby floor opened just a bit as Donato moved past on his way to an elevator.

"You have guests," a male voice whispered. "Two very rough-looking Americans."

"Police?"

"I smell big-time Mafia," the neighbor replied. "And a lot of trouble."

"Orazio is upstairs?"

"Unhappily."

"The boy has worms in his skull," Donato commented in a quiet voice. "He knows nothing."

"You do, Jimmy." The man paused. "And now foreign torpedoes have the right address."

"Can they do the impossible?" Donato asked, glancing toward the elevator. "Make a rock speak?"

"Leave at once," the voice advised firmly. "There will never be another opportunity."

"Close the door, Sebastiano," Donato told him. "Keep out of this business."

He turned away and headed for a meeting with Ralph Cecchi and Anthony Pisano.

Condominio Fernanda
Rapallo, Italy
9:10 p.m.
Tuesday, June 12, 1979

LABADI: Franco was pissed off when I got upstairs to his room. He told me that two guys had just left. They had delivered orders, and a message blaming him for lousy results. Franco was steaming.

GARTH: What about the orders?

LABADI: Senator Kennedy would be dropped on the night of June fourth at the Ambassador Hotel. No more excuses. Experts had planned the operation. A successful hit was guaranteed.

GARTH: Napoli's people had become involved.

LABADI: I assumed. Two sharp professionals had been all over the hotel. Maps showed rooms and corridors and kitchens and lobbies and elevators and stairs and toilets and fire exits. They had the entire place detailed.

GARTH: How could they predict Kennedy's moves in the hotel that night?

LABADI: Bits and pieces of information came from Ambassador employees, the press, the Kennedy workers, even the police and security guards.

GARTH: I was there on June fourth. Plotting Robert Kennedy's moves would have been nearly impossible.

LABADI: Franco said—

GARTH: At ten P.M. nobody had definite information about the California vote. But television was predicting a victory. Kennedy was in the Royal Suite on the fifth floor with his entourage debating a move downstairs to the Embassy Room for a victory announcement. He was uncertain of his own schedule and timing on the night of June fourth.

LABADI: I can only talk about Franco's briefing.

GARTH: Did Franco give you a detailed plan? Or just orders for Joan and Sirhan?

LABADI: Kennedy was destined for absolute elimination at the Ambassador Hotel on June fourth.

GARTH: How?

LABADI: Franco claimed that every logical and illogical spot in the hotel would be switched on.

GARTH: Elaborate.

LABADI: He mentioned the Royal Suite and said that Kennedy would eventually come down the five floors to make a statement in the Embassy Room. They would be primed for him. But no hit was scheduled until after the Senator's announcement. Sirhan and Joan would be in the service pantry behind the room. Without a doubt Kennedy's execution chamber, according to Franco.

GARTH: Why so damn positive?

LABADI: I told you before. The entire hotel was sketched on paper. A freight elevator comes down from the fifth floor to a kitchen behind the Embassy Room. A short walk through the service-pantry corridor would bring Kennedy to his platform and rostrum. He would pick this route instead of battling his way in and out of the Embassy Room mobs. Anyway, that's how Franco's experts had things figured.

GARTH: Suppose Kennedy had finished his announcement and

gone straight through the room fighting crowds and to hell with using the back way?

LABADI: Franco claimed the place was switched on. They were primed for him.

GARTH: Meaning?

LABADI: He didn't explain. I had nothing to do with overall tactics. The pantry was my responsibility.

GARTH: Joe Napoli would never have brought his own men to a Kennedy assassination. And hiring outsiders or more Sirhan types would have increased the risk of a leak and charges of direct involvement. The Rajah would have been a lot brighter than that.

LABADI: Agreed.

GARTH: What did Franco mean by switched on and primed?

LABADI: I can only guess.

GARTH: A hidden bomb? A flash of lightning? Poison gas? A Napoli secret weapon?

LABADI: Don't fuck around! You knew going in that I was only a minor participant! Franco was careful! He told me exactly what I had to know and nothing more!

GARTH: Calm down.

LABADI: Accept my story or push the damn button!

GARTH: Keep talking.

LABADI: For some reason they were almost positive that Robert Kennedy would leave the Embassy Room the back way. I was told to impress on Joan that Sirhan's last chance would be in the pantry. No more excuses. Important people were anticipating a completed mission.

GARTH: Did you explain that other rooms would be switched on and primed?

LABADI: No. I detailed the freight elevators and the Embassy Room and the pantry. Just the way Franco had briefed me, using my own sketches and background information supplied by the organization's experts.

GARTH: Did Franco identify other locations?

LABADI: The Ambassador Ballroom.

GARTH: Any others?

LABADI: The Colonial Room.

GARTH: Were you responsible for advising Joan about purchasing a gun and ammunition for Sirhan?

LABADI: According to one of Joan's reports, Sirhan had an Iver Johnson Cadet model twenty-two-caliber eight-shot revolver. He bought the weapon just before they started to become close friends in early March of 1968.

GARTH: Sirhan used a pop gun for the assassination.

LABADI: Franco never complained.

GARTH: Who selected the ammunition?

LABADI: On June first in Pasadena, Sirhan picked up two boxes of twenty-two-caliber Mini-Mag hollow points. The muzzle velocity is about twenty-five percent stronger than the average twenty-two-caliber bullet.

GARTH: Did Joan have a gun?

LABADI: Yes.

GARTH: What type and caliber?

LABADI: I don't know. Evidently a small pistol. Built to fit her purse. Joan never discussed the weapon.

GARTH: Events on the fourth?

LABADI: I met with Joan at ten in the morning and spent about an hour briefing her. The girl understood everything—a very sharp operator. I asked her to go over the plans with Sirhan before lunch.

GARTH: And the killer on this date?

LABADI: Target practice with his Iver Johnson and Mini-Mags at the San Gabriel Valley Gun Club, in Fish Canyon. Joan reported that Sirhan left the range at five o'clock. Went for dinner at Bob's Big Boy near Pasadena City College. We have to assume that he was in the hotel at nine o'clock as Franco had planned.

GARTH: Did Joan ever discuss Sirhan on a personal basis? How was he reacting to the assassination scheme? What did she think of him?

LABADI: The girl only made formal reports. Although one time she did mention that he was a very complicated person. A mix of good and evil.

GARTH: Was he blowing off about Jews and Arabs?

LABADI: Very little.

GARTH: Hatred of Robert Kennedy?

LABADI: No.

GARTH: Anything?

LABADI: Money and recognition. Joan once remarked about a heavy list of things he wanted for himself and his family. He would gamble on the longest shot in order to collect his fortune and become somebody.

GARTH: Joseph Napoli is one of America's most experienced hoods. I can assure you that he would have planned the hit with more sophistication. A small caliber, a packed room, and no opportunity to escape—amateur night on Wilshire Boulevard!

LABADI: Practical strategy for the organization.

GARTH: A clumsy job.

LABADI: Exactly. Unlike anything Napoli or other professionals would have set up. A lunatic or a fanatic had suddenly decided to eliminate Kennedy.

GARTH: Escape?

LABADI: Franco told me that the New Yorkers had discussed it with Joan at the beginning. I was never briefed.

GARTH: What do you figure?

LABADI: Big money and front-page recognition for doing time.

GARTH: Ever hear of the death penalty?

LABADI: I always felt that they instructed Joan, and the girl convinced Sirhan that he would never have to inhale the gas at San Quentin.

GARTH: Based on what?

LABADI: Diminished capacity.

GARTH: When did you become a lawyer?

LABADI: Franco mentioned it. Claimed that Sirhan might beat the rap because he would be judged a looney. I assumed that

Joan pitched this to him. The guy was sharp and capable of doing a great acting job.

GARTH: Even a successful diminished capacity plea wouldn't have kept this man out of prison. Do you believe that Sirhan was prepared to face death or a long jail term for money and recognition?

LABADI: He was a gambler—bet against the odds. Maybe the cash was deposited with his family. Death penalty? A remote chance. If so, Mama and the boys would have a taste of security. An easier life, provided by Sirhan—another form of recognition. Mama's hero. A way to get back at his father. Jail term? Completion or parole eventually. With a bankroll stashed at home.

GARTH: Speculation. And time is running out. Get back to Joan and her instructions on the fourth.

LABADI: Franco's organization had prepared credentials: "Kennedy for President, Pasadena-Altadena." Legitimate admission to all rooms for Joan. I handed them over.

GARTH: Sirhan?

LABADI: Only the girl.

GARTH: And?

LABADI: Joan would get to the hotel at eight P.M. Hang around like other workers and supporters. Compile tips about Kennedy's progress and movements. She didn't need any reminders to stay alert and keep a low profile.

GARTH: And Sirhan?

LABADI: She would instruct him. Don't park close to the hotel. Be on the premises around nine o'clock.

GARTH: And?

LABADI: Sirhan mingles with the crowd. Keeps his nose clean. Watches television monitors. Listens to the Kennedy supporters and campaign workers. Waits for signs of a victory move.

GARTH: And Joan?

LABADI: In the Embassy Room.

GARTH: They were familiar with the pantry area?

LABADI: Etched on their brains.

GARTH: The maps and sketches?

LABADI: And a couple of dry runs before the event.

GARTH: What made Franco's people so damn certain that the pantry would be accessible?

LABADI: Prior information. And they were right, according to Joan in her final report.

GARTH: Let's hear it.

LABADI: As you know, the Embassy Room was packed on the night of the murder. Over twelve hundred people waited for Robert Kennedy's victory appearance, Joan included. Sirhan had presumably entered the hotel at nine p.m. His 1956 white and pink Fire Flite De Soto was parked a half-block south of Wilshire, on New Hampshire Street. Three blocks from the Ambassador.

GARTH: Keep talking.

LABADI: The rest went perfectly. Franco's experts had called the shots. Kennedy came down the back way, used the freight elevator and kitchen and service pantry corridor to enter the Embassy Room.

GARTH: Joan?

LABADI: Waited for Kennedy to appear.

GARTH: Sirhan?

LABADI: Picked it up on a monitor near the Ambassador Ballroom. Went directly to the Colonial Room, out the rear door. Followed his route through the kitchen and on to the corridor directly behind the Embassy Room. He waited in the shadows.

GARTH: Joan?

LABADI: After Kennedy's entrance—cheers and songs and lights and bedlam—Joan moved out easily. Past Sirhan in the corridor behind Kennedy's stage. She continued through double doors to her assigned location in the pantry. Sirhan waited in the corridor.

GARTH: Did Joan see others in the pantry area?

LABADI: Yes, including a Kennedy worker getting away from the Embassy Room heat. The experts were right. Access to the pantry was never difficult—people had been going in and out freely all night.

GARTH: According to Joan.

LABADI: Yes.

GARTH: And?

LABADI: Robert Kennedy finished his announcement. Workers and press ran into the corridor, dashed past Sirhan heading for their next stop, avoiding crowds by using the kitchen route.

GARTH: They were rushing to the Colonial Room.

LABADI: I guess. Anyway, Sirhan followed through double doors to Joan in the pantry. The girl reported that the others had swept by her without a hesitation.

GARTH: What's this mark on your chart?

LABADI: Joan was positioned behind a tray rack. Sirhan waited in front. They were silent. No open contact, following Franco's instructions.

GARTH: Did Joan say anything about his condition?

LABADI: A few words.

GARTH: Was he in a trance?

LABADI: No.

GARTH: Drunk?

LABADI: No.

GARTH: What?

LABADI: Cool and determined and very anxious to eliminate Senator Robert Kennedy.

GARTH: The Iver Johnson?

LABADI: In his waistband on the left side.

GARTH: Describe Kennedy's entrance.

LABADI: Kennedy walked through the double doors of the pantry. He stopped and shook hands with a few kitchen boys near some stainless steel warming tables. Reporters, photographers, and members of his entourage were around. Then he took a few more steps, paused again, and turned to his left. He shook hands with a waiter and a kitchen porter. Time now for the hit. According to Joan's report, Sirhan glanced back at her. They smiled at each other. He moved calmly and deliberately away from the rack, stepped toward Kennedy, pulled the gun from his waistband, and fired at very close range. Two quick shots. Joan reported that a man leaped, grabbed Sirhan's gun hand, and wrestled him onto a steam table while he continued firing. Joan opened her purse and took out a weapon.

GARTH: She fired?

LABADI: Joan claimed that Kennedy was struggling to rise up after the second blast. His right hand was moving. The target was alive. In the rush and confusion and focus on the assassin and the wounded, she aimed and fired, just as a group of people rammed the tray rack while grappling with Sirhan. Her bullet went astray. Joan dumped the gun and closed the purse without being noticed.

GARTH: Did her bullet strike the wall?

LABADI: Joan was positive that it hit in the area of the pantry's swinging doors. She recalled that people were rushing in when the bullet went crazy and nearly hit them. At least the gun was pointed that way as she fired.

GARTH: What time?

LABADI: Approximately twelve-fifteen a.m., June fifth, 1968.

GARTH: Finish the report.

LABADI: More shots. Others jumped Sirhan. Joan saw Kennedy on the floor; blood was flowing out the right side of his head below the ear. Screams, panic, confusion. Joan moved carefully toward the pantry doors. She observed three or four wounded in addition to Robert Kennedy. A man was sprawled flat on his back with a bullet hole in the forehead.

GARTH: Keep rolling.

LABADI: Joan eased out of the pantry at the height of the uproar, before the police arrived. Men were still battling with Sirhan on the table. The guy's strength amazed her.

GARTH: Any trouble leaving?

LABADI: None. People were running in and out of the place. And the Embassy Room was chaotic.

GARTH: How did she leave the neighborhood?

LABADI: Joan hailed a taxi at Wilshire and Catalina. Went home. Telephoned me at two a.m. I met her in a safe joint a half-hour later. She gave me the final report.

GARTH: Had Sirhan been paid in full?

LABADI: No. Joan just said that additional money would be given to him immediately after Robert Kennedy's death.

GARTH: By whom?

LABADI: Joan.

GARTH: Delivered where?

LABADI: I don't know. The New Yorkers had instructed her at the beginning. Maybe somebody in his family received payment. It was none of my business.

GARTH: Did you hear from Joan after her final report?

LABADI: Never.

GARTH: What about Franco?

LABADI: Promptly.

GARTH: Well?

LABADI: I got a phone call from him at one-fifteen a.m. on the morning of June fifth. He was excited about the results. But he wanted me to ring him immediately after my session with Joan. He explained that high-level members of the organization were following Robert Kennedy's progress. The Senator had just been admitted to Good Samaritan after a police escort from Central Receiving Hospital.

GARTH: What happened after your meeting with Joan?

LABADI: I reported and Franco was satisfied. He promised to call me back when they received definite information about Kennedy's condition.

GARTH: And?

LABADI: Franco had been drinking when he phoned at two-thirty a.m. on June sixth. Kennedy died at one-forty-four. I picked up compliments. Franco said he would have my final payment the next day. We arranged for a meeting at nine the next night—Friday, June seventh. The joint on North Vermont.

GARTH: Did he appear?

LABADI: Yes. Nearly stoned out of his mind. Claimed his people were very appreciative. Franco handed me a white envelope. Five thousand dollars. Plus one thousand as a bonus. The guy ordered drinks and started putting them away. I paced myself.

GARTH: Clever boy.

LABADI: By half past nine he was tight. Mumbling about his own bonus and a promotion in the organization.

GARTH: Did he mention Joe Napoli?

LABADI: No. But while he lushed and babbled an idea was forming in back of my head. I called the photo chick over and she took a few Polaroid shots of Franco and myself drinking at the table. He didn't even notice.

GARTH: What idea?

LABADI: I'll explain later. Franco was damn nearly out cold by ten-thirty. He got mean. A very tough expression. Started blasting his job and the organization. Repeated the words "ungrateful bastards."

GARTH: You questioned his loyalty.

LABADI: Couldn't figure him. The man never gave a thing away to me—even with booze. Well, he was really beginning to go under around ten-forty-five. Garbled something about an early-morning flight. Asked me to get him back to his room as quickly as possible.

GARTH: And you obliged?

LABADI: Right. I phoned a cab. Dragged him out, jammed him in, and had a rough time getting him up the damn stairway to his place.

GARTH: Was Franco conscious?

LABADI: Barely. After minutes of fumbling he gave me the right key. We entered. I plopped him on the bed, and he went into a deep sleep at once, holding on to a thin black case. The one he brought to the joint.

GARTH: How tempting.

LABADI: Franco's bags were packed and ready to go. Closets and drawers had been emptied.

GARTH: What about his thin black case?

LABADI: He was in another world. I had dropped Franco's keys on a bureau after opening the door. One of them sprung his case and there was gold inside. My idea became a plot at once.

GARTH: Tell me.

LABADI: Open the last envelope. Read the material later. This bright Franco character was obviously about to splatter Joseph Napoli. The guy had been compiling evidence, and I found a pile of it in a sealed folder. Was he making a deal with Beppe Sandalo of Houston? Or some American government investigators?

GARTH: Jesus Christ!

LABADI: Everything you need. Copies of letters from Caracas to Gino Corletto and Carmine Peci. Handwritten and signed by Joseph Napoli. Loaded with damaging information. A precious gift for the American Justice Department and a bonanza for immigration.

GARTH: What's this?

LABADI: A sample of income and payoffs on Napoli's books. Drugs, prostitution, loan schemes, and labor racketeering. Read about pension fund fraud and kickbacks. Bribery and the names of government officials. The works.

GARTH: Powerful stuff!

LABADI: Really? Listen to a few recorded taps on Gino Corletto's phone. Napoli burying himself. Proof that he was linked to the killing of President John Kennedy. Other names are included. You also have Napoli confirming without a doubt that he was behind the murder of Robert. He's like a maniac on one call. Shows the man's hatred of the Kennedy family. And his fears too. Robert Kennedy as Attorney General was enough of a headache. Napoli figured that Robert as President would be a disaster for him and the organization. On one call Napoli mentions that Robert would probably use the White House to avenge his brother's death. Against the Napoli organization and the others involved.

GARTH: This is a very charming photograph.

LABADI: A group shot in front of Napoli's pool. Joseph, Corletto, Peci, De Luca, Pisano and Frank Sindona. Better known as Franco to me.

GARTH: I like this one.

LABADI: Franco and myself in the joint on North Vermont. Helps to back up many things.

GARTH: Here's your passport and other documents.

LABADI: Wrong. You have a copy of Muazzam Labadi's passport along with other identification. I am now somebody else.

GARTH: Did you run with Franco's evidence?

LABADI: I had worked out an escape plan just before the Ambassador job. Cost me plenty. A Jordanian acquaintance lined up a room in Newark, a freighter at the dock, and connections in Beirut. Sailing time was June ninth or tenth.

GARTH: You took off for Jersey?

LABADI: Right. I was bolted in my Newark room with the Joe Napoli papers on June eighth.

GARTH: What about your idea?

LABADI: A double-cross. Get paid twice. Find a buyer for the Joe Napoli assassination story. Close a quick deal before the run to Beirut.

GARTH: Your customers?

LABADI: My old employers, the Agency. But there was a problem
           —Draper was out of the country. I would have to deal
           with the bastard Albert Polk. No time for alternatives;
           this was the eighth of June. I contacted him and we met
           for some drinks at a remote place in Newark. Three P.M.
           I explained that the murder of Robert Kennedy was a
           conspiracy, plotted by a leader of organized crime. For a
           lump sum and the usual guarantees I would provide the
           details. Names, dates, locations, plus a folder of court-
           house material, including phone taps, which I didn't have
           with me.

GARTH: Your deal?

LABADI: Fifty thousand in cash, payable before midnight. And the
           usual guarantees.

GARTH: Meaning?

LABADI: Able to remain in the shadows forever as an untouchable.
           No questioning, harassment, arrest, or prosecution. Just
           as before.

GARTH: His reaction?

LABADI: At first Polk ridiculed the entire package. He asked two
           questions and received satisfactory answers, so then he
           was interested. But he said he would have to consult with
           his superiors, because of the large payoff and the explo-
           sive subject matter. Polk also wanted to alter the proce-
           dures—asked me to come to the office with him. I refused.
           The game was never played that way. Finally, he urged
           me to phone him at five p.m. at a special number. Polk
           claimed that he would have answers.

GARTH: Did he?

LABADI: Yes. A fifty-thousand-dollar payment was out of the ques-
           tion. In fact, no money would be handed over until the
           bastard evaluated my information and the folder. But
           guarantees would be honored as usual. Polk suggested an
           eight p.m. meeting at a railroad coffeehouse on the out-

skirts of Newark. A cash payment, based on the value of my evidence, would be made before midnight.

GARTH: And?

LABADI: I griped. Refused. Wanted an unreturnable deposit of five thousand. An incentive to sound off and open the folder. Then Polk could evaluate and pay the rest before midnight. As long as the balance was civilized. Anyway, regardless of the problems, I would be five thousand dollars ahead.

GARTH: He bought your approach?

LABADI: Eventually.

GARTH: Why trust Polk?

LABADI: I didn't. But Draper and Polk were the only agents who knew me personally as an informant. I couldn't have gone to anyone else—too much of a gamble. Possible red tape and complications. Might have delayed my sailing date on June ninth or tenth. Besides, Polk was crooked. I figured the guy would be easier to manage.

GARTH: How?

LABADI: By talking straight about his back-room deals. I told him to expect immediate destruction if law enforcement or the Agency decided to visit the railyard coffeehouse to play funny games with me.

GARTH: Reaction?

LABADI: He went crazy in his usual quiet way. Denied all charges, threatened legally and physically. He vowed to sort me out later. But he confirmed our eight o'clock rendezvous on my terms.

GARTH: Did he show?

LABADI: No.

GARTH: Funny games?

LABADI: Yes. But not what I figured as a possibility.

GARTH: What did he arrange?

LABADI: Our veteran Central Intelligence Agency officer processed the assassination tip and fingered me. However, the man did not operate with the United States government. I saw two cars pull up, front and back of the coffeehouse. A Mafia hit squad: Pisano and De Luca were included. This filthy bastard Polk had alerted Joseph Napoli.

GARTH: Only a few minutes to record.

LABADI: I used the toilet window and got away. My freighter left for Beirut early the next morning. You know the rest.

GARTH: What about the girl?

LABADI: I read in an English newspaper dated June twentieth, 1968, that a young whore and dope addict by the name of Rita Collins had been found raped and sliced down the middle in a dark Boston alley. Police listed her as the fifth victim of a sex maniac who had been operating in the area. I studied her pictures. Without a doubt the girl was Joan. Napoli experts had probably staged the murder.

GARTH: Will you reply to one Factory question?

LABADI: Never heard of the place.

GARTH: Just sketch your route to Perinaldo.

LABADI: Turn off the machine.

Garth clicked off, moved the switch to rewind, and faced the mummy while the audio tape whirred back. "The Factory operation is very important," he persisted. "You've covered more dangerous subjects this evening."

"Factory members are still handling me," the voice responded wearily. "I don't want problems—now or in the future. Besides, you have more than enough material to sign off my end of the deal, and I'm hot and tired and we're running late on a bad night."

The journalist organized his envelopes and watched Labadi's testimony fill the plastic reel. "I'll analyze and evaluate your information with others," Garth said formally. "Everything looks and sounds too perfect at the moment."

"Your envelopes and tapes will reopen Bobby Kennedy's murder case and finish Joseph Napoli," the voice assured. "How exciting for me to watch developments as a complete outsider. May we both have good luck and successful ventures."

"Fucking creep!" Garth turned off the machine and collected his tape. "Worse than Sirhan or Joan or Franco or Polk or Joseph Napoli." He made a bundle out of the plastic reels and envelopes. "You pimped, and sucked on the edges, avoiding danger, collecting blood money and whoring for more. If your crap is authentic—" He picked up the evidence. "Good luck and success? To a goddamn animal? May you be trapped and convicted and punished with all the others. I would like to yank away the bandages and beat your new fucking head to a pulp. Ever think about the victim—Robert Kennedy? As a man, a father, a politician? His achievements and potential? What role he might have played in world history? *Did you think?*"

"Pick up my cardboard notes and rip them up later," said the voice. "We're finished." He pressed the button on his chair and Bono entered the room at once.

"Session over?" he asked.

"Yes," the mummy replied. "Thompson has envelopes and audio tapes."

"Any complaints?" Bono asked. "Zaki?"

"No."

"Thompson?"

"No."

"Rand's agreement has been honored," the Italian said. "Now we follow through."

At 9:45 p.m. on June 12, 1979, a sealed envelope was pressed into the gauze of the mummy's hand. "Your new passport and other documents," said Bono. "Good luck."

The man once known as Muazzam Labadi was led out of the room by the Factory's swaggering young hood. Garth watched helplessly. The identity change was now absolute. A moment later, the guard entered and repeated Mario's final orders. "Follow me back to your room," he said. "Wait there a half-hour until the patient is out and on his way to another location. Then leave on your own. We have no further business."

In the adjoining room, Garth paused, and glanced out a front window overlooking Via Tubino. Some of Fernanda's residents were loading heavy suitcases and boxes into cars and vans.

"No panic," the guard said. "A quiet evacuation just to avoid trouble."

21

It was a large apartment with high ceilings and old Italian furnishings. Giovanni Andretta sat thinking behind a cluttered desk in the living room. A glass of wine had been emptied. Elderly and round-shouldered, Andretta wore a dark sweater which contrasted with his full crop of snow-white hair.

He had just received a phone call from Orazio Torissi, the dumb boat assistant in Sestri Levante. Jimmy Donato had given the old man's address and Factory responsibilities to Pisano and Ralph Cecchi. Donato was busted up and unconscious on the floor, and Napoli's boys were en route to Genoa.

The old man poured more wine. After a sip, he calmly lifted the receiver, and dialed a private number in Sestri Levante. A deep voice answered. "Yes?"

"Giulio?"

"Yes."

"Donato just lectured two big American gangsters." The old man spoke without emotion. "Joe Napoli's helpers."

"Bastard."

"The Rajah wants a patient who had a recent face job," he explained. "Muazzam Labadi."

"Why?"

"I don't know." Andretta tasted his wine. "We're going to make them very happy."

"How?"

"Get over to Donato's place right away," the old man ordered. "Take tools and some help. Jab a needle and wrap him like after surgery. Carry a new American passport and the regular documents. Use the Bradford stuff that's already in order. Haul Donato fast to Rapallo. Labadi is out and on his way now. In fact, the place should be vacant when you arrive. Prop Jimmy on Labadi's bed and fasten the Bradford envelope to his gauze. Jab another needle to keep him under. Make the scene look right. For example, a nurse is around somewhere, and others too. Understand? Hustle back to Levante when you finish."

"And you?"

"I'll wait," Andretta replied. "Let them knock me around for a while until I decide to crack a little at a time. First the drop address in Rapallo. Then I croak that Labadi is now Bradford recuperating at Fernanda. Jimmy gets a symbolic punishment. The Rajah is a happy man. And we protect our client as usual. A beautiful ending."

"What do you mean?"

"Order Santovito to activate the emergency plans. Dismantle the Factory. Ignite everything on paper. And give formal notice to all personnel. Two operations were completed today. Have the patients moved to safe houses for recuperation. Get both of them on the road along with Abu Zaki. But that's it. No further jobs. Regardless of pressure or urgency. We're closing down."

"Can you give a reason?"

"I'm old and tired," Andretta replied. "And the backers are worried and restless and losing interest fast. Pressure from Joe Napoli is all they need."

"Want muscle in Genoa?"

"No," he answered without a pause. "Just instruct Santovito and handle Donato right away."

"Count on me."

"I always have, Giulio," the old man told him. "We'll feast when the dust settles."

Andretta eased the receiver down, filled his glass, and waited for the American hit squad.

Condominio Fernanda
Rapallo, Italy
10 p.m.
Tuesday, June 12, 1979

Mario's guard took his position in a hallway chair near Garth's room. The journalist entered and was surprised to discover a very nervous Rosa Gambino packing a case with Fernanda odds and ends. She moved unsteadily. Tension had whitewashed her complexion.

"Abu Zaki is being escorted to a new safe house," she announced formally. "You should be leaving Fernanda on your own before a quarter after ten."

She motioned with her eyes, walked briskly to a closet, and Garth followed. Metal hangers were jangled to cover her low-pitched dialogue.

"Two large envelopes are in the middle bureau drawer," Rosa whispered. "Under your shirts."

"Copies of Zaki's new passport and documents?" Excitement forced him to control the volume. "His name and face?"

"Everything," Rosa answered shakily. "Also deep background on the Factory."

"How did you—?"

"There are many problems." She leaned forward and breathed every word. "A Factory insider has talked. He is being wrapped and delivered here as Zaki. A symbolic execution. Mafia gunmen from America want your traveler. Probably for reasons which you have explained to me. This address will be given."

"When?"

A startled expression on Rosa's face made him turn abruptly.

Mario had entered the room. The short, heavy-set Factory worker closed the door, walked to a table, and perched himself arrogantly on the edge.

"Sit down," he instructed, glancing at two chairs. "I want to conduct a brief meeting."

Rosa complied at once. Garth hesitated, took note of Mario's impatient expression, and figured that argument would be dangerous and ill-timed. He sat next to Rosa as the hefty Italian began his report.

"All tenants and employees of Fernanda have moved out." Mario announced. "Except for a boy downstairs who'll be around for last-minute errands."

"I know the arrangements," Rosa insisted nervously. "You are disrupting my schedule."

"Bono has delivered Abu Zaki to another location," Mario went on, ignoring Rosa's comment. "And I have just dumped your hall-way guard."

"Excellent," said Garth. "When can I leave?"

"After we review a final item of business." Mario eased down from the table and stepped closer to Rosa and Garth. "The Factory has reported a theft," he explained ominously. "Copies of Zaki's new passport and other documents."

"What!" Garth faked astonishment. "Do you have suspects in mind?"

"Yes," Mario replied. "A prime one."

"I'm sure that Zaki's papers were misplaced during the alert." Rosa was fighting hard to smother her emotions. "Probably the result of confusion."

"The heist was tracked immediately to a member of the records department." Mario calmly removed a gun from a jacket holster and Garth noticed a silencer attached. "Arnaldo Bocca confessed," the Italian reported, glaring at Rosa, and then at his watch. "He was executed at nine-fifty-five p.m."

The woman moaned from deep inside, covered her face with both hands, and lowered her head. Keeping a steady eye on Garth,

Mario walked behind Rosa's chair and pressed the gun barrel against her temple.

"Where are the Zaki papers?" he asked coldly. "I don't have any time for delays."

"Lower the pistol," Garth advised. "Violence won't force her to cooperate."

"Be quiet and wait your turn," Mario cautioned. "The signora is first on my list."

Once again he demanded Zaki's papers and, just as before, the woman failed to react in any way. Her head was bowed low, and her long black hair flowed nearly to the carpet, blocking out her face and her thoughts and her feelings.

"Your time is almost up." Mario's revolver clicked to firing position. "Where are Zaki's papers?"

Rosa, apparently oblivious to his demand, did not budge or utter a sound. Mario began to apply pressure on the gun's trigger. *"Now!"* he yelled. *"Or your head will splatter!"*

Garth was convinced. "Put that goddamn weapon away," he said firmly. "I have the Zaki material."

Quiet descended over the room. Mario looked up and glared at the reporter. Rosa was still hunched over, unresponsive and lost in another place.

"Deliver it fast," Mario threatened, keeping the gun flush up against Rosa's head. "Both of you have serious problems."

Garth stood, walked a few steps to the bureau, and opened the middle drawer. He reached under the shirts and pulled out a large envelope. At the same instant, he heard two muffled shots, turned quickly, and watched Rosa Gambino slide to the floor.

The reporter stared in amazement. Blood oozed and gushed and covered her face and hair, and she lay dying in a pool of it within seconds.

"I want two envelopes." Mario waved the revolver until Garth turned away and concentrated on the drawer again. "This weapon is aimed directly at your back," he reminded. "Give me Zaki's papers immediately or join the signora."

Garth's heart was pounding as he noticed the Smith and Wesson on the right-hand side of the drawer. The woman had positioned it for quick action. She'd also supplied boxes of ammunition, and one of them had been opened. He prayed for luck and courage.

"Zaki's documents!" The Factory worker inched closer. *"Do you want me to get them?"*

Cold perspiration was moistening Garth's forehead. He picked up both envelopes with his left hand and gripped the revolver firmly in his right. Without a pause, he spun about, and fired three quick rounds at the unsuspecting Italian. One shot from Mario went astray because of the impact.

Garth watched mesmerized as pieces of flesh and bone were torn away from the victim's head. Surprise forced Mario's eyes and mouth open to an exaggerated degree. They froze that way as he did a slow-motion drop to the carpet next to Rosa. In a moment they were drenched in each other's blood, and Garth was on his own in Fernanda, unable to look away from the grotesque sight he had created.

He was jolted out of his trance by the sound of fast running in the hall. *"Mario! Mario!"* It was the errand boy from downstairs heading toward the room. Garth rushed to the door and slammed the bolt, just in time. *"Mario! Mario!"* The boy yanked violently on the handle and then pounded with force. *"Mario!"* he screamed.

Breathing unevenly, Garth leaned against the wood, and remained silent until he heard the young employee leave, apparently knocking into furniture on his dash through the apartment. Moments later the front door of 304 banged shut, and he was alone with two corpses.

Garth listened with his ear pressed to the door. Silence. He felt certain that the apartment was vacant. After opening the door quietly, he walked the hall, a feather step at a time. The kitchen, living room, and dining room gave the impression of having been used very recently, but no one was around. Garth tried the phones and discovered that they were disconnected or the lines had been cut.

Still dazed and weak-kneed from the shootings, his nerves were blasted again as he came to an abrupt halt outside the room where Muazzam Labadi had been recuperating. The door was open. He entered and faced a sleeping mummy propped in the bed with a sealed envelope locked in its gauze-wrapped fist.

This must be the informer who'd talked, now a victim to be executed by the American Mafia. Props were arranged on a table: medicine and water and straws and books and other items designed to make this appear a real sickroom. They gave the impression that a doctor or a nurse or an orderly was on the premises somewhere. Garth inhaled the fumes of hospital alcohol and disinfectant, and thoughts of Ellie chilled him. And he realized how deeply he'd become involved with the Factory since he'd met Rand in the Café de Beaulieu only nine days ago.

His urge to examine the mummy's papers evaporated when he heard a car start up and a garage door open. Garth moved quickly down the hall to the large inspection room overlooking Via Tubino. He peered out the window just as the Fernanda errand boy sped away in the gray 1974 Fiat.

Garth noticed a station wagon parked in front of the condominio entrance and assumed that it belonged to Mario. A fast exit was now the journalist's prime concern. He looked at his watch, and the time check sent him flashing back to his own room.

Death was not an unusual sight to Garth. He'd been covering murders and suicides and accidents for years. Yet his legs buckled and his stomach turned as he saw again the blood-covered victims on the floor. Luckily Rosa was face down, and this helped. The woman had been used, set up for annihilation, and Garth expected to be hounded by conscience for the rest of his days and nights. But for now, in order to keep going he reminded himself that both Rosa Gambino and Mario had been working outside the law, giving shelter and aid to criminals, terrorists, and assassins. Garth blocked them out temporarily and prepared for his escape.

He found his briefcase on a table. Labadi's confessional tapes, documents, photographs, and the Napoli phone taps were placed inside. Garth opened the stolen Factory envelopes and made a fast inspection. They contained Muazzam Labadi's new face and identity: a photograph—hardly any resemblance, a copy of his new American passport, other documents. Everything needed to hunt the man down. There were also pages of Factory records, deep background. Automatically he looked over at Rosa's corpse.

The Factory material was added to Labadi's tapes and papers. This was a sizzling hydrogen bomb—fresh evidence that Sirhan was not the lone assassin of Senator Robert F. Kennedy. And it was the means to apprehend a key conspirator. Possible deportation or worse for Joe Napoli and a few members of his organization. Frightening allegations against an official in the Central Intelligence Agency. Documented proof about the existence of a highly professional identity-changing facility in Europe. And more.

Garth closed the briefcase, locked it securely, and then jammed the key into a trouser pocket. The game had changed, he told himself. Fantasy had become reality beyond his wildest expectations. Now commercial publication, recognition for Ellie, a good job for himself, big money and security, had all become meaningless. The potent evidence in his case would have to be protected and delivered to the American government at the highest levels as quickly as possible.

Squeamishly, the reporter knelt beside Mario, avoided his blood, and removed the Italian's keys. Garth did not look at Rosa as he stuffed them in his jacket and got to his feet.

The gun and a box of ammunition helped bulge his pockets. With a firm hold on the briefcase and a packed suitcase, he walked to the door, listened carefully, and then went, deciding not to glance back.

As he passed the inspection room, Garth heard a car pulling up to the Fernanda entrance, making an unusually quiet approach. He moved inside and looked out the window. Two vehicles had parked and switched off headlights. Garth examined the hazy outlines of drivers and men. A visit from the police after neighbors had reported the sound of gunfire? Surely not here on Via Tubino, where the families were probably born and raised to ignore other people's business.

Three men left each car, and the drivers remained. Garth made a swift inspection as the gorillas neared the building. Their appearance and behavior told the reporter that he was trapped, by the American Mafia.

In his room, Garth was calming his nerves and reviewing the dangerous backyard escape plan, his only chance of survival. He wore tailored denim and a lightweight safari jacket with buttoned pockets: it would have to be his wardrobe until the end of the run. He tossed the packed suitcase, a burden, into a closet. Then he switched off the lights and operated by moonglow.

Keeping a firm grip on the briefcase handle, Garth opened the window, took a final look at Rosa, and stepped out on the rusty balcony. He closed the window, assuming that the Mafia had already started breaking and entering apartment 304 in Condominio Fernanda.

Using one hand, as planned, Garth dangled from the lower rung of the balcony. He swung out, then back, and dropped to a similar balcony on the floor below. Crouched, rigid, and hardly breathing, he waited for a sign of trouble. The apartment was still quiet and dark. Garth's first maneuver had worked perfectly.

The second was a disaster. While hanging from a corroded bar, he noticed a row of tall flower pots on the balcony railing below; an obstacle course, too great a risk of noise and detection. The journalist swung out, then back—and then out again, releasing his grip on the rung. He soared clear of the building and fell nearly two floors to a grass- and weed-padded patch of ground.

Severe pains in his arms, legs, and head brought on a dizzying black haze and waves of nausea. Finally, realizing his vulnerability in the moonlight, Garth managed to drag himself to shadows under a tree. The briefcase was in good shape. He tapped the revolver in his pocket. And just for a moment he leaned on the bark, closed his eyes, and trembled uncontrollably.

Eight muffled gunshots from a third-floor room brought Garth to attention. The Mafia had executed a Factory informer, and they were probably applauding and congratulating themselves for hitting Napoli's target, Muazzam Labadi. One down and Steven Garth to go, he could almost hear the killers pledging.

After the gunfire, an elderly woman in the next building poked her head out a window, looked over at the Fernanda for a second, and then ducked inside. There were no other visible reactions from the backyard neighbors. Garth figured that he was right about the Via Tubino families.

The reporter pulled his bruised torso up as a light went on in his room. Using the tree for cover, he watched male figures pass the window gesturing broadly and speaking animatedly. The Napoli people must have been discussing the bodies of Rosa and Mario, and the disappearance of Labadi's companion. One man opened the window, surveyed the yards briefly, and then closed it, while continuing to jabber in Italian. About two minutes later the room went dark, and Garth assumed that the visitors had gone. An apartment occupied by three fresh corpses would be considered an unsuitable resting place for members of the American underworld. Especially in Italy.

Besides, they had to find Labadi's companion. A smart reporter handling an explosive feature would never linger. And if he was responsible for the mess on the carpet, that was a good reason to leave twice as fast. Also, the garage door was open and a vehicle was missing. The station wagon, parked near the entrance, probably belonged to one of the dead Italians.

Garth's rationalizing ended abruptly as two cars started up out front. Battling pain and nausea, he contemplated his next move as the Mafia pulled away from the Fernanda.

One thing was definite: the backyard escape route would have to be altered because of his physical condition. Garth inventoried the negatives: a bright moon, dogs, cats, flashlights, rows of hedges, a wooden fence, an open lawn, shotguns. Too many risks for a limping intruder, a wounded and groaning—nearly unconscious—trespasser.

Garth decided to creep around the right side of the Fernanda, walk straight to Mario's vehicle, and to hell with positioned gunmen or watchdogs left behind by Napoli's visitors, or even law enforcement. A blind alley. The original plan would have allowed him to observe and go the other way if he'd spotted suspicious traffic or people near the building.

The reporter made certain of his weapon, took a firmer hold on the evidence, and limped away from the tree. Assignment: Guard the history-book material and guarantee a safe delivery to the proper American officials.

Garth moved cautiously around the dark right side of the Fernanda. The pain was excruciating, and he was forced to smother a need to cry out. Finally he reached Via Tubino and the area of the front entrance. He hugged the wall of a dimly lit corner and surveyed the place. Mario's vehicle was parked across the street. There were no other cars nearby. Everything appeared to be quiet and normal.

Even so, Garth knew that gunmen could be hiding, waiting to drop him on sight. He imagined the killers behind trees and bushes, Napoli's experts anticipating his move to the station wagon. Or they might be in cars at the bottom of Via Tubino, ready to follow or to slaughter him through the glass of his windshield.

Knifelike pains in his stomach doubled him over, and he nearly fell to the ground. There were no alternatives. Garth pulled away from the wall, and staggered toward Mario's vehicle, ready to face the consequences.

He removed the keys from his pocket and fumbled with the door, expecting shouts or fists or bullets. There were no incidents of any kind. At last he had the door open, and Garth was inside and behind the wheel. He placed the briefcase and the weapon on the floor within easy reach, locked windows and doors securely. He angled the rearview mirror and started the engine. A gauge indicated that he had enough gasoline for a long journey. At 12:15 a.m. on June 13, 1979, Garth was rolling down Via Tubino in a station wagon full of secrets.

●

"WHAT'S MADAME GARTH'S condition now?" James Hatfield asked on the Hotel Negresco phone, late in the evening of November 9. "Any improvement?"

"The same," Léon Dumas replied. "Total paralysis and severe head pains."

"Awake?"

"Out cold."

"Did your specialist turn up?"

"Dr. Joubert is expected before midnight," he answered. "You'll receive a call when he arrives."

"Good," said Hatfield. "Brandon Patterson of London will be at your place sometime tomorrow."

"An honor."

"Yes."

"Have you finished Madame Garth's work?" Dumas suppressed a yawn. "Dr. Vassolo is anxious to examine the papers."

"I'm still reading," Hatfield replied a bit testily. "We'll discuss the contents later."

"Better hurry," Dumas warned in a sarcastic voice. "Eleanor Garth feels the Mafia has an option."

"Phone when Joubert arrives," Hatfield told him bluntly. "I have long-distance coming through."

Kenneth Tyler, an American Justice Department veteran, was on the line returning Jim Hatfield's call to Paris. Tyler had been attending government meetings for a week. The literary agent and the popular Washington official were old friends.

"When are you leaving?" Hatfield asked. "I might meet you for a drink."

"Great," said Tyler. "We finish up on the seventeenth. Any problems?"

"No," Hatfield answered. "Just a possibility that I'll want you to read a manuscript."

"Another technical piece?"

"Fiction."

The line went silent for a moment. "A pleasure," Tyler said finally. "But why me?"

"I have a Robert Kennedy assassination story," Hatfield went on. "Sirhan and the CIA and the Mafia."

"God help us!" Tyler exclaimed. "Another one?"

"This is a little different," Hatfield said quietly. "Eleanor Garth wrote it."

"Eleanor?" Ken Tyler paused. "I thought she was crippled and hospitalized."

"A very sick woman," Hatfield agreed. "Regardless, I have a feeling this property might need an official examination because of certain delicate accusations."

"No harm in looking," said Tyler. "Bring it along."

"Depends on my instincts after flipping the last page," Hatfield stated. "I won't build a candy mountain and squander your time."

"Get up here," Tyler insisted, his voice warm and pleasant. "With or without a conspiracy."

"Thanks," said Hatfield. "I'll let you know."

"Where is Steve Garth?" Tyler inquired after some thought. "Any news?"

"No," Hatfield replied. "They claim he deserted Eleanor about five months ago. I had lunch with him just the day before he's supposed to have run out on her. It's hard to believe that's what happened."

"She was driving him insane."

"Probably."

"I had lunch with Garth just before they ran to Europe," the official confided. "His eyes were sunk, his face was gloomy, and hell was brewing under that rough exterior. I can visualize what developed over the years."

"An unlikely deserter."

"Who knows?"

"Do you honestly believe that Steve deserted?" Jim Hatfield prodded again. "Knowing Eleanor's condition?"

"Maybe," the official answered. "His boxer's physique might have covered many weaknesses. Sometimes a man like Garth reaches saturation point, and the only thing he can do is run." There was a pause. "Eleanor must have been a very difficult bundle," Tyler added.

"No doubt."

"Any clues about Steve in the manuscript?"

"Many references." Hatfield's reply was evasive. "Although the book is fiction."

"Of course," said Tyler. "Now you have me all geared up for a presentation."

"I'll call," Hatfield assured him. "Thanks again, Ken."

With Tyler's opinions fresh in mind, Jim Hatfield picked up *Sandcastle*, and returned to the events of the previous June.

22

Garth was speeding on the autostrada. Past Genoa, Arenzano, Varazze, Albisola. He had coasted to the foot of Via Tubino and made a left without a problem, but still it was difficult to ignore the feeling that he was a moving target being followed by expert gunmen.

The journey had become a nightmare. Cold sweat dampened every part of his body, Garth's vision had blurred, his stomach was upset. Unsteady legs rested on the pedals and trembling hands gripped the wheel. Very bright headlights glaring just behind him added to his uneasiness. He slowed, but the car refused to pass him. Garth veered abruptly to the far right, and the vehicle followed, with lights blazing. A definite tail, he figured, trying other maneuvers. He could not shake the pursuer.

Garth's breathing was now forced and uneven. Then he felt a tightening across his chest, and a dagger-sharp ache in his left arm. Nerves? A muscle? A heart attack? He was near panic when, moments later, he noticed a sign ahead, a cutoff for Savona. Garth eased right and circled off the autostrada. He took a quick look in the rearview mirror. All cars had sped past.

His pains and fears had increased by 1:20 a.m. The reporter was lost in the town of Savona, Italy. Every house and store was bolted, and the streets were deserted, except for an occasional drunk. Driving in circles and growing weaker, Garth was tempted to ring a bell and plead for help. He needed medical attention. And, of course, a telephone. It was urgent for him to call Ellie, find out her condition, and pass on instructions. This reminded him of the briefcase and the contents and his predicament. The chest pains and other symptoms would have to be endured. He made a futile attempt to get back on the autostrada.

Unable to locate the route, Garth ended up in a slum area of town on a dark back street. He pulled to a curb, parked, rolled up the window, made certain of each lock, shoved the briefcase under the front seat, and put the gun in his jacket pocket. He slumped low and closed his eyes. It was difficult to ignore the easy way out: the practical options, including the Savona police, local hospitals, the American consul in Genoa. But he thought of red tape and ignorance and delays and complications and his fears about trusting anyone other than the proper American officials at the highest government levels.

A blanket of soft velvet began to dull his thinking and ease his pain and cover his anguish. And, moments later, Steven Garth was asleep.

A finger tapped on the car window. Again. Again. His eyes opened quickly and blinked at the sight of a grinning young black man. The crouched figure was motioning urgently to roll down the glass. After the scene had registered, Garth was alert, with his right hand in the jacket pocket. A fast time check revealed 1:45 a.m. It had been a short nap. Gripping the Smith and Wesson, he reached over, and lowered the window a few inches.

"Are you sick?" the man asked in rotten Italian. "You were howling when I moved past the car."

Even in the dark, Garth could tell that he was sober and certainly not a street tramp, or a beggar.

"You are parked in a very rough neighborhood." His face was closer to the window. "Better take off."

"Thank you," said Garth, hardly recognizing the feeble sound of his own voice. "Is there a phone anywhere?"

"Yes." The lanky black man narrowed his eyes, scratched his chin, and peered through the opening with greater interest. "You have to be American," he blurted in English.

"Right."

"What a fuckin' shot in the head." The black man appeared to be impressed and excited. "My name is Polo. I'm from Long Island, New York."

"A pleasure," Garth mumbled. "I need a telephone."

"Along with other things." Polo eyed him curiously. "I work around the corner. A private nightclub. Great place. Everybody is cool. The owner is fantastic. Use our phone and anything else you like. Be my guest.'

The reporter was measuring the risks and the alternatives. A knife of pain in his chest forced a decision. He leaned over and unlocked the door.

"Man, you are really beat up," said Polo. Garth's fingers tightened on the briefcase and the gun as the black man supported him down the street, around the corner to a narrow alley. A sign under a flickering red arrow publicized La Chunga.

It was the usual private cellar joint. Two muscle types with black hair and dark clothes were at the door. Carpeted stairs led down to a modern bar with stools and presentable hookers. One was doing business and the others were applying nail polish. A butch-looking girl mixed drinks. Neatly set tables in the center of the room were empty. Partitioned booths lined the walls. Four whores munched sandwiches and gulped wine in the first, while paying customers were being heated up in the second and third. A waiter stood with arms folded gazing blankly at the only couple using the dance area. A wide-hipped prostitute was rubbing herself against a small man's crotch in the near-zero lighting. Gaudy patterns revolving on the walls and ceiling furnished the necessary disco effects. The soft rock music and faint odor of cheap perfume added the final touches. La Chunga waiting for action in the early-morning hours.

Garth and Polo were sitting in a partitioned booth. The young black man was of average height and build, with a smooth complexion, good features, close-cropped hair, and a pleasant attitude. He was neatly dressed in a sports outfit. They evidently liked him in the club. Polo received winks and smiles from whores and the permanent employees.

"I want to clean up." Garth was feeling better after draining a large bourbon. "Do you have a room?"

"Over there." He pointed to a door next to the bar. "Want me to help?"

"No," Garth replied. "Thanks anyway."

Holding the briefcase and wearing his jacket, Garth stood and limped across the dance floor. He knew that every unattached hooker and all the members of the staff were checking him with interest, curiosity, and suspicion.

Garth locked the washroom door, removed his jacket cautiously, and hung it on a peg. His breathing was normal and the chest pains had gone. Bruises and sprains were much easier to cope with. Luckily, he had landed on thick grass behind the Fernanda and nothing seemed to be fractured, although he was worried about the bones in his right foot. He could arrange for a complete physical after the official delivery.

After washing, combing his tangled hair, and smoothing out the wrinkles in his denim trousers and shirt, he unlocked the briefcase and glanced at the material inside. Excitement churned again. The bombs were ticking in place. He opened an envelope and removed six hundred-dollar bills—part of his expense money. The case was locked again. Garth put on his jacket, shoved the cash into one of the pockets, and fingered the gun in the other. A flash of Rosa and Mario bleeding on the carpet sobered him for a moment. But his thoughts were interrupted abruptly by the rattling of the washroom door handle.

Garth returned to his seat in the booth. "You look real fine now," Polo complimented with a smile. "Ready for a gorgeous piece of woman?"

"I need a telephone," Garth replied in a formal manner. "And privacy."

"The chief has both in his office," Polo stated. "Let me fix something."

"Obviously I'll pay for all charges," Garth explained. "Plus a bonus."

"You don't have to strain, man," Polo advised. "The owner is a fantastic guy."

The amiable young black stood and walked confidently to a far corner of the dimly lit room.

Garth sipped a drink and listened to music. A prostitute at the bar finished her manicure and stared in his direction. Garth avoided contact. Business was picking up at La Chunga, and he was becoming impatient. The hooker's steady gaze added to his annoyance. A waiter returned, filled Polo's glass, his own, and left the bottle.

"Excuse me, sir," he whispered. "A young lady would like to join you for a drink."

"The one at the bar?"

"Yes, sir," the waiter replied. "Tina is a beauty from Rome who speaks perfect English."

"Bring Tina champagne," said Garth, anticipating the owner's favor. "And explain that I prefer drinking alone."

"Yes, sir."

Polo returned smiling. "You have a telephone and privacy," he said. "Come with me."

Garth followed the young black man across the room. The whore at the bar raised her drink in salute as they passed. Garth nodded politely.

They entered an office which had just enough space for a glass-topped desk, two chairs, nude photographs of women, and a fat, bald Italian man in his late fifties.

"Al Cortini," Polo announced with genuine respect. "My friend hasn't volunteered a name yet."

"Unimportant," barked the dressed-up pimp with sneaky eyes as he extended a hand and shook Garth's vigorously. "Treat my office like your own," he said, motioning to a phone on the desk. "Glad I can help."

"Thank you." Garth was anxious to begin. "I'll keep a record and finish quickly."

"Plenty of time," said the "fantastic" owner. "Me and Polo will hire a table." He laughed and took the black man by the arm. "The food and the broads are clean in our joint."

Polo glanced around and winked as they left the office.

Steven Garth's first call was to Hospital Saint Roch in Nice, where he received a bewildering message. Madame Garth had been discharged. She was not at her apartment in Beaulieu-sur-Mer; contact Dr. Roger Lambert at his office or home for the patient's new address; there were no other details in the hospital records.

Concerned, Garth opened the briefcase, removed a thick address book, and then locked the case again.

The doctor's villa phone was finally answered by a sleepy maid after many rings. Dr. Lambert had gone to Nice on an emergency. Garth introduced himself and requested Ellie's address.

"I'm sorry," the woman apologized in a fuzzy voice. "Only the doctor has this information."

"*Where is Madame Garth?*" His nerves were jangling. "*I demand an explanation!*"

The maid insisted that she did not have any facts. "Dr. Lambert is expected about three o'clock," she informed him placatingly. "Want to leave a number?"

Garth hesitated for a moment, "No," he blasted. "I'll call back." He slammed the receiver and left the closet-sized office at 2:35 a.m.

Cortini, Polo, and the hooker from Rome were chattering and laughing and draining his bottle when Garth approached the table. He was upset and tired and not in the mood to play grab-ass in a back alley.

"That was fast," the owner commented. "Business over?"

"No," Garth answered. "I have to phone again at three, with your permission."

"Anything you want." Cortini shoved over and made room for him next to the beauty known as Tina. "Relax and drink and take advantage of our personal services."

The girl was young, tall, dark-haired and flashy. Her legs and breasts were attractively shaped and clearly visible. Garth was mainly disturbed by her large painted eyes. They continued to study him with unusual interest.

"Are you a secret agent?" Tina moved close and scraped her brightly polished nails across his leg. "That fucking briefcase is glued to your hand."

He inched away and made certain that no one pressed against his jacket pockets. Six hundred-dollar bills were on the girl's side and a weapon rested next to Cortini.

"Forgive my boldness." Tina exaggerated a pout. "You must be having a rough time."

"I am," said Garth. "Please understand."

"We do," Cortini broke in, giving an eye signal to a waiter. "Have a few drinks and use my office at three." He glanced over at the Roman whore. "The man has problems."

Polo agreed, and Tina understood, and bourbon arrived—with champagne too—and the La Chunga group drank and chattered and laughed, while Garth paced himself and sat waiting quietly. He was still bothered by Tina's occasional squints at his briefcase and jacket. Finally, at three, he excused himself, and left for Cortini's office to phone Dr. Roger Lambert.

23

La Chunga
Savona, Italy
3:10 a.m.
Wednesday, June 13, 1979

At last the doctor was on the line, and Garth felt relieved as he listened to a report on Ellie's partial remission. Although her movements were slow and unsteady, she made her own way or used a cane, but never a wheelchair. Her mental state had improved, except for anxious periods due to her husband's absence and lack of news. She adored the beauty and isolation of the villa. Dr. Lambert explained his friend's generosity, the hospital transfer, and the reason for cooperating with Ellie's demand for secrecy.

"She will be thrilled to hear from you," he predicted. "The best medicine in the world."

After thanking Dr. Lambert, Garth wrote down the address and phone number of Eleanor's temporary residence, in Saint-Jean-Cap-Ferrat, France. He dialed and heard her voice strong and more alive than it had been in years. He ignored the disease and pictured her elegant figure and confident bearing. Once again he felt bedazzled by animated green eyes, long silken hair, and classic features. Happier days came to mind as they spoke of love and being apart and prayers for an early reunion.

And then, before Eleanor could inquire, Garth explained that his assignment might have produced staggering results.

"Can you discuss them?"

"No," he answered. "Wrong place."

"I understand." Excitement forced her to pause. "Are we onto something, Steven?"

"Affirmative," he replied. "Possibly more than you imagined at the beginning."

"Oh, God," she whispered. "Dear God."

"Ellie?"

"Yes."

"I need addresses and unlisted phone numbers." Garth pushed along. "Do you have the book?"

"Right next to me on a table."

"Fine," said Garth. "Dennis Greenway and Warren Sullivan in Le Cannet and Nice."

Moments later, after furnishing the information, Ellie asked, "Are you coming here?"

"Not directly," Garth answered. "I want to meet with Dennis or Warren at once."

"I see." Eleanor lowered her voice. "Are you in France?"

"Just over the border," he said evasively. "Skip the exact location."

"Of course."

"Be patient," he advised. "This is delicate business, and we have to operate in a certain way."

"What do I tell Hatfield and the others?"

"You heard from me," Garth answered. "There is one more job opportunity to be investigated."

"A feeble explanation."

"So what?" He was anxious to proceed. "Our main concern is the assignment."

"Yes."

"Expect a call after Greenway or Sullivan." He paused. "Be alert and suspicious."

"You know me."

"And take care of yourself," he added. "I'm bringing home a very important package."

Warm sentiments were exchanged before the conversation ended with farewells and hopes again for an early reunion.

Sitting at the owner's desk, feeling bubble-headed and weary, Garth looked at the addresses and phone numbers, and thought about his two contacts. Greenway, the former State Department official, was a man he admired and trusted. They had met frequently during Garth's best reporting days. Later, Greenway had been a reliable source of information for Eleanor's second novel, the controversial Washington thriller. If the influential senior man was in France, at his Le Cannet villa, Garth would beg to visit immediately for advice and cooperation.

Warren Sullivan, of the American Consulate in Nice, was another friend, but Garth was dubious about processing explosive material through lower-ranked government officials working abroad. Dennis Greenway, a retired veteran, was his first choice.

After many rings, Greenway was on the phone, half asleep and shocked to hear the voice of Steven Garth.

"I need an immediate appointment," he explained. "This is a matter of urgency."

"Have you gone mad?" Greenway had evidently noticed a clock. "What's the problem?"

Garth revealed no details as he made his claim to material, tapes, and documents which had to be examined at once by the United States government at the highest level.

Greenway reacted after a pause. "Tapes and documents?" The former official was incredulous. "Excuse me, Steven, but mystery is a bit difficult to handle at this hour."

"Please allow me to visit and explain," Garth went on. "The material is ultrasensitive."

"Contact the proper authorities," said Greenway. "I have no right to become involved."

Garth persisted, emphasizing the importance of his material, the need for speed, his fear of trusting others, the urgency of a safe delivery to recommended government officials at a top level, and the personal dangers involved while he acted as courier.

"I risked my life to gather this evidence," Garth said with deep intensity. "And some nasty people are chasing me now." He swallowed hard because of a dry throat. "Your expert advice and cooperation would be appreciated."

At the other end of the line, Greenway was silent for a moment while he flashed back on Steven Garth. He'd known him as a calm, even-tempered, rational man, unlikely to be phoning anyone in the early-morning hours about tapes and documents and personal risks, unless there were very good reasons. Eventually, the former official consented to see Garth, and to honor his request for secrecy until further notice. "I just arrived from Arlington last night," he explained. "My villa staff won't be on the premises until late afternoon or evening. I'm alone, but I'll brew some coffee and make breakfast. When do you expect to arrive?"

"Probably five-thirty or six," Garth replied. "I'm driving from Italy."

"Oh, yes." There was a pause. "Here are the directions to my place."

Garth scribbled the route to Villa San Giorgio in Le Cannet France, thanked Dennis Greenway, put down the receiver, and left the office moving fast.

Tina was sipping champagne alone at his table. Garth, in a hurry, sat a distance away from her.

"Want to make arrangements?" she asked. "My place is down the road a few blocks."

"No, thank you." Garth motioned for a check, and the waiter nodded. "I have to leave now."

"Really?" Tina put down her glass indignantly. "After you fucked my chances of negotiating elsewhere?"

"Polo invited you to my table," said Garth firmly. "And nobody used chains."

"Filthy bastard." She poured more champagne. "You owe me some apology money."

Garth ignored her as the waiter approached and placed his tab under a bottle.

"Signor Cortini figured it in dollars for you," he said. "The last quart is on the house."

Garth made an instant decision as he registered the $420 total. The usual clip-joint protests had to be avoided. A fast and smooth exit was his only concern. He reached into his jacket pocket and came out with six hundred-dollar notes. He handed five to the waiter and put one back. "Service is covered," Garth reminded. "Your boss has eighty bucks for the use of his office."

"And I rate a hundred," said Tina. "You fucked me out of doing business this morning."

The briefcase was at Garth's side as he paid the bill. Suddenly, he wheeled about as Tina grabbed the handle and pulled it close to her. "A hundred dollars," she taunted. "Or I keep your secrets."

Garth was paralyzed, a stone figure, unable to react.

"Are you a bank robber, a gambler, a pornographic freak, a drug pusher, a spy?" Tina sat on the case and laughed mockingly. "Is my ass resting on money, dirty pictures, grass, or maps and charts?"

"I want the briefcase," he said icily. "Right now."

"Pay me," the whore demanded. "You've got a hundred stashed in that jacket." She wagged a finger at him. "Don't jerk around or my price will go up."

"Hand over the briefcase," said Garth menacingly. "I'm warning you."

"*Cortini!*" the whore screamed. "*This fucking American refuses to pay his dues!*"

In moments, Cortini and Polo had arrived, followed by waiters. Others in the club were staring over from the bar, tables, and dance floor.

"What's the problem, Tina?" the owner asked. "The man already settled his bill."

"Not with me," she argued. "He owes a legitimate debt of one hundred dollars."

"The briefcase." Garth was running out of patience. "You're asking for serious trouble."

"We never threaten ladies in here," Cortini explained, losing most of his charm. "Do you have the briefcase, Tina?"

"Yes."

"Where?"

"Under my ass," the whore replied. "And it stays there until this bastard pays one hundred dollars."

Al Cortini laughed, and Polo laughed, and the waiters laughed, and the rest of the club joined them.

"I want two hundred now," Tina decided. "Get it up before my price changes again."

"See what I mean?" Cortini laughed with the others. "A real tough businesswoman."

At that precise moment, Steven Garth's face became a killer's mask, cruel and determined. He pulled the gun from his pocket and jammed the muzzle against the whore's throat. "Lift your ass," he ordered. "And give me the briefcase."

Cortini, Polo, the waiters, and the others in the club were stunned. Tina was petrified. *"Give me the case!"* he bellowed, pressing the gun deeper into her flesh. *"Or die right now!"*

La Chunga's owner, taking a careful look at Garth's eyes and steady hand, waved his muscle team back to the door. The room was quiet as Tina got up and stood rigidly. Garth took a firm grip on the briefcase while pointing his weapon directly at Cortini. "The problem is solved," he announced. "I want to leave now."

"Go ahead," said the owner, inspecting him suspiciously. "We can't afford trouble here."

With the gun in firing position and the briefcase at his side, Garth limped across the room heading for the steps. *"Open up for him!"* Cortini yelled to his bouncers.

Polo, the whores, the customers, staff members, and the owner gazed intently as the battered American found his way out of La Chunga.

Ten minutes later he was on the autostrada speeding toward

France and Le Cannet, for an early-morning session at Dennis Greenway's Villa San Giorgio.

A villa
Suburb of Genoa, Italy
5:00 a.m.
Wednesday, June 13, 1979

Gabriel De Luca's perpetual frown had disappeared temporarily and the deep creases in his forehead were less noticeable. The Mafia worrier had just phoned a report to Gino Corletto in the States. "That's very good," Corletto had said—Napoli's key agents seldom praised troops during an operation. "Joe expects a quick finish," he'd added. "Call late today."

De Luca had presented a full report: Muazzam Labadi, sculpted and bandaged as George Bradford, had been eliminated in a Rapallo Factory drop. A phone tap on Eleanor Garth's temporary residence at Saint-Jean-Cap-Ferrat, organized by Andrew Tolkin, had picked up Steven Garth's call from Savona and revealed that the reporter's Labadi material was virgin, sealed, waiting for an expert—probably Dennis Greenway or Warren Sullivan. Tolkin knew both men personally, and officially. Pisano and Cecchi had already been dispatched to Villa San Giorgio and two others were headed for Nice —Garth was en route to one place or the other. They would park, hide, observe, and wait; De Luca agreed with Tolkin that the intelligence officer was in a position to move in close and line up Napoli's target using a sophisticated approach. Later, at the proper time, in the right place, Gino's strong-arms would use their own methods to gather up the damaging evidence and neutralize Steven H. Garth.

De Luca had received instructions to remain in Genoa on a hookup with Corletto. Jefferson Boland and a surveillance group were still assigned to Eleanor Garth's villa at Cap-Ferrat.

"We're coming down the stretch," De Luca said aloud to himself; and then, out of habit, he frowned and looked worried.

24

Villa San Giorgio
Le Cannet, France
Early morning
Wednesday, June 13, 1979

Bleary-eyed and near collapse, Steven Garth drove on a quiet tree-lined road past impressive estates until he reached a pair of iron gates marked "San Giorgio." They were open. He circled on gravel and stopped in front of an old peaceful-looking structure set in neatly landscaped grounds.

Garth pressed his forehead on the steering wheel and closed his eyes tightly, but jagged patterns of red and green refused to disappear. Pain and nausea and a feeling that his body was going numb forced him to straighten up and reach for the door handle.

"Relax on the couch," Greenway ordered. "We'll discuss your problems after a hot breakfast."

The former government official was a tall silver-haired man in his late sixties. His features were soft and plump, with cold gray eyes and a humorless expression. He looked an athletic type, who had run out of condition. But his deep-voiced authoritative manner, his expertise and reliability, were all being used to advantage in his Washington law offices. A widower and childless, Dennis P. Greenway had always been rather fatherly toward Eleanor, and her journalist husband.

•

The eggs and bacon were fried perfectly and the coffee was hot and delicious. Greenway made apologies for the late-arriving staff, but it was obvious that the man knew his own way around the kitchen. Garth needed breakfast. His empty and quivering insides were still burning from La Chunga's forty-proof diet.

"Now I want some explanations." Greenway watched the reporter scrape his plate with buttered toast. "You look horrible. And I'm quite disturbed about that mysterious phone call." He filled their mugs again. "Tapes and documents which have to be inspected at the highest government levels?" He stared at Garth's briefcase propped on the chair beside him. "Just what the hell are you talking about, Steven?"

"Are the doors and windows locked?" Garth was serious. "Mind if we check the front and back?"

Greenway studied him thoughtfully. "Now I demand explanations, my friend." He pushed the coffee away. "Why are you hiding like a thief?"

"I might have been followed."

"By whom?"

"A variety of killers."

"For what reason?"

"The material in this briefcase." He grabbed the handle. "My tapes and documents."

"Some kind of evidence?" Greenway became impatient. "What do you have in that damn bag?"

"A Robert Kennedy conspiracy," the reporter blurted. "And the destruction of Joseph Napoli."

After looking stunned for a moment, Greenway made his decision and got up. "There are precautions to be taken," he said. "Then we'll use my upstairs office for a conference."

Saint-Jean-Cap-Ferrat
France
Early morning
Wednesday, June 13, 1979

Eleanor Garth adjusted her pillow and stared up the ceiling. Remission. Steven was nearby delivering headlines, and her limbs were functioning well enough for a dignified reunion. At least she would be able to visit him in an upright position, with a minimum of wobbling, stammering, and foot-dragging.

Thoughts of him stirred her emotions. Acting impulsively, she reached for the address book, found the number, lifted the receiver, and dialed Dennis Greenway at Villa San Giorgio.

Ellie pressed a button, sat up in bed, and waited. A neatly uniformed French woman appeared.

"Good morning, Annie," Ellie said joyfully. "Please help me dress."

The maid returned the greeting, went to a closet, and began to remove a lounging robe and slippers.

"No, dear." Ellie gestured negatively. "I have an appointment outside this morning."

Annie looked at her with a baffled expression as she gave her instructions. Each item of clothing was selected by Ellie without hesitation. During the lonely days and nights, she had imagined and rehearsed this meeting with her husband, playing both cripple and victim in remission. She was programmed to go either way.

"Leave my things on the chair and wait." Ellie rose to her feet and walked a determined step at a time, heading for the bathroom. "I expect to be ready and quite presentable in less than an hour," she proclaimed, looking back at the fascinated maid. "What a vain bitch," she added in English, knowing that Annie understood the language.

Using a dressing-table mirror, she accentuated her green eyes and high cheekbones and brushed her long brown hair to a perfect shine. In fact, she did everything possible to transform herself into a likeness of the woman Steven Garth had married.

"Tony and Ralph will have another customer," Boland reported to De Luca after watching a taxi speed Ellie away from the Saint-Jean villa. "Madame Garth just left."

"Stupid reporter," De Luca commented. "Didn't he figure that we'd be on her ass?"

"How would the guy know she took off?" Boland replied. "She phoned a number, a man's voice answered, Madame Garth listened and then hung up."

"Checking if Greenway was home."

"I assume," said Boland. "About an hour later, a French girl dialed for a taxi and booked a ride to Le Cannet."

"For the Garth woman alone?"

"Yeah," Boland replied. "Want us to follow?"

"Unnecessary," said De Luca. "Let her believe that she drove away clean."

Villa San Giorgio
Le Cannet, France
Morning
Wednesday, June 13, 1979

Muazzam Labadi's voice chilled Garth again as the audio tape rolled for Dennis Greenway. The former State Department official was absorbed in the conspiracy dialogue. Garth had recounted his adventure, most of it, before pushing the button. Edgar Rand and Jefferson Boland and Rosa Gambino and Mario and the Factory. The Napoli papers were examined cursorily; Greenway would look at them in detail later. Recordings of phone taps between Napoli and Gino Corletto too would be heard later.

Greenway's skeptical attitude had given way to curiosity and then to astonishment, and now the lawyer was deeply involved with the material and the story, reminding Garth that he had admitted his participation in criminal activities, including the shooting of a man, and that he failed to notify law enforcement or representatives of the American or foreign governments at the time.

He had agreed that the journalist's briefcase would have to be handled with care.

Garth knew Greenway well, trusted him, and respected him; but he had not mentioned one important aspect of the package, and he would remain secretive about it until all the evidence was on the desk of some high-ranking American official in Washington, D.C.

Garth had vowed that nobody would be told that Labadi had left the condominio, or that he had a file on the new Labadi: name, face, a copy of his American passport, and other documents. This vital information would remain in his case until the right moment. Rosa Gambino had been killed for attempting to obtain these identity papers, and Steven Garth had been forced to blast Mario in self-defense.

Greenway stopped the machine at the sound of a buzzer. There was someone outside the iron gates. His grounds were surrounded by a fence of spiked metal, a feeble barrier, useless against a determined intruder, but troublemakers would never announce themselves. He pressed an intercom button. "Yes?"

"Dennis Greenway?"

"Who is this?"

"Eleanor," said a female voice. "Eleanor Garth."

Possibly because of weakness and injury and an accumulation of incredible happenings, Garth lived the next twenty minutes in a daze, hardly able to believe his wife was really there. Greenway had flipped a switch, gates had opened, a taxi had driven up, and the beautiful woman had appeared, a vision from the past, a snapshot from their album. She had moved to him unaided, and they had embraced and kissed and held each other tightly, and it was a reminder of healthy times, productive times, irreplaceable times.

The impact of Ellie's dramatic appearance—upright, confident, and moving freely, with multiple sclerosis in remission—began to fade as they sat a little later in Greenway's office.

Steven was concerned that Ellie might have been followed during her taxi ride from Saint-Jean. "They were probably watching the house day and night." His tone was all business now. "You took a chance, Ellie."

"No one knew about the Ferrat move," she told him. "We left the hospital secretly."

"You're dealing with professionals." Garth looked around at Greenway. "I'm sure they had the information right away."

"How about it, Ellie?" Greenway asked. "Was anything following you from the Cap?"

"I am not a fool." Eleanor's posture was erect and normal, and Steven watched her admiringly. "The route from the villa was clear in the early-morning hours. No other vehicles were in sight until we reached the Pont and the lower corniche. And believe me, I was alert, on my guard, all the way. I would have ordered a wild goose chase if anything suspicious had been following us."

Steven stifled his doubts; it was too late now for lectures. Instead he stupefied Eleanor by outlining his story and describing the contents of his briefcase. As before, he avoided mentioning the Factory copies of Muazzam Labadi's new face, passport, and other documents in Greenway's hearing. He would brief Ellie later.

Greenway finished the audio tape on low volume, and Ellie listened, spellbound.

"Disturbing," he remarked. "Especially combined with the rest of your material."

"An understatement," she said, her pale skin reddened by excitement. "Can I hear the beginning?"

"Later." Steven Garth's eyes were on the lawyer. "Where do I make a delivery?"

"Paris," he answered quickly, as though plans had already been formulated. "The American Ambassador is my friend. Your briefcase will be inspected under tight security. His advice and cooperation are vital. The Ambassador can set a meeting with your high-ranking officials in the United States."

"When?"

"I'll phone," the lawyer declared. "You should be on the Nice to Paris flight at one-thirty this afternoon."

The wind had picked up speed. A mistral. Andrew Tolkin drove along the quiet tree-lined road leading to Villa San Giorgio. He spotted Tony Pisano's black Mercedes parked on a dusty side turning —a concealed location, although the occupants had a good enough view of Greenway's entrance through gaps in the branches of trees. The Central Intelligence officer turned left and rolled to a noiseless halt, across from Pisano in a spot just as obscured.

Tolkin got out of his car, walked briskly to the Mercedes, and climbed into the back seat next to Jefferson Boland. Ralph Cecchi had been driving. A solemn-faced Pisano was on his right.

"Like cancer," he remarked without looking back. "The longer you wait the faster it spreads. We eliminated Labadi and now three or more targets are in that house."

"Be patient," warned Tolkin. "Follow instructions."

"I'm worried," said Pisano. "They might have contacted police or government already." He turned and faced the agent. "There's a car full of professionals behind this villa. We're sitting here in front. Greenway's wall is an easy climb. The mistral is a perfect cover." He swung around and glared at Cecchi. "Maybe we rush the damn place and finish our business."

"Ignorance!" Tolkin removed his glasses. "I suggest that you listen to me!"

Hard and fast, the agent pushed his angle. He had the only keys to Villa San Giorgio: a personal relationship with Greenway, credentials, a reason to enter the front door instead of scaling fences. Without a doubt, the material was still virgin. Greenway and Steven Garth would insist on face-to-face high level conferences, a tight security plan, guarantees of immunity, and other legal promises for the journalist in advance. Tolkin assured Pisano that details would never be revealed on a telephone. He scoffed at wall-climbing and a massacre on the premises. A gendarmerie was nearby. San Giorgio's owner was an experienced lawyer and a former government official; he probably had the villa and grounds bristling with alarm contraptions. But Tolkin's main point was that he had a plan, a sophisticated operation in two phases. First, a CIA-type maneuver, designed to set up the victims and the material. Then, with risks lowered and success guaranteed, Pisano and his men would finish the assignment in their own way.

An unusually subdued and haggard-looking Jefferson Boland and the arrogant young Ralph Cecchi listened with Tony Pisano to Tolkin's sketchy operational briefing.

"I want to borrow Cecchi," Tolkin proceeded. "They won't know him."

"For what?" asked Pisano.

"My driver and helper on a Nice assignment," the agent replied. "We announce at the gates, enter, and Cecchi waits in the car while I visit Greenway."

"Just like that," said Pisano. "The man has guests."

"And I have a legitimate reason for appearing." Tolkin rubbed his glasses with a handkerchief. "You will understand later."

"A typical spook piece of business," Cecchi remarked, glancing around for the first time. "What happens to Pisano and the rest of our boys?"

"They wait," Tolkin replied bluntly. 'I expect to come out of that villa in fifteen or twenty minutes. I'll give Cecchi a detailed report on the situation inside, along with blueprints for the next critical move."

"How do I broadcast this information?" Cecchi mocked. "Use a loudspeaker?"

"You will go on an errand for me." Andrew Tolkin replaced his glasses and adjusted them carefully. "Stop here and give my report to Pisano."

"Double-talk!" the young hood exploded. "You haven't told us anything!"

"Wait until I come out of the villa." The agent was preparing to leave. "Are you with me, Cecchi?"

Cecchi looked at his boss and received a nod. "Joseph Napoli is very anxious," lectured Pisano as Tolkin and Cecchi reached for the doors. "And Corletto is squeezing." He eased down in his seat and frowned. "God help your CIA ass if we fail today."

Through a gap in the swaying branches of a tree, Pisano and Boland watched Cecchi bring Tolkin's car to a halt at the Villa's iron gates. Tolkin leaned out of the passenger window and spoke into a metal box. After a slight delay, the gates opened, and the vehicle rode over gravel to the front entrance of San Giorgio as the gates closed behind them.

Although dust and leaves were beginning to swirl, Andrew Tolkin could be seen getting out of the automobile, gesturing to his driver, and marching up steps to the front door. Pisano and Boland had to squint as they focused on a confident-looking agent buzzing and waiting for a reply. Moments later the door opened and Tolkin disappeared inside.

"A cold and slimy piece of work," Boland whispered almost to himself. "With training, experience, intelligence, and a very large set of balls."

Pisano ignored him.

25

Villa San Giorgio
Le Cannet, France
10 a.m.
Wednesday, June 13, 1979

Startled by the voice on the intercom, Greenway explained quickly to his guests that Andrew Tolkin was in the diplomatic service, a man known to him, a respected veteran now assigned to Paris. Even so, he suggested that the Garths lock the upstairs office and remain quiet until the mystery of Tolkin's unexpected visit had been solved.

"I'll come right to the point, Dennis," said the agent. "Steven and Eleanor Garth are here and we have official interest."

They were using the living room, seated face to face, conversing in a formal manner.

"What's this business about?" Greenway was puzzled and upset by Tolkin's sudden appearance. "I have a right to know."

"Everything I say here is absolutely confidential," emphasized Tolkin, then he told Greenway of his assignment in Nice and the reports of a drug storage and distribution center, links between terrorism and organized crime, his cooperation with the Federal Bureau of Investigation, the Bureau's push to gather evidence against Joseph Napoli, and a feeling that the Rajah might be involved with the National Patriotic Brigade and others in a new *French Connection* type of heroin network.

"Thanks for the candid rundown," said Greenway, a bit shocked by the CIA man's willingness to disclose so much privileged information. "But why are you looking for Steven and Ellie Garth?"

"We had leads on a character named Edgar Rand," Tolkin replied. "Rand and Steven Garth both disappeared on the same date." He went on to explain that on June 7 an Agency source had reported that Rand, known as the Major, was linked to many of the elements being investigated by the CIA and to foreign organizations. Direct tips about his relationship with an identity-switch Factory had placed Edgar Rand high on Andrew Tolkin's list. Previous rumors had indicated that organized crime and a network of terrorist groups were sharing responsibility for maintaining the facility. Napoli and Sandalo had been fingered as American participants.

Rand had vanished from his apartment on June 6. An informer operating in the Beaulieu-sur-Mer area claimed that Edgar Rand had met recently with Steven Garth, a former reporter. Other leads had connected Garth and Rand. Tolkin's men had firmly established that Garth also disappeared on the sixth. Along with other moves, Garth's wife, Eleanor, had been placed under constant surveillance. On the eleventh of June, Madame Garth was removed from Hospital Saint Roch and delivered to a villa on Cap-Ferrat.

"Her phone was tapped immediately," the agent concluded. "And that's why I'm here this morning, Dennis."

The lawyer stared, giving the impression that he was digesting the information, evaluating the material. "Congratulations on your promptness," he remarked finally. "And thanks again for discussing the Agency's business in such an open manner."

"I know what to conceal," Tolkin replied. "Mainly you should understand my reasons for being here and wanting to speak with the reporter."

"A logical explanation," Greenway assured him. "Wait here and allow me to confer with Steven and Ellie."

"Have you opened the package?"

"Package?"

"On Garth's tapped call from Italy," Tolkin reminded, "he

mentioned a very explosive package."

"Yes," Greenway confessed, after some thought. "I have opened the package."

"Anything?"

"Tapes and documents," the lawyer replied. "You arrived during my inspection."

"Speak to Garth." Tolkin was a picture of composure. "This is quite an important development for us. I would also like to examine the material. Any objections?"

"Probably," Greenway replied without hesitating. "For a start, Garth will be furious about his wife's surveillance and your tap on her villa phone."

"The man was an investigative reporter," Tolkin countered. "He knows the game."

"Regardless, we're flying his briefcase to Paris, Andrew." The former State Department official glanced at his watch. "Garth wants the material on a high-level desk in Washington."

"Why Paris?"

"Cooperation from the Ambassador," Greenway replied. "A friend of mine."

"A practical step." Tolkin's pale and lifeless complexion died a little more. "I want to explain my official position in this very delicate Garth affair."

Ellie and Steven conferred quietly in the upstairs office. He shocked her again by revealing that his briefcase contained the name, face, passport, and other documents belonging to the man once known as Muazzam Labadi.

"The key to our discovery," Garth whispered. "A secret until I meet the official in charge."

"A quick look?"

"Later," he replied. "We'll keep the file sealed."

Garth found he wanted to talk about Rosa Gambino, and he told Ellie of her background, motivation, and courage. But he jumped to Mario and the death scene without admitting his guilt in bed. Ellie would probably judge for herself and push the verdict aside, at least temporarily.

"I killed a man and there were no witnesses," said Garth concernedly. "And that was only a part of my involvement with hoods and terrorists."

"You were covering an unprecedented story," she reassured him.

"Without notifying police or government representatives," Garth reminded. "That's why the material has to be processed by qualified Washington officials right away. Leaks and questioning and red tape along the way might set me up for a booking and charges and flashy publicity. And we'll delay or ruin the entire mission."

"Or increase the commercial value," Ellie said excitedly. "I can't see anyone prosecuting Steven Garth. A man who risked his life to deliver a briefcase full of history-making journalism."

He winced and stared at her, and understood that the multiple sclerosis, active or in remission, had left deep wounds and ugly scars, physically and emotionally. He looked closer at Ellie's abrupt transformation from invalid to sophisticated partner again. This was a replica with many flaws. Her lovely eyes glared harder than before, and the edges of her mouth curved downward. Lacking warmth, her voice reminded him that bitterness, selfishness, and desperation would continue to permeate Ellie's thoughts and feelings, regardless of attacks or holidays.

"Prosecution by the law is just one worry," Garth stated. "Our lives are in danger." He watched her eyes carefully. "The American Mafia wants us very badly."

"We're in good hands now, Steven." Eleanor motioned to rows of framed diplomas, awards, and photographs on Greenway's office walls. "Dennis and his government contacts know how to deal with Napoli and organized crime."

"You're underestimating the Rajah," said Garth. "And the stuff in my briefcase."

"And now a working official is downstairs," she continued, just as though Garth had not spoken. "We'll have adequate protection, my dear."

"Listen to me." His voice was rough. "Dennis Greenway and his friends will be trusted up to a point."

"You're suspicious of Dennis?"

"No," Garth answered. "But he is still not the man responsible for processing this evidence."

"Christ, don't screw up a miracle, Steven."

"What?"

"Our gold mine." She leaned forward in the chair. "A book, and recognition for both of us."

"The material will be delivered to the American government," he pointed out firmly. "I don't know about the commercial angles. But there should be a way to profit later on." Garth studied his wife's resentful expression. "The officials will advise," he added.

"How thrilling for you, Steven." Ellie lingered on each word. "A Pulitzer and new job offers from Ackerman and the others. You'll have them waiting in line."

"Stop." Garth's mind and body had been pushed far beyond their usual tolerance levels. "Are you doing a Cayuga Lake?"

"No," she answered, managing to be pleasant. "Just begging for an opportunity."

"We'll promote some kind of a book, Ellie," Garth assured her. "After the material has been dissected in Washington."

"Good." Ellie smiled. "Just remember our critical situation when the applause begins."

"Let's stay alive," Garth said harshly. "The rewards are paid on delivery."

"As usual."

"Are you able to type today?"

"Yes." Ellie wiggled her thumbs and fingers. "Why?"

"Shorthand?"

"I can manage." She looked at him curiously. "Are you offering me a job?"

"Yes." He stood and walked to Greenway's tape machine.

"We'll make transcriptions of Labadi's confession and Joseph Napoli's phone taps. Seal them in your purse. Keep the room bolted and the volume low. You'll have enough time. Our Paris flight is at one-thirty."

"When do I begin?"

"On a cue from me." Garth moved to the office door and put his ear against the wood. "After we're properly introduced to the early-morning visitor." He turned a key. "The diplomat is now on his way up the stairs with Dennis Greenway."

They were sitting in the office. Greenway had reviewed Andrew Tolkin's impressive background, emphasizing his ability, reputation, and length of government service; he'd also commented on their years of friendship and a productive working relationship. Ellie and Steven watched and listened attentively.

"Andrew has been straight with me," said Greenway. "The facts will be reported to you just as openly."

He began an explanation of Tolkin's job in Nice and his involvement with the Factory, Rand's disappearance, leads on Steven Garth's involvement, Ellie's surveillance, and taps on her phone.

"Did you have a judicial warrant?" Garth fumed. "Approval of the Attorney General?"

"No," Tolkin replied, at ease. "We acted independently."

"Are we agents of a foreign power?" he continued. "Saboteurs or international terrorists?"

Greenway made an attempt to quiet him. "Please understand the importance of Tolkin's assignment. Linking terrorism and organized crime, sniffing new drug routes, checking on a Factory, and helping the FBI destroy Joseph Napoli." He glanced at Eleanor Garth. "Can you blame Andrew for chasing every lead?"

Tolkin spoke before Ellie could reply. "Our people are also concerned about your safety. Italian and American Mafia hit squads have orders—"

"Thanks for the warning." Garth was cold and impatient. "Why are you here, Mr. Tolkin?"

"I need your cooperation," Tolkin replied evenly. "We're on a very difficult assignment."

"My briefcase is going from Paris to Washington," Garth stated. "Deal with your superiors."

But Greenway was again supporting Tolkin, explaining that he was in a position to contact others and have Garth detained for questioning. Sharp moves by Tolkin could result in a quick legal grab of the briefcase for inspection and possible confiscation as evidence. In other words, the veteran diplomat with the ashen skin and rimless glasses could be a source of real trouble if Garth persisted in flicking him away.

"I've explained that the briefcase contains startling tapes and documents." Greenway watched the reporter's fist tighten on the handle. "Possibly evidence which Tolkin's group and the FBI have been looking for."

"Possibly?" Ellie's tone ridiculed Greenway's use of the word. "Why do you minimize the importance of our property?"

Garth's eyes flashed over to her. *"Eleanor!"*

Greenway edged into the debate. "Are you prepared to grant inspection rights to Andrew Tolkin, Steven?"

"No," Garth slammed back firmly. "I refuse."

"Will you answer his questions?" Greenway inquired without pushing too hard. "About Rand, the Factory, and the material in your briefcase?"

"No," he said adamantly. "We travel Paris to Washington on a direct route."

Eleanor frowned, Tolkin looked impassive, and Greenway cleared his throat in preparation for a brief lecture. The former State Department official had anticipated Garth's reactions, and Tolkin had been primed.

"Andrew is going along with our decision to meet the Ambassador in Paris," said Dennis Greenway. "Believe me, my friend is in a position to disrupt our quiet plans instantly by contacting his superiors or an FBI task force official who is eager for Joseph Napoli evidence. Now listen, Steven, Andrew will accept your refusal to allow questions or inspection. But he and his assistant will accompany you on the one-thirty Paris flight."

It was understandable, Greenway argued, because this was Tolkin's assignment. Ellie, Steven, his story, the material, should be within his reach until the Ambassador closed the doors of his embassy office for Garth's 3:30 p.m. meeting. Only an irresponsible operator would have kissed off a suspect, witnesses, and a briefcase full of possible evidence.

Greenway went on talking, saying that Tolkin and his man insisted on staying close because of a Mafia hunt and other threatening prospects. Killers were searching for Garth and his briefcase in Rapallo and Genoa, according to the latest information received by Tolkin's people. These smart chasers might suddenly appear on target without advance signals. Tolkin and his man would supply additional protection. The government had many obvious reasons for guaranteeing a safe journey to Paris.

"My superior expects me back tomorrow anyway," said Tolkin. "I have to bring him up to date on the Nice assignment."

"What about today, Andrew?" Greenway inquired. "Are you going to report our situation?"

"Yes," Tolkin replied dutifully. "But not until Garth finishes his meeting with the Ambassador."

"That's very kind of you." Greenway looked at Ellie and Steven. "Andrew is permitting a head start without any disruption."

Ellie nodded her thanks, and Steven continued to study the man with growing interest.

"We should begin making preparations." Greenway addressed Andy Tolkin. "Are you waiting here until flight time?"

"My assistant is parked outside the door of the villa," explained Tolkin. "I'll go out and instruct him to pick up my files and my bag from the Negresco and return in time for the drive to the airport."

"While you sit here and keep an eye on us," Garth snarled. "A continuation of the Agency's monitoring procedures."

"Be reasonable, Steven," Greenway advised. "Would you react any differently in these circumstances?"

"Actually, I would like the use of a room, Dennis," said Tolkin, unperturbed by Garth's comments. "My own reports on Nice have to be cleaned up for Paris."

"The downstairs study," Greenway proposed amiably. "I'll phone Air France and book two extra seats, wake my secretary and check the Claridge desk for messages, and then sit in a tub of hot water until this unexpected and totally unreal episode begins to float away or register." He rose to his feet and spoke to Garth. "You'll need legal counsel every inch of the way. My vacation is ruined. Expect a staggering tab when this damn affair is over."

"Bless you, Dennis," said Ellie. "I know we'll find a way to repay—"

"Great," the lawyer interrupted. "And what's on your immediate agenda, Steven?"

"We have business to conduct up here." Garth looked at Ellie. "Strictly private," he added.

In the black Mercedes outside the San Giorgio gates, Jefferson Boland and Anthony Pisano were still able to get a fuzzy view of the entrance, although the mistral had gained force. Boland sat upright on the back seat, fidgety, uneasy in the presence of Gino Corletto's deadly right hand. Slumped low beside the wheel, Pisano glowered at the villa while dragging on an unlit cigarette.

"Here comes Tolkin," Boland announced excitedly. "Walking like he owns the fucking place."

Both men squinted hard through dust and swaying branches as the agent paraded down the steps and moved to the car for a talk with his "assistant," Ralph Cecchi.

26

Villa San Giorgio
Le Cannet, France
10:45 a.m.
Wednesday, June 13, 1979

Andrew Tolkin climbed into the front seat of his car and sat next to Cecchi.

"You're late," said the young hood angrily. "I've been sweating my balls off here."

"Unimportant." Tolkin waved the palms of both hands. "This is crucial business. Listen to me carefully, absorb and memorize every word, and deliver an accurate report to Pisano. Understand that Joseph Napoli's survival will depend on the effectiveness of the next phase."

Tolkin explained that four targets were inside the Villa San Giorgio. Steven Garth, Eleanor Garth, Dennis Greenway, and a full briefcase. Tapes and documents had been mentioned—a possible Labadi confession before his execution in Rapallo. Maybe even some copies of the Frank Sindona double-cross. A death whistle for the organization. Greenway had referred to the material as startling, and the reporter had refused questions or inspection. The woman had stressed the importance of the property. Tolkin believed her.

He repeated the discussion about Paris. A quiet meeting with the Ambassador at the Embassy, at 3:30 p.m. And, hopefully, a rapid delivery of the briefcase to high-level Washington officials. The agent reminded Cecchi to tell Pisano that no representatives of police or government had seen the material, because Garth was saving it for the upper rungs. The evidence was virgin outside the gates of San Giorgio.

Other points were noted for Cecchi's report to Pisano. Garth had a weapon in his jacket pocket, the agent had spotted it while they were meeting upstairs. But he was positive Garth would leave the weapon behind, understanding the risks of detention and trouble at the airport.

Each detail was spelled out. Greenway traveling as the legal counsel. Tolkin's assignment in Nice, assisted by Cecchi, and the reasons for their flight with the others. Every point made in the villa was repeated slowly and carefully for Pisano's benefit.

"All of us are booked on Air France at one-thirty," Tolkin said. "Our targets will be ready."

"I don't get you." Ralph stared blankly. "How do we conduct business?"

"Make notes." The agent handed over a pad and pencil. "This is my plan for extermination."

"We should rush the place now," said Cecchi. "Why complicate things?"

"San Giorgio is on the alert," Tolkin snapped. "They have at least one weapon, a phone, neighbors, a gendarmerie, probably some villa help, and alarm systems." His forehead veins were beginning to swell. "Make notes," he repeated angrily. "Pisano will follow my lead."

The agent repeated his excuse for leaving the villa. His assistant was being instructed to go to the Negresco Hotel in Nice, pick up folders and a packed travel bag before returning to San Giorgio, waiting for passengers, and driving to the airport in time for the Paris flight at 1:30 p.m.

After Tolkin's briefing, Cecchi would, of course, make his exit, circle the area briskly, and eventually park on the dusty side road behind the Mercedes. Pisano would receive a word-for-word accounting. Cecchi's Negresco props were already in the car: two large sealed envelopes in the glove compartment and a packed traveling bag in the trunk. Cecchi would complete his business with Pisano and return to Villa San Giorgio on time for the airport journey.

"Make notes," Tolkin warned again. "This plan will have to be clocked and executed like a military operation."

Depart Greenway's villa at twelve noon. Casually and at the proper moment Andrew Tolkin will explain to the others that a brief stop en route is necessary. Just a few minutes off course. The Negresco files have to be delivered personally. Tolkin's helper is waiting.

Cut off just before reaching the airport. N 202. The road to Digne. Drive over a ramp and continue for approximately five minutes until a sign appears. Black and white letters. "Schober Céramiques." A narrow dirt lane marked private is on the right at the fringe of an industrial section. Take it and go downhill for a short distance.

Park in front of a wooden shack. The office. One room. A cement-block house-type workshop is located nearby. The grounds are strewn with tools and ceramic pieces. An isolated operation in a deep ravine below the other manufacturing plants. However, nothing should arouse the passengers' suspicions, because Schober is typical of commercial layouts in the region. And Cecchi's detour will be handled sharply, just a few minutes from the airport.

Tolkin is familiar with Schober Céramiques and the rest of the area because of the Nice assignment and recent developments. The old ceramic plant is safe and deserted until 3:30 p.m. Time of arrival: 12:45 p.m. Tolkin will be holding envelopes for his man as they pull up to the office. After a brief apology and a promise to return in seconds, he will move out quickly and disappear into the wooden hut.

Tolkin knows the location of a key to a vehicle parked at the rear exit. The owner is a contact employed by Schober. He will climb in, start fast, and make a run back to N 202, going for Nice.

All four targets, Dennis Greenway, Steven Garth, Eleanor Garth, and the briefcase end up in Pisano's hands. An easy play.

Ideal conditions. The agent is convinced that appropriate plans will be formulated based on the details provided.

A tip for Pisano. High-powered factory equipment blasts steam on the grounds overlooking Schober's plant from 1:15 to 1:20 p.m., precisely. Every afternoon. Automatically controlled. Enough noise for Pisano to cover a gunshot or a hydrogen bomb.

The agent made sure that Cecchi had all the details in order. He forced a repeat and checked the young hood's notes. He emphasized the blasting time—1:15 to 1:20 p.m.—and warned that Napoli's existence and many others, including his own, would now depend on Pisano's handling of the second phase at Schober Céramiques.

"Even nature is going for him," said Andrew Tolkin as the wind howled and lashed at the San Giorgio palms. "See you back here at noon, Cecchi."

Greenway had booked two extra seats, contacted his Washington secretary, and was now accepting the Garth affair as reality while bathing in hot water. Tolkin had shut himself in a study on the ground floor. Steven and Ellie Garth were upstairs battling with a tape machine, shorthand, and a typewriter, in order to complete a paper version of the Labadi recordings.

It was 11:35 a.m.

Cecchi, chewing gum nervously, sat alone in the agent's car on the dusty side road. He was reviewing his instructions from Tolkin and Pisano before announcing himself at the villa entrance.

Tolkin's messages had been delivered to Pisano after Cecchi had driven him to a nearby apartment. The place was owned by friends of Gabe De Luca, and the woman and her daughter were given enough money for a luxury hotel when Pisano and Cecchi arrived. Jefferson Boland remained on duty, although one of the surveillance group had to be pulled from the other car because the former CIA informant was a question mark acting on his own.

Pisano's long-distance call had roused Gino Corletto out of bed, but the Mafia leader did not object. They had been waiting for news.

A detailed rundown of Tolkin's observations and plans were passed on to Gino, who made no comment. After listening in silence, he asked Pisano for the Le Cannet number, and told him to wait for a quick call back. Fifteen minutes later, Pisano was jolted by the voice of the Rajah, Joseph Napoli himself.

He had pronounced Tolkin's basic plan acceptable, but in order to guarantee elimination of all targets and damaging evidence, the Rajah had added new dimensions. The final act, requiring the aid of a trusted expert on the villa surveillance team, would be kept secret, known only by the expert, Pisano, and Cecchi. Joe Napoli wanted to be phoned directly as soon as the business arrangements were completed. Success was expected. Failure or a delay of any kind would mean a death sentence for every person involved.

Pisano had called Gabe De Luca in Genoa while Cecchi was still at the apartment. He was instructed to wrap things up and report to Le Cannet. The Garth operation would probably be over before his arrival.

Pisano, Boland, and the surveillance cars were gone, working on the next phase at Schober Céramiques. Ralph Cecchi glanced at two large envelopes and a traveling bag resting on the front seat. He checked his watch, started the motor, and drove along the windswept dirt road heading for the gates of San Giorgio.

It was twelve noon.

The passengers were being driven to Nice Airport by Ralph Cecchi. Tolkin was beside him. Greenway, Steven Garth, and Eleanor sat quietly in the back.

The reporter's dark-ringed eyes watered under heavy lids. All the knocks and bruises and sprains were being aggravated by tension and fatigue. He gripped the briefcase handle and told himself that minor discomfort was a small price to pay for the incredible Labadi material: evidence which might rid America of Joseph Napoli, expose a Robert Kennedy conspiracy, and permit the government to apprehend a faceless man, the supplier, a knowledgeable witness. And then his mind drifted away from public service to private enterprise. Flashes of the Negresco lunch with James Hatfield curdled his insides again, and he thumbed his nose at Ackerman, Rowland, and the other leading journal bastards as he pictured them drooling for him, waiting in line, marveling at his reportorial ability, offering fat employment contracts and incentives. The Labadi material would enable him to care for Ellie properly and re-establish his dignity back home in America.

Garth pulled at the collar of a blue sports shirt, a loan from Greenway along with socks and underwear. After a bath and a shave, he had borrowed the items, politely refusing trousers because of their circus fit. The Ambassador would have to receive him with tattered denims and a safari jacket. His gun had been, as Tolkin had predicted, stashed in the lawyer's safe.

Ellie clung to his arm and worried about a familiar tingling sensation in both hands, a reminder of a premonition that her next attack would be devastating, crippling, final. The Labadi material was a book. Her book. She must protect the commercial angles. To hell with quiet applause from government officials. Garth's future was now secure. Ackerman or Rowland or somebody big would grab him as soon as his journalistic accomplishment became known. Without a book, Ellie could see herself as a rotting invalid, a dying failure, being spoon-fed to oblivion by a celebrated husband. Actually, she reasoned, the briefcase was fifty percent her property. Garth had been pushed, as usual, or he would have ignored Major Edgar Rand.

A shorthand transcript of Labadi's confession was in her purse. Eleanor's fingers had tired, and her mind had gone fuzzy about halfway through. But she had managed to complete an accurate record of the Kennedy conspiracy a few minutes before Andrew Tolkin's man had returned to the villa. As the car sped toward Nice she regretted that there was not enough time to produce a written record of the Gino Corletto–Joseph Napoli phone taps; although she had listened with Greenway, and they had both examined the Frank Sindona papers, without, however, having an opportunity to study any of the electrifying charges against the Mafia leader. A photostat copier and another tape machine would have simplified matters. They would now have to wait for the Embassy's facilities in Paris and to forget Steven's warning about carrying all the eggs in one briefcase without keeping a duplicate record of some kind while en route.

"Remember to stop." Andrew Tolkin held up envelopes for Cecchi. "Kemp is waiting for these."

The driver nodded. Garth looked at his watch. It was 12:35 p.m. "What the hell are you talking about?" he asked roughly. "We're on a direct run."

Tolkin was patient and casual as he turned and faced Garth. "I have to deliver these files personally. Our group is working in the area. Quite urgent. Just minutes off course." He went back to his former position. "We'll be on time for the one-thirty flight."

Garth stared at Greenway until the lawyer shrugged, indicating that he was not concerned about the detour.

"Where is this place?" Garth demanded, unsettled by the change of plans.

"Route N 202," Tolkin answered, with eyes straight ahead. "The road to Digne."

"Just before the airport," Ralph Cecchi added formally. "We'll cut off and ride a few kilometers to Schober Céramiques." He looked in the rearview mirror. "I don't understand the problem."

"Steven is weary and on edge," said Greenway. "You can imagine what the man has been through, Andrew."

"Of course," said Tolkin, peering out the window for a landmark as the mistral roared and clouded the air with swirling debris. "We should be at N 202 in about five minutes."

The driver and the passengers were silent as they approached the cutoff for Digne. Garth's eyes had been fixed on the back of Andrew Tolkin's neck.

"Do you know a man by the name of Sanford Draper?" The question from the reporter was blunt and unexpected. Both Dennis Greenway and Ellie stared at him. Cecchi drove without reacting.

Andrew Tolkin did not move his head when he spoke. "Draper

is my superior in Paris," he replied calmly. "I hope to introduce you later today."

"What about Sandcastle?" Garth's voice was unsteady. "Did you and Draper participate?"

Greenway broke in harshly. "Use a little discretion, Steven," he admonished. "You have no right to interrogate Andrew Tolkin."

"I'm curious about everyone and everything," he snapped back. "You can't blame me."

Ellie squeezed his arm. "At least spare the government." She glanced toward the front. "Mr. Tolkin has been very cooperative."

"Without a doubt," the lawyer agreed. "You can ask questions in Paris."

"Route N 202," Cecchi announced in bus-driver fashion as they pulled off the main road. "We have a fast run to Schober."

"And then what?" Garth was still disturbed about the unexpected detour. "You owed us a briefing in advance."

"The man is delivering his package," Greenway blasted. "Are you looking for trouble?"

"Dennis is correct." Tolkin removed his glasses, edged flush up against the door, and faced Garth. "Ask your questions in Paris," he repeated.

"I will," said the reporter. "Believe me."

"This is extraordinary," Tolkin remarked. And as the man spoke, Garth noticed what others had seen before. Without glasses, Tolkin's blue eyes were clear and piercing, and his expression was freakishly youthful for someone nearing sixty. "Don't juggle roles, Garth," the agent cautioned. "Keep in mind that you should be on a witness stand responding to official injuries."

Ralph Cecchi sped the car over the ramp on N 202. Minutes later he geared down as they approached a weather-battered sign, a swaying black-lettered indicator partially obscured by flying dust. Schober Céramiques. He squinted and made a quick right turn onto a narrow dirt lane. They were on the fringe of the local industrial district, which now resembled the Sahara at the peak of a windstorm.

After going downhill on this bumpy private road, they stopped at a dead end in front of a wooden hut. Layers of blinding dust almost obliterated a small, ruggedly built workshop nearby. The grounds were littered with tools, ceramic pieces, and swirling trash. Andrew Tolkin had described the place accurately. Schober's operation was isolated in a ravine far below the other plants. Yet it was typical of most commercial layouts in the district, and a brief stop here would never have aroused suspicions in ordinary circumstances.

"I'll return in a few minutes," Tolkin advised the driver. Then, with the envelopes under his arm, he glanced back at the others while reaching for the car door. "We'll be on time for Paris," the CIA man assured them.

At exactly 12:45 p.m. they watched him leave, stride hard against the roaring wind, and enter Schober's office.

The hut's only room was constructed of splintered, uneven planks. A small window lit the place by day and kerosene lamps provided night lights. A beat-up mahogany desk, three uncomfortable straight-backed chairs, and a grease-stained rug were the furnishings. Schober's hut was used by the plant foreman and his ceramics workers.

Andrew Tolkin opened the door, and stood motionless as the wind ripped into the wooden shack carrying the dust and filth it had swept off the grounds.

"Close the fucking thing!" a voice ordered. "And put your back against the wall!"

Tolkin stared in amazement at a revolver which Jefferson Boland was aiming directly at his chest.

"*Follow instructions!*" Boland yelled. "*I'm warning you!*"

Deciding to obey, the agent pressed the door closed against the raging mistral and then faced Boland again.

"*Squat next to the wall!*" the southerner ordered. "*Raise your arms up high!*"

Tolkin's reactions had gone from disbelief to bewilderment to anger. "Explain this insanity, Boland." He moved a step toward his former informant. "What the hell are you doing?"

"*Tolkin!*" Boland prepared to fire. "*Get back to that wall and squat with your hands up!*"

Boland's leathery complexion had turned ashen, and sweat dripped from his crew-cut hair. But Tolkin also observed that a very nervous finger was resting on the trigger of his weapon, a sign to give away points for the moment.

Solemnly the agent lifted his arms high and moved back to the crude planking. With the gun at ready, Jefferson Boland searched him and found that Tolkin, as usual, was unarmed.

"*Get down low!*" Boland ordered. "*Back against the wall, hands up, and mouth shut!*"

Tolkin lowered himself to a crouched position on the floor with his arms up and his back against the wall. "I'm obeying," the agent said quietly. "Will you please explain—"

"*Mouth shut!*" Boland's revolver was an inch away from Tolkin's head. "*You'll understand in a few minutes!*"

27

Schober Céramiques
Outskirts of Nice, France
12:50 p.m.
Wednesday, June 13, 1979

In Tolkin's car outside the hut, Garth was becoming anxious. Even Greenway and Ellie had been fidgeting and checking watches. Cecchi showed his indifference by drumming a rock beat on the steering wheel.

"A mistake," Garth complained. "We should never have allowed a detour."

"Tolkin will be out in a minute," Ellie predicted, attempting to calm Steven as well as herself. "The airport is a few kilometers down the road."

"Everything is fine," said Greenway, leaning forward to address the driver. "Unless this mistral slows up traffic." He watched the young Mafia lieutenant unbutton his neatly tailored jacket. "Do you anticipate a problem?"

"Not for us," he answered, removing a pistol from a shoulder holster. "We're just going for a short walk."

Their reactions—Greenway's astonishment, Eleanor's panic, and Garth's anger—had been blended with other emotions by the time they were forced to leave the car and march toward Schober's hut. Ralph Cecchi was behind them holding a gun and a briefcase, gained only after Steven's refusal to give up the Labadi evidence had almost cost Eleanor her life. The professional killer had aimed for her throat and would have fired without hesitation if Garth had held on to the case. The threat to his wife, and Greenway's pleading had eased the reporter's grip on a journalistic triumph.

Dirt and grains of sand tore into their faces as they battled the wind. Ellie and Greenway had questioned Cecchi without any success. The lawyer had threatened and warned, spelling out the consequences of detaining and harming the group—especially Andrew Tolkin, a government official. Cecchi had laughed, then ordered silence.

Garth held Ellie's arm as they pushed forward, confused and shocked by the development, imagining the dangers facing them in the hut, agonizing over the loss of Garth's briefcase. For an instant their eyes met, and it was the same as conversing for hours. Both of them—perhaps for slightly different reasons—were now ready to kill and to risk death for the Labadi evidence.

Inside the Schober office, Cecchi sat on the edge of the desk and watched Boland frisk Greenway and the reporter. Discovering nothing, Boland told them to crouch against the planks beside Tolkin. Two aimed weapons and young Cecchi's quiet threats urged them along.

"Don't put your goddamn hands on me," said Ellie as Boland waited for orders. "And I refuse to squat anywhere."

"Get the lady a chair," Cecchi decreed. "I already felt her purse," he added. "There's no hardware inside."

Ellie sat, joining the others at the end of the line next to Garth and the Schober rear door.

"You had better have answers, Cecchi," Andrew Tolkin blurted. "Everyone is going to pay dearly for this humiliation."

"Sit behind the desk, Jefferson," Cecchi ordered, refusing to acknowledge the agent's statement. "Kill the next person who says a word."

The prisoners could see that Boland was quivering and sweating, completely unnerved, as he took his assigned position. Ralph gave him the pistol, and Jefferson now had two weapons leveled at the opposite wall of the shack.

Garth made an effort to rise up, and Greenway pulled him back as Cecchi opened the briefcase. The young underworld protégé checked for weapons, found none, snapped the latch, and handed the Labadi evidence to Jefferson Boland.

"Keep this in the middle drawer," he ordered. "And guard it with your life."

"That's enough!" Tolkin stormed. "How could Pisano—"

"Quiet!" Cecchi glanced at Boland. "One more word and you shoot to kill." He watched the nervous guard stash the briefcase and resume his two-gun pose. "You have a contract, Jefferson."

"I know," the southerner drawled. "Don't worry, Ralphie."

Just before one o'clock, Cecchi moved away from the desk and stepped closer to Andrew Tolkin.

"I'll explain a few things quickly," he said. "Make a comment or ask a question and Boland will do his job."

Cecchi claimed that FBI and CIA signals had put local police and other law enforcement agencies on their backs. "These people are swarming all over the area because of your fucking drug chase," he told the agent. "We're supposed to be involved."

Ellie, Steven, and Greenway were staring at Tolkin, knowing now that—years ago—he had been Muazzam Labadi's unscrupulous contact, the evil bastard known as Albert Polk.

"Pisano won't risk hauling the briefcase to Le Cannet or anywhere else," Cecchi was saying. "Boland has special instructions for a safe delivery after he completes this Schober business."

Tolkin was about to speak. "Not a word," Cecchi threatened. "Or Jefferson will demonstrate his new reliability."

Cecchi moved toward the front door of the shack. "This was your plan, Tolkin." He paused, turned, and faced the agent once more. "My boss just altered the original version."

Ellie and Greenway absorbed Ralph Cecchi's words and Andrew Tolkin's reactions. Watching them, Steven Garth could see fear, anxiety, and confusion still etched on their faces. Oddly enough, his own apprehension had diminished since entering the hut. Boland was obviously an edgy and reluctant jailer, and the briefcase was still on the premises within reach. The reasons for leaving the vital material in shaky hands had failed to convince Garth, but it was Cecchi's business, and possibly his own good fortune.

"Jefferson has been collecting for over nine years," the young hood was reminding Tolkin. "Working both sides of the fence."

Always well paid, safe, and immune. Cecchi's boss had finally decided to give him responsibility, a chance for direct involvement, an opportunity to earn his money from just one source. Boland had vowed loyal behavior and a closed mouth.

"The Labadi disease and every carrier will be eliminated for good," Cecchi continued. "Boland has been assigned this job—your second phase, Tolkin."

They glanced at the informer, erect in his chair, programmed, a robot, two guns covering his targets, eyes blinking repeatedly as the perspiration flowed.

Cecchi's face was grim when he looked at Ellie and Steven Garth and Dennis Greenway. "Pity you tripped over this information." He focused on the reporter, groped for words, and ended up by saying, "We have no choice." He also explained that two expert riflemen with telescopic sights were concealed on the grounds directly above the Schober hut. Anybody managing to break free would become an instant corpse. And a car, loaded with armed men, was blocking the end of the dirt lane from Schober's working area where it led on to Route N 202. Other measures had been taken to guarantee the completion of Boland's assignment.

"Boland has the key to your vehicle parked out back," Cecchi informed Tolkin. "He'll meet us when the job is over."

Preparing for an exit, Ralph Cecchi brushed dust from his clothing and stared at the agitated executioner. "Be smart, Jefferson," he cautioned. "Everyone is in position and waiting for results."

Boland nodded slowly, keeping his guns in place and his eyes on the four captives.

Cecchi turned, opened the front door, braced himself against the violent mistral, and left Schober's dilapidated office without glancing back.

At 1:05 p.m., Boland coughed up phlegm, swallowed it, and wiped his damp forehead with a sleeve. "I'm warning you." He tightened his grip on the pistols. "Don't give me any trouble. You'll drop dead if I see a funny move."

"Listen to me," Tolkin pleaded. "Cecchi has a bullet waiting for you."

"*Shut up!*" Boland's voice wavered as much as his aim. "*Obey the rules!*"

"I wrote them!" The agent faced the others, ignoring threats and desk-pounding by Boland. "Pisano will kill this man after his assignment here in the office."

"You should know," Garth snarled. "Right, Albert Polk?"

Tolkin concentrated on Boland. "At one-fifteen, the factory equipment starts to blast automatically." The CIA agent rose from his crouched position. "Using this noise as a cover, you execute us, grab the car, and head for N 202."

"On the floor, Tolkin!" Boland stood and pointed a gun at the man. "Unless you want to die early."

"But that vehicle parked outside is your hearse," Tolkin went on, refusing to obey. "Cecchi and his boys will riddle you at the N 202 intersection. Don't be a fool. We know too much. Look how they double-crossed me."

"Boland!" Garth had been studying the executioner's waverings. "Time is running out," he warned. "Will you listen to a reasonable proposition?"

"*No!*" Boland was cracking, and it showed. "*I have to go with Pisano!*"

"Wrong!" Garth responded at once. "Take advantage of a last-minute opportunity!" He got up slowly, keeping his back against the wall, and then Greenway followed. Boland eyed them suspiciously for a moment but tolerated the move. Looking light-headed, the executioner sat in the desk chair and propped both guns in front of him on a direct firing line. "Talk fast," he demanded. "I'll kill anybody who acts in a sneaky manner."

Ellie, the lawyer, and even Tolkin listened attentively as Garth made a fast, sincere, convincing pitch for their freedom. In his reasonable proposition he emphasized Greenway's background as a prominent Washington attorney and a former senior official in the American State Department—an influential man willing to help in many ways if Boland would cooperate.

He spoke passionately about the Labadi tapes and documents in his briefcase, the confession, evidence against Joe Napoli, and other secrets. (Though he still avoided mentioning the files showing the conspirator's new identity.)

Feverishly Garth dramatized every angle, including an escape with the briefcase and Tolkin, a suspect, as prisoner. Together, Greenway, the reporter, and Eleanor would be able to convince the government that Boland was a hero. A man who saved their lives— and saved a taped confession that would guarantee an official investigation and a possible reopening of the Robert Kennedy assassination case before Sirhan's release on parole. It would also, during an important FBI probe, provide shocking evidence against Joe Napoli and his organization. Perhaps even the proof needed for prison terms and deportation.

"Give the briefcase to Cecchi or Pisano and the contents will be destroyed!" Garth went on huskily. "A staggering loss for the United States!" He found that he was speaking eloquently, almost preaching, about responsibility and Senator Robert Kennedy, about Sirhan and Napoli—even about history!

"Too late!" Boland was on target, resigned to follow through without enthusiasm. "I have a deal with Napoli. You heard Cecchi —they've got expert riflemen with telescopic sights just above us." He looked at his watch. "And Pisano's car is blocking the road out to N 202."

As the seconds ticked past 1:10, Garth made a final try. Pisano was obviously planning Boland's funeral after Schober Céramiques. Why not take the risks now? Forget the car parked outside. Keeping a gun on Tolkin, the group could sneak out the rear exit, and to hell with telescopic riflemen. Gamble with a blinding dust storm instead of with Anthony Pisano.

They could make a run for the workshop nearby, disappear on foot going in the opposite direction of Route N 202; Garth had noticed trees at that end of the industrial area.

Or he could wait for the blasting at 1:15. Shoot over the captives' heads and use the same procedure. Everyone out the rear door, make a run for the workshop, head in the opposite direction to the car. Snake past the telescopic rifles in a blanket of swirling dust.

"No!" Boland's features were contorted as he glanced at his watch and stood. *"It's almost time!"*

Greenway was a veteran of crisis diplomacy, although he had never before negotiated at gunpoint with his own life at stake. The pressure showed in his eyes and manner.

"You'll have risks either way," the lawyer told Boland. "The odds favor escape." Swiftly he mentioned government protection, immunity, a major contribution to history, and possible financial rewards. Pisano's plan offered him complicity in Mafia operations, the rap for at least four killings, and God knew what else—if not certain death, at N 202 or later by Napoli's enforcers.

"Fire at the godamn wall!" he shouted. "And run with us!"

At that moment, 1:12 p.m., Tolkin left his position and took a step forward.

"Get back!" the executioner warned, aiming a gun directly at his chest. *"Or I'll fire right now!"*

Tolkin stopped. "You have three targets," he advised. "Kill them as planned. I have vital Agency information for Joseph Napoli. Eliminate the others at one-fifteen and head for Pisano's car with me and the briefcase. An urgent intelligence report has been snagged for the Rajah and his organization."

As Tolkin jabbered and started another cautious move forward, and Boland pointed the weapons and threatened, Eleanor gripped the rear door handle and turned it slowly. Only Greenway and her husband noticed.

Seconds later, Tolkin was at the edge of the desk, where he faced the trembling southerner. "Jefferson, you know you can count on my official assistance if there are problems with your employers." He pressed his lips together in an approximation of a smile. "Based on experience, we both know that operating with Pisano alone is a very dangerous game." The agent, somber now, leaned closer and whispered. "Give me the weapons, Jefferson." He reached out authoritatively. "You will never have the courage to follow through."

In a flash of unexpected action, a heavy pistol butt suddenly crashed against Tolkin's rimless glasses, and he stood upright and motionless while blood poured from his eyes and nose.

At the same time, the rear door opened, filling the room with a cyclonic whirl of brown powder. Tolkin dropped as Garth shoved Eleanor out into the raging mistral.

On the ground, biting dust, she watched the office door close instantly. Fearing the rifles overhead Eleanor pulled herself up and hobbled quickly to the workshop—there she'd be behind thick cement, shielded from the wind and out of telescopic range. She peered around the corner and squinted at the hut. Less than a minute to go. A feeling deep inside told her that Jefferson Boland would fire to miss, leave a wounded Tolkin, and run with Dennis, Steven, and the briefcase.

At the end of the dirt road leading to N 202, Anthony Pisano and Ralph Cecchi waited in the black Mercedes. The young hood was behind the wheel.

"The briefcase should have been sent home," Cecchi said quietly. "Nobody really inspected the contents."

"The Rajah wants everything to dissolve." Pisano was stern-faced and impatient. "No chance for leaks or copies." The Mafia leader glanced at the storm lashing outside the window. "He's got an FBI probe, Sandalo, and other troubles. All Joe needs floating around is Garth's briefcase."

Pisano lifted his watch, read 1:14:30 p.m., and nodded. Cecchi started the engine, looked at the dust-blurred Schober works outline in the rearview mirror, and said, "*Addio.*"

From behind the corner of the ruggedly built workshop, Eleanor was able to lean out and keep her eyes on the hut. At precisely 1:15 p.m., she heard the roar and hiss of steam being blasted from the factory above. An instant later she counted ten muffled shots. She gazed anxiously at the Schober office, ignoring the danger of telescopic sights. Hardly breathing, and with her nerves gone wild, Eleanor shivered and stared and prayed that the door would open, allowing Boland's hostages to escape clutching the briefcase.

Without any notice, a glaring, eyeball-shriveling light was followed by a deafening explosion. *Pulverizing the wooden hut!! A chemical smell! A roaring fire! Burning and burning and burning and burning!* Consuming the unrecognizable bits and pieces of Steven H. Garth, Dennis P. Greenway, Jefferson Boland, Andrew Tolkin, and the briefcase, a confession, wiretaps, documentation, and the new face and identity of Muazzam Labadi, a conspirator in the assassination of Robert Kennedy.

Joe Napoli's targets and Garth's evidence had been dissolved as ordered, without a scrap remaining. The material would never be used by the FBI or the INS or any other enemy, including Beppe Sandalo.

Eleanor had screamed long and loud without being heard, and her fall behind the crumbling workshop had gashed both knees and her left arm, yet she had felt nothing. A few minutes after the explosion, she crawled past the edge of the damaged building in order to inspect the Schober office, Steven's crematorium.

Mistral winds had fanned the blaze, transforming wood and flesh and tape and paper to ashes: dust mixed with dust, being tossed crazily in all directions, and some touched her face, and she howled, although the sound blended with the loud excited voices of others as they hurried down from the industrial plants above the ravine.

●

THE REST OF ELEANOR'S MANUSCRIPT was difficult to read because of smudges, blotches, scrawling and jumbled phrases. At three o'clock in the morning of November 10, James Hatfield was still awake in his rooms at the Negresco, deciphering references to stumbling past crowds and fire engines at the explosion scene and later being picked up in a daze on Route N 202. A family of German tourists had driven her to the emergency-room door of Saint Roch before continuing on their way.

And at about the same time that she would have been entering Saint Roch, there seemed to have been a phone call to a regional daily newspaper. The National Patriotic Brigades, an Italian organization, had claimed responsibility for the explosion at Schober Céramiques. According to the anonymous male voice, the hut had been used as a front for a CIA undercover team, and the caller had warned that a list of other agents would be eliminated by the Brigades as part of a new campaign.

Hatfield found scribbled mentions of grief over Steve's heroic death and a fear of the Mafia. Ramblings about pain, drugs, anxiety, and frustration as her MS symptoms became more advanced, crippling, and unbearable. She worried about having enough time for completion of a detailed manuscript, and the strength to protect it against theft or reproduction.

There was, however, a paragraph Eleanor appeared to have polished carefully, perhaps intending it as the last one in her last book:

> The young Italian smiled after calling the newspaper. He left the booth, entered a waiting vehicle, and headed for Le Cannet. Anthony Pisano, Ralph Cecchi, and Gabe De Luca were gathered for a victory celebration. Every grain of the crumbled Sandcastle had blown away on the grounds of Schober Céramiques, and Joseph Napoli was pleased.

A few of her Kennedy conspiracy notes were legible: references to a payoff in Sirhan's diary, and an Ambassador Hotel headwaiter's claim that he saw a bullet lodged in the center divider between two swinging doors leading into the pantry. She believed nine shots had been fired. The one-inch outer facing of the dividers was removed shortly after the assassination, subjected to an X-ray check, and then destroyed after no bullets could be found. Eleanor seemed to be questioning the speed and wisdom of the Los Angeles Police Department.

There were muddled Labadi references: a faceless man on the loose, a slow ticking bomb with the explosive power to eliminate Napoli and disrupt the Sirhan release. Along with his knowledge of the conspiracy, he might have copied the Sindona evidence and the Napoli phone taps and the other documents which had vanished in the explosion at Schober Céramiques. Perhaps one day for reasons of his own, guilt or something else, the man formerly known as Muazzam Labadi would have the courage to step forward and risk punishment by the government and the Mafia in order to square the records with Joseph Napoli and Sirhan Sirhan.

And Eleanor complained about being harassed by the underworld at Saint Roch and Les Mimosas, while doctors and staff considered her to be insane. Her fingers were obviously trembling, and her coordination was going, as she described the various hiding places she'd used for the manuscript as work progressed. The closing lines had become terribly garbled.

But the final page was a scribbled tribute to Steven: a hero, a journalist, and—

The telephone rang, and Hatfield was on the line with Dr. Roger Lambert calling from Les Mimosas.

"Eleanor Garth is dead," the physician stated bluntly.

At a café on the Champs Elysées in Paris, James Hatfield was sipping coffee with Kenneth Tyler of the Justice Department. It was November 18, six days after the literary agent had delivered a copy of Eleanor's manuscript. Before he could do that, he had had to make arrangements for the transportation of her body to Pasadena, California, where distant relatives would supervise the funeral. With *Sandcastle* on Tyler's desk, Hatfield had flown back to London for a series of conferences. He was now in Paris again, ready for an opinion.

"Brandon Patterson is a fine doctor," said Tyler, munching on a croissant. "Did he agree with the cause of death?"

"He accepted a cerebral hemorrhage." Hatfield replied without much enthusiasm. "Although Roger Lambert, Vassolo, Dumas, Joubert, and the other Frenchmen failed to impress him."

"And you?"

"Never confident," said Hatfield. "Who knows what really led to Eleanor's mysterious head pains?" He thought for a moment. "I should have pulled her away from them at the beginning."

"The Sandcastle influence." Tyler smiled. "Garth concocted an exciting fantasy."

Kenneth Tyler was a short, compactly built man with a jovial attitude and a very direct approach. His eyes gazed steadily from behind tinted glasses as he outlined his impression of Eleanor's work. In his opinion the woman must have been driving her husband up the wall, both before and during her illness. Finally Steve had reached his limits, and packed and run for parts unknown, on June 6, 1979.

Eleanor was shattered, lost, confused, helpless—and very ill, both mentally and physically. Instead of the big sleep, which was not her style, she had concocted an adventure: a plot designed to kill many real birds with one fictional stone.

Tyler tapped the envelope. "This is a good mixture of experience and talent, of medication and imagination and pain. And of her husband's research library. She used everything she could, and came up with a clever blend of fact and fantasy—the basis of what she prayed would be another best-seller. She needed one, for obvious reasons—"

"Ellie did not have access to Steven's research at Saint Roch or Les Mimosas," Jim Hatfield interrupted. "And I doubt very much if the library could have been folded under a pillow."

"They moved her to a villa," Tyler reminded. "The facts were probably organized there."

"Only a couple of days," said Hatfield. "Not enough time for a thorough job."

"Who knows?" The official shrugged. "Her book was obviously researched."

"Go ahead, Ken." Hatfield was anxious to move along. "Cover other points."

Tyler repeated that Garth was basically a weak man, dominated by Eleanor, uncomfortable with others—professionally and socially. In her fiction, the woman had transformed him into a man of action, courageous, rugged, determined, pushing whores around dingy joints, facing up to bad guys, screwing beautiful terrorists, guarding his secrets with loaded pistols, and risking his life for justice, and self-esteem. Eleanor's personal treatment for a crippled body and a wounded ego. Better to be dumped by superman than an unemployed reporter.

"In my opinion," stated Tyler, brushing crumbs off his jacket with a napkin, "Eleanor Garth superimposed the fantasy husband on a realistic background and then added her own imaginative padding to create a novel."

"A few questions?"

"Of course."

"The Robert Kennedy conspiracy."

"No such thing."

"I mean Eleanor's book."

"That's different."

"I recall that witnesses did see a girl resembling Joan with Sirhan at various places," said Hatfield. "And there were rumors that Robert Kennedy was stalked."

"What's your question?"

"Labadi's fictional confession," Hatfield went on. "Were the author's statements preposterous?"

The official removed a notepad from his pocket and flipped to a page. On May 20, 1968, a bartender at Robbie's Restaurant in Pomona, California, did see a man he thought to be Sirhan, forcing his way up the stairs during a Robert Kennedy appearance. A girl resembling Joan in Eleanor's manuscript was at his side. Both of them had acted suspiciously. After questioning by the Los Angeles police, the bartender refused to swear under oath that the man was Sirhan, and the investigation was dropped.

A professor of psychology at the University of California, Los Angeles, and his wife had contacted the police insisting that they had noticed Sirhan after a Kennedy rally at the Los Angeles Sports Arena, on May 24. They also claimed that he had acted in a suspicious manner. The report had been noted by the Los Angeles Police Department.

At his trial, Sirhan testified that he was present at a rally for Kennedy at the Ambassador Hotel on Sunday, June 2.

"Eleanor based her Labadi stalking revelations on three leads which the Los Angeles police had evidently considered to be flimsy or unreliable," said Tyler.

"Why?"

"I did not conduct the investigation."

"Maybe they scared hell out of the bartender who saw the girl with Sirhan in Pomona," said Hatfield, playing devil's advocate, a bad piece of casting, but Eleanor rated a full hearing, because of Dr. Serge Vassolo's files. "They should have checked for a girl without a sworn oath."

"Everybody saw a girl," Ken Tyler recalled. "Especially in a polka-dot dress."

A young worker for Kennedy, Sandy Serrano, reported seeing a girl fleeing the scene. Thomas Vincent Di Pierro, a member of the kitchen crew, noticed a girl in a polka-dot dress standing behind a pantry tray table, with Sirhan in front, moments before Kennedy was shot, and they appeared to be together. An insurance company executive reported seeing a girl with Sirhan on a target practice range in May, at Rancho, California.

"Did the girls resemble Joan in Eleanor's manuscript?"

"Close enough."

"Why did the police disregard these reports?"

"Various reasons," said Tyler. "Some witnesses backed down and changed their stories while being questioned, others refused to swear under oath, one failed to recognize Sirhan in a picture file." He sipped his coffee. "I am in no position to go deeper without a full-scale investigation. An unwarranted effort based on Eleanor's material."

"Did Sirhan go to San Diego on June third?" Hatfield prodded. "The El Cortez Hotel?"

"Nothing officially listed."

"What about Eleanor's references to a payoff in the Sirhan diary?"

Again Kenneth Tyler checked his notepad. "They were based on facts." He gave a résumé: Whenever Robert Kennedy's name appeared in the diary it was always accompanied by "please pay to the order of Sirhan." This line was never written anywhere else in the diary, except on the pages where Sirhan mentioned "kill" or "Kennedy." Another entry was obviously a repeat of instructions to forget all promises of money: "RFK must die RFK must be killed Robert F. Kennedy must be assassinated before 5 June 68 Robert F. Kennedy must be assassinated I have never heard please pay to the order of of of of of of of of of of of this or that 80000." Sirhan Sirhan was never able to explain the references to money in his diary.

"I don't understand why the cops and the prosecution failed to exert more pressure for logical responses." Hatfield counted on Tyler's even disposition. "Sirhan's Rosicrucian trances were accepted as a cover for everything."

"The man *was* found guilty," Tyler reminded. "And sentenced to death."

"Was Joseph Napoli ever suspected of being a conspirator in the assassination of Robert Kennedy?"

"There has never been solid evidence linking him."

"President John Kennedy?"

"There is a possibility that a conspiracy led to the murder of John Kennedy," Tyler admitted. "Joseph Napoli and some other members of organized crime have been mentioned as participants."

"Why?"

"Electronic surveillance material accumulated by the Bureau proves that major underworld figures were hurt by the actions of our department," he answered. "They vowed revenge against John Kennedy and his brother Robert, the Attorney General."

"Napoli and Sandalo were—"

"The House Select Committee on Assassinations will complete a report and make it public very soon," Tyler interrupted. "Now let's concentrate on Eleanor's manuscript."

"We are," Hatfield whipped back. "You've admitted that Joe Napoli was mentioned as a possible conspirator in the killing of President Kennedy and that he vowed revenge against John and his brother. Muazzam Labadi's fictional confession is logical. Joe Napoli would have had many reasons to assassinate Robert Kennedy if the Senator was moving toward the Presidency. More pressure from your department and a possibility that Robert would use the office against the suspects to avenge his brother's death."

"Sorry, Jim," Tyler said patiently. "There is no official evidence linking Napoli to the assassination of Robert Kennedy."

"I'm just clearing my brain." Hatfield finished his coffee and ordered two more. "What about Eleanor's pitch about there being nine shots?"

"The experts counted eight bullets," Tyler replied. "There is nothing to support a ninth shot."

"Was Eleanor correct about the destruction of a panel?" he asked. "The divider between two swinging pantry doors?"

"Yes," Tyler answered, "after no trace of bullets could be found. The original wood under the removed facing was inspected by John van de Kamp, Los Angeles District Attorney. He reported that no spent bullets or fragments were located. And he did not find tangible evidence of any previous spent bullet."

"But that inspection took place more than seven years after the Senator was killed there."

"Eight bullets, James." Tyler smiled as the coffee arrived. *"Sand-castle* has influenced you."

"I'm upset over Eleanor's death." Hatfield glared into his cup as he stirred sugar. "And certain aspects of this damn story have been disturbing and quite baffling."

"Get them off your chest," Tyler advised. "I stayed over a day in order to help."

Hatfield fired questions, and the official supplied answers. He'd had Eleanor's manuscript for almost a week and had made cursory checks on the major questions it raised. Edgar Rand, a real person who owned a shack in Perinaldo, Italy, had vanished from his Beaulieu-sur-Mer apartment on June 6. The Major owed six months rent and damages for a cracked table and a missing white scatter rug. A government investigator, acting on tips, believed that Rand was in the States, living quietly under an assumed name, hiding from a group of creditors— including the IRS and a former wife looking for back alimony. No Factory or Mafia connections had been discovered. A further check would be ordered because of his tax problems.

American and European Intelligence had been tracking leads on the Factory for years. In 1974, Steve Garth had been working as an investigative reporter on a story involving terrorism and the possible existence of a key identity-switching operation in southern Italy. Therefore, Eleanor had known about it and wrote Factory fiction—based on truth.

Mario, Rosa Gambino, Giovanni Andretta, Victor Donato, his brother Jimmy, and the other Factory connections were presumably imaginary characters. There were no records showing that any of these people existed.

"Fictitious names, Ken," said Hatfield. "Did anyone check the Genoa and Rapallo areas?"

Again Tyler was forced to sit back and lecture. A Factory search had been in progress for years. Suspects resembling the Ellie Garth characters would have been fingered by the American and European police and government agencies by now. "She made them up." Tyler concluded. "And did a very good job."

Italian police had no reports of two gunshot deaths or of a bullet-riddled mummy on Via Tubino in Rapallo. The Condominio Fernanda was a phony address.

The authorities in Savona had never heard of Eleanor's rough joint, La Chunga.

Many former government officials were prominent lawyers with villas on the Côte d'Azur. There was no Dennis P. Greenway—a figment of the author's imagination—to spend holidays at the Villa San Giorgio, in Le Cannet. Gendarmes had no record of a missing American who was vacationing in the south of France.

Hatfield was about to question Tyler's statements about the lawyer but decided against it.

Muazzam Labadi, or Abu Zaki, was disposed of immediately by Tyler. He was complete fabrication, the key to Eleanor's imaginative plot—a good example of writing fiction based on published research.

Franco, or Frank Sindona, was a fictitious name, but he did resemble a former member of the Joseph Napoli organization. The young hood was found shot through the head in a parked car on June 8, 1968, after the Rajah had caught him feeding information to Beppe Sandalo. There was nothing in the files to show that the man had tapped Napoli's phone or copied revealing documents for an explosive folder. Eleanor must have made up this exciting piece of business.

"How would she have known about Napoli's action?" Hatfield asked. "An insignificant gangster double-cross."

"Probably Garth's files," Tyler replied. "That's all I can figure."

"Labadi's confession was incorrect," Hatfield mused. "He thought Sindona was alive."

"Eleanor was incorrect, Jim," said Tyler, grinning him back to reality. "Or Garth's research files were a little screwed up."

"What about Pisano, De Luca, and Cecchi?"

"Fictitious names," the official replied. "But they do fit three of Gino Corletto's lieutenants." He buttered another roll. "Eleanor invented their foreign assignments in *Sandcastle.*"

"Andrew Tolkin, Sanford Draper, and Jefferson Boland."

Tyler frowned, put down his croissant, and explained that the Central Intelligence Agency, rightfully so, had refused to discuss agents and helpers operating in France, or anywhere else. Tolkin, Draper, and Boland were names unknown to members of the American Embassy staff in Paris.

"Her story about Tolkin, the Mafia, and the Senator's killing is a bit outlandish, to say the least." Tyler's eyes were on the literary agent. "Don't you agree, Jim?"

"Wilder reports are circulating about the CIA," said Hatfield thoughtfully. "Anything seems possible these days."

The official gave his friend a sympathetic look. "You need a little time to accept Eleanor's unexpected death," Tyler commented. "All this *Sandcastle* business will read easier."

"No doubt." Hatfield paused and asked his next question with less intensity. "Was there a government drug investigation in the Nice area?"

"Yes," Tyler replied without hesitating. "And I'll admit that her knowledge of the operation and the references to an FBI probe were slightly bothersome."

Eleanor had been accurate about reports of a drug storage and distribution center in the Nice area, a link between terrorism and organized crime, the FBI's drive to gather evidence against Joseph Napoli, and a feeling that the Rajah and his organization might be involved with the National Patriotic Brigades of Italy and others in a new *French Connection* kind of heroin network.

"There were a few news leaks in Washington and Paris." Tyler smiled. "I guess she picked them up." He nodded his balding head respectfully. "Quite a woman."

"Baffling," Jim Hatfield said. "Schober Céramiques was destroyed for real on the thirteenth, and the National Patriotic Brigades did claim to be responsible."

"Correct."

"News reports stated that approximately twenty-five kilograms of TNT were used," Hatfield went on. "Also chemicals. Their bomb was exploded by remote control. A spokesman for the group claimed that five of their enemies had been eliminated, and the terrorists refused to be more specific."

"Facts."

"The corpses were torn and scorched beyond recognition," said Hatfield, proceeding slowly. "Official identification of the five victims will never be recorded."

"So?"

"Were they agents operating in the Nice area?"

"Irrelevant," Ken Tyler replied after some thought. "Here's a perfect example of the author's technique. Eleanor placed Steve Garth and her other imaginary characters in the Schober hut. They blew away as dust in a factual setting." He reached for the large envelope. "I repeat —a clever juggling act by a woman struggling for attention in the last days of her life."

Jim Hatfield nodded, took back the manuscript, and positioned it carefully in a briefcase resting by his chair. "You don't see the need to go any further in Washington?"

"No, Jim," Tyler replied honestly. "The material is fiction based on published information."

"It might be troublesome for the Agency people and others in the administration," said Hatfield as he motioned for the waiter. "You know, digging up the past and rattling skeletons."

Tyler looked at him incredulously. "Jim, Ellie did not come up with another Watergate, believe me." The waiter brought their check and left. "Are you referring to a cover-up?"

"No," Hatfield answered. "Just an unpleasant assignment for the government employees."

Ken Tyler continued to stare as the literary agent put money on the table. "Do you honestly believe Eleanor Garth's fantastic story?"

"You were right," said Hatfield, ignoring the blunt question. "I need time to accept her unexpected death."

"Will you try for a publication deal?" Tyler asked, breaking the quiet. "A book of fiction?"

"I might hire a writer and get it shaped up," Hatfield stated without great enthusiasm. "But not right away."

"Be careful," Tyler warned seriously. "Joseph Napoli detests *Sandcastle*-type accusations in fact or fiction. Eleanor's book attacks him from every possible angle. And the Rajah would not appreciate being tagged as the organizer of Robert F. Kennedy's assassination. It would be a dangerous, irresponsible charge, regardless of Eleanor's mental and physical state and a publisher's use of name changes and disclaimers."

"Thanks for the advice," Hatfield told him, meaning it. "We'll stay alert if the project ever goes ahead."

"And Sirhan Sirhan acted on his own, Jim," Tyler reminded as he watched the literary agent pick up his briefcase. "There is no evidence of a conspiracy."

"Message received," said Hatfield, smiling for the first time. "You've been very kind and helpful." They shook hands. "I really appreciate it, Ken."

"Contact me at once if you trip over Eleanor Garth's faceless man," the official joked. "His conspiracy knowledge and the Frank Sindona package would represent the miracle our investigators have been praying for during this probe." They stood, and Tyler pointed to James Hatfield's briefcase. "Damn pity you're carrying fantasy back to the States."

James Hatfield walked slowly on Third Avenue after finishing dinner with a client. It was the evening of June 23, 1980. Abscam and Brilab, the Justice Department's code-named ambitious two-pronged attack on labor union fraud and political corruption, were over. Destructive evidence had been turned up against a variety of political figures. A few had already been subpoenaed to appear before federal grand juries.

The special task force—an undercover splinter group with official orders to concentrate on building evidence against Joe Napoli—had not produced spectacular results. Hatfield had clipped a recent newspaper photo of Napoli and his group making a triumphant exit from a packed southwestern hearing room. The arrogant, unsmiling Rajah and his lieutenants had been questioned for hours. Harold Richardson and his FBI unit had needed Eleanor Garth's miracle.

Sirhan had been granted a four-month reduction in his life sentence after the convicted assassin of Senator Kennedy told a parole board that he had been offered asylum in Libya. His new release date would now be November 1, 1984, instead of March 1, 1985. James Hatfield had read that further reductions in Sirhan's prison term were being considered. In addition, newspapers had reported that a New York–based Arab-American group was starting a campaign to win an earlier release for the assassin. Leaders of the organization argued that Sirhan had been in prison since June 5, 1968. He was nearing the thirteen-year mark, a period matching the average terms now being served by others convicted of first degree murder in California. To hold him longer would be a vendetta and revenge, and not justice. They felt that an early release would be assured if the victim had been Joe Smith instead of Robert Kennedy.

Hatfield crossed 67th Street and moved toward 68th with his mind on Sirhan's parole board and his supporters, and then he thought of the murder and the trial and the jury which had condemned the assassin to death—a fate he avoided by luck when California abolished the death penalty and changed his sentence to life on June 16, 1972, thus making him eligible for parole, like other convicted murderers, while setting up a major problem for any future board attempting to cancel his release date without new circumstances or evidence.

The literary agent stopped a taxi at 70th, climbed in, and gave his Riverside Drive address. He closed his eyes and pictured Eleanor Garth.

And this brought him back to Muazzam Labadi, Joan and Franco, the Kennedy confession, the Sindona papers, and the Joe Napoli phone taps; and he cursed the ghouls of multiple sclerosis for creating fantasy when truth might have portioned out justice by eliminating the Rajah and disrupting the Sirhan parole.

At ten o'clock, James Hatfield unlocked the front door of his exclusive apartment building, pressed a light switch, and moved to an elevator, which also required a key after dark. He waited until the heavy front door had closed and latched automatically. Then he clicked a mechanism to operational and pushed a button for the elevator, just as a quiet voice stopped his breathing for an instant.

"James Hatfield?"

The agent glanced in the direction of a large indoor plant near the dimly lit emergency stairway. A man was hidden in the corner. Hatfield debated his next move as the elevator arrived on the lobby floor.

"I'm here to advise you about something." The whisper had a sense of urgency. "Better listen."

With his nerves on edge, Hatfield moved to the stranger in the dark corner, reasoning that a call for help or a quick dash for home would only aggravate the situation.

"Speak up," Hatfield demanded, battling for control. "Who are you?"

The grim blond intruder, of medium height and build, took a step forward. "Don't publish Eleanor Garth's manuscript," he cautioned, "without my help and cooperation."

Shock and fear gave way to anger as Hatfield imagined his visitor congratulating the Rajah as they filed out of the hearing room sneering again at law enforcement, federal agencies, and the American people.

"I do not take orders from Joseph Napoli," Hatfield stated firmly. "Eleanor Garth's property is my business."

"Are you ready to die for a stack of paper?" the man asked seriously. "Napoli is an expert."

"Leave this building at once," Hatfield insisted, shaken by the blunt threat. "I'm going upstairs to call the police."

"Don't be a fool," the visitor warned harshly as the agent turned away. "You're gambling without chips."

Jim Hatfield stopped, thought for a moment, and walked back to the man. "How did you become familiar with the details of my property?"

"Rumors," the man answered. "They spread and magnify."

"Why didn't Napoli threaten me before?" the agent inquired with growing interest. "I've had Eleanor Garth's manuscript for almost eight months."

"She was a physical and mental wreck," the man replied in a knowing fashion. "Her story would have been laughed away by the authorities."

"What are you doing here now?" Hatfield asked. "Eleanor's papers have never been changed and the woman is dead."

'Marketing," the stranger answered instantly. "A published version could be troublesome."

"Rumors again?"

"A hunch and gossip," the voice responded coldly. "The new release date for Sirhan gives you a timely property."

"That's enough!"

"I could help," the intruder said, breaking Hatfield's mood. "Let me study Eleanor Garth's papers in your presence, and I'll react, evaluate, and decide about cooperation."

"What the hell are you proposing?"

"Garth's work is either based on truth or horse manure," he stated arrogantly. "Do you want a verdict?"

"Impudent bastard," Hatfield remarked angrily. "I would rather destroy every page than use you as an editor."

"Then burn the fucking story!" His veneer was beginning to crack. "My last warning!"

Hatfield was now certain. "We've talked before," he stated bluntly. "I know your voice."

"Right."

"Where?"

"France," the stranger admitted without haggling. "My name is Cliff Dwyer."

"Oh, yes." Hatfield's temper was brewing. "Cliff Dwyer of King Features."

"No," the stranger admitted. "I only used the King name to do business with you."

"A special piece on Eleanor Garth."

"I wanted to read the manuscript," he continued. "And find out how much she actually knew."

They both heard a key turning in the front door. "Be smart and natural," the visitor whispered hoarsely. "I don't want any trouble."

A young well-dressed couple entered, greeted Hatfield, and made use of the elevator on the lobby floor.

"Listen to me," Hatfield ordered after they were alone in the dark corner. "I don't know whether you're a lunatic, a bum off the streets, or a member of the Napoli organization. The evidence points to Joe Napoli. So I'll make a brief speech, and when it's over you'll leave this apartment and get the hell out of my life. I never want to see or hear you again. Do you understand the message?"

There was no response. "You can rest easy," the agent said in a detached tone. "Tell Joseph Napoli that I've canceled all plans to edit and market Eleanor Garth's work. The material has been locked in private storage files and the contents will never be discussed again."

There was no response. "In addition, the entire manuscript has already been checked and investigated by the Justice Department, and the results should also please Napoli's followers. Garth's work is fiction based on public information. Sirhan acted on his own when he assassinated Senator Kennedy. There is no evidence of a conspiracy. In other words, the United States government has no interest in Eleanor Garth's fantasy."

"Blind, stupid idiots," the stranger remarked, or at least it sounded that way to Hatfield. "Earplugs and hidden motives."

"What did you say?"

"Joseph Napoli is guilty, Hatfield," the stranger whispered. "I have the *facts!*"

The agent stood motionless, confused, mesmerized, unable to respond.

"And Robert Kennedy's assassin leaves Soledad in a week, or a month, or a year," the man pressed on. "A flight to Libya with a brain full of secrets." His voice was bitter as he cursed Sirhan for taking a life and cheating death. Like Joseph Napoli, he would be able to move freely and strike others without ever facing truth or justice.

"Will Edward Kennedy be safe in the future?" the man in the dark corner asked quietly. "Napoli and Qaddafi would be very logical paymasters."

"How do you intend to change this situation?" Hatfield strained for a better look. "Ordinary citizens are helpless."

The intruder was not listening to Hatfield's question; he seemed intent on his own thoughts as he spoke bitterly about living victims, witnesses, conspirators, and employees, active and retired, hiding knowledge and scars. And he predicted that someday very soon one of the involved ones, with a good reason, could be motivated to step forward, admit his guilt, accept the punishment, and deliver all the proof needed to reopen the Sirhan trial, eliminate Joe Napoli, and hold Robert Kennedy's assassin in prison for the rest of his life—

"I am disappointed and unhappy with my existence," he stated grimly. "Joe Napoli, Sirhan, and others like them are being set free without experiencing the proper amount of suffering."

Although dull lighting and shadows hazed the image, Hatfield studied the visitor's gaunt and bony face, dark-circled eyes, and flesh stretched tightly without a crease or a blemish.

A jumble of spine-tingling guesses cluttered the agent's brain as he inched forward, entering the hiding place behind the leaves and branches.

"Maybe I do need your assistance," Hatfield stated carefully. "Eleanor Garth's papers are in the office files. Will you report tomorrow morning?"

For the first time the blond stranger appeared to be unconcerned about revealing himself in the glow of the overhead lighting. A frayed collar, shabby jacket, worn, ill-fitting pants, and battered shoes reminded Hatfield of street-bum clothing.

"I'll think about your offer tonight," the man said, forming his words awkwardly. "A decision to go ahead will change my life in many ways."

"You've been hounding me for an opportunity!"

Hatfield stared at the man's features and decided that they were plastic, waxlike, unreal. Was the effect being created by shadow patterns, nerves, and imagination?

A noise at the front door ended his inspection abruptly and prompted the visitor to straighten up and make ready for a hasty exit.

"My real name is not Cliff Dwyer," he said, backing toward the entrance. "I don't work for King Features, Rajah Napoli, or anyone else." A large bearded man was opening the door as the visitor added, "I'm a drifter, a phantom, a free-lance character who knows the score."

He wheeled about and dashed past the bewildered tenant as Hatfield followed close behind.

"Wait!" The literary agent stood in front of the apartment building and watched the mysterious figure run, then switch to a quick walk, and finally disappear around a corner.

After gazing thoughtfully at the empty pavements, Hatfield turned slowly and went back inside the lobby, hardly aware that the door was still being held open by his neighbor.

"A thief?" the man asked excitedly as they approached the elevator. "Breaking and entering?"

Hatfield's eyes were fixed on the tenant's key as it made a click for the elevator.

"Jim?"

"What?"

"That bum who ran out of the lobby," he inquired again. "A thief?"

"No." The words clogged in Hatfield's throat. "I know who he is."